SYMPATHY FOR THE DEVIL

A MORRIS AND CHASTAIN
SUPERNATURAL INVESTIGATION

JUSTIN GUSTAINIS

D1390994

SOLARIS

First published 2011 by Solaris
an imprint of Rebellion Publishing Ltd,
Riverside House, Osney Mead,
Oxford, OX2 0ES, UK

www.solarisbooks.com

ISBN: 978 1 907992 02 5

10 9 8 7 6 5 4 3 2 1

A CIP catalogue record for this book is available from the
British Library.

Designed & typeset by Rebellion Publishing

Printed in the UK

To Betsy Brown,
Cotton Mater's most unlikely descendant.
Because I keep my promises.

"The best trick the Devil ever pulled
was convincing the world
that he didn't exist."

– Roger 'Verbal' Kint
in *The Usual Suspects*

"Easy is the descent into Hell."

– Virgil, *The Aeneid*

"When you dance with the Devil,
the Devil don't change.
The Devil changes you."

– Max California
in *8MM*

I

INFESTATION

Prologue

HIS VOICE, BOOMING though the state-of-the-art sound system, filled the hall and reached out to the people sitting in the cramped seats, as if he were speaking to each one of them individually.

"And so, my friends, even though our efforts have accomplished much, let us not fall victim to the comforting illusion that no battles remain to be fought. The war for the heart and soul of America will go on. Make no mistake about it, a hard and bloody fight it will be, and the victory of virtue is by no means assured."

He paused, looking out at the crowd, the grave expression on his face a testament to the concern he felt for his nation and its future. Then his face, almost but not quite handsome, broke into a reassuring smile.

"But although there is no unassailable guarantee of success in our endeavors, of this much I *am* certain: that with God's help, you and I, all of us who fight for right, will find within ourselves the strength we seek for the struggle!"

The audience erupted into applause and cheers, as they had done four times already.

In the press gallery, *The Boston Globe* looked up from its laptop and said to *The New York Times*, "Knows how to push their buttons, doesn't he?"

"Not hard to do with *this* crowd," *The Times* replied with a shrug. "Throw the animals a little red meat, and they'll jump through all kinds of hoops for you."

The Globe smiled slightly. "Does your editor mind you referring to the devout reactionaries of Believers United as 'animals'?"

"Not as long as I don't do it in print."

The two men resumed typing their stories as the applause from the 5,822 attendees at the Believers United annual convention rolled on like a mighty river. On stage, the man behind the podium was basking in their approval.

A few minutes later, as the speaker launched into his peroration, *The Times* asked, in a bored voice, "Think he's got a chance?"

"What, for the Big Enchilada?"

"Uh-huh."

"Nope," *The Globe* said dispassionately. "Not a chance in Hell."

AT THE RECEPTION following the speech, those members of Believers United who had made a minimum $10,000 tax-deductible contribution were given the opportunity to consume high-cholesterol hors d'oeuvres, wash them down with domestic champagne, and exchange a handshake and a few words with the guest of honor, Senator Howard Stark.

Since the paying guests numbered 108, the funds raised amounted to a tidy sum. By prior agreement, the money would be split down the middle: half into the coffers of Believers United, and the rest to the 'Stark for President' Campaign Committee.

Half a million dollars, give or take, for two hours of schmoozing sounds like easy money, but the Junior Senator from Ohio earned it. He did not resort to the repertory of techniques that every politico learns early on – the bright but meaningless smile, the quick, firm double-pump handshake, the artfully vague phrases that might mean anything and hence meant nothing at all. A typical politician would have used all of those tricks in a situation like this, but Stark was not a typical politician. The support of the Christian Right was going to be vital if he was ever going to use '1600 Pennsylvania Avenue' as a return address, and Stark knew he couldn't afford to go on automatic pilot. If Stark let his eyes glaze over, these people would notice, and remember. They were touchy about respect, and, as Stark was soon reminded, passionate about their concerns.

"More than a million babies every year, Senator, butchered in those abortion mills!"

"Since they've got that Brady law on the books, it's just a matter of time before the storm troopers come knocking on people's doors and confiscating our guns, you just wait and see if they don't!"

"And the man admitted he was a queer, right there in front of the School Board and everything, and they still *couldn't fire him."*

"Won't let a kid say the Lord's Prayer in school, but nobody minds if he smokes a marijuana joint outside on the playground. Hell, some of these hippie teachers would probably join him…"

To each guest Stark gave a handshake, a smile, and a few moments of his attention, whether he felt the speaker deserved it or not. Stark was sincere in his opposition to both abortion and increased gun control, but privately unsure about the degree of menace posed to the nation by gay marriage or the use of fetal stem cells in medical research.

It went on like that for the full two hours, and not once did Stark let his concentration wander. And so he was understandably relieved when his Chief of Staff drifted over and said softly in his ear, "We've put in our time, as agreed, and we *do* have that other appointment later. Do you want to get going, or are you having too much fun?"

Without changing his pleasant expression, Stark replied, in a near-whisper, "By all means, let's get out of here, before all this self-righteousness gives me hives."

His Chief of Staff gave the barest hint of a bow, and a murmured "*Fiat voluntas tua, Domine,*" before turning to address the room in a clear and commanding voice. "Ladies and gentlemen, it was really great of you to invite us here tonight. I know the Senator would stay to talk with you all night, if I let him. But somebody's got to be the bad guy and make sure he gets his rest, so that he can have his wits about him when he goes back to telling the President how to run the country, tomorrow."

There was good-natured laughter in response, partly at the corny humor, but mostly at the idea that the label 'bad guy' could possibly refer to Mary Margaret Doyle, the tall, charming, and beautiful woman who had just paved the way for her boss's departure. And so, after a few final words with Believers United Director Miles Miller, Senator Howard Stark made his exit. As he did so, his Chief of Staff was at his elbow – a position she had occupied since Stark's days as a freshman member of the Ohio legislature.

MARY MARGARET DOYLE drove with the same quiet competence that she brought to everything she did. It had been quiet in the car for a while, but as the headlights picked out a sign reading 'Welcome to Rhode Island,' Stark said, "Let's hope the media doesn't get wind of this little errand of ours. Laughingstocks don't get elected President in this country. Well, give or take Jimmy Carter."

"The media won't know anything about it," she replied, with calm assurance. "Right now you're in your suite at the Copley Plaza, alone, suffering from a bad headache, probably brought on by all of the MSG in those awful hors d'oeuvres at the reception. You have given orders that you are not to be disturbed, under any circumstances, before breakfast time tomorrow."

"Great, terrific," he said sarcastically. "So if something major hits the fan overnight, something that we should issue a statement about right away, we won't even find out about it until 7:00 in the morning?"

Mary Margaret sighed. "'*Woe unto ye, oh ye of little faith*,'" she said. "In the unlikely event that something hits the fan, as you so elegantly put it, one of our staff people, either back at the hotel or in Washington, will hear about it. They have orders to call my phone, which is right here." She tapped the black leather bag on the seat next to her, an immense Italian-made thing large enough to serve her as both purse and briefcase. "I have no doubt that our people, properly instructed by phone, would be able to cope with your hypothetical emergency for the ninety minutes or so it would take us to return to

13

Boston, drafting your hypothetical statement en route. Then we're back in the Copley Plaza through a rear door, up to the 18th floor in a service elevator to which I have obtained a key, and back in our respective rooms, in plenty of time for you to issue a statement or get in front of the cameras, as needed."

"You think of everything," Stark said grumpily. "Too bad, while you were at it, you couldn't manage to think up a more convenient time for us to go on this wild goose chase."

"The man said that Halloween night was an excellent time for it. The balance of forces is favorable, or something like that. Besides," she said, "if you really think it's a wild goose chase, then why are you here? Why aren't you back in your room, on the bed with your shoes off, watching boxing on HBO?"

There was no response. Finally, Stark said, "If what you've heard is true, if this el-Ghaffar guy can really do what he says he can do, then the implications could be just… staggering."

"The national security implications, you mean." There was a touch of mockery in her voice now.

"Yes, damn it, that's exactly what I mean," Stark said. "What did you think, that I want to use this guy to find buried treasure, or something? Last I looked, the value of assets in the blind trust was something like six and a half mill, not counting the house in Chagrin Falls and a couple of other properties."

"It's just over 7.2 million now," she said. "The quarterly statement arrived last week, and has been sitting in your 'In' box. You really should read your mail more often."

"You know, sometimes you can be a real fucking pain, M.M."

"So can you, Senator, especially when you use that kind of language, knowing full well that *I don't like it*."

There was stony silence for the next three-tenths of a mile. Then Stark took in a deep breath, let it out and said, "I'm sorry, M.M. I just can't shake the feeling that this whole thing is going to be a colossal waste of time, and it's got me kind of cranky. But I'm sorry for the way I spoke."

"I'm sorry, too," she said. "I expect I *was* being something of a pain, at that. And you might be right: it *could* turn out to be a fool's errand. But everything I've been able to find out says there's something to it."

"Conjuring demons," Stark said, shaking his head. "Just like in the movies."

She nodded. "Yes, I know. It sounds like very bad late-night TV – except that it might just possibly be for real."

They continued south on Route 95, which soon brought them to the outskirts of Providence, although they did not take any of the exits leading into Rhode Island's capital city.

"Lovecraft country," Stark said, as if to himself.

Mary Margaret Doyle's brow furrowed. "Excuse me?"

"H.P. Lovecraft. He used to live in Providence."

"Is that someone I should know? He's doesn't work on the Hill, does he?"

Stark gave a growl of laughter. "No, he's been dead a long time. Lovecraft was a writer. Still quite well known, in some circles."

"I don't think I've ever come across his work," she said. Clearly, if she hadn't read Lovecraft, he wasn't worth reading.

"Good to know that there are some gaps even in a Vassar education," Stark said. "Lovecraft wrote a lot of stories, back in the Twenties and Thirties. Pulp fiction, I guess you could call it, but well done, nonetheless."

"That's interesting." Her tone said otherwise.

Stark ignored her sarcasm. "Lovecraft wrote a lot of his stories about this race of creatures he called the Great Old Ones."

"Sounds like the Foreign Relations Committee," she said, smiling.

"Lovecraft's guys were even older than some of my esteemed colleagues," he said. "The Old Ones were supposedly on Earth long before man. They were immensely powerful, almost like gods. Eventually, some savvy humans found a way to control them, to lock them away where they couldn't do us any harm. But in Lovecraft's stories, the damn things keep getting loose, despite man's best efforts."

Mary Margaret Doyle drove in silence for half a mile or so, then asked her boss, "Is there a moral in there somewhere? Some point you're trying to make, however obliquely?"

"No, I don't think so," Stark said.

"I mean, if you don't want to go through with this, I can take the next exit and turn around. We can stop for coffee somewhere and then head back to Boston. Believe me, I'd understand. I'm a little frightened at the prospect of doing this, myself."

Frightened did it. "No, keep going, damn it," he said. "We started this, we'll see it through. If this guy turns out to be a fraud, it'll be something we can laugh about later, maybe."

"Maybe," she said softly. "Maybe we will."

They left Interstate 95 a little south of Warwick. After

that, it was all secondary roads, past innumerable fields bordered by low stone walls. The frost covering the plots of farmland twinkled and sparked in the moonlight.

There were few road signs to guide them, but Mary Margaret Doyle never hesitated at any intersections or forks in the road. Finally, a little west of Kingston, she slowed the car and began peering at the road's right shoulder. A few moments later, she murmured, "Ah, there we are," and made a right turn that took the car down a narrow dirt road, tall pine trees lining both sides like sentinels.

"We're almost there," she said.

"Good," Stark replied, and almost sounded as if he meant it.

ANOTHER QUARTER-MILE brought them to the clearing, and the house that stood within it. If Stark was expecting Castle Dracula, he was disappointed. The place looked like it might have once been a farmhouse, although what there was to farm in the middle of this forest was anybody's guess. In the abundant light from the full moon, he could see that the building was not quite ramshackle – the outside walls badly needed re-staining, but were all upright nonetheless; the roof appeared to be missing a few shingles, but was still intact; the porch steps groaned when subjected to Stark's weight, but they did not break.

Since Mary Margaret Doyle had set this meeting up, he let her do the knocking at the weathered front door. It was opened almost immediately.

The man silhouetted in the doorway smiled. "Miss Doyle, I presume," he said smoothly. "What a pleasure to meet you in person, at last. Please – come in."

They entered what seemed to be a living room, its rugs faded, the furniture old and a little shabby. As their host turned back from closing the door, Mary Margaret Doyle said, "Dr. Hassan el-Ghaffar, I'd like you to meet Senator Howard Stark."

The men shook hands. Hassan el-Ghaffar, who looked to be about fifty, was over six feet tall with a build that was slim bordering on skinny. His hair, black with a few touches of gray, was combed straight back from his forehead. The skin tone was on the swarthy side, and his face bore a few tiny craters that spoke of an early acquaintance with chicken pox, or maybe smallpox. A carefully-trimmed goatee covered el-Ghaffar's chin and upper lip. The only incongruity was the pale blue eyes, a color sometimes seen among the Berbers of Northern Africa.

"I am delighted you could be here this evening, Senator," el-Ghaffar was saying. "And Miss Doyle, too, of course." The last was said almost as an afterthought, which led Stark to suspect that the man shared the common Arab attitude toward women. *Too bad for him*, Stark thought. Any man who underestimated Mary Margaret Doyle usually regretted it sooner or later.

"I'm not entirely sure if 'delight' describes my own feelings about this evening, Doctor," Stark said. "I suppose that will depend on what you have to show us."

"Ah, a skeptic!" el-Ghaffar said with an enthusiasm that Stark suspected was rehearsed. "I derive great satisfaction from introducing skeptics to the mysteries of the Nether World. It is always interesting to watch them readjust their *weltanschauung* to the new reality that is revealed to them."

18

"Readjust their *what*?" Stark was not going to be intimidated by some intellectual's command of ten-dollar words.

"'World view,'" Mary Margaret Doyle said absently. "Literally, it refers to a comprehensive way of seeing the world, as well as humanity's place within it."

Both men turned and looked at her.

"Well, whether my world view is due for adjusting remains to be seen, Doctor." Stark said. "But if you're willing to make the attempt, I'm willing to observe."

"Of course, of course," el-Ghaffar said. "I think you will find it an interesting experience. Rather like that enjoyed by those observing the first test of the Manhattan Project." He gestured toward a door in the living room's far wall. "Come, let us descend."

As el-Ghaffar led them down the creaking basement stairs, Stark said, "It's interesting you should mention the Manhattan Project. I saw a documentary last month on the Discovery Channel or someplace. I hadn't realized before then just how much uncertainty there was about the test explosion, out there in New Mexico."

"Really?" el-Ghaffar said. "They didn't know what would happen when they set off the bomb?"

"Apparently not. I gather there were serious disagreements among the scientists. Enrico Fermi, I think it was, was betting that the nuclear blast would set the atmosphere on fire and burn up all the planet's oxygen."

"I hope the others were smart enough to take his bet," Mary Margaret Doyle said, stepping gingerly in her two-inch heels.

"Why 'smart'?" Stark asked. "You figure they should have known Fermi was wrong?"

"No," she said. "They should have known that if he

19

was right, they wouldn't have to worry about paying up."

The two men laughed, perhaps a little louder than the witticism deserved.

"Well, you need have no such fears about this little demonstration, Senator," el-Ghaffar said. They had reached the bottom of the stairs now. "This is not the first time I have performed a summoning, and there is no real danger involved, as long as we follow a few elementary safety procedures."

The basement, which consisted of one room, was larger than Stark would have guessed. It might have been designed as a 'rec room' by the architect long ago, but it was clear that whatever went on in there now would not be considered 'recreation' by anyone – except maybe Johannes Faustus.

There was the pentagram, of course. Stark had done enough reading to recognize one, and this specimen was at least ten feet across. It had been drawn on the concrete floor using a liquid that appeared brown in the uncertain light. At each point of the star was a squat red candle, unlit, about eight inches high.

The altar was off to the right, covered with a scarlet cloth into which a variety of symbols had been woven in black. Stark thought he recognized a few of them, like the figure eight on its side that was the Greek symbol for infinity, but most of the rest were a mystery.

Atop the altar were a small charcoal brazier, a copper bell, several small ceramic bowls, an old-looking book bound in cracked leather, two candles similar to those surrounding the pentagram, and a long sword with a curved blade. Stark recognized the sword as an Arab implement called a scimitar.

On the floor behind the altar was a circle about three feet in diameter, the same color as the pentagram. Ten feet to the left, two more circles were inscribed on the concrete. It was to these that Hassan el-Ghaffar led his guests.

"Senator, if you will take your position within this circle here," he said, gesturing. "And Miss Doyle, inside this one, if you please."

Dr. el-Ghaffar stepped back a couple of paces. "Very good," he said. "Now, in a moment I will seal each of your circles." He held up a cautionary hand. "Nothing that will induce claustrophobia, I assure you. But you will each be effectively protected against the demon that I will summon. It will not be able to escape from the confines of the pentagram in any case, but one always takes extra precautions when playing with fire, so to speak." He grinned briefly, the gleaming white teeth an odd contrast with the black goatee and café-au-lait complexion.

If that smile's meant to be reassuring, Stark thought, *then I think it needs a little work. He's as nervous as a cat in a room full of rocking chairs.*

El-Ghaffar picked up a canvas sack the size of a ten-pound bag of flour. Bending at the waist, he carefully poured what looked like sand around the perimeter of Stark's circle, then Mary Margaret Doyle's, before repeating the procedure on the larger circle behind the altar. The sand, if that's what it was, appeared to be shot through with small bits of blue stone. Stark noticed that el-Ghaffar was careful to create an unbroken circle each time he laid the sand down on the concrete floor.

"Once I start the summoning," el-Ghaffar said, straightening up, "do not leave your circle for any reason, until the ritual is completed, the demon has been dismissed, and I tell you it is safe. This is *vitally* important." He looked each of them in the eyes. "If you disregard my instructions, you will place yourselves in very great hazard."

"What kind of hazard?" Stark demanded. "You just said that this demon that's supposedly going to show up will be trapped inside the pentagram, right? So what does it matter whether I stay inside the circle or walk around the room on my hands, holding a rose between my teeth?"

"I am a cautious man, Senator," el-Ghaffar said. The patience in his voice was clearly forced. "It is true that this work involves some risks, but they are always calculated risks, which means I employ every protection available."

"That's what I don't get," Stark said. "What *are* the risks? What's the worst that could happen if something goes wrong?"

"The worst that could happen?" The Arab shook his head. "Senator, I ask you to believe me when I tell you this: you do not want to know."

"Well, why –"

El-Ghaffar held up his hand. "Please! I would enjoy discussing this issue with you at length, but our time grows short. We must be ready to begin by midnight. So let me ask you this: have you seen that famous movie about the shark, *Jaws*?"

A shrug from Stark. "Sure."

"Then I ask you to consider what you would do if you were in the position of the young man in that film, being lowered into the sea in a shark cage. This water, remember, contains an immense Great White, to which you would be little more than an appetizer, if it could reach you. Now, you are in the cage, you trust the cage, the manufacturer claims that it is proof against any shark in the world. But, as you are about to be lowered

22

into the water, someone asks you if you would like a tube of shark repellent, just for a little extra protection. Tell me, Senator – would you refuse it?"

The two men stared at each other for several seconds. Then Stark shrugged. "You draw a nice analogy, Doctor, although I'm not sure you've established your premise." He sighed, then said, "All right, no more questions for now. We'll stay in our circles until you say otherwise. Right, M.M.?"

Mary Margaret Doyle had been silent throughout this contest of wills. "Of course we shall," she said. "I never contemplated anything else."

El-Ghaffar checked his watch and walked quickly over to the altar, saying, "There is still time, but I must hurry."

A steamer trunk sat on the floor fifteen feet behind the altar. El-Ghaffar reached in and brought out a garment of black cloth with red adornments. With a quick, practiced motion, he slipped it over his head and passed his arms through the armholes so that the robe fell into place, its hem just above the floor. Stark noticed that the symbols on the robe were the same as those on the altar cloth; only the color scheme was reversed. El-Ghaffar then came up with a skullcap in the same scarlet color as the altar cloth. As the Arab carefully positioned the cap atop his head, Stark noticed that it bore the 'infinity' symbol in black, exactly in the center.

El-Ghaffar took his position behind the altar, making sure that both his feet were well within the circle. He opened the ancient-looking book to a page that had been marked with a black ribbon. Looking over at his guests, he said, "I will perform the ceremony in Arabic, since my *grimoire*" – he reverently touched the book – "is written in that language. Also, it is my native tongue

23

and I am least likely to make any mistakes that way. It will be incomprehensible to you, but be patient. You will find things becoming interesting before long."

El-Ghaffar produced an ordinary plastic lighter and lit the altar's two candles. Then he passed his left hand over them several times, reciting something in a language that Stark assumed was Arabic, although the words themselves meant nothing to him.

El-Ghaffar suddenly stopped speaking, drew in a deep breath through his nostrils, and blew it out forcefully through his mouth.

Seems kinda dumb, blowing out the candles, Stark thought, *after just going through all the trouble of lighting the damn things.*

But the candles were not extinguished by el-Ghaffar's vigorous exhalation. Instead, *something* appeared to flash through the air from the altar candles over to where the pentagram had been drawn on the floor. An instant later, the five candles at the pentagram's points sprouted tiny blossoms of flame and were soon burning brightly.

Stark stared at the newly-ignited candles for a second, then shifted his gaze in time to catch the glance that the Arab sent his way.

Yeah, I thought so. Wants to see how well the conjuring trick is going over. Well, it's not bad, although I think Penn and Teller were doing something like it last year in Vegas. You're going to have to do better than that, buddy-boy, if you want to impress me.

Nothing very intriguing happened over the next half-hour. El-Ghaffar read aloud from his *grimoire*, rang the bell periodically – always for five times on each occasion – made mysterious gestures in the air and generally bored Stark half to death.

24

Then, finally, he lit the brazier.

He first dropped in powders from the ceramic bowls. Stark noticed that each substance was of a different color: first there was blue, followed by green, then brown, then, finally, red. After adding the last ingredient, el-Ghaffar held his hands, palms down, over the brazier, read another few words from the book, then clapped his hands together, hard.

The material in the brazier burst into flame. It burned brightly for a few moments, then subsided to a glow that gave vent to a rather thick, gray smoke.

Stark had been watching closely. *That's a little better. I didn't see anything drop into the bowl while he was clapping. Of course, some substances will spontaneously combust when you combine them. Or maybe there's a heating element hidden inside that brazier. But it's a pretty good trick, anyway.*

El-Ghaffar's voice was louder now, and had taken on a rhythmic quality. Among the incomprehensible Arabic words, Stark now heard one that he recognized. He'd seen plenty of news footage of various Arab crowds denouncing America as 'the great Satan,' so the word *Shaitan* was familiar to him.

There were no windows in the basement, or visible ventilation ducts. Even so, the smoke from the brazier was moving now, flowing inexorably toward the pentagram some twenty feet away.

Now you're talking, or, rather, chanting. I can't figure this trick out at all. Wonder if M.M knows how he's doing it?

Stark glanced at Mary Margaret Doyle and saw that her expression was grim. Her eyes were narrowed, and a vein in her neck was visibly pulsing. Stark decided to save his smartass questions for later.

The gray smoke was gathering in the center of the pentagram and had grown noticeably thicker. El-Ghaffar's chanting was reduced to one word now, and he was saying it over and over, louder and louder: "Sargatanas. Sargatanas. *Sargatanas Sargatanas!* **Sargatanas! Sargatanas! SARGATANAS!**"

The smoke in the pentagram's center was swirling, congealing, forming and reforming, and finally took on a shape that was vaguely humanoid. Then the gray mist began to dissipate, leaving the figure in plain view.

Stark's suspicion that he had been watching a cleverly produced magician's illusion disappeared along with the smoke that had been shrouding the pentagram. His skepticism had been replaced by a blend of awe and fear and disgust.

The center of the pentagram was occupied by a rotting corpse. At least, it *should* have been a corpse, except that it was standing, apparently under its own power, and the head was questing back and forth, as if it could see all three of them even though the eye sockets contained nothing but a steady stream of maggots issuing from the putrescent skull cavity.

The figure was naked, which gave Stark ample opportunity to observe the precise condition of its decaying flesh, to note the places where the flesh had disappeared completely to reveal white bone, and to consider the number and variety of necrophages (beetles, worms, and the maggots, among others) that were finding the unquiet corpse a tasty treat.

The grotesque sight had been present only for a few seconds when its odor hit them like a great polluted tide – an amalgam of rot and filth and shit and decay that almost made Stark vomit.

"Hearken unto me, disobedient one!" el-Ghaffar said

sternly. "Thou wert summoned, as per agreement, and bidden to assume a pleasing form. Do so – *now!*"

The thing in the pentagram answered in a voice that was deep and cultured, like James Earl Jones at his most charming. "My form is pleasing to *me*."

"Well, it pleases neither me nor my companions," el-Ghaffar said. "Change now, lest I smite thee!" He picked up the long, curved sword from the altar and held the blade an inch or so above one of the candles.

"Peace, peace, I hear and obey." For Stark, it was the height of incongruity to hear that voice, so alive and vigorous, coming from something that you might find buried deep in a Mafia-owned landfill.

Then, in an instant, the image of decay and death was gone, replaced by something that was manifestly, defiantly alive. The sculptors of ancient Athens could not have envisioned a figure of human perfection to rival what now stood in the center of the pentagram. The man stood about six feet, with a cap of tight black curls that matched the eyebrows which perched elegantly above piercing blue eyes. The body was literally perfect – muscular, tight, tan, and toned, without a scar or blemish.

"Thy form is now much more pleasing to the eye, not to mention the nose," el-Ghaffar said. "Whilst thou art briefly among us, great Sargatanas, I will ask of thee certain simple tasks, well within thy powers to perform." He gestured toward Stark and Mary Margaret Doyle. "These companions of mine would know of thy power, thy wisdom, thy knowledge of this world's affairs, even of those things which certain Kings and Princes regard as their most closely-held secrets. In return, I shall reward thee as promised in our bargain, made freely and duly signed by us both, in mutual obligation."

"I don't think that will be necessary."

The voice was Mary Margaret Doyle's, the first time she had spoken since the ritual started. Both men stared at her in amazement which quickly turned to shock as, almost casually, she stepped outside the circle.

Stark was mystified. She had appeared to be taking this business seriously from the beginning, whereas Stark's suspicion had evolved into tentative belief only in the last few minutes.

Is she trying to debunk this whole thing? Is el-Ghaffar a fraud, after all? Did she notice something that I've missed?

If Stark was confused, el-Ghaffar looked stupefied. He gaped as Mary Margaret Doyle walked briskly over to the pentagram. The demon trapped inside it seemed to be the only one who did not find her behavior unusual. Instead, he appeared to be watching with great interest.

She approached one of the candles burning at the pentagram's five points, and, after a moment's hesitation, kicked it over.

This brought Hassan el-Ghaffar out of his shocked silence. "You stupid cow, what are you *doing?*" he screeched. "Put that back where it was, immediately! Quickly, before it goes out! Do you hear me, you fucking *cunt?*"

Mary Margaret Doyle turned to look at el-Ghaffar. Instead of the shocked and angry expression that Stark expected, there was a wide smile on her face.

"Goes out?" she said pleasantly. "You mean, like this?" The smile remained in place as she raised her left foot again – and stomped the flame into extinction.

A sudden release of energy knocked all three of the humans off their feet. There was no sound of detonation, no flying debris, just a force of immense power that burst from the center of the pentagram, and if there was any noise at all, it was something that resembled a cry of triumph, although it was a sound that had never issued from any human throat.

El-Ghaffar was the first to regain his feet. He did so slowly, awkwardly, like a punch-drunk boxer determined to answer the bell for the last round. Blinking rapidly, he looked toward the pentagram, where the four remaining candles had been reduced to smoking pools of melted wax. The same fate had befallen the two candles atop the altar. And there was an even more important change in the basement.

The center of the pentagram was empty.

Mary Margaret Doyle stood up next, in a single, fluid motion, and began brushing bits of dirt off her expensive blue suit. El-Ghaffar looked at her, but the rage was gone from his face, replaced by a look of shocked incomprehension.

Howard Stark was just getting to his feet as el-Ghaffar said, "We should... all be dead. There are accounts on record, going back centuries, stories of demons who were conjured and then somehow got free of their fetters."

Stark dusted himself off without speaking, left the now useless protective circle, and walked stiffly toward the altar. His face bore no expression.

"All these stories, these legends," el-Ghaffar continued in a monotone, "say the same thing: after the demon escaped, it slaughtered every person in the conjuring chamber, usually with extreme cruelty and mutilation."

Stark had reached the altar, but el-Ghaffar paid him little mind. If he noticed Stark's hand closing on the handle of the scimitar, he gave no sign of it.

"It makes no sense, when you consider the malign nature of demons," el-Ghaffar said. "I can't understand why Sargatanas failed to kill us all."

"It's simple, really," Stark said, in a deep, harsh baritone that was utterly unlike his normal voice. "This time, there are bigger stakes involved."

In his addled state, el-Ghaffar was slow to understand. In the three or four seconds it took him to comprehend what had happened, something that had until recently been Howard Stark took two steps forward, the scimitar in its right hand. The Arab's mouth was just starting to open in a scream when Stark's arm swung in a low, vicious arc.

There was a wet sound of impact, followed a moment later by a high-pitched scream. El-Ghaffar stared in horror as his intestines began to slide out through the long, spurting slash that had just been made in his belly. After a few seconds he looked up at them, his face showing a mixture of pain, horror and despair as he realized that, this time, the shark cage had failed him utterly. Then he collapsed to the concrete floor.

The thing that had once been Senator Howard Stark turned to look at Mary Margaret Doyle. She stared back, her eyes wide, her body rigid as a marble statue. Then the smile lit up her face again.

"That was nicely done," she said. "You've got quite a stroke there."

Stark's mouth smiled in turn. "Once we are alone, in the hotel, I will show you other strokes that I am capable of. All night long, for a beginning."

"I should certainly hope so," she said.

Stark's head turned to look at el-Ghaffar, who lay in a spreading pool of blood, mouth opening and closing like a hooked fish awaiting the gaff. "I could have killed him at once, but it amuses me to give him a small foretaste of Hell. He thinks that he suffers now – he will soon learn the true meaning of suffering."

Mary Margaret Doyle looked at el-Ghaffar with the same indifference she would give to a dead dog alongside the road. "We shouldn't be away from Boston too long. As you said, there are bigger stakes involved, Senator – or should I say, *Mr. President*."

The thing that had once been Howard Stark chuckled softly. "I like the sound of that title. I could get used to it."

She gave her head a toss. "If all goes according to plan, you'll have the opportunity to do so."

It nodded Stark's head a couple of times. "Yes, the prospects are good, and will yet improve. We have you to thank for that. My Father is pleased with you. When the Final Victory is ours, you will be rewarded."

She bowed her head humbly. But when she straightened up, there was a wicked gleam in her eyes. "Perhaps you can provide a foretaste of my reward, in the meantime." "

"It will be interesting to see just how strong your... appetites are. Perhaps, even in this poor flesh, I will prove too much for you."

"That sounds like a challenge," she said, her voice husky with lust. "And I *do* love a challenge. Shall we go?"

At the base of the stairs, she looked back at El-Ghaffar's still-twitching form. "What about him?"

"Have no concern. He will be attended to."

They climbed the stairs, and soon there was the sound from outside of a car starting. Three minutes later, the first rat crept into the basement through a gap in the house's foundation. Its whiskers twitched as it sniffed the damp air. The smell of blood was fresh and strong, and the rat was hungry.

It did not stay hungry long. Nor did its many relatives

Chapter 1

TROUBLE WITH THE manly parts tended to run in Ron Brooks' family. His father had died of prostate cancer, as had an uncle. So when Brooks started having to strain to take a leak, he wasted no time consulting his family doctor, who gave him a referral to a urologist.

The specialist ordered a battery of tests, which were performed during a two-day hospital stay. Some of the procedures were embarrassing, others painful, and a few were both. But Ron Brooks went through it all without complaint, and made an appointment with the urologist to discuss the results a week later.

Hyman Reiss – M.D., B.C.U. – had given bad news to a lot of patients over his sixteen-year medical career. Therefore, he was always happy to be the bearer of good tidings – even if the recipient *was* a politician, a species that Dr. Reiss privately ranked slightly below the tapeworm.

Reiss was double-checking the patient's test results and making annotations in the margins when his intercom buzzed softly. "Mr. Brooks is here for his appointment, Doctor," his receptionist's voice said. "Did you want him in an examining room?"

"No, Kathy, bring him back here, would you?"

A few moments later, there was a soft tap on the closed door of Reiss' office. "Come on in," he called.

The door opened to reveal the receptionist and a man whom Reiss thought vaguely resembled the actor Charles Durning. Kathy politely motioned Brooks inside, then departed, closing the door after her.

"'Morning, Congressman," Reiss said. "Come on in. Have a seat."

Brooks sat down in the padded visitor's chair, but gingerly, as if his goods were still sore from the procedures. "You don't need to call me 'Congressman,' Doctor," Brooks said. "'Ron' is fine, and a heck of a lot better than what my opponent called me in the last election."

Reiss laughed politely. He sometimes found himself beating around the bush when delivering bad news to a patient, but never did so when the prognosis was favorable. "All right, Ron," he said, "let me answer the question you really want to ask: You do not, I repeat, *not* have cancer."

Brooks grinned then, with far more wattage than he'd mustered a few seconds earlier, but the smile faded as his natural caution took over. "This isn't one of those 'good news, bad news' deals, is it Doc?"

"Absolutely not," Reiss told him. "You have an enlarged prostate gland, which is what's been causing your problems with urination. It is not cancerous, nor is it a pre-cancerous condition. In fact, it's a minor but common problem among men in your age group. You're what – 54?"

"Fifty-three," Brooks said. "Until September, anyway."

"Well, it's a common condition among guys your age. The prostate gland enlarges, for reasons that science still hasn't figured out yet, and this partially blocks the urethra, the tube through which urine flows when you empty your bladder – which is why you've been having some difficulty going to the bathroom."

"Will it get worse?"

"Hard to say," Reiss told him. "In some men, the prostate continues to enlarge, eventually blocking the urethra completely, in which case we have to operate – a minor surgical procedure, I assure you. In other cases, the swelling of the gland stabilizes at a level the patient can live with, despite some difficulty with urination."

"Does it ever shrink back to its normal size?" Brooks asked hopefully.

"Without treatment, hardly ever. But there are some new drugs available that have been efficacious with some patients. We can try you on one, if you wish, and see how things develop."

Ron Brooks (R-NY) left Dr. Reiss' office considerably more cheerful than when he had arrived. He was not going to die – not anytime soon, anyway.

Brooks was not an especially religious man, but he was inclined to take Dr. Reiss' diagnosis as a sign – an indication that he should move ahead with plans that had been in his mind for some time, but which had been put on hold when the prostate problem developed.

He was going to do it. He would have to move fast to catch up with the other contenders, but fortunately his 'exploratory committee' had been raising money for months. Ron Brooks was going to run for President.

DEPUTY STAN MEEHAN brought his cruiser to a slow stop in the driveway of the isolated farmhouse, gravel crunching under his tires like small bones breaking.

Near as Stan could figure, this was the place he was looking for. He'd taken two wrong turns on his way out here. A city boy born and bred, he could never figure out why somebody would live out in the boonies who didn't have to. Stan was used to people and the noises that they made; spending all his time amidst the quiet of the country would have driven him bonkers.

As Stan got out of the cruiser and closed the door, it occurred to him that this patch of country seemed... different, somehow. It bothered him for a moment, until he figured out what it was: no birds. A place with this many trees around ought to be alive with birdsong, even this time of year. But it was quiet as the grave.

He scanned the half-bare branches, and saw not a damn thing. Stan knew from TV that birds will flee a predator, even if it poses no direct threat to them.

There's no bears in these parts, far as I know. No bobcats, neither. What the hell is big and bad enough to make all the birds get out of Dodge?

Stan gave a mental shrug and turned back to the house. His gaze took in the missing shingles, the wood that hadn't seen stain for several seasons, the broken windowpane repaired with a piece of cardboard.

Beat-up old place. I hear these professors make a pretty good living, even if they do only work about twelve hours a week. What's this guy do with his money, if he don't spend any on his house?

The Prof apparently hadn't shown up to teach his classes for a couple of days. He hadn't called in sick, and wasn't answering his phone, either. Bob Richman, head of Campus Security at URI, had called the Washington County Sheriff's Office and asked them to take a look-see, which is what had got Stan Meehan sent out here to the back end of nowhere.

Stan checked the copy of the report that had been faxed over. The guy was 47, supposedly.

Kind of young for a heart attack or a stroke. Maybe he slipped on a piece of soap in the shower and cracked his skull. That can happen to ya at any age. Hell, Ellie's cousin Frank did it a couple of years ago, and he was what, 28?

A photo had also been sent, and was stapled to the report. Stan looked at it closely for the first time. The dark-eyed, dark haired man with the goatee who stared back at him looked mid-forties, all right.

Stan peered at the name written on the report, which he hadn't really paid attention to, focused as he was on just finding the damn place. Hassan el-Ghaffar.

What the hell kind of name is that? Arab? Oh, shit!

What would some guy with an Arab name be up to, living way out here where nobody could see what he was doing? And a damn professor, too. The form didn't say what department at URI this el-Ghaffar taught in. Physics, maybe? Chemistry?

Stan felt his heart start to beat faster. This was just like 24, his favorite TV show, where every season another damn Arab terrorist was planning to blow up a city or assassinate the President. Hot damn! Could be Stan Meehan was about to get famous.

Unless the bad guys got him first. Stan unsnapped the leather strap that kept his .45 Colt Commander snug in its holster. He'd better be ready for anything.

He walked up the steps to the porch, the old wood creaking under his weight. He listened hard for signs of life inside the house, but heard nothing.

Stan knocked firmly three times on the front door, shaking loose a few small chips of peeling white paint. Then he quickly stepped to one side, just like he had seen Jack Bauer do. You had to be careful at times like this, in case the bad guys decided to open up right through the door at you.

No bullets punctured the old wood of the door; no gunshots disturbed the almost-eerie quiet. Stan wasn't sure whether he was glad or disappointed.

The six weeks of training he had received prior to joining the Sheriff's Department had not included instruction on how to kick a door in, but Stan had seen it done often enough on TV and in the movies. You had to plant one foot, make sure you were balanced, then slam the other foot into the door, just above the knob. *Bam* – door's open! But, just to be thorough, he figured he ought to try the knob first.

It turned easily in his hand. Relief and frustration once again warred within him.

Stan pushed the door slowly open with his left hand, the right one firmly grasping the butt of his weapon.

"Police officer!" he said loudly. "Anybody home?"

Silence greeted him, instead of bloodthirsty jihadists with automatic weapons. Stan noticed that the furniture was of a piece with the house's exterior – old, beat-up, and neglected. He checked the other rooms, and could tell with a glance that each was empty of life.

There was a door just off the living room which Stan thought might lead to the basement. He opened it carefully, and found that he was right. A light had been left on to illuminate stairs that led downward, but it was the smell that really got his attention. He coughed a couple of times, then covered his nose and mouth with one hand. He knew what he had here, now. Stan had uncovered a few ripe corpses in his four-year career with the law – mostly old folks living alone who hadn't been missed for a few days after they'd passed on – and in one memorable instance, for a whole week.

No terrorists making atom bombs this time. Stan would have bet money that there was a shower or bathtub down there where this el-Ghaffar dude had slipped, fallen, and died. He sighed behind the hand that covered his lower face. He couldn't call for the meat wagon until he had made a visual confirmation. That was procedure, and he'd have a hard time living it down if the smell turned out to be from a dead dog instead of a man.

He took a deep inhale of relatively fresh air, held his breath, and started down the steps, as quickly as safety would allow. With any luck, he could eyeball the corpse and get back out of the basement before he had to breathe the corruption from close up.

The third step down gave Stan his first view of the basement – a small section of concrete floor. The next step gave him a wider view of the floor, and his first hint that things were not as he'd expected. He could see circles and a big star painted on the gray concrete, and some partly-burned candles lying around.

What the fuck is this? Occult stuff?

By the fifth step, Stan knew he had a problem. He could see a man's feet in black shoes, toes pointed up. All well and good. But he could also tell that the corpse lay in the middle of a big, irregular brown stain that was almost certainly blood.

But it was his next step that introduced him to the real horror show.

The torso and head of what appeared to be an adult male was covered by what at first looked like a fur coat. Stan thought for a second that somebody had draped the coat over the body like a shroud, but then he realized that the fur coat was moving.

39

Stan took one more step down, and that was when the rats heard him, or smelled him, or whatever it is that rats do. They immediately scattered – all except for one of the bastards, the biggest rat that Stan had ever seen. A full-sized tomcat might have hesitated to take the damn thing on. It stood on its hind legs and faced him defiantly, something that looked like an uncooked sausage link clutched in its jaws.

The next few seconds were busy ones for Stan Meehan. In the first couple, he realized that what this immense rodent was holding and refusing to give up was almost certainly a length of human intestine. The rat then apparently decided on flight over fight and scurried away, taking its meal along. The next two or three seconds allowed Stan to get his first good look at what the rats had been dining on. Stan turned then, all thoughts of holding his breath forgotten, not even noticing the foul smell that permeated the basement. Four more seconds got him back up the stairs and through the basement door, which he slammed loudly behind him. In another two, he was bent over the kitchen sink, puking up everything he had eaten for lunch, breakfast, and a midnight snack last night, or so it seemed.

Stan knew you weren't supposed to contaminate a crime scene with anything, least of all your own vomit, but he hadn't had any choice in the matter. At least he hadn't left a mess for the other cops to kid him about – like they wouldn't have tossed *their* cookies, if they'd seen what Stan just did.

After a while, he realized he was done. Even the dry heaves had stopped. He ran some water to wash his stomach contents down the drain and splashed some of it over his face to wash away the detritus. He turned off the water, wiped his face with a handkerchief, then made his unsteady way outside and back to his cruiser.

Stan reached in and pulled his police radio from its plastic holder. He pushed the 'Transmit' button and started to speak, but this brought on a coughing fit. He spat on the ground a couple of times, cleared his throat, and tried again.

"Dispatch, this is Five, over."

Marge Lunsford's voice came back almost immediately. "This is Dispatch, how ya doing, Stan?" Radio procedure around the Sheriff's Office tended to be pretty casual.

Stan tried to make himself focus, to get the image of what he'd seen in the basement out of his mind so that he could function like a cop instead of a scared little kid.

"Uh, Marge, I'm gonna give you my twenty in a minute – as well as I can, anyway. It's gonna be tricky, 'cause I'm out here in the boonies about sixteen miles west of Kingston."

"No, problem, Stan-o. We can use your vehicle's GPS to pinpoint your location, if we have to. What's up?"

"I need somebody from the Coroner's Office, along with an ambulance. Also, some forensics people from BCI better get out here, too."

Marge's voice lost its light tone. "What's the matter Stan? Is it that professor guy you were looking for – El Gaffer, or something?"

"Affirmative. I'm at his house now."

"I assume you found him deceased."

"I – I'm not sure."

There was a brief silence over the air. "Say again?"

"I mean, I'm sure he's dead, or somebody is. But I can't make a positive ID on the body."

"How come? I know you've got a photo – URI faxed it over, and I know I attached it to the Missing Persons Report before I gave it to you."

"Affirmative, I have the photo. But it's no good, I mean I'm sure they sent the right picture, but it's no good for an ID of the vic."

"I'm not following you, Stan."

"Because he doesn't have a face no more!"

Chapter 2

MARY MARGARET DOYLE looked up from the *Washington Post's* editorial page and said, "The pundits seem to be of the opinion that we haven't got a prayer."

The demon Sargatanas used Howard Stark's mouth to produce a tiny smile. "In my case," it said, "that is literally true – and has been so for a period of time longer than you could possibly comprehend."

"It's just an expression," she said hastily. "I meant no offense."

"I know."

"But the pundits have a point, damn them."

Sargatanas shrugged. "Damnation? That might be arranged."

She touched his face softly. "I know, my sweet, I know. But later, after The Plan succeeds."

"You still think that it will?"

"I only know that it must. Therefore, it will."

"I like your attitude. It is rare among humankind."

"Yes. Yes, I expect it is."

Sargatanas walked over to the window of Stark's condo and looked out onto M Street. "You're the political expert. So, tell me – why is the campaign not catching fire? No pun intended, of course."

"The main reason is that the field of candidates is a lot bigger than anyone expected."

"And why is that?" His voice was didactic, professorial.

"Because the recession came on so suddenly, and hit so hard, a lot of Republicans have concluded that the Democrats are vulnerable this time out. So, as a result, there are six other serious candidates besides you, not counting the usual fringe fascists. Many of your competitors have bigger reputations and better connections – and, consequently, larger war chests."

"The so-called 'Un-Magnificent Seven.'"

She nodded. "Another pundit's not-so-clever pun. The six others, and you." She grinned then. "This is not to say that you're not pretty magnificent yourself."

He inclined his head in a slight bow. "But that does not solve our problem, and it *must* be solved. Otherwise there will be displeasure, from a source whose displeasure is something to be greatly feared."

"Yes, I understand that," she said and began to pace a slow circuit of the living room. After a few minutes she said, musingly, "We have to find a way to make you stand out from the herd."

He nodded. "Yes, all right, you are the expert in such matters. But there is another approach to the problem which we should also consider seriously."

She stopped pacing and looked at him. "And what is that?" she asked, not at all certain that she wanted to hear the answer.

"The Seven, whether magnificent or not, are far too many." A small smile appeared on what had once been Howard Stark's face. "There is an expression used, I believe, by professional hunters in your world. I think they call it *thinning the herd*."

IT WAS FRIDAY night in New York City – the town where, as Huey Lewis has famously claimed, you can find half a million things to do, even at 2:45 a.m. – and Libby Chastain was bored.

It had been a busy week in the white magic business. Libby had been so preoccupied attending to the urgent needs of several clients, she had neglected to make plans for her downtime. But all the spells had been cast, all the evil curses dispelled, all the pesky spirits banished. And now the weekend was here, and Libby found herself with nothing to do, and nobody to do it with. *Crap*.

There was a new exhibit at MOMA that she wanted to see. Libby didn't mind going to museums alone; but MOMA had closed at 5:00, which meant that her dose of high culture would have to wait until tomorrow. *Double crap*.

She called a couple of her friends, well aware that such short notice meant slight odds of success, and was not really surprised when all she got were a series of voice mails. *Well, at least somebody's going out tonight. Have fun, kids*.

Then, after a brief hesitation, she tried Quincey Morris in Austin. She hadn't seen him since that nasty business in Idaho a few months back. Quincey had saved her life then, at no small risk to his own, but talking about it had seemed awkward to both of them, so they stopped. *So, okay – nothing says we have to bring up that stuff*.

The sound of a phone ringing buzzed in Libby's ear. At the fifth ring, there was a click.

"Howdy. You have reached Quincey Morris Investigations. If you've got this number, then you know what I do. If you want me to do it for you, then wait for the beep and leave a detailed message. I'll get back to you as soon as possible. Y'all take care, now."

A few seconds later, a brief tone sounded. Libby tried to keep the frustration out of her voice. It wasn't Quincey's fault that he wasn't around when she was feeling needy.

"Hey, Tex, it's me. Nothing urgent – I just called to see how you were doing. Give me a call sometime, when you have a chance. And stay the hell out of Idaho. Bye."

As she closed her phone, Libby wondered if that last thing she'd said had been a tad untactful. Quincey'd had a brush with Hell in Idaho, and still carried a burn scar on his neck to prove it. She knew it still bothered him – and not just physically. Truth be told, it bothered Libby as well, but she never spoke about it to him.

Until now – and in an answering machine message, to boot. Way to go, Libby.

She shook her head, put the phone down, and walked over to one of her condo's large windows. She stared down at the traffic without really seeing it.

There were a couple of nice bars within a few blocks from here – quiet, respectable places where she could nurse a drink and probably get picked up, if she wished.

No, bad idea. Libby had gone that route a few times over the years, with men and women both, and each encounter had left her feeling empty and depressed.

Being somebody's fucktoy for an evening isn't an uplifting experience – even when it's mutual.

Anyway, if it was simply a matter of being horny, Libby had a Hitachi Magic Wand (the world's best vibrator, whose name gave her no end of amusement)

46

and a good imagination. But she was saving that for bedtime. Nothing like three or four good, hard, guilt-free orgasms to help a girl sleep soundly.

Walking slowly through the living room, hands in the deep pockets of her bathrobe, Libby glanced at her plasma-screen TV. She had the best cable package available in the city, but she had done some surfing a little while ago, and found herself agreeing with the country song lyric that went 'a hundred fifty channels, and not a damn thing on.'

As she padded through the kitchen, her glance fell on the refrigerator. There was a full bottle of Grey Goose in the freezer, she remembered. Some ice-cold vodka might taste pretty good about now.

Too good, most likely. There was some alcoholism in Libby's family, and although she lived a mostly temperate life – to practice magic effectively, you have to – she was still wary of developing bad habits. Even witches weren't immune to the weaknesses of mankind. Drinking when you were alone and bored was the first step down a path that Libby had no wish to travel. She kept moving.

Well, there was always the Internet, thank Goddess. Libby went into the bedroom, sat at her desk, and logged on.

Like most Internet users, Libby knew where to find free porn on the Web, but most of that stuff bored her now. When you've seen one porn site (well, okay, a couple of hundred) you'd pretty much seen it all.

She went to a few news sites and scanned the day's headlines. The world, it seemed, was still going to Hell in a handbasket. Only the rate of travel seemed to vary.

Then she watched movie trailers for a while. Libby liked the little 'coming attractions' featurettes, even for movies she would never be inclined to see. She admired the artistry involved in taking two hours of Hollywood crap and, in just two minutes, making it look like something that might actually be worth spending eight bucks on.

After viewing all the new trailers that interested her, Libby decided to see if anything was happening in her profession – anything that had made its way into the public press, at least. So she Googled 'witchcraft.'

Lots of Halloween stories, of course, even though Samhain had come and gone. Some Harry Potter stuff, as usual. A parents' group in Lexington, Kentucky, was demanding that local school libraries ban the book series, on the grounds that it encouraged their children to practice the dark arts.

Libby snorted. She knew of a coven of black witches operating near Lexington whose activities made the Harry Potter books look like innocent fairy tales. She and Quincey Morris had clashed with them a few years ago, after the coven had kidnapped a local girl with the intent of inducting her into their circle by force.

Libby and Quincey had rescued the girl before too much harm had been done to her. She had recovered fully. The same could not be said for some of her captors. The survivors, Libby had heard, did not abandon their art – but had become much more discreet in its practice.

Hallmark was coming out with a line of Wiccan greeting cards. *And about time, too.* She made a mental note to send a blessing in the general direction of the Hallmark Company headquarters, and to maybe buy a few of the cards to send to her sister witches, who might get a kick out of them.

A blogger at a New Age web site had a piece called 'How Witchcraft Really Works.' By the third paragraph, she was smiling a little. By the seventh, she was giggling, and before she finished the essay – which had it all so wrong, wrong, wrong – Libby Chastain was laughing out loud. She bookmarked the page to read again the next time she was feeling down, and noticed that her mood had improved considerably. Maybe the folks at *Reader's Digest* had been right, and laughter really *was* the best medicine.

Then she came upon an article from the *Providence Journal* that prompted no laughter from her. None at all.

PROFESSOR FOUND DEAD; OCCULT CONNECTION SUSPECTED

East Kingston, RI. Nov. 4. State Police are labeling as 'suspicious' the death of a URI professor whose body was found in the basement of his rural Narragansett County home yesterday.

The body of Dr. Hassan el-Ghaffar, 47, was discovered by a Sheriff's deputy who was sent to the home after University Police reported that the professor, who taught Anthropology, had failed to show up for his scheduled classes.

A Bureau of Criminal Investigation official, who spoke off the record because he was not authorized to discuss the case publicly, said that el-Ghaffar's body was found in a large basement room containing an altar, atop which were numerous objects often used by Satanists. On the floor near the corpse was a drawn pentagram, a symbol often associated with occultists and those practicing witchcraft.

The official said that el-Ghaffar's death was almost certainly a homicide, although the Coroner's Office has not yet released its report on the case. Identification of the body, which apparently had been in the basement for several days, was made by dental records, the official said, since the corpse had 'become disfigured due to infestation by local wildlife.'

After finishing the article, Libby continued to stare at the screen. There was probably nothing supernatural involved in this Rhode Island business, anyway. People who became interested in black magic were often none too stable to begin with. Few of them were interested in undertaking the years of study necessary to become proficient in the dark arts, fortunately.

Although sometimes they can learn just enough to get themselves killed.

Nobody had hired Libby to worry about it, and there was probably nothing to be concerned about, anyway – except to local law enforcement. Some budding psychopaths got buzzed on meth, and tried to conjure up something evil. When it didn't work, they turned on one of their own.

But the one who had been turned on had been a professor, a Ph.D. This el-Ghaffar was apparently a man who had already devoted years of study to learning – what?

When Libby finally went to bed, her sleep was troubled, three good orgasms notwithstanding. She kept wondering whether that pentagram had actually contained something from the Other Side – and if so, what had become of it?

Chapter 3

DR. REISS' ASSESSMENT turned out to be right on the money; Ron Brooks never did develop cancer – but, a month later, his prostate killed him, anyway.

The medication was slowly doing its job of shrinking Brooks' enlarged prostate gland, but the pills had one annoying side effect: stimulation of the kidneys, leading to increased urine production. As a result, Brooks' sleep was usually disrupted several times by the demands of his uncomfortably full bladder.

On the December night that he died, Brooks had gone to bed early. The Iowa Caucuses, which marked the start of the long and grueling presidential primary season, were about a month away. From that point on, sleep would be a luxury. Brooks arose at 1:43, awakened by the need to take a leak. This would be his first trip to the bathroom since retiring for the evening a little before 10:00. It would also be his last.

As he slipped out of the warm queen-size bed, Brooks was careful not to disturb his wife, Evelyn, who was snoring gently a few inches away. He trudged along the twenty feet or so of carpeted hallway that led to the upstairs bathroom. He had always hated bedroom slippers, so as he stepped into the darkened bathroom, it was his bare feet that first told him that something was wrong.

Water. Cold water. Christ, a lot of cold water, all over the floor, it feels like. What the hell's happened?

Then Ron Brooks did what almost anyone would have done in similar circumstances. Still standing in the inch or so of water on the floor, he reached out for the bathroom light switch, found it, and flicked it on.

"I GOT LAID off last June," Len Kowal said, his rough voice low and sad. "Mold-All Plastics. Machinist. Twenty-two years, I was there."

Quincey Morris didn't know what to say to that, so he just nodded.

"What Len means is, we got no health insurance," Helen Kowal said. "They kept up his benefits for six weeks after they let him go, but after that..."

"So that's why you haven't been able to get medical treatment for Susie," Morris said.

"We been to the hospital with her twice. To the ER. They asked a lot of questions, then they did some tests that we had to put on our MasterCard." She shrugged her thin shoulders. "We're still paying, a little each month."

"Did the tests find anything?"

"No, not a thing. So they wanted to admit her, and do even more. But once we said we had no insurance..." Another shrug.

"Tried to mortgage the place," Len Kowal rumbled. "None of the banks would give us the time of day. Mortgage crisis, they said. Nobody's lending money, nobody's buying houses." He looked away and said to the wall, "And our credit number, it maybe ain't so good, either."

"I'm not a doctor," Morris said gently. "If it really is a medical problem, I'm afraid there isn't anything I can do to help."

"We understand that, Mr. Morris," Helen Kowal said, her eyes rimmed red from crying. "But we thought at least you could tell us if it's... that other thing we talked about."

She doesn't want to say it, Morris thought. *Can't hardly blame her for that.*

He was rapidly coming to the conclusion that this trip was going to be a waste of time, but the knowledge made him more depressed than irritated. The likelihood was that the girl was suffering from some disorder of the nervous system, or worse.

Good news, Mrs. Kowal: your daughter isn't possessed by an entity from Hell, after all. The downside is, she has a brain tumor the size of a golf ball. We're giving her six months, at the outside.

"Would you at least look at her?" Helen Kowal said. "Maybe talk to her a little bit?"

It would have been cruel to refuse. Anyway, he had come all the way up from Texas, and there was always the outside chance...

"Sure, I can do that," Morris said, and stood. Helen Kowal rose also, but her husband remained seated in the worn, overstuffed armchair that had probably been 'Dad's chair' for twenty years or more. He did not look at Morris.

"Her room is upstairs," Helen Kowal said. "This way."

Two flights of threadbare, creaking stairs led to the big house's second story. At the landing between staircases,

53

Helen Kowal paused, waiting for Morris to catch up. As he reached her, Morris said, "I guess your husband isn't coming with us?"

She shook her head. "He don't go in there anymore. The things she does... no father should see his daughter that way."

Morris nodded, as if he understood completely. But he was puzzled as he followed Helen Kowal up the remaining stairs and along a carpeted hallway.

She stopped at a door of brown wood that looked newer than the jamb that held it in place. The doorknob was surrounded by the metal plate of a heavy security lock. Helen Kowal reached into the side pocket of her housedress and produced a key ring.

"This didn't come with the house, did it?" Morris said quietly.

"No," she told him, sliding a key into the lock's thin aperture. "We had it installed after."

The door opened smoothly on oiled hinges.

The large room would have made a Spartan feel right at home. It contained a bed, a plastic commode with a roll of toilet paper on the floor next to it, and the girl, who lay in the bed, covers pulled up to her chin.

Morris had thought that Helen Kowal would perform introductions, to put the girl at ease with the stranger. Instead, she simply closed the door and stood with her back against it, arms folded as if to ward off a chill.

Morris walked slowly toward the bed.

Mrs. K. didn't relock the door. Maybe she's afraid it would stop us from getting out fast, if we need to.

Susan Kowal, age seventeen, calmly watched him approach. All he could see of her was a thin face and a mop of medium-brown hair, tangled and matted as if it hadn't been either combed or washed in quite a while. Her body was just a vague shape under the gray, stained blanket.

I don't know what's wrong with this poor kid, but keeping her in here is tantamount to child abuse. The parents don't know any better, but there's got to be a better place for her than this fucking prison cell.

He stopped at the foot of the bed and rested his hands lightly on the metal frame. "Hi, Susan," he said pleasantly. "My name's Quincey Morris."

"Hi, Mr. Morris. Are you a doctor?" Her voice was high, a natural soprano.

"No, I'm not. But I was visiting your folks, and they asked me to come up and say hello. I figured you hadn't had much company, lately."

Her mouth twitched in what Morris supposed was intended as a smile. "Not too much, no."

"How long have you been…?" Morris found himself searching for a tactful way to describe her circumstances. No point in upsetting her.

"The Prisoner of Zenda?" Her voice was mild, without bitterness. "I'm not sure. The trees are bare, aren't they? They had all their leaves when Mummy and Daddy put that big lock on the door. It was hot out, too."

Mummy and Daddy? Dear God – this kid needs a doctor, maybe a series of them. Not an exorcist.

It looked as if her hands were moving under the blanket. Was she scratching herself? Bedbugs wouldn't be hard to imagine in this hellhole.

He wondered if having an itch was like yawning – one person starts and, before you know it, you're doing it too. Morris had a healed burn scar on his neck, half hidden by his collar. Given the circumstances under which he'd received it, he did his best to forget it was

55

there. These days, he was succeeding more often than not. But sometimes it itched a little. Like right now.

"Your Mom and Dad tell me that you've been having some pretty serious problems lately. What do you think is –"

The girl threw her head back, eyes shut tight, breath coming fast between her clenched teeth.

"Susan, what's wrong?" Morris asked urgently. "Are you in pain? Should I –"

Jaw still tight she growled at him, "No, I'm *coming*! Oh, yes, yes, yessssss…"

Quincey Morris had seen a lot of life's seamier side. If asked a minute earlier, he would have told you that he'd lost the capacity to blush. But he would have been wrong. He felt his face reddening as he averted his eyes to stare at his hands, fingers clenching the bed frame.

Morris understood now why her father had not accompanied them. If she did this all the time, it would be a Freudian nightmare for him every time he got near her.

Is that why they've locked her up? The kid's got some kind of emotional disorder prompting compulsive masturbation, and the parents are so ashamed they won't even try to deal with it?

And yet, they had invited Morris here – into their home, into the girl's room. If it was such a dirty family secret, why share it with a stranger?

Maybe they're so old-school-Polish-Catholic, they figure only the devil could make a girl be so sexual, in such a public way? Is that what the nuns taught them, forty years ago?

He could hear that the girl's breathing was returning to normal, and decided that he could look her in the face again.

"Sorry for the interruption," she said matter-of-factly. "That one kind of snuck up on me."

"You do that a lot?" He tried to match her casual tone. "Masturbate, I mean?"

"Every chance I get," she said, and winked at him. "Which, at my age, is pretty much all the time."

Morris didn't know what to say to that.

"Isn't the female body wonderful?" She might have been discussing a new shade of lipstick she'd discovered. "I can just come, and come, and come, over and over. Sometimes my poor pussy gets so swollen it's sore, and I have to take a break. But after a few hours sleep, I'm good to go again."

Morris had faced vampires, werewolves, black witches, zombies and the very fires of Hell. But a teenage girl's sexuality run wild was something he was not prepared for, by either training or experience. Where was Libby Chastain when he needed her?

"I reckon that –" Morris stopped, cleared his throat, started again. "I reckon that most girls your age must masturbate sometimes," he said. "Some, they probably do it a lot of the time. It's normal, a part of life. But I'm guessing that most of them keep it kinda private, you know? A personal thing."

"Yes, I suppose they do, the poor dears. But I can't seem to help myself, Mr. Morris." Her eyes were wide. "It's like there's something inside me, making me do it. I *just can't stop*. It's like the devil's got hold of me, or something."

So *that's where the parents got the notion she was possessed – the girl thought so, herself*. Morris wondered if her shame over this hypersexuality, fed by a nice big case of Catholic guilt, was so profound that she had reached a psychotic state where she felt Satan himself was inside her, controlling her, making her act so wickedly.

Morris knew more than he ever wanted to about Satan and his ways, and he was fairly certain that making teenage girls in Michigan play with themselves was pretty low on the Evil One's agenda.

"Susan, I think maybe you need –"

"Oh, gosh, Mr. Morris, he's doing it again! Look!"

With one quick jerk of her legs she kicked the covers aside, to reveal that she was naked underneath them, both hands busy, busy.

Morris wasn't able to stop himself from one quick glance toward her groin, where he saw she had what looked like the standard female equipment, even if it was being put to rather vigorous use. Embarrassed for both of them, he turned his back on her.

"Susan, why don't you put the covers back? Please?" He tried not to look at Mrs. Kowal, who was still standing at the door, head down, weeping softly. "You don't need to show yourself to me like this."

"But it's so much fun!" Her voice was mocking. "It turns you on, doesn't it? Huh? Doesn't it?" She was breathing in short gasps now, and Morris tried to banish from his mind the image of her tight, young body, and what she was doing, right behind him.

Maybe once she was done, he could persuade her to get under the blanket again. He wanted to find out more about where this idea of a demon inside her had come from.

"Why don't... you... turn around... Mr. Morris?" Morris was trying not to listen to her gasping voice, and the wet sounds that accompanied it. "Show me that... hard cock... in your pants. Take... it out and... fuck me hard! Come on!"

Okay, that's it. I'm only making it worse.

Morris began walking toward the door. He was starting to wonder if the girl was exhibiting Klüver-Bucy Syndrome. He'd have to ask Mrs. Kowal whether Susan had recently recovered from encephalitis, or received a severe head injury. Maybe he could find a local psychiatrist who would work *pro bono* and try to help this poor kid. Oddly, the scar on his neck was itching like crazy. It hadn't done that since the burn healed, months ago.

Mrs. Kowal had the door open, and had already slipped out into the hall. Morris was almost out of the room when he heard the girl's voice say, "Next time, bring Libby with you! I hear she licks pussy *reeaal* nice!"

Chapter 4

THE WASHINGTON POST had the story first; one of the crime reporters always kept a police scanner going, and Mrs. Brooks' semi-hysterical call to 911 had resulted in both an ambulance and a D.C. prowl car being dispatched to the residence. The crime reporter working the graveyard, a newbie named Miles Kincannon, had recognized the name, and alerted the night editor.

So the *Post* got the scoop, if that's what it was, then the wire services moved it twelve minutes later. But CNN was first to get it on the air.

At 6:01 a.m., the female anchor aimed her blonde good looks at the camera and said, "This is Headline News and I'm Kyra Baldwin. Thank you for joining us this morning. Our top story: the nation's capital is reeling after the reported death early this morning of Representative Ron Brooks, a Republican member of the House from New York, and one of the early front-runners in the race for his party's presidential nomination.

"For more on the story, we now go live to John Rendell in Washington."

Rendell was a thirtyish, handsome black man with short hair and a thin mustache. The camera showed him standing outdoors in a residential area, the uncertain light of approaching dawn supplemented by the news crew's own harsh illumination. The reporter's breath was visible in the cold air as he spoke into the microphone held in one gloved hand. "Kyra, I'm standing in front of the Georgetown home of Congressman Ron Brooks, who was electrocuted here early this morning, in what police are describing as a freak accident."

Then came a videotaped segment focusing on a man identified at the bottom of the screen as 'Martin Hanratty, D.C. Police Spokesman.' Hanratty was a thin man with pewter-gray hair and stooped posture. His beak of a nose and bushy eyebrows gave him a defiant look, and he glared at the forest of microphones and miniature tape recorders in front of him as if he found them a personal affront.

"District police officers were dispatched to the residence of Representative Ronald J. Brooks at 1:58 this morning, in response to a 911 emergency call placed by a woman who identified herself as Mrs. Evelyn Brooks." Hanratty referred frequently to a yellow legal pad that he held in one hand like a talisman. "An EMT unit was also dispatched at the same time. The police officers, who arrived first, found the house in darkness as the result of an apparent power failure. They were admitted to the house by Mrs. Brooks and, employing flashlights, were led upstairs to a man who was lying on the floor of a bathroom in an unresponsive state."

Hanratty paused to turn a page of his legal pad. "The EMT unit arrived a few minutes later. They attempted to resuscitate Congressman Brooks at the scene, but were not successful. Another attempt was made to resuscitate him in the ambulance while en route to Bethesda Naval Hospital. This attempt was also unsuccessful. A third attempt was made in the emergency room of Bethesda Naval Hospital, but without favorable result. Congressman Brooks was pronounced dead at the hospital at 2:44 this morning."

Hanratty stopped and let the hand holding the yellow pad fall to his side. The shouted questions began again, a trickle that threatened to quickly become a flood. Again, Hanratty ignored them. "Any inquiries concerning the medical aspects of Congressman Brooks' unfortunate demise should be directed to the appropriate personnel at Bethesda Naval Hospital. Questions concerning the investigation into his death should be directed to the Federal Bureau of Investigation, which assumed jurisdiction of the case at 3:35 this morning." The questions came in a torrent then. Hanratty stared at the frantic reporters impassively for a moment, then turned on his heel and walked away from the microphone without saying another word.

A moment later, the reporter reappeared on the screen. "Kyra, officially, the FBI team investigating this tragedy will have no comment until its report is issued, probably several weeks from now. However, sources close to the investigation are expressing the belief that Congressman Brooks' death was an accident, brought about by the confluence of two unlikely events: a leaky pipe under the sink, and a defective light switch in the bathroom that caused electricity from the house current to come into contact with the Congressman when he flipped the switch on, while standing in about an inch of water. However, I want to stress here that this comes from off-the-record assessment, confirmation of which will have to wait release of the official FBI report."

The reporter paused for effect, then concluded, "Live from Georgetown in the nation's capital, this is John Rendell for CNN Headline News. Back to you, Kyra."

"Thank you, John," the anchorwoman said into the camera. "After the break, we'll be talking with CNN political consultant Jeff Bloomfield, to get his assessment of how Representative Brooks' death will impact the Republican presidential race. We'll be right back – stay with us."

"MR. MORRIS? THE Archbishop will see you now. If you'll come with me?"

Morris followed the young Monsignor down a carpeted hallway and into an anteroom of dark wood, leather furniture, and gilt-framed oil paintings of the Archbishop's predecessors. Morris wondered if the humility, piety and wisdom visible in those faces reflected decades spent in God's service, or the work of an especially skilled series of artists.

The Archdiocese of Detroit ministered to the spiritual needs of Catholics in four counties in Southeastern Michigan. One of those counties contains the town of Leesburg, from which Morris had recently come.

A very thin, middle-aged woman looked up from her computer and said to the Monsignor, "Go on in – he's expecting you."

Archbishop Thomas Stanton stood up from his desk, a professionally pleasant smile on his face. He said, "Mr. Morris, glad to meet you," and extended a hand in greeting.

As Morris sat in one of the armchairs facing the large oak desk, the Archbishop said, "I hope you don't mind – I've asked Monsignor Costello to sit in on our talk.

He's my closest advisor, and eminently trustworthy."

"Of course," Morris said, as if he had a choice. Costello took the chair on Morris's right, but turned it a little so that he could see both his boss and the visitor at the same time.

"Archbishop Esperanza speaks well of you, Mr. Morris," Stanton said. "I can't say that I know Jorge very well, but we've met a couple of times at NCCB meetings."

He didn't bother to explain that NCCB was the National Council of Catholic Bishops. Either he assumed that Morris knew, or he didn't much care.

"He told me, when he called last week, that you've rendered valuable service to the Diocese of El Paso on more than one occasion." Stanton sat back in his chair and studied Morris for a few moments. "But he was rather vague as to what those services were."

"Archbishop Esperanza is a man of great discretion," Morris said evenly. This was a dilemma he had faced before. If he talked about the dark and bloody work he'd done on behalf of the diocese, down there in South Texas, it might help establish his *bona fides* here in Detroit. Or it could get him branded a lunatic, and treated to what Morris's father had liked to call 'the bum's rush' – right out the front door. Since he knew nothing about Archbishop Stanton, who was new in the job, discretion on that subject seemed like a good idea.

Stanton drummed his fingers on the padded arm of his chair. His tone was a little less friendly when he said, "I agreed to fit you into my schedule at short notice as a courtesy to my brother Bishop. But I have another appointment in fifteen minutes, so I'm sure you'll pardon me if I dispense with the pleasantries and ask you just what it is you want."

Short notice? I had to wait nine days to get in to see you, you sanctimonious prick. "Fair enough," Morris said aloud. "I want you to authorize an exorcism."

Stanton's gray eyebrows slowly rose. "Do you, now?"

"Or, at least, I'd like you to order an expedited investigation, as a prelude to authorizing an exorcism. I believe you'll find a clear case of demonic possession – involving a teenage girl in Leesburg."

"Leesburg…"

"A small town just north of Poultny, your Excellency," Monsignor Costello said. "Population between two and three thousand, I believe."

The sign welcoming visitors to Leesburg, Morris remembered, had said the town numbered 2,643 souls. He began to see why Stanton kept Costello around.

"Of course." Stanton nodded, as if he had known it all along. "And what is it about this young lady in Leesburg that leads you to believe an exorcism is warranted, Mr. Morris? Have you performed exorcisms, yourself?" The question was more a challenge than a request for information. Morris was used to that, too.

"No, of course I haven't. I'm not a member of the clergy."

"That hasn't stopped some individuals, if the news reports can be believed," Stanton said.

"Well, it stops *me*. A true exorcist, of whatever faith, needs years of preparation – including training, meditation, and prayer. Anybody else who tries it is either a fool or a fraud, or both."

Stanton was apparently not used to being addressed in such a tone. When he spoke again, his tone was cold enough to skate on. "Then perhaps you can at least answer my question. What leads you to believe that this girl needs an exorcism?"

"Two things. One, she has betrayed knowledge she couldn't possibly have."

"What knowledge?" Monsignor Costello asked.

"She made an insulting reference to my... business associate, Elizabeth Chastain. I had never mentioned her to either the girl or her parents."

"That's all?" Costello wasn't bothering to hide his skepticism. "Surely there are a dozen ways the girl could have heard of your associate, especially in this Internet age."

"I'd be inclined to agree." Morris kept his voice even. "Except that the family doesn't have Internet access in their house. They can't afford it."

Costello shrugged his thin shoulders. "At school, then. She simply used a computer at her school library."

"The girl is home-schooled. Always has been."

"Then one of her little friends." Costello did not quite sneer. "Perhaps their parents are more affluent, and have the Internet at home."

"The information the girl had isn't publicly available, but let's not play Twenty Questions over this, Monsignor. There's a second reason I believe an exorcism may be necessary, and it's a little harder to explain away."

Morris loosened his tie, then undid the collar button of his blue shirt, and the button below it. He used one finger to pull down his collar, turning in his chair so the two men could see what had been hidden underneath.

After a moment, Monsignor Costello said, "That's a nasty looking burn, Mr. Morris, and it was quite painful to receive, I'm sure. But I fail to see its relevance."

As Morris returned to a normal sitting position, Stanton said, "The burn looks quite recent. Are you claiming the girl gave it to you?"

"No," Morris said. "Not directly."

The two clergymen looked at each other, but before either could speak, Morris said, "You should know that I received that burn four months ago. Apart from the scar, it had healed completely. Until yesterday."

Stanton looked pointedly at his watch. "Your time is almost up, Mr. Morris. It you were planning to start making sense, I'd recommend you do it now."

Morris nodded grimly. "Then you'd best know," he said, "exactly where that burn came from."

Chapter 5

IN THE CONDO on M Street, the TV was tuned to MSNBC. By now, all the news outlets were carrying the Ron Brooks story.

"That was nicely done," Sargatanas said. He touched the remote control, cutting off Chris Matthews in mid-sentence.

"Thank you," Mary Margaret Doyle replied. "But it was your plan – or, should I say 'scheme?' I merely carried it out. The hardest part was the spell for the bathroom light switch. I'm just a novice at magic, as you know. But your instructions were very clear."

"And you're certain you were not spotted leaving?"

"Quite sure. As you predicted, the house's fuse box shorted out after Brooks fried himself, and Mrs. Brooks was too busy having hysterics to hear me leaving in the dark."

The demon nodded with satisfaction. "Well, I'd say that we've made a good beginning."

"Yes, we have. But I can't keep doing this. It's too dangerous."

"I don't *expect* you to keep doing it, as I told you earlier. If we kill off *all* of the competition, even the stupid authorities will become suspicious, eventually."

"There are other ways to 'thin the herd,' as you put it, and I think they seem very promising. But I can't keep playing the role of hatchet man to carry them out."

A sardonic smile appeared on the demon's human face. "Not losing your nerve, surely?"

"Don't you worry about my nerve!" she snapped, but as soon as she'd said it, the part of her brain where the self-preservation instinct resided kicked in, reminding her of how very unwise it would be to offend this creature.

She took a deliberate deep breath, and when she spoke again her tone was much more reasonable. "What I meant was, I'm too well known – in political circles, at least. I'm very closely tied to you, to Stark, I mean, and the campaign. If something should go wrong, if my involvement in these... activities should become public, it would be very difficult for you to preserve deniability."

He understood immediately, of course. "So, in an approximation of 'plain English,' you mean if you get caught putting cyanide in some old fart of a Senator's Ovaltine, I would not be able to deny all knowledge of your clumsy intrigues, throw your fat ass to the wolves, and bring the campaign to a successful conclusion without your fumbling assistance."

The insults, she knew, were punishment for her brief insolence. That was all right.

He continued, "I assume you brought this problem up because you have some notion as to how it might be solved?"

She nodded, tight-lipped. "I do."

He sat back in his chair, waved an indulgent hand. "Enlighten me, then."

"If I can't play hatchet man, then we need someone else to do it. Not a thug – someone who can work discreetly, but effectively, and whose involvement with the campaign can be convincingly denied, if need be."

"And someone who can be himself removed quietly, once his usefulness to us is over."

"Yes, exactly."

"Do you have someone in mind?"

"I do, yes. I've compiled a dossier for you to read. It's locked in my desk – excuse me for just a moment."

Halfway across the room, she stopped, looking back over her shoulder. "Do you really think I have a fat ass?"

He glanced at his watch. "Let's take a look at this dossier of yours. Then, I think we will still have time for me to answer you. In a way that will leave no doubt whatever in your mind – or elsewhere."

She continued on to her office, walking a little faster now.

"AND THEN THEY threw me out on my ass," Quincey Morris said.

"Did they really?" Paul Hannigan, S.J., blew on the surface of his double skinny latte. "About time somebody did."

The Starbucks was half empty at this time of morning, so it was possible to have a conversation without shouting. Considering the subject under discussion, that was just as well.

"Not literally, of course. I don't think the Chancery actually has bouncers on staff." Morris took a sip of his double espresso. "Although some of the nuns I saw over there might've handled the job pretty well.

The Archbishop just made it very clear that our little interview was over. His pet Monsignor showed me the door."

"You can't hardly blame him, can you, Quincey? Some dude they never even heard of waltzes in there with a story like that? You wouldn't be the first nut to show up at a Chancery, asking for something right out of a comic book. Happens all the time."

"I *did* have an introduction from the Bishop of El Paso," Morris said.

Hannigan shrugged. "Even Bishops make mistakes. At least, that's the way Stanton's probably looking at it."

"How about you, Paul?" Morris looked at the old Jesuit. "Do *you* think I'm a nut?"

Hannigan gave him half a smile. "Shit, I've thought that for years." Then the smile faded. "Which doesn't necessarily mean that there isn't really a creature from Hell down there in Leesburg."

"So, you'll do an exorcism? Religious orders don't come under the Bishop's authority. You guys can do whatever you want."

"It's always the Jesuits," Hannigan said, shaking his head. "Ever since that damn movie, everybody thinks that the Jebs are the go-to guys for demonic possession. Why didn't you ask the fucking Dominicans?"

"I don't know any Dominicans," Morris said. "Anyway, I don't like that bunch. Never have."

"How come? As a religions order, they're no better or worse than anybody else. Except the Jesuits, of course, who are better than everybody."

"*Domine cani*," Morris said. "*The Hounds of the Lord.*"

Hannigan drank some coffee and stared at Morris over the rim of his cup. He put the drink down and said,

"Tomas de Torquemada is a long time dead, Quincey. The Spanish Inquisition closed up shop centuries ago."

"Still, that order has a lot of blood on its hands."

"Generational guilt is bullshit, my friend. The Church doesn't believe in it anymore. We've even let the Jews off the hook for killing Christ, in case you hadn't heard. Only took us about two thousand years to get around to it, too."

"We've all got our prejudices, Paul," Morris said. "I never claimed to be perfect. Anyway, the Dominicans aren't here – but you are. And you're the only exorcist I know. So, what do you say? Are you gonna help this poor kid, or not?"

Hannigan stared into his cup for several seconds, then said, "I'll have to go down there and see for myself."

"But, I –"

"I believe everything you've said, Quincey. However, if I request permission for an exorcism, the first question I'm going to get is 'Have you seen the victim yourself?'" Hannigan shook his head. "For something like this, second-hand information just won't cut it."

"Okay, so you drive down to Leesburg, and check the kid out."

"That's going to take some time," Hannigan said. "I have to apply for authorization to conduct an investigation, and the process itself could take a week to ten days. You know how bureaucracies work – even Jesuit bureaucracies."

"All too well," Morris said. "So, after you investigate, assuming you don't decide I'm delusional, what then?"

"I'll talk to my rector, tell him what I know, then see what he says. He may want you to come in, too."

Morris smiled. "You sure he won't think I'm another nut who's wandered in off the streets?"

"No, he won't – especially after I tell him about some of the shit you and I have been through together."

Chapter 6

THE BIG MAN bumped his forehead on the cracked vinyl of the seat in front of him, and came awake with a start, blinking. There'd been nobody sitting there – the bus only had seven or eight passengers – so he didn't have to contend with some granny bent out of shape because his head had nudged her shoulder.

Just as well. I don't think I could handle a pissed-off Girl Scout right about now. His head was pounding like a drum set in one of those Japanese Taiko concerts. *Taiko? And how the fuck do I know about that? Am I Japanese?*

He turned to the window next to him. His head hurt too much to focus his eyes on the stores and office buildings that were passing by at a steady pace, but there was enough light inside the bus to check out his reflection in the grime-streaked window. The face that looked blankly back at him was white, not Asian. It was a thin face, with a nose that looked like it might have been broken once or twice, topped by disorderly brown hair. He couldn't tell the color of the eyes that looked back at him, but he saw they were deep set, with pronounced hollows underneath.

He looked around the bus's interior, using small head movements so as not to call attention to himself by gawking.

Wait a second – what do I care if somebody notices me or not? Am I that shy? Or maybe I'm on the run. But from WHO?

He closed his eyes for a few seconds, willing his mind to be still. Then he checked out the advertisements that lined the bus's interior above the windows. 'CBS: The one to watch for comedy' was superimposed over the face of some doofus he didn't recognize. 'Pezzini's dry cleaning – 24-hour service GUARANTEED' was next, followed by 'WTTG-TV, FOX 5. Now showing *Friends* weekdays at 4:00.' All of which meant he was riding a beat-up old city bus through the darkened streets of Somewhere, USA.

So far, so good. The genius has figured out what country he's in, even if he doesn't know how he got here.

He thought about asking one of the other passengers for some basic info. There was a dumpy middle-aged woman with a scarf over her hair four seats down on the opposite side. He could plop down in the seat next to her, try for a charming smile, then say, *Excuse me, ma'am. I seem to have misplaced my life. Can you tell me what city this is – oh, and today's date, including the year?*

She'd probably decide he was a psycho and start screaming. Then the driver would stop the bus and tell him to get the fuck out.

Which didn't seem like such a bad idea, now that he thought about it – not bothering the woman, but getting off the bus. He had no idea where the thing was headed, and couldn't think of any reason he should stick around to find out.

A couple of minutes later he was on the sidewalk, buttoning his overcoat against the evening chill. There were no other pedestrians, which meant it must be late. It occurred to him to check for a watch, and he had one on his left wrist. Looked like a nice one, too. The hands said it was 12:11. Peering at the face, he learned that it was an Omega Seamaster, whatever that was. More interesting was the little window set into the dial that was showing the number 6. So if the watch was accurate, it was 12:11 a.m., the sixth of... something. The cold air meant that it wasn't summer, but beyond that he had no clue.

He figured around ten minutes had gone by since he'd woken up in the bus, which meant that he had returned to the world at just about midnight. He thought that fact was interesting, but couldn't have said why.

He figured he'd better start walking.

Less than a minute later he came upon one of those newspaper vending machines – you put in your 50 cents, lift up the lid, and take a paper. He checked his pants for change but found none. However, a folded copy of the paper was pressed up against the glass as a teaser. He bent down and found himself staring at the front page of *The Washington Post*. He was less interested in the headline (PRESIDENT OPPOSES BUDGET CUTS) than he was in the date.

January 5.

He stepped back looking thoughtful.

Doesn't mean I'm in D.C. necessarily. The Post *serves a big area, including a good chunk of Maryland and northern Virginia.* He had gotten tired of wondering how he knew stuff like that, so he just accepted the fact that he did. He started walking again.

So it's January 6th, and I'm in the D.C. metro area. So fucking what?

His headache had eased, but in its place he'd been getting flashes of… things. Faces, sounds, landscapes. Each one came and went so fast he couldn't get a firm grasp on it. But the faces, what he'd seen of them, were contorted and ugly, and the sounds echoing through his head sounded like voices screaming.

Flashbacks? But from what? Was I in a war someplace?

Up ahead, he saw a brightly-lit plate glass window. As he drew closer, he saw neon that read 'Capital Café' and, below, 'Open 24 hrs.'

He checked his hip pocket, felt a familiar bulge, and pulled out a new-looking black leather wallet. Checking the bill compartment, he saw twenties and at least one fifty. *Good.* Coffee, along with a chance to sit down and think about things sounded pretty appealing, and he increased his pace a little. His hands were getting cold, so he put them in his coat pockets – and almost stopped dead in his tracks, because there was an object in each pocket, and the scary thing was that he'd known what each one was at once, without looking.

The right pocket was heavier, and his hand had closed around the object it contained without hesitation, as if it had done so a hundred times. The other pocket was lighter, but the shape and weight of its contents were also familiar to him.

As if he didn't have enough to puzzle over – minor stuff like who he was and where he had come from – now there was this. Okay, fine. Fuck it. He could sit in the Capital Café over a nice cup of joe and try to figure out what the hell he was doing in or near the nation's capitol with a heavy-caliber automatic and a silencer.

* * *

77

"She's exhibiting some of the signs," Hannigan said. "Verbal aggression, mixed with a lot of obscenity. 'Why don't you take that holy cock of yours and fuck yourself with it, blah, blah, blah.' Shows aversion to the mention of Our Savior's name, and claims to find holy water painful – but there's no actual searing of the flesh. No speaking in a foreign language, no revealing of knowledge she shouldn't have, apart from what Quincey's reported. No levitation, or any other dramatic stuff. Oh, and she plays with herself constantly, for whatever significance that has." Hannigan shook his head slowly. "This is either one clever demon, or something that's not possession at all."

Despite its secular-sounding name, the University of Detroit is operated by the Society of Jesus. The Jesuit Rector at UD was a skinny, mostly bald priest named Francis Strubeck. His face had the wrinkles you'd expect from a man in his sixties, and they became more prominent when he frowned. Strubeck had been doing a lot of frowning over the last fifteen minutes.

Once Hannigan had finished, Strubeck sat there and looked at him for a few moments before saying, "So your mind is uncertain about what we're dealing with. What does your gut tell you, Paul?"

Hannigan didn't answer at once. He let his gaze take a slow stroll around the oak-paneled room that was Strubeck's study, taking in the many books, the small religious icons perched on various shelves, the stark silver crucifix that adorned one wall.

"My gut says it's possession," Hannigan said. There's an aura of evil in that room that doesn't come from mental illness, no matter how severe."

Strubeck nodded gravely. Turning to Morris he said, "We know so much more about the human mind today

78

than we did in generations past. So many conditions that were once thought to represent possession we now have medical names for – Tourette's syndrome, epilepsy, schizophrenia. Medical names and medical treatments, which are often quite successful. Yet despite all this science, the number of exorcisms authorized by the Church worldwide every year is at least three times what it was in 1950. Why is that, do you think?"

"Maybe the power of evil in the world keeps growing," Morris said, "and so the good guys have to try harder in order to fight it. Exorcism is one of the ways to fight."

"We try harder." Strubeck produced a wry smile. "Makes us sound like a car rental company."

The smile disappeared as he turned back to Hannigan. "I have great respect for your gut reaction, Paul. But it still troubles me that the girl hasn't had a complete medical workup, to rule out the usual organic causes. And a thorough psychological evaluation, as well."

"I don't like it either," Hannigan said. "But the family can't afford it. The father was laid off months ago, so they have no medical insurance, and what's left of their savings doesn't amount to much. They've been living on unemployment, and whatever Mrs. Kowal can scrounge from babysitting."

"They told me that they tried to mortgage the house," Morris said. "But, the market being what it is…."

"The Order could always pay for the tests," Hannigan said. "If you have a spare six or seven grand in the budget."

Strubeck's eyebrows rose. "It costs that much?"

Hannigan nodded.

"There's one additional factor that may help you make a decision," Morris told him. "Of course, that depends on whether you believe what I'm going to tell you, or decide that I'm delusional, like they apparently did at the Chancery."

Strubeck looked at him curiously. "Let's say that I'm prepared to keep an open mind, Mr. Morris. Please – proceed."

It took Morris just under twenty minutes to summarize certain events that he, Libby Chastain, and several other people (some now dead) had gone through at Walter Grobius's Idaho estate.

When he was done, Strubeck said, "What you've told us is consistent with what I've heard about that business up there in Idaho. Although nobody in the Order seems to know very much."

"Now that you know what really happened, I'd be obliged if you'd keep it to yourself," Morris said. "I can't begin to list the number of laws that we broke that night, in the process of..."

"Saving the world?" Hannigan said, and there was no irony in his voice at all.

Morris shrugged. "Call it that, if you want. Whatever it was, we all paid a price for it."

"And your price was being touched with Hellfire," Strubeck said.

"Far as I knew, it was completely healed, apart from the scar."

"Until your contact with that young lady in Leesburg," Strubeck said.

"Exactly."

Ultimately, Strubeck's decision may have been influenced by a factor neither of the other two men knew about: he was dying.

The diagnosis of terminal melanoma had been made two months ago. Strubeck had informed his immediate superior in the Jesuit order, but told no one else – he wasn't interested in receiving anybody's pity. Besides, knowledge of his condition might well have reduced his ability to get things done in the months he had left before the disease made work impossible. He had obtained brochures from several hospices, but kept them out of sight when others were around.

Under other circumstances, Strubeck might have taken a 'wait and see' attitude toward the case in Leesburg. He could have sent another Jesuit down there for an assessment, or tried to find a hospital willing to give the girl a thorough mental health workup in return for a big helping of Jesuit good will. But Strubeck's time for waiting and seeing was fast running out. And his faith in medical science to solve problems was not what it had once been.

He looked at Hannigan and said, "All right, Paul. Do it. Save her, if you can."

Chapter 7

THE CAPITAL CAFÉ wasn't exactly teeming with customers at 12:36 in the morning. A couple of college age guys sat near the window, eating sandwiches and talking quietly. One of them, a redhead with the build of a hockey player, looked like he was coming off a very bad drunk. Three tables over, a 30-ish blonde who looked like a hooker coming off shift was putting away a plate of scrambled eggs and making eye contact with nobody. In one corner, a pencil-thin black guy who might have been homeless was dawdling over a bowl of soup, as if he were trying to make it last until dawn.

After getting his large black coffee, the man with the gun in his coat had picked a chair that placed his back against a wall and gave him a view of the whole place, with clear lines of sight to the front door, both lavatories, and a set of swinging doors that probably led to the kitchen. He couldn't have told you why any of this mattered – it just did.

Letting his coffee cool, he pulled out the wallet again and began to methodically sift through its contents.

Cash on hand amounted to $180, plus the change from the ten he'd used to pay for the coffee. He also had an Amex card, a Visa and a Diner's Club, all in the name of Malachi Peters.

Any sense of financial security he might have derived from these evaporated when he saw that each one had expired – *in 1982* – apart from Amex, which had held out until July of '83 before breathing its last.

A compartment behind the credit cards yielded a driver's license in the name of Malachi Ezekiel Peters, with an address in Brooklyn, NYC. The photo more or less matched his memory of the reflection that he'd examined in the window of the bus.

The license had expired in 1984.

He looked for a car registration, but apparently Malachi Peters didn't own a car. He did own a card from the New York Public Library (expired), a Playboy Club membership card (ditto), a charge card at Brooks Brothers (likewise dead) and a Social Security card. That one, at least, lacked an end date – a Social Security card doesn't expire until you do.

In the other side of the wallet, another compartment, yielded a pocket calendar for 1982, along with an appointment card from Jerome Fletcher, D.D.S. Malachi Peters had been due for a routine exam and cleaning on November 8, 1982. He supposed the dentist had been pissed when Peters didn't show up – or had he?

Last was a membership card from the National Rifle Association. It had expired like all the rest of the stuff, but he was interested to learn from it that Malachi E.Peters was designated a 'Distinguished Expert – Pistol.'

Apparently, he knew how to use that gun in his coat pocket – or he had, once.

Replacing these treasures in the wallet, it occurred to him what he *hadn't* found. No pictures – if he'd had a wife, kids, parents, or even friends, you couldn't tell from the wallet contents. No letters from anybody, either. No professional correspondence, unless Dr. Fletcher's reminder card counted. There was no hint of what Malachi Peters did for a living. Although the pistol and silencer he was carrying did suggest some unpleasant possibilities.

His attention was diverted from the wallet when the coffee shop's door opened. A white-haired man in the black suit and clerical collar of a Catholic priest came in and stepped up to the counter.

Figuring that he probably wouldn't be called upon to shoot the padre, Peters returned to thinking about the wallet and its contents. He had forgotten about the priest entirely, until the old guy slid into the empty chair directly opposite him.

Peters looked up and scowled. "Whatever you're selling, peddle it someplace else, Father. I came in here for coffee, not pie in the sky."

The priest gave him an impish smile. In an Irish accent right out of some old movie, he said, "Ah, well, a pity that. 'Tis always a shame to see a man pass up his chance of salvation, and thereby risk falling into the clutches of the wicked demons in Hell."

And just for half an instant, his face *changed*. The transformation came and went so fast, Peters wasn't even sure he'd seen it. In fact, he was hoping he hadn't, because his impression of what he thought he'd seen was of an inhuman visage so terrible it would give Dracula nightmares for a month.

Peters realized the back of his head was pressed against the wall behind him. Without even realizing it, he'd recoiled from the sight, so horrible that it cannot be described in any language known to this world.

A small smile appeared on the kindly old face. "Now that I've acquired your full attention, Mr. Peters, there are some pressing matters for us to discuss." He leaned forward, and his breath was indescribably rank. "First among which, as far as you're concerned, is how you might avoid being condemned to Hell." The blue eyes twinkled at Peters. "For a second time, I mean."

"*YOU'RE ALL GOING to fry in Hell! All of you!*"

The exorcism of Susan Kowal began at 9:16 a.m. on Tuesday, January 9th. It ended at 11:41 p.m. the same day.

"*Your faith isn't worth shit! And neither is the One you pretend to worship!*"

Demons, Morris knew from experience, did not go gently into that good night. In fact, since it wasn't a good night at all, but Hell itself, that the creature was being sent to, it shouldn't be surprising that the thing usually fights hard to stay on this earthly plane.

"*You're all going to roast for eternity, like big fat pigs! And I'll be the one turning the spit!*"

Hannigan had brought with him three Jesuit seminarians in their early twenties. They were a year or so away from ordination and had volunteered to assist with the exorcism ritual. He also brought Quincey Morris.

The seminarians were all tall and slim with dark hair. Morris had difficulty telling them apart, so in his own mind he called them Hughie, Dewey, and Louie. When Hannigan made introductions, Morris had been struck by how young they looked – young, and innocent. He hoped one of them wouldn't lose his nerve when things started to get intense.

Apart from the demon's obscene verbal abuse, the exorcism didn't resemble the famous movie very much. The being inside Susan Kowal did not spew pea soup, or anything resembling it. The bed did not levitate; the girl did not defy human anatomy by pivoting her head 360 degrees.

But it was still a nasty experience. Nasty and ugly and stressful on all concerned.

And it didn't work.

Not the first time, anyway. Hannigan had told them before it all began that the ritual might not succeed the first time. There was ample precedent for that.

Morris had asked what the record number of attempts was.

"For a successful one? I believe it's nine."

"I'm not sure I want to know what the record is for an unsuccessful one," Morris said.

"I'll tell you anyway," Hannigan had said. "It's seventeen."

"After seventeen, they gave up?"

"No. The exorcist died."

"*Numquan certiore havet mater!*"

After screaming foul obscenities at them in English for hours, the demon switched to Latin. If there had been any doubt, this confirmed for Hannigan and Morris that they were dealing with the real deal, and not an extreme case of Tourette's Syndrome – there was nothing in Susan Kowal's history to suggest that she had ever been exposed to the ancient language.

Morris had picked up enough Latin at Princeton to understand what the demon was saying, although he had never done any of those things with his mother that the demon was suggesting.

Hannigan and the seminarians were each dressed in a black, ankle-length cassock covered with a white surplice – a tunic-like garment that has its roots in the Middle Ages. Hannigan alone had the addition of a purple stole draped over his shoulders. Morris, not being clergy, wore a dark suit – although he took the precaution of removing his tie. It didn't take long for the surplices, and Morris's jacket, to become stained with sweat – and not just because it was warm in Susan Kowal's bedroom.

The prayers went on. Hannigan led them, and periodically sprinkled holy water on the girl. Morris joined in the responses, for all the good it might do, saying "Have mercy on us," "Pray for us," or "Deliver us, oh Lord," as called for.

When, at the end of each ritual, it was clear that the demon still remained, Hannigan would call for a brief break, drink a little water, and begin again. And again.

After a while, the demon tired of Latin and switched its screechings back to English. Morris tried not to pay attention. By then, the foul curses and blasphemies had lost their shock value, anyway.

Then, midway through the fourth administration of the ritual, the demon inside Susan Kowal said something that got Morris's attention, since it was a break in the pattern of threats and obscenities.

"*Even if you win, you lose, you pathetic faggots. One greater than I is here already, and soon he will have the power to bring this world of yours to an end. Then you will all be sent to Hell, where my brothers and I will be waiting! And then the torment will be yours to suffer – for eternity!*"

Morris tried to focus on the responses, but by now he was saying them by rote. This left a good part of his mind free to puzzle over what the demon had just said. You can't believe anything a demon tells you, ever, and Morris knew he should probably give this stuff as much credence as he did the demon's earlier blasphemy about what Jesus had supposedly done with His twelve disciples. But still...

It was after the fifth unsuccessful exorcism that someone noticed the girl's wrists were bleeding.

They had tied her to the bedposts before beginning, of course. That was standard practice. Morris hadn't been happy about that part, but he understood the necessity, which was only confirmed by the girl's behavior once the ritual began. Considering how viciously the demon had fought them verbally, it didn't take a genius to imagine what it would have done with the girl's fists, feet and teeth, given the opportunity.

The exorcist may not harm the person possessed, no matter how strong the impulse to do so, except in unavoidable self-defense. Susan Kowal was the victim here, and hitting her in response to the demon's abuse would make as much sense as attacking a ventriloquist's dummy after it had 'said' something to piss you off.

Morris and the seminarians understood that as well as Hannigan did. None of them had responded violently to the demon's imprecations, although the seminarians had sometimes sent glares in the girl's direction, in response to some particularly foul reference or suggestion.

But now the bed sheet was stained red under where Susan Kowal's hands were bound, and it was easy to see why. The demon's struggles had caused the ropes to rub the girl's wrists raw and bloody. Her ankles were almost as bad. Morris wondered if she was able to feel the pain. If not, she would certainly experience it in full once the demon had departed.

Hannigan was troubled by the severe rope burns – not only from his natural compassion, but out of concern that they violated the Church's 'Thou shalt not harm the victim' injunction.

"Should we maybe bandage her wrists?" Dewey asked. The five of them stood in a rough circle in the corner that was farthest away from the bed.

Hannigan clicked his tongue in self-annoyance. "I meant to bring along a first aid kit – for our sakes, if not for hers. But I haven't done an exorcism in quite a while, and I forgot it. Shit."

"I remember seeing a Rexall at the edge of town as we drove in," Hughie said. "If you'd like to take a longer break, I can –"

"*No!*" Hannigan snapped, startling them. He closed his eyes for a moment, then took a deep breath and let it out. "Sorry. But we're getting close. The demon is weakening – I can *feel* it! We can't stop now – even for twenty minutes."

"Could… could we hold her down, instead of tying her?" Louie asked. "At least that would stop the damage from getting worse."

"But demons often show unnatural strength," Hughie said. "It might be able to throw us off, which would only make matters worse."

Hannigan chewed his lower lip for a few moments. "No, if this demon had the power to impart supernatural strength to the girl, it would have done so by now, by breaking the ropes and attacking us. I don't think that's an issue here." He looked at Morris. "What do you think, Quincey?"

"If we hold her, it'll be easier on Susan, and harder on us." He gave a tired smile. "But we signed on to be tough, right?"

They did it one limb at a time. Kneeling next to the bed, one of them would get a good grip on an ankle or wrist, then someone else would untie the knots. Morris was the last man in place, taking the girl's right wrist after Dewie had assumed a good grip her left.

"Remember what I told you earlier," Hannigan had said before they broke their circle. "Don't look into her eyes. It may be an unnecessary precaution, but in this room we take *every* precaution, understand?"

They were almost done, thank God.

Chapter 8

NESTOR GREENE LET himself into Room 833 at the Hyatt Regency using the card-key they'd sent him. He had no luggage, but since he hadn't registered at the desk downstairs, none of the hotel staff should care. Besides, he wasn't planning to stay the night. And if someone saw him and concluded that he was here for a nooner with some bored Congressional wife, that wouldn't do his reputation any harm.

You couldn't blacken Nestor Greene's reputation with anything less than a charge of serial murder. Even then, it might depend on how many victims you were talking about, and whether they were really, you know, *bad*.

He was greeted by an empty room. Greene went so far as to check the bathroom, but resisted the temptation to open the closet or peek under the bed. He had a strong streak of paranoia, but it was not completely without foundation. Nestor Greene's work had made him a lot of enemies.

Just because you're paranoid doesn't mean they're not really out to get you. Who had said that? Somebody from the Seventies, he thought. Ancient history.

He strolled around the room, too restless to sit still. As he passed the big mirror, towering over the chest of drawers like Kubrick's monolith, he paused to check himself out. As usual, he was pleased by what he saw. His Hermes tie needed a little straightening, but the rest of it – the suit (Oxford), the shirt (Ascot Chang), the pocket handkerchief (Hermes, again) – was perfect. The black hair was a little long to be fashionable, but he liked the way a few strands kept drooping down into his eyes; he thought it made him look boyish – a trick that was getting harder to pull off, now that he had reached his 40th birthday.

He'd never even considered getting the kind of Marine Corps brush cut that so many guys his age thought was becoming. It was all the rage, he'd noticed, among the younger AAs on the Hill and the lower-level members of the White House Staff. Whatever else Nestor Greene was, he was no one's Administrative Assistant. And as for the White House, there was no one there these days who would even think about putting him on the payroll – officially, at any rate.

He was ambling over to the window to check the view when, from behind him, there came the sound of a door opening. Turning, he saw the connecting door swing wide, and a woman walked in from the next room. She wore a tailored business suit and a serious expression. The black briefcase she carried looked expensive.

The woman was tall, with red hair and rather severe good looks that reminded Greene of Sister Mary Boniface, a nun he'd had a crush on as a boy. He immediately felt attracted to her, and, because of the kind of man he was, instantly distrusted the attraction.

"Mr. Green," she said with a measured smile. "It's good of you to come." She did not offer to shake hands.

Greene's answering smile was equally controlled. "I'm afraid that goodness had nothing to do with it, but the thousand dollars, your pardon, I should say the *non-refundable* thousand dollars, did play a considerable role in my decision." His voice was slow and measured, rich with the honeyed accent of the American South. Continuing to look at her, Greene tilted his head a little to one side. "But I do believe you have the advantage of me, madam."

She put her briefcase down on the bed. "No, I don't," she said matter-of-factly, and let the smile turn cold. "You recognized me the moment I walked in; I could see it in your face. It's just as well, really – if you were so out of touch with things as to *not* recognize me, then I very much doubt that I would have any use for your services, and this little interview would already be over."

After a few seconds, he bowed his head forward an inch or two. "Well, now, it would appear that you've skewered me rather nicely. I must either admit to having been guilty of some slight prevarication, or disqualify myself from the enviable opportunity to become associated, even if only professionally, with a lovely and charmin' – and, may I say, *clever* – lady such as yourself."

"While you're solving your dilemma, which I'm afraid you'll have to do within the next thirty seconds, perhaps you can answer a question for me."

He gestured graciously. "I am at your disposal, madam."

"Is that genteel accent and manner of yours for real? Or do you have a DVD of *Gone with the Wind* at home that's about to wear out from overuse?"

He did not seem to take offense. "Oh, I believe that I can lay honest claim to my rather quaint way of speakin'.

You see, although I was born in rural Louisiana, in what some folks around those parts uncharitably refer to as 'cracker country,' my mother, rest her soul, insisted that I spend most of my formative years in a Catholic boarding school in New Orleans." He paused to brush the hair out of his eyes. "The good Sisters, I'm afraid, had some rather old-fashioned notions about Southern gentlemen and how they ought to conduct themselves. And since their punishments for what they considered improper speech and behavior tended to be both painful and humiliating, a Southern gentleman is what I became – in my speech and manners, at any rate."

"I see," she said, and glanced at her watch.

"However," he continued, "since those sheltered days of my youth, I have had occasion to experience rather more of the world and its ways, such that –" He paused, then went on, in a flat tone that contained no trace of accent whatever, unless East Coast Bitter can be considered an accent "– such that I can pretty much employ whatever lingo the situation calls for. And if this is the way you'd prefer to talk business, Ms. Doyle, you'll find that it's okay with me."

She nodded, as if to herself, then gestured toward the room's only armchair. "Why don't we sit down?"

Mary Margaret Doyle took a seat on the edge of the bed and opened her briefcase. As she rummaged inside, she asked, "Why did you say at first that you didn't recognize me?"

"I wanted to see what you were going to call yourself. If you used your own name, fine. If not, I'd know who you were anyway, and you wouldn't know that I knew."

"Even if it had worked, it's a pretty small advantage."

"Several small ones can add up to one big one. Sometimes, anyway."

She nodded again, and Greene thought he perceived a small measure of satisfaction in the movement. "So, where did you lose the Tennessee Williams accent?" she asked. "At Dartmouth?"

"That's right, although I didn't so much lose it as pick up a second one."

"You were involved in politics there, weren't you? Student politics, I mean."

"I never ran for anything myself, but I managed a couple of campaigns for friends of mine who wanted to be Student Body President, in different years."

"They won, didn't they? Both of them."

"They did, yes."

There were allegations, afterward, of certain... improprieties on your part."

"An allegation," he said primly, "is, by definition, a claim made without proof to back it up."

"Yes, to be sure." The set of her mouth had changed subtly, suggesting amusement. "After Dartmouth, it was Harvard Law School?"

"For a while, yes."

"You left when, exactly?"

"Middle of my second year."

"Not for academic reasons, surely?"

"No, not hardly," he said. "I received a job offer that was too good to resist, so I didn't – resist, that is. That's what all this *auld lang syne* is leading up to, I assume? A job offer?"

"That remains to be seen," she replied coolly. "Now, tell me about this offer you received at Harvard. Who made it?"

"A guy I'd met through my roommate. He was from Texas, originally, and the guy he introduced me to had started making a name for himself in political circles down there. By the time I knew him, he was a major player, even though he was only five or six years older than me."

"His name was…"

"Karl Rove."

"George W. Bush's personal Machiavelli? How interesting! What kind of position did he have in mind for you?"

"I don't think there ever was a formal job description. So I asked him, 'Karl just what are you hiring me to do?' And he looks at me, and this big grin spreads across his face, and he says, 'Whatever is necessary, boy. Whatever is necessary.'"

"And so you took the job."

"Yes, and I spent the year 2000 doing whatever Karl Rove thought was necessary. Officially, I was assigned to what's called 'Opposition Research.'"

"Is that a synonym for what used to be called 'dirty tricks'?"

"I'm sure I wouldn't know," he said.

"Well, you must have been good at it, since it launched your career as a… political consultant. So, what did you do for W's campaign?"

"There were actually a couple things that I'm –"

"Briefly, if you please." She was looking at her watch.

"All right," he said tightly. "How about one word? Do you think that might be *brief* enough for you?"

"That would depend on the word, wouldn't it?"

"Then suppose you try this one: *Florida.*"

"The state that decided the election."

"That's the one."

She leaned forward, for the first time. "The Democrats demanded a recount."

"Indeed they did. And a Federal District judge agreed with them, much to the dismay of Jim Baker, whom

Daddy Bush sent down to handle things. You never *heard* such language."

You might be surprised, she thought. Then, aloud: "The Supreme Court overturned the ruling though, didn't they? They stopped the recount, and, since Bush was ahead, he was declared the winner. Game over."

"Exactly."

"You're not telling me that you got to somebody on the Court?"

He gave her a tiny smile. "No, that was reaching a little too high, even for Karl. Or me."

"What, then?"

"The Supreme Court's ruling was based on the conclusion that the recount process was unreliable. Machines were breaking down, ballots were getting lost. In some places, every vote for Gore was challenged as soon as it was counted. The Court had it right: it *was* a mess."

"And that was you."

"Me, and a few guys I brought down with me. And some local help that we picked up. We had no shortage of cash to spread around."

"So, you screwed up the recount, giving the Justices…"

"The excuse that some of them were looking for. Just because we couldn't get to the Court directly doesn't mean that the Bushes didn't have friends there."

She nodded. There was silence in the room for a few seconds, then Mary Margaret Doyle said, "Valerie Plame."

If she was expecting a reaction, the only one she got was a slow raising of Nestor Greene's eyebrows. "Yes? What about her?"

"During the run-up to the Iraq war, somebody leaked that she was CIA. The White House's revenge for the

Op-Ed her husband wrote, claiming that the 'weapons of mass destruction' were a myth."

"Yes, I remember."

"That was you, wasn't it?"

The gentleman planter accent was back as Nestor Greene said, with a smile, "I have no knowledge of any such operation or activity, madam. Nor, if I had, would I be presently disposed to discuss it."

"*WHAT'S THIS – A holy gangbang? Oh, what fun!*

As before, none of them responded to the taunts, and once the girl was secured, Hannigan began the ritual again. Morris thought that the priest may have been right about the demon's hold beginning to loosen. Its blasphemies were fewer this time, and uttered with somewhat less enthusiasm.

When it came time for the sprinkling of holy water, Hannigan did what he had done all the other times. He removed the wand-like *aspergillum* from the small silver bucket holding the holy water (the *aspersorium*) and shook it over the girl's form. But this time, the circular tip came loose and flew under its own momentum a short distance through the air to land softly on the girl's stomach.

Hannigan stopped chanting and made that small, annoyed sound with his tongue again. He closed the prayer book after marking the page with a ribbon, and came around the bed.

What happened next took only a few seconds, but had several discrete, identifiable steps – identifiable, that is, after it was too late.

One: Susan Kowal's head turned toward Morris. In a voice that was an exact match for Libby Chastain's, it said, "Quincey!"

Two: Without thinking, Morris turned and looked at the girl. Like all of them, he'd had a long and stress-filled day, and was not at his most alert.

Three: Morris locked eyes with Susan Kowan, and those eyes were not human at all. What he saw in them cannot be described in words, but an approximation would be to say that Quincey Morris was given a brief, unfiltered glimpse of Hell.

Four: Rev. Paul Hannigan reached the side of the bed where Morris knelt and bent forward, reaching for the small sphere that was the sprinkler's tip.

Five: Susan Kowal's form twisted slightly away from Morris's side of the bed, causing the sprinkler tip to roll off her chest unto the bed, on the side opposite where Hannigan was now bending over.

Six: The scar on Morris's neck began to burn, far more painfully than it had that wild night in Idaho when he had been touched by Hellfire. To Morris, it felt as if a red-hot branding iron were being applied to the side of his neck – and then it got worse.

Seven: Hannigan, seeing where the tip had gone, did what anyone else would have done in such circumstances – he leaned a little farther forward, so that he could reach across Susan Kowal.

Eight: Morris, with a grunt of agony, released his grip on Susan Kowal's right arm and clutched the site of the burn on his neck.

Nine: With the speed and determination of a striking black mamba, Susan Kowal's right hand, two fingers extended, streaked toward the priest's face, less than two feet away.

Ten: those straight, rigid fingers reached Paul Hannigan's eyeballs – and kept right on going.

Chapter 9

PETERS STARED AT the man sitting across from him. "Who are you? *What* are you?"

"You have no memory at all, do you?"

"Not of anything before the last half hour or so." Peters looked up at the other's deceptively benign face. "I've been getting flashes. Faces. Sounds – screaming, mostly. Otherwise, I can't remember shit. I've been looking through the stuff in my wallet – at least, I assume it's mine, since my picture's on the driver's license. But it might as well be something I found on the street. None of it means anything to me."

The 'priest' nodded slowly. "Yes, we were afraid of that. It's so rare to send one of you back, we weren't sure how the transition would affect you. One theory held that you'd arrive incurably insane, although it seems that's been avoided, at least. Those among the brethren who might know the effects for certain are precisely the ones we couldn't ask, lest they find out about our little… project."

Peters held his head in both hands, as if afraid it was about to explode. "Look, if you're trying to drive me crazy, congratulations – 'cause you're well on the way. If you want something from me, and I guess you do, you'll have to explain it in terms that I can understand. For pity's sake –"

The priest gave a laugh that was utterly devoid of humor. "You're speaking to the wrong one about pity, I'm afraid."

"So, that means you're... the Devil?"

The other sighed heavily. "I'd forgotten what stupid creatures you Eve-spawn are, since I rarely converse with any of you, back in my domain. Do you actually think yourself worthy to receive the attention of the Lord of Darkness, you impudent maggot?"

"I'm sorry, I didn't –"

"I am Astaroth, a Crowned Prince of the Netherworld. If we were back there, you would address me as Lord Astaroth. But one shouldn't stand on formality on this side, I suppose."

"So, 'back there' is Hell?"

"There may be hope for you yet. Yes, Hell, Gehenna, Pandemonium, Hades – 'where their worm dieth not, and the fire is not quenched.'"

"That sounds like a quote, the last part."

"It is. Mark 9:48, to be precise. Now let us move on to more important matters."

"Matters like what I'm doing here."

"Exactly. You were sent back because we – some of us – thought you could be useful. In your first sojourn on this plane, after all, you were a professional murderer."

Peters' eyes narrowed. "You mean, like a hit man?" He was thinking about the pistol and silencer in his coat.

"In a sense. You committed your murders – sixteen, all told – in the service of the United States government, which allowed you to rationalize them to yourself as acts of patriotism. Of course, at your Judgment, that excuse worked about as well as it ever does – which is to say, not at all. You were judged guilty of Murder without Repentance, and your soul was turned over to us. All very routine. That was in 1983, as you reckon time on this side."

"And you've sent me back here, because you want me to kill somebody else."

"Indeed. There is no shortage of murderers in Hell, as you might imagine. But one capable of carrying out an assassination skillfully, dispassionately, and on command is harder to find – and many of them are in areas that are under the control of... others. Since we wanted an American, in order to blend in, you were determined to be the best of those available."

"And who is it you expect me to skillfully and dispassionately kill?"

"A Senator, who would be President. His name is Howard Stark."

"So, WHAT DID you think of our political mercenary?" the demon, Sargatanas, asked.

"I think he'll do," Mary Margaret Doyle said, slipping off her shoes. "He's had quite a lot of experience with the rougher side of the business, and he seems to be utterly without scruple. Oh, and he needs the money. He hasn't had a job worth mentioning since Bush left office."

"He's unwilling to compromise his... *principles* and work for the Democrats?" He sounded amused at the prospect.

"His only principles are the ones printed by the U.S. Mint. No, he's radioactive. He did one too many dirty jobs for the Bushies – mostly for Cheney, I understand – and word got around town. When you're so dirty that even Karl Rove won't take your calls anymore…"

She presented her back to him, lifting her hair off her shoulders. "Help me with this zipper, will you? I want to shower and change before the fund-raising dinner."

"Hold still a moment. There."

"Thank you."

"The only thing I dislike about human politics is that it sometimes makes me homesick," the demon said.

She was bent over, sliding her pantyhose down her calves when suddenly she felt him, pressing against her. "Why don't you stay like that for the moment," he said, his voice suddenly husky. "In fact, you might bend over just a little more."

WHEN A MEMBER of Congress dies without a physician in attendance, the FBI is called in. The investigation may involve no more than a couple of witness interviews and a quick read-through of the autopsy report, but the Bureau always gets its two cents in.

Such routine tasks, when they occur in or near the nation's capitol, are given to the D.C. field office – which is an entirely separate operation from the main FBI Headquarters in the Hoover Building. Special Agents Blaise and Garvin got the job by virtue of being the only team in the office when the Special Agent in Charge got the call.

Melanie Blaise was the senior agent of the pair, so she was the one who showed FBI creds to the police detective guarding the door of Brooks's house.

Her partner Bill Garvin, followed her inside. Physically, they were an odd pair. Melanie Blaise, who had barely made the Bureau's minimum height requirement, wore her raven-black hair as long as the Bureau regs would permit and still had the wiry build of the gymnast she had been during her four years at Ohio State. Garvin was six-two and a weight-lifter in his spare time. His blond hair was cut well within the official limits.

Their walk through the house was slow and thoughtful. Eventually, they climbed the stairs leading to the bathroom where Brooks had died. The hallway was well-lit by sunshine streaming through a skylight overhead.

Garvin looked toward the darkened bathroom at the end of the hall. "Power off, you reckon, Princess?"

Once, during a long stakeout, Melanie had mentioned that her parents had paid for a genealogy search when she was small, and found that the family was very distantly related to some minor European royalty. Garvin had been calling her 'Princess' ever since – in private. She had threatened to eviscerate him if he ever did it around anyone else.

She looked around, found a light switch, and flicked it. Nothing. "Power's turned off."

"Good," Garvin said. "One guy's been electrocuted around here already, which is one too many. Don't want to add to the total."

The floor of the Brooks' bathroom was still wet. Although light came in through a small window, they got out the flashlights they always carried and scanned the room carefully, noting the still dripping pipe joint under the sink. Then they looked at the light switch, now a small mass of melted, blackened plastic.

"My Mom used to warn me about turning on a light with wet hands," Garvin said. "But then, my Mom believed the *Weekly World News*." He shook his head.

"I didn't think it was possible to fry yourself with a light switch, even standing in water, like Brooks was."

"It isn't," Melanie said. "At least, it isn't supposed to be. I did a quick Internet search before we left the office. The stuff they make light switches out of these days doesn't conduct electricity."

"Except that it does. Or it did."

"Must have been a manufacturer's defect. That, or the electrician installing it screwed up. Either way, Mrs. Brooks has the basis for a nice, fat lawsuit, whatever consolation that holds."

"I reckon so." Garvin was from the Tidewater area of Virginia, and Southernisms sometimes crept into his speech.

They checked to be sure the house's security system was functioning, although the likelihood of an intruder having something to do with Brooks' death seemed slight, under the circumstances.

Back at the office, they did a quick 'Rock, Paper, Scissors' to decide who would stay late and write up the brief report about Representative Ron Brooks's death. Blaise's scissored fingers beat Garvin's flat-handed paper. "The victory's yours, Princess," he said, and pulled up a chair.

"Good," she said. "I'm meeting someone for a drink, and now I won't have to call and say I'm running late."

Garvin turned on his PC and waited for it to boot up. "New boyfriend?"

"I wish. It's Colleen O'Donnell, from Quantico." Melanie Blaise pulled on her black overcoat. "We were in the same class at the Academy. She's in town giving a deposition at Justice. We're gonna have a few drinks, and" – she flashed him a wicked grin – "badmouth our partners behind their backs."

"Quantico, huh? She's teaching at the Academy now?"

"No, she's in Behavioral Science."

Garvin blinked. "Oh. One of *them*."

"Yup, one of *them*. And if your ears start burning half an hour from now, at least you'll know why. *Ciao*."

Chapter 10

THE EARLY PART of the week was busy for Libby Chastain. Monday brought her a client whose daughter had run away two years ago. The parents had already tried the police, the FBI, and a series of private investigators. Finally, they called Libby.

She used several personal objects the girl had left behind as the basis for a complicated scrying spell. Then she went to work with a series of maps and a magically-charged pendulum. Hours of work over a map of the U.S. turned up nothing, so Libby widened her focus to North America, and got a hit. Juarez, Mexico.

It took her a while to find a detailed map of Juarez on the Internet. She printed it out, then went back to work. The pendulum stopped at a point that could represent anything within a four-block area.

So she went to Google Earth. Who needs magic when you've got technology?

Libby printed out the image for the area she wanted, uttered a brief incantation, and picked up the pendulum again. Its thin point swung, hovered, then stopped – over one, specific house.

To be sure, Libby did it twice more. Same house, each time.

Later, handing over the printed satellite image to the parents, Libby said, "I won't sugar-coat this. She's in a bad part of town. A twenty-year-old girl, alone, far from home – she could be in a pretty bad situation down there. You should be prepared for it."

"Maybe she was only visiting that area," the mother said tentatively. "It's possible that she lives somewhere... nicer, isn't it?"

"Possible, but not probable, I'm afraid. I scryed the image three times over a 24-hour period." Libby tried to make her voice gentle. "I got the same result every time."

"I suppose you want your money," the father said. Fear and worry had made him rude. Libby was used to such reactions, and didn't fire back.

"No, Mr. Deshayne. Not yet. You've paid me half in advance, as agreed. You can send me the rest once you get back from Mexico."

I hope what you find there doesn't make you wish you'd stayed home.

Back in her condo, Libby said a prayer to the Goddess, asking for the parents' safety and success on their journey. Then she checked her calendar, and found the rest of the week empty.

She remembered that she had tried to reach Quincey Morris several weeks ago, and failed – and he had never called her back. She opened her phone and pressed the icon that would send a call through to Quincey.

"Howdy. You have reached Quincey Morris investigations..."

Libby said a bad word and terminated the call. A

frown sprouted on her face, and rapidly grew. It wasn't like Quincey not to check his messages regularly, and it was *really* not like him to get a message from Libby and not reply.

Libby stood there, staring at nothing.

Maybe a little more scrying is in order. If I can find out where he is, I might be able to figure out whether he's in trouble, or on vacation.

She needed a personal item. She and Quincey weren't in the habit of exchanging trinkets, but he had once spent a night at Libby's place, sleeping on the couch. There had to be something.

But there wasn't. She thought of using a locater spell to see if something would turn up, then realized the folly of that idea.

I'd need a personal item from Quincey to make the spell work, and that's what I'm fucking looking for in the first place. Shit!

Libby thought for a few minutes more, then decided a trip to Texas was in order. She might be able to pick up Quincey's trail, then she could decide whether to follow it.

Somebody takes care of his hamster – what's his name, Carnacki? Probably a neighbor kid does it. Maybe he knows where Quincey's off to.

And if this turned out to be a wild goose chase, Austin was a pretty nice town – for Texas. Libby was sure she could find something interesting to do there.

She got online and started looking for airline ticket bargains.

Pity I don't really fly a broom. It would make stuff like this sooo much easier.

* * *

MALACHI PETERS LOOKED at the demon Astaroth. "Okay if I go get another coffee?" he asked. "Sounds like we're gonna be here a while."

"Here – take mine." Astaroth pushed his coffee cup across the table.

"Thanks. But it's, um, cold by now."

The demon touched the cup with his index finger. A whisper of steam began to rise from it immediately. "Not any more," he said, with a tiny smile.

Peters stared at the hot cup of coffee for a second, then reached for a packet of sugar. "Thanks," he said. As he stirred the cup he asked, "So why does Hell want this Senator dead? I would have thought most of those guys would be on your side, whether they knew it or not."

"Oh, they are," Astaroth said. "More than you might imagine. And this one, Stark, even more so."

Peters blew across the surface of his cup then sipped, waiting for more.

"Senator Stark, you see, is playing unwilling host to one of my... brethren." The last word was said with a twist of irony. "Sargatanas, one of my subordinates."

"You're saying you sent him?"

"No, I did not. He was chosen by others, as an insult to me, because I am known to oppose this dangerous scheme – even though my Lord Lucifer was persuaded to authorize it."

Peters put his cup down, frowning. "Authorize? Persuade? I don't mean to be stupid, but you've lost me again. I thought Lucifer was in charge down there, and everyone else did what he said."

"No, it's not that simple. As you used to know full well. My Lord Lucifer is the most powerful of us, it is true. But he is not all-powerful. Others, who were once great angels before... everything changed, served as his generals during the Great Rebellion. We were almost his equals then, and the same holds true in Hell. Which means there are more intrigues, plots, and betrayals in the Netherworld than you would have found in the palace of the Emperor Nero."

"So some of you in Hell favored sending Sargatanas over here, and others were opposed, you being part of the second group?"

"Precisely."

"Why were you against it?"

"Because it just might succeed."

SPECIAL AGENT MELANIE Blaise had arranged to meet Special Agent Colleen O'Donnell at a restaurant called Mac's Place, just off Dupont Circle. Although squeezed between two new-looking office buildings, Mac's Place looked like it hadn't changed in more than forty years, which was the truth.

Melanie Blaise stepped inside and waited for her eyes to adjust to the gloom. The lights were kept deliberately low, and the tables were spaced far enough apart so that you could have a conversation at a normal tone without sharing it with other customers. The German-born bartender was skilled and fast, and he knew more Washington gossip than most people who worked on Capitol Hill.

And then there was the maitre d', another German by birth, who had been there since they built the place. He had the posture of a Prussian General, the dignity of a bishop, and the memory of a Mafia godfather.

As Melanie's vision adjusted she could see him approaching with his slow, measured tread.

"Good afternoon, Miss Blaise," he said with a stiff bow that seemed perfectly natural. "It is good to see you again. We have not had the pleasure of your custom for some time."

"It's nice to see you again, Herr Horst. I guess it's been more than a year, hasn't it?"

"Eleven months, I believe," he said with a slight smile. "Your colleague, Agent O'Donnell, arrived a few minutes ago. If you would follow me, please?"

He led her to the table where he summoned a waiter to take her drink order, and disappeared back into the gloom.

She ordered a Scotch and soda, then turned to her friend and said, "Still sitting with your back to the wall, I see."

"It's a good rule," Colleen O'Donnell said. "If Wild Bill Hickock had followed it, he might've lived to a ripe old age. Or, at least, died with some dignity."

"Dignity or not, you still stop breathing when it happens." Melanie shrugged off her coat and tossed it on an empty chair. "So, how've you been, kiddo?"

"Not bad. Still fighting the good fight against the forces of evil. You?"

"About the same," Melanie said, "although I sometimes think the forces of evil are winning."

Her drink arrived, and Melanie took a sip, peering at Colleen over the rim of the glass. Then she put it down on the coaster and said, "What's wrong? Why are you looking at me like that?"

112

Chapter 11

QUINCEY MORRIS LIVED in a sprawling old Victorian house in the Bryker Woods section of Austin. As Libby's cab pulled up in front of it, a little after 10:00 in the morning, she felt her heartbeat accelerate.

She'd flown into town the night before, checked into the Hyatt, and called Quincey again. Still no luck.

Squinting against the slant of morning sunlight, Libby walked slowly up the red brick sidewalk leading to the house. She followed it around to the back, where she knew she'd find the clients' entrance. A peek through a garage window showed that his blue Mustang was in there. That didn't mean anything; if he were out of town on a case, he could have taken a cab to the airport.

The client door had a pewter knocker which was also a charm against demons. Libby should know – she'd installed it two years earlier. She knocked three times, waited, then gave it three more. *Nada.*

There was also a buzzer. She pressed the button, and kept her thumb on it for a count of thirty. More nothing.

Just means he's not home, that's all. No big deal. Probably.

The door was locked, of course, but Libby had come prepared to deal with locks. A brief incantation later, the knob was turning in her hand. There were wards around the doorframe, designed to repel anyone who came there to do Quincey harm. Libby had set those up, too, and they did not trouble her as she stepped inside.

She closed the door behind her and stood in Quincey's empty office. The room was pleasantly cool, which meant the central air conditioning was on.

It must cost a nice piece of change to cool a place this size. Why spend the money on an empty house? Not like Quincey to throw money away. Did he just forget? That's not like him, either.

Then Libby realized that she could hear voices, coming from several rooms away.

She had a black leather handbag hanging from her shoulder that contained a few things that you'd expect to find in any American woman's purse – and quite a few items that you wouldn't. She reached inside for the telescoping wand that had saved her life in Idaho. She extended the wand to its full length of fourteen inches, and a few whispered words made it active and ready for use. Libby didn't know who – or what – was in the house with her, but she wanted to be ready for trouble.

She left the office and walked softly down a hallway as she followed the sound of people talking. It seemed to be coming from the living room. As Libby got closer, she was able to make out the words. A man's voice, not Quincey's, was saying, "… tell ya, Billy, this here's about the worst wasp infestation I've ever seen. We're gonna have to be extra careful when we take this nest down, 'cause these suckers will attack en masse if we…"

Television. It's some dumb TV show. Did Quincey leave the set on?

114

Just because the TV was playing didn't mean that nobody was home. Quite the contrary, in fact.

Maybe somebody's house sitting? Can't be. Quincey wouldn't let somebody just have the run of this place. Would he?

She continued her stealthy journey down the hall until she was one step away from the living room entrance. Libby took a deep breath and let it out. Then she took that next step, turning to face into the room as she did so.

Libby Chastain stood in the entrance to Quincey Morris's living room, ready for anything – anything, that is, except for what she actually found.

HE LOOKED ACROSS the table at the demon Astaroth, whose disguise as a kindly old priest was so perfect that Peters was afraid some half-drunk Catholic coming off a bender was going to wander into the Capitol Café and ask this Prince of Hell to hear his confession.

"You're enjoying this, aren't you?" he said to the demon. "Messing with my head, feeding me information a little at a time, as cryptically as possible, to confuse the shit out of me."

Peters held up both hands, palms out, as if warding off a blow. "Okay, okay, you do what you're gonna do. I'm gonna hang in there and wait you out, because I know it's in your best interest that I understand what's going on. Since you want me to succeed in killing this Senator Stark for you, eventually you'll tell me what I need to know. In the meantime, have your fun – I can't stop you anyway."

The demon in priest's clothing nodded a couple of times. "Yes you're right, I have been enjoying myself with you. Torment is, after all, part of my nature. But we *are* wasting time, which you were wise not to say out loud."

He leaned over the table until his face was only a foot away from Peters. "We want you to kill Stark," the demon said, "because we want the plan to put him in the White House to fail."

"Who's 'we,' if you don't mind my asking."

"Me, Baal, Asmodeus, a few others who are capable of looking beyond the short-term gain and consider the ultimate consequences of this madness."

Peters just nodded.

"The immediate benefit of the plan's success is obvious," Astaroth said.

Not obvious to me, it isn't. Peters nodded again.

"Stark, controlled by Sargatanas, becomes President, then uses the powers of the office to destroy you apes-with-souls once and for all. It won't be done with the kind of speed and certainty that an all-out nuclear exchange with the Soviets would have achieved, but there are still many paths to the goal. The President commands the armed forces, and hasn't had to bother with a declaration of war since 1941 – and ah, what a year *that* was."

"But Congress can still impeach him, if he does anything too –" Peters stopped, blinking rapidly. "How did I know that? Maybe things are starting to come back, after all."

"And about fucking time, too," Astaroth said. "Even if the fools in Congress were to act, by the time they could begin impeachment proceedings, it would be too late. The wheels would already be in motion, and unstoppable. Sargatanas would have almost an embarrassment of options. Worldwide release of some bioweapon perhaps, or a simultaneous nuclear attack on Russia and China, with immediate retaliation to follow. The precise means don't matter. The fact is, he would have the power to get it done."

"Yeah, I can see that," Peters said. "What I don't get is why you and the others are opposed to it. I don't remember anything much about Hell yet, but it seems to me like the kind of thing you guys would cheer."

"In some respects, you are quite correct. The destruction of you foul creatures, whose creation was the cause of the Rebellion that led to us being cast down, is a consummation devoutly to be wished. But there is one likely consequence of such a cleansing that we could *not* control, and which most of us do *not* want to bring about."

Peters just raised his eyebrows and waited.

"In a word," the demon said, "Armageddon."

COLLEEN O'DONNELL WAS glad to see Melanie again. There had been twelve women in their class at the FBI Academy, and they had tended to stick together – among 80 men and the macho culture of the Bureau, there had been little choice, if you wanted to get through with your sanity and self-esteem intact.

Colleen had been a witch for years before she'd applied to the FBI, and she had not been afraid to use a little white magic from time to time during the course to help the other women, and herself. Nothing dramatic: a steadying of the hands during firearms qualifications, a little boost to the endurance while struggling through the obstacle course, a strengthening of resolve during those times when the pressure came on hard and the men (some of them, anyway) were watching and waiting for you to cry and quit.

It was due in only a very small part to Colleen's magical aid that every woman in her class had graduated. The same had not been true for the men. Colleen had not used magic against them – you can't use white magic to hurt others; that's one of the key distinctions in magic between the good guys (and gals) and the bad ones. Still, she and Melanie had exchanged a private high-five at the news that Joe Pavone (who liked to refer to the female students, among his buddies, as the Dykey Dirty Dozen) had failed Legal Procedures and been kicked out of the class.

The only thing to spoil Colleen's happiness in seeing her friend again was that today Melanie Blaise reeked of black magic.

It wasn't anything that the staff or patrons of Mac's Place would ever notice. Although Colleen thought of it as a smell, what she was experiencing was the psychic response of a trained sensitive in the presence of a spiritual malignity. In other words, black magic is so evil, it sticks to people like an aroma, and to a trained sensitive like Colleen it smells like nothing else in the world.

That's why she was staring, so intently that Melanie had noticed and been prompted to ask, "Why are you looking at me like that?"

No way could Melanie Blaise have taken up black witchcraft. No fucking way.

Melanie had put her drink down and was now looking across the table intently. "Colleen? Is something wrong?"

She couldn't have gone over to the Other Side. For one thing, she isn't twisted enough. Sure, she's got a nasty sense of humor, but it takes a lot more than that to embrace Evil as a lifestyle. I don't know what the fuck is going on here, but it's not that.

Colleen thought fast. Maybe she could make the gloom of Mac's Place work to her advantage. She tried for a reassuring smile.

"No, Mel, I'm sorry, I wasn't looking at you. See those two guys who are just being seated, over your left shoulder?"

Melanie glanced at the two men, then looked back. "What about 'em? They look like a couple of lobbyists, to me. But neither one's got two heads, far as I can tell. I thought I'd grown one for a second, the way you were staring."

Colleen shook her head. "The one with the glasses looked for a minute like a guy whose photo I've seen on the wall at Quantico."

Melanie's face went still. "Serial killer, you mean? Or something... worse?" She had heard stories about some of the cases that Behavioral Science was said to be investigating these days.

"Doesn't matter – he's not the guy. I'm sure of it, now that he's closer and I can get a decent look at him. Sorry for the drama."

Colleen took a sip from her Scotch and water, and tried for a casual tone. "So – watcha been up to, lately?"

Chapter 12

NESTOR GREENE CHECKED his post office box every few days, hoping for an opportunity to make some money exercising his unusual skills – although those had been increasingly rare over the last seven months or so. Mostly what he got these days was junk mail and bills, both of which went into the same post office wastebasket.

But today, he had received a package.

Nestor Greene's salvation came wrapped in brown paper, and was the size of a shoebox. He waited to open it until he was back in his car, a silver-gray Jag XJ-6 that he'd bought four years ago, when he was flush. No one had been afraid to hire him then.

The box contained money and a sealed business-size envelope. He counted the money first, saving the envelope for dessert.

The cash amounted to ten thousand dollars, a figure he found so pleasing that he immediately counted the bills again.

Now the envelope. He used his car key to open the flap, which came up without much resistance, as if it had been glued only lightly. He tilted the envelope, and out fell three old Polaroid photos and a folded sheet of paper.

Nestor Greene looked at the pictures first. The colors were a bit faded by time, but the images remained clear enough: you could see who was doing what to whom. The faces in each shot were plainly visible, and one face in particular, which appeared in all three pictures, drew Greene's attention. It looked like a younger version of someone he had seen before but could not quite bring to mind.

Then he unfolded the sheet of paper that appeared to be a hand-written letter on engraved stationary. The ink, like the pictures, was pale with age but perfectly legible.

Greene looked back at the three photos, staring again at the face that had seemed vaguely familiar. It wasn't vague any longer.

"Well, well," he murmured. "So that's what we used to do for fun, back in the old days. Naughty boy. And we let someone take pictures of it all. Naughty *stupid* boy."

He slid the Polaroids and letter back in the envelope, replaced the envelope and money in the shoebox, and sat quietly, scratching his chin.

There were several ways he could play this to achieve the result his new employer wanted. Each approach promised its own interesting set of repercussions.

Greene leaned forward, started the Jaguar's engine, and watched the side-view mirror for a gap in the traffic. He would go home, relax a little, and consider the possibilities. He should be able to reach a decision by this evening; tomorrow he would act on it.

Nestor Greene waited until there were no cars coming

up behind him, then pulled away from the curb. The powerful engine took the gray Jag quietly away, like a shark moving through still water.

LIBBY CHASTAIN'S PERCEPTIONS were already in high gear, and she absorbed the sight of Quincey Morris's living room in one second of total, frightening, *gestalt*. All her senses were providing data, which her finely-trained mind processed at lightning speed.

Smell: booze, marijuana, stale food, body odor, and vomit. Libby's nose wrinkled.

Hearing: the idiots on TV, of course. The ever-present hum of the air conditioning. And snoring, coming from the unconscious man who lay on the couch.

Sight: empty pizza delivery boxes, piled haphazardly in one corner. At least a dozen of those little white cartons that you get from Chinese take-out. Several of these were on the floor near a wastebasket, as if someone had tried to score points from a distance, and had not cared whether they went in or not. More cartons on the coffee table, along with two Jack Daniels bottles – one empty, the other about a third full. A small hand mirror, on which were two short lines of... *cocaine*? And on the sofa, snoring away like a miniature wood chipper – the man himself. Quincey Morris, scion of a long line of monster fighters, the terror of vampires, werewolves, and black witches worldwide, honors graduate of Princeton University and one of the finest men Libby Chastain had ever known. Clad now in a ripped forest-green T-shirt and faded Levis with the zipper half down, both abundantly stained. One foot bare, the other in a filthy black sock. A three or four day growth of beard on the not-quite-handsome face.

Touch: Libby's left hand, the one not holding the wand, was curled into a fist so tight that the manicured fingernails were digging into her palm.

Taste: It had been hours since breakfast, but there was now a definite, distinct taste in Libby Chastain's mouth, and she recognized it for what is was: the coppery taste of fear.

MELANIE BLAISE SAT back, her chair creaking a little. It was comfortable, but well-used and maybe a little worn down – kind of like Mac's Place itself.

"Haven't been up to much, recently" she told Colleen O'Donnell. "Not recently. More paperwork than anything else." She smiled a little. "Can we still call it paperwork, when there's so little paper involved? Maybe *electron-work* is more appropriate these days."

"Call it whatever you want," Colleen said. "It's still bureaucratic bullshit, most of it."

"Amen to that, sister." Melanie shook her head a little ruefully. "But it's still better than staying in Akron and making my slow way up the corporate ladder at B.F. Goodrich until I'd hit my head on the glass ceiling. Of course, all I knew about the Bureau then was from movies and TV. I thought it was all going to be car chases and shootouts with desperate international criminals."

Colleen gave her a small smile. "Disappointed?"

"I was, a little – until my first real shootout. You can do all the arrest problems in Hogan's Alley that you want. The real thing is still different."

Colleen nodded. "Real bullets, real adrenaline, real danger."

"And real blood. Gabe McWirter was determined not to be taken alive. He'd gone down for bank robbery twice already, and the third conviction would be mandatory life. I guess he knew that."

"So he got his wish."

"Yeah, he did. I think he figured to take one of us with him, though. He ran at me, rather than Garvin. Maybe he figured a woman might hesitate, or something. Bastard looked surprised when I double-tapped him with my Glock."

Melanie's fresh drink had arrived, and she took a sip before continuing. "I was okay, you know, while it was going down. The training really *does* take over, which I guess is the whole point of it. But about an hour later, I got the shakes so bad I couldn't even stand. Fortunately, I was able to get into a stall in the ladies room before it got too bad. Nobody saw anything."

"No shootouts recently though, huh?" Colleen could still smell the fetid odor of black magic on her friend, and was determined to find out its origin.

"Nope, which is fine with me. Garvin and I spent most of last week in court, giving testimony in the Delicata kidnapping case. Guy's lawyer seemed to think he's Perry Mason – kept each of us on the stand for-fucking-*ever*."

Colleen contented herself with "Um-hmm," and waited. She didn't want to push too hard, although she would use Voice on Melanie if she couldn't get information any other way. She hated to employ magic with friends, but black sorcery is serious business. She had to know its source.

"Oh, and we caught a dead Congressman this morning," Melanie said.

"That must have been tricky," Colleen said. "How far did he fall?"

"No, dummy, the guy died in his house. You know the drill – he wasn't under medical care when he croaked, so somebody had to check it out. At least it got us out of the office."

"Whose political *corpus* was *delecti*?" Colleen asked casually.

"Brooks, Ronald J. R-NY. From someplace upstate. I think."

"Heart attack?"

"Uh-uh. Freak accident. He got up in the middle of the night to take a whiz, not knowing that a leaky pipe had caused some water to pool on the bathroom floor. He was standing in it when he flicked the switch. And that's all she wrote."

Colleen's brow furrowed. "That's not supposed to happen."

"I bet the Congressman thought so too, in his last moments."

"No, I mean electrical switches these days are purposely designed not to do shit like that. That's why they're made of plastic or ceramic instead of metal – they can't conduct electricity."

"Yeah, I know. Our best guess is that the switch was defective. The widow probably has grounds for a suit against the manufacturer, if she wants to pursue it. *I* sure as hell would."

Colleen frowned into her drink for a few seconds before saying, "Ronald Brooks. That name's been in the news for something recently. Did he get caught with his hand in the political cookie jar, or something?"

"Not that I know of," Melanie told her. "But he *was* running for President."

Colleen nodded. "*That's* where I heard his name. One of the 'Un-Magnificent Seven,' right?"

"There's six, now."

"Right," Colleen said, with a vague feeling of unease that she couldn't explain. "And then there were six."

"ARMAGEDDON," MALACHI PETERS repeated. "That word sounds familiar, but I don't…"

"The final battle between the forces of light and darkness," Astaroth told him. "It's supposed to coincide with the Second Coming, which I've always thought sounds like a reference to some virgin's honeymoon. In any case, it is prophesied to result in the ultimate defeat of my Lord Satan and us, his humble followers."

"No offense, but I thought you guys had already been defeated," Peters said.

"Yes, I know. But this is supposed to involve a deeper pit, hotter fires, and I don't know what all. The scriptural references are not exactly clear."

"And you believe that's what happens – you lose again?"

"Not at all," the demon said. "Or, rather, not necessarily. What the other side calls *prophecy* we call *propaganda* – a word that the Church itself invented. By the same token, even a broken watch is right twice a day."

"So you're not sure."

"Quite right. There is too much at stake – all we have built, both here and in Hell, over the millennia. No, if there is to be such a war, it is we who will choose the time. And the time is *not* now."

"So, let's say I manage to kill Stark – then what happens?"

"Sargatanas will be returned home, where he will face the most obscene punishments I can devise. He is my minion, after all, and I can be *very* creative."

"Why does he have to go back? *You're* here, in human form that you took on yourself. You didn't have to possess anybody."

"I am permitted on this plane for one revolution of the planet. Twenty-four hours, no more. Then I must return. It is the Law."

"Whose law? Satan's, or...?" Stark glanced toward the ceiling for a moment.

"It is no concern of yours, worm. Focus instead on the reason why you were allowed to leave the place of torment. You must kill Stark, lest he become your pitiful country's next – and last – President."

"Under the circumstances," Peters said, "I'm sure you won't be offended when I ask, 'What's in it for me?'"

The demon shrugged, a little too casually for Peters's liking. "You'll be allowed to remain here, of course. One damned soul, more or less, is of no consequence. There are an uncountable number of you in Hell already, with millions more coming every day. No one will miss you, least of all me."

"Uh-huh. Allowed to remain for how long? Until I live out my natural lifespan? Then what? Another judgment – or back to the fire, no matter what?"

The demon laid a long index finger along his jaw and thought – or appeared to. "You know that's an interesting question. There's very little precedent for something like this, and I can't access that which doesn't exist, as I told you." He smiled at Peters without showing any teeth. "I suppose we'll just have to hold that question in abeyance, for the time being. I'm sure it will work itself out."

Before Peters could protest, the demon said mildly, "Or, I could take you back with me right now, this very second. I'm sure there must be some other American

127

assassin in Hell who would roast his own mother over a slow fire for the chance of even a few seconds' respite from eternal torment."

"No, no," Peters said hastily. "It's okay. I'll take my chances."

"A wise choice," Astaroth said. "By the by, how's your memory?"

"Stuff's coming back," he said. "I can remember college, sort of. My parents. Signing on with the Company after graduation." He paused. "My wife."

"Yes, the fair Cecelia. And get any thought of looking her up out of your head – she was killed by a drunk driver, in 1991."

Peters closed his eyes, kept them shut as he said, "I see."

"It may interest you to know, however, that she is *not* among our guests."

Peters opened his eyes and looked at him.

"That's right, Peters. She made it. All the way to the Promised Land." The last words were said with a sneer, but Peters felt his heart lift. For the first time since coming back to this world, he felt like smiling.

"Now, then," Astaroth said, "down to brass tacks. Take a few days for your memory to return fully, as I have no doubt it will. And get yourself oriented to the Twenty-First Century. You'll find that quite a lot has changed since you, uh, left. You're no good to me, unless you're fully functional. Then get started on your task."

"That's going to pose some problems," Peters said. "All I've only got on me is a bunch of expired credit cards and a hundred eighty-some bucks in cash. That wasn't a lot of money even in the Eighties – I imagine it's worth even less now."

"Really?" The demon raised his eyebrows. "Perhaps you should look again."

Peters reached for his wallet and found that it felt thicker than he remembered. Opening it, he saw that it was full of bills, all of which seemed to be hundreds.

"Five thousand dollars," Astaroth said. "And every time you open that wallet, it will contain the same amount, no matter how much you have removed from it previously. You can use it to accumulate cash, if you need to. And those credit cards, which are all up-to-date, should serve you well. Each one has a credit limit that you probably could not exceed, even if you tried."

Peters looked. The expired pieces of plastic he'd found the last time had all been replaced with new-looking credit cards, some of which he didn't even recognize. "That seems very... generous," he said.

"Generosity is not in my nature, as you should be able to deduce, even if you can't remember it," the demon said. "You will have expenses – you will be surprised what a truly accurate assault rifle costs these days, for instance, and the price of plastic explosive is outrageous. Besides, in order to get close to a U.S. Senator, you may have to play the part of a wealthy man. And now you are one – for the time being, at least."

Astaroth tapped the back of Peter's hand that still held the bulging wallet. "However, if you start spending that wealth on whores and cocaine instead of getting on with the job, I'll know about it. And you will find yourself back in Hell so fast, it will makes your ears bleed. And there I will devote my *very* special attentions to you, for the next thousand years or so. Have I made myself clear?"

"Crystal," Peters said. "What kind of timeframe do I have to operate in?"

"The one provided by the American election cycle. I don't care when or how you kill him, but Stark must *not* take the oath of office next January."

"You seem pretty sure he'll win. Can demons see the future?"

Astaroth shook his human head. "No, that is an ability we have never possessed, more's the pity."

"But you figure his chances are pretty good," Peters said.

"Being one of my *brethren*, he has certain... advantages that the other candidates lack. And he has that bitch Doyle working with him. She is almost as ruthless as he is, which is a compliment I haven't paid to a human since the days of the Third Reich. Yes, I think he'll win."

"But what if he doesn't? Just for the sake of, um discussion." Peters had been about to use the word 'argument,' but decided that might be unwise. "What if I haven't gotten to him by election day, and he loses? Do you still want him dead?"

"Oh, absolutely. Quite apart from the fact that he'd probably start planning for the next election immediately, which he might well win, the sooner that Sargatanas is back in Hades and enjoying my *hospitality*, the better I will like it."

The way that Astaroth had uttered 'hospitality' made Peters glad that the demon wasn't thinking about him when he said it. "All right, then – either way, he's a dead man."

"Very good." The demon let a gentle smile appear on his priestly face. "And once that's accomplished, we'll see what's to be done about you."

He pushed his chair back and stood up. "Come on," he said, "let's get out of here. You have work to do, and

I want to see if I can find a nun to despoil before I have to return home. I imagine all the altar boys are in bed, by now, alas."

Chapter 13

SHE KNEW THAT Morris was still alive; the chainsaw sound of his snores showed *that* as well as anything would have. Still, Libby Chastain knelt next to the sofa and checked his pulse: a little slow, but steady.

By his own account, Quincey had been something of a party boy at college, like many of his contemporaries. But for him, Libby knew, graduating from Princeton had meant the end of keg parties and pub crawls and the beginning of his training to join the family business. And when your family's business involves dealing with entities euphemistically known as 'creatures of the night,' and the slightest mistake can get you killed – or worse – then self-indulgence just isn't an option.

And Quincey had understood that – had known it down to his core. In the years they had known each other, Libby had never seen Quincey drunk, or high, or wired. He had never, to her knowledge, consumed more than two bourbon-and-waters in one sitting, and that only occasionally.

Libby knew the kind of horrors Quincey had faced – she had seen many of them along with him. Nothing had driven him to this kind of mindless, solitary orgy of self-indulgence. She needed to know what that traumatic experience had been. Only with that knowledge could she help Quincey heal.

She set about bringing him back to the land of the living – the body for a start, and then the spirit. The first of those two tasks was going to be the easier one.

Libby Chastain sighed, opened her bag, and began to sort through the contents.

THE AQUINAS INSTITUTE of Theology in St. Louis is located in a building that is both short and broad. The two-story structure once housed the Standard Adding Machine Company, inventors of the ten-key adding machine – a fact considered important enough by somebody to have the building declared a National Historic Landmark.

There is an elevator connecting the first and second floors, but Father Martin Finlay took the stairs. He liked to keep himself in reasonably good shape, and his heavy teaching responsibilities had cut significantly into his gym time. That, and the exorcisms.

Finlay wore the white ankle length tunic and white hooded surplice that are hallmarks of the Dominican Order. The black beads of his 20-decade rosary clacked softly against each other as he walked the length of the second-floor hall to the President's office at the north end. As it happened, The Rev. Arthur Voytek was not only President of the Institute, but the Prior Provincial, as well. Finlay was glad of that – it meant that only one man would be pissed off at him today, instead of two.

The outer door to the President's office was an impressive slab of polished mahogany. Finlay went through without knocking.

Inside, a man in his late twenties, who also wore the robes of the Order, sat at a desk frowning at a computer monitor. He looked up when the door opened.

"Good morning, Brother Frank," Finlay said. "I believe I'm expected."

The young man glanced at a large appointment book that lay next to his computer. "Indeed you are, Father. I'll let him know you're here."

Two minutes later, Finlay was sitting in front of Rev. Arthur Voytek, O.P., whose black hair, square jaw and rough-hewn face always looked to Finlay as if they'd been borrowed from some character actor in the movies. *Here's hoping he's not gonna be playing the heavy today,* Finlay thought, as he handed over the plain No. 10 envelope he'd brought with him.

"Under the circumstances," Finlay told his boss, "I figured I'd best give this to you personally."

"Since it's not my birthday, I've got a feeling that doesn't mean good news," Voytek said, with a ghost of a smile. The unsealed envelope contained a single sheet of paper. Voytek unfolded it and read quickly. Then he read it again. With a sigh, he dropped the sheet onto his desk and sat back in his chair.

"I never know what to say at times like this," he said. "'Congratulations' doesn't seem quite appropriate, but I can't bring myself around to something like 'How could you?', either."

"For what it's worth," Finlay said, "that was very hard to write. Maybe the second-hardest thing I've ever had to write in my life."

"That invites me to ask what occupies the position of Number One, so I will. Just nosy, I guess."

"The eulogy for my mother's funeral mass."

"Well, at least the occasion involved this time is more joyous." Voytek chewed a fingernail, a habit, Finlay knew, he'd been trying to break his entire life. "I won't insult you by asking if you've thought this through, Marty."

"My confessor and I have just about worn it out from talking about it. I've discussed it with a couple of old friends, too. And I've prayed over it for countless hours, Arthur."

Voytek nodded. "Who's the lucky girl – anybody I know?"

"Her name's Judith Racine. She heads the County Social Services office downtown." Finlay hesitated, then said, "She's a former nun."

Voytek nodded again. "I wish you both every happiness. And I mean that from the bottom of my heart."

Finlay smiled for the first time since entering the room. "I know you do, Arthur. Thank you."

They were quiet for a bit, then Voytek said, "Did the exorcisms have anything to do with it, Marty? I have no doubt that you're in love with the lady, but I wondered if that aspect of your work has…"

"Burned me out?" Finlay touched his rosary, as if he found comfort there. "I've thought about that… and it's hard to say. The stress involved in an exorcism is immense."

"I can imagine," Voytek said.

"And, although I've never declined an assignment, I can't say that I don't look forward to the day when I know that part of my life is behind me. Maybe the nightmares will stop then." Finlay shook his big head slowly. "I don't know, Arthur. If it's played a role in my decision to request release from my vows, I'm not consciously aware of it. But who knows what the subconscious influences are?"

"Indeed. And I hope you understand that what I'm about to say is not an attempt to 'guilt' you in any way." Voytek paused for a second. "You're the last exorcist the Order has left in North America, Marty."

"I wasn't aware of that," Finlay said quietly – then, more strongly, "Not that it affects my decision."

"No, of course not. I wouldn't expect it to."

"How did I get to be the last one? I thought there were… three or four of us."

"There were. But Father Tobin retired last year."

"That's right, I forgot. It was in the newsletter."

"Right. And frankly, he's too old to handle the challenge of an exorcism now. The man is 74, Marty."

"I agree – someone that age should not be performing exorcisms."

"And Father Echols, another of our exorcists, was killed in a car crash last New Year's Eve. Some fool of a drunk driver…"

"Really? I must have missed the news of his passing. Oh, wait, that's right. Last New Year's I was in Ohio, performing the exorcism of that poor woman. What was her name – Elvira Jernigan. I wasn't following the news, either the Order's or anybody else's. I didn't know about poor Father Echols."

"Here's something else you probably don't know," Voytek said. "Gerald Hooper has been diagnosed with stage four liver cancer. The doctors say six months, maximum."

"Dear Lord," Finlay said. "So, I'm the last of the Mohicans, as it were."

"For the time being, yes. The Master of the Order has asked Rome to send over at least one, preferably three, qualified exorcists to this side of the Atlantic. But even if they agree, these things take time."

"Yes, I know."

Voytek nudged the sheet of paper on his desk. "So do these requests for release from vows. I'll send it through in tomorrow's mail, with my recommendation that your petition be granted. But it could take six months, or even longer, to work its way through the bureaucracy."

"I expected as much," Finlay said. "I've researched the process pretty thoroughly. There isn't any chance the order could refuse, is there?"

"I've never heard of that happening, in all my years of service. The Order won't keep any man against his will, Marty. It goes against all our principles."

"Still, I'm glad to hear you say it."

"I hope you're prepared to continue in your priestly duties until the release becomes official, Marty."

"Of course I will. I'm teaching three classes of grad students. I wouldn't dream of leaving them hanging by making an exit in the middle of the semester."

"Your sense of responsibility is as admirable as always," Voytek said, with no trace of sarcasm. "And what about exorcisms? Should the need arise, I mean."

Finlay didn't answer immediately. Instead, he studied a crease in his cassock as if it were the most interesting thing in the world. "Judith and I have discussed this," he said, finally. "I told her I was planning to decline any further requests for exorcisms, for the sake of my mental health – and hers. But that was before I knew that I was the only game in town."

He studied the crease a bit more. "I'm going to pray that no poor souls are afflicted by the minions of Satan over the next six months – or if they are, that the Jesuits will handle it. But if it becomes necessary..." Finlay took in a big breath and let it out. "I'll be your exorcist – for a little while longer."

FOR ITS SIZE, the nation's capital can lay claim to an usually large number of drinking establishments – but then politics, some say, is thirsty work. Peabody's Bar and Grille is located a couple of blocks from M Street, the street known as Lobbyist's Row. It's one of the many establishments to occupy the mediocre middle among the District's bars. It was midway between upscale and sleazy, which is why Nestor Greene occasionally used it for business purposes. You could bring, or meet, almost anybody there without drawing undue attention.

Greene walked into Peabody's a little after 3:00 in the afternoon and stood just inside the door for a few moments, letting his eyes adjust to the gloom, which was only slightly abated by the glass-enclosed candles burning on each table. Even in Washington, most bars experience this slack period, between the departure of the lunch lushes and the arrival of the Happy Hour crowd. Consequently, once his night vision had kicked in, Nestor Greene had no trouble spotting the person he had come to meet.

He slid into the booth and looked across the table at the man who sat with one big hand curled around the half-empty glass of beer in front of him. Al Mundenar's curly black hair was still worn short, Greene noticed, and the moustache was badly in need of a trim, as usual. The gray pinstripe suit looked handmade – which it would almost have to be, to accommodate the breadth of those shoulders.

"How's it going, Al?" Greene said. "Sorry you had to wait. Parking is a royal pain around here, as usual."

"Why didn't you walk over?" his companion rumbled softly. "That's what I did."

Nestor Greene, who loathed physical exercise, smiled and said, "It's a little cold for a southern boy like me to be outdoors. Besides, we can't all be athletes."

"I'm not an athlete, either. Not any more. Doesn't mean I let myself get soft." Al Mundenar had spent just over three years as a defensive back for the Minnesota Vikings. The second game of his third season had produced the knee injury that ended his career, but Mundenar wasn't complaining. His new occupation was just as financially rewarding as the old one, and infinitely easier on the connective tissue.

A waitress approached, took Greene's order for a Dewar's and water, and departed. Greene watched her ass wiggle in the tight skirt for a moment, then turned back to his companion. "Haven't seen your byline for a while," he said.

"Naw, I'm mostly an editor these days. You'd be amazed how many of these fucking kids we get, fresh out of college, can't write a sentence that makes any sense. So I edit copy a lot, and sometimes, if it's a slow week, they let me write headlines."

"'Elvis Speaks to Me through My Dog'," Greene murmured. 'Face of Jesus Found on Dark Side of the Moon'. And my all-time favorite, 'Dwarf Rapes Nun, Flees in UFO'."

"That last one's not ours," Mundenar said. "Sounds more like the *Weekly World News*. Or it would, if they were still in business."

"How about, 'Presidential Wannabe Has Homo History'? Think you could sell some papers with that? Or maybe something a bit more pithy: 'Governor Sucks Dick'?"

"Couldn't go with that second one," Mundenar said, seriously. "It's a family paper, after all."

Greene raised an eyebrow. "Oh? And which one might that be – the Addams Family?"

Mundenar took a sip of his beer and put the glass down. "Did you come here to diss my work – which, coming from a slimeball like you would be the biggest case of 'pots and kettles' since Jimmy Swaggart was on the air denouncing porn – or do you want to do business?"

"I'm always ready for business," Greene said, "but, in this case, most of the business has already been done, as you well know. I've already been on the phone with McGreevy in Lauderdale, and we've made our deal. All you're supposed to do is eyeball the material to ensure its authenticity, and then it's the sole property of *The National Tatler* – in return for that check you've got in your pocket, of course."

Mundenar stared hard at Greene for a long moment – a look that more than one NFL quarterback would have recognized. Then the big man smiled, but not in a way that promised undying friendship. "Well, if all I am is the errand boy in this deal, we might as well get the errand over with. Let's see what you've got."

Greene produced the three Polaroid photos and placed them side by side on the table.

Mundenar peered at the pictures, going back and forth between them, for at least a full minute. Then he produced a small, square magnifying lens with a built-in light – the kind that the elderly use to read restaurant menus. He examined the photos more closely, concentrating on the faces. Then from his coat pocket he pulled out a sheet of paper that appeared to be computer-printed copy of a head-and-shoulder photo, the details enlarged considerably.

"What's that?" Greene asked.

"I had a fella I know scan this from a college yearbook. Dartmouth, 1978."

"Chesbro's graduating class."

"That's right, smart guy. I wanted a better idea of what he looked like, back then. People can change a lot in thirty-some years."

Mundenar examined both sets of images for the next minute or so, making frequent use of his magnifying glass. Finally he looked up and said, "I was told there was something else, too."

"Yes, there's this." Greene pulled from the envelope the single sheet of gray personal stationary and placed it next to the Polaroids.

Mundenar read the letter twice, taking his time about it.

"How sweet," he said. Then he looked at Greene and lightly slapped the table with his huge right hand. "Okay, it looks like it is what you said it would be. Guess we have a deal."

Mundenar reached into an inside pocket and produced a certified check. He placed it, face up, in front of Greene. "Satisfactory?"

Greene peered at it for a moment, then nodded. "That's the figure I agreed to." His left hand had just touched the green rectangle of paper when Mundenar's paw clamped down on top of it.

"You know, I was just thinking," Mundenar said, with a small, tight smile, "one of these days we ought to do a story on *you*. You're not important enough for the front page, of course – not any more. We usually reserve that for the story on whatever bimbo is fucking some politico this week. But we might find room for something juicy on an inside page, what do you think?"

"I think you ought to let go of my hand," Greene said calmly.

"Sure, sure, just a minute. That story I was thinking about, we could call it, 'The Dirty Tricks King that Nobody Knows,' or something like that. Maybe throw in a photo or two of you as well, *Nessie*. Could be that somebody might provide us with a picture of *you* sucking cock, or doing something else nasty. Wouldn't that be funny?"

"A riot, absolutely," Green said equably. "But be sure you discuss this story idea of yours with McGreevy before you invest a lot of mental energy in it. He might tell you that it's a really *bad* idea. He might even mention that I know where an *awful* lot of bodies are buried – including a few that he might not want to see dug up." Greene finished the sentence with a broad gesture, which brought the hand close to the candle burning in its translucent container. In one smooth movement, he plucked the candle from its glass globe, tilted it, and poured about a tablespoon of hot wax onto the back of Mundenar's big, hairy hand.

Leaving Peabody's a few seconds later, Nestor Greene wondered which was going to give him more pleasure for the rest of the day: the figure inscribed on the check in his pocket, or the memory of his last sight of Al Mundenar's face.

Chapter 14

"QUINCEY? CAN YOU hear me? Quincey?"

Libby Chastain was tired. The spell she had worked on Morris required a lot of direct contact, not unlike the 'healing touch' that some mystics are reputed to have. Time-consuming it was, and hard on the knees, but the spell had been successful. She had drawn out of Morris's bloodstream most of the alcohol that had caused him to pass out, turning it into vapor which she had then burned away with a snap of her fingers. She then removed the toxins that the liver produces as it digests alcohol. It is the toxins, not the alcohol, that cause a hangover. There was no point in sobering him up if he couldn't talk because his head was pounding out the drum solo from 'In-a-gadda-da-vida.'

"Quincey? Time to come up from the dark now. Come to my voice, Quincey. Follow the sound of my voice."

Morris made a sound that was a mixture of equal parts sigh and groan. His eyelashes fluttered then, blinking rapidly, he opened his eyes.

He turned his head toward Libby Chastain and she saw his pupils dilate in recognition. He stared at her for

143

a few seconds then said, softly, "Ah, shit."

Libby leaned back a little, to escape his breath as much as anything else. "Charmer," she said with a little smile. "I bet you say that to all the girls."

Morris moved his head around, as if checking that it was still attached. "I oughta feel like death, just lightly warmed over," he croaked. "As I recall, I sure as hell earned it."

"Yes, I expect so. But I was able to give you a little help with that. Think you can sit up?"

"Let's find out."

Moving slowly, stiffly, as if unsure what parts of his body still worked properly, Morris brought himself upright.

"Very good." Libby handed him a tall glass full of clear liquid. "Here – drink this. Take your time."

Morris looked at her. "More magic?'

"Sure. A magical potion combining hydrogen and oxygen, in a ratio of two-to-one."

Morris's brow furrowed. Clearly, he wasn't tracking well, yet.

"It's water, Quincey. Just water. You've got to be dehydrated."

As he drank, Libby took another look around the shambles of a room.

"Seems like it was quite a party," she said. "Everything but a trained monkey and bunch of hookers."

Morris moved a half-full bottle of Jack Daniels aside and put his empty glass on the coffee table.

"The trained monkey was already booked," he said, looking at the floor. "The hookers, they left – what's today, Tuesday?"

"Wednesday."

"They left Sunday, sometime. I think."

Libby snorted. "I'm surprised I can't smell the stale perfume, or… whatever."

"That's because all of our business transactions were carried out upstairs." He still wouldn't look at her.

"Prostitutes, Quincey?" She kept her voice mild. "Cheap hookers?"

"Uh-uh. They weren't cheap, I can tell you that much. I'd say they were two of the most expensive working girls in this town, which is saying something. Don't forget, Austin's the state capitol – got the governor and the whole administration, plus the State Lege, and all those lobbyists, too. Makes for a high-class clientele, which requires high-class service. Hell, one of the ladies, if I can use that expression, said she was second year at the law school – and I believed her. I said that she ought to be real good at practicing law, because she was already knew how to screw her clients, and she told me –"

"*Quincey.*" Libby's voice had some snap behind it. His words had been coming faster and faster, and she had sensed the incipient hysteria behind them.

Morris stopped talking. He took in a big breath and let it out slowly. "Sorry."

Libby put a gentle hand on his arm. "It's all right." She squeezed the arm for a moment before letting it go. "I'm not judging you, Quincey. I'm the last person in the world to do that. But, high-class or not, I hope you and those working girls practiced safe sex."

Morris nodded. "Condoms every time. They insisted, whether I gave a damn or not."

Libby just stared at him. "Whether you *gave a damn*? Are you fucking *serious*?" She grasped his arm again, and this time the grip was not so gentle. "You ever hear of AIDS, Quincey? It was in all the *papers*."

145

Morris said nothing. After a moment, she let his arm go.

"I mean, they've got some wonderful drugs these days," she said, "and maybe a cure is on the horizon, but right now, that disease is still a death sentence."

"I'm aware of that."

"Well, then?"

"The only thing wrong with it as a death sentence," Morris said bleakly, "is that it would take too fucking long."

Libby's stare lasted longer this time. When she spoke, her voice was soft. "I think you'd better tell me. I know something happened, and I know that it must have been horrible, to lead you into a state like this. But I want to help you, Quincey – and I can't help unless I know."

"I don't know if anybody stocks the kind of help that I need – even you, Libby," Morris said. "But if you'll fetch me another cold glass of this hydrogen and oxygen mixture, I'll tell you. That'll explain my little" – he waved a tired hand around the room – "orgy of self indulgence here, even if it doesn't excuse it."

Libby Chastain was almost to the kitchen when she heard him say, "It'll also explain why I'm getting out of the ghostbuster business. For good."

IOWA IN JANUARY is about half as charming as Hell with the fires out. That, at least, was the opinion of Hugh 'Bat' Masterson, and since he had already spent the last three days amid the snow and ice of the Hawkeye State, he figured he was entitled to it.

Masterson slid the Glock 9 into his belt holster and then slipped on his jacket. A quick glance in the motel room's mirror told him that no telltale bulges were visible.

Not that if fucking matters. We're supposed to be armed, and everybody knows it. Who cares if some fucking farmer sees the outline of the piece underneath my coat?

Masterson was in a bad mood, and had been ever since getting word that he was assigned to the Stark protection detail. In the Service, the person you were assigned to protect was a good (if unofficial) indication of your place in the agent pecking order. The most highly regarded agents were assigned to the President, or POTUS ('Eagle' in the current radio code, although who all that cryptic stuff was supposed to fool was something Masterson had never figured out).

Using that logic, you might assume that the Vice President's security detail should be the Number Two most prestigious job, but you'd be wrong. Although the role of the Vice President had improved since John Nance Garner had declared his job to be 'Not worth a bucket of warm piss,' the VOTUS (more code) assignment was a long way from being the second most important job in Washington. That fell to the Secretary of State, followed (in most administrations) by Secretary of Defense.

At the bottom of this artificial hierarchy were the wannabe presidential candidates every four years. Most of the men (and, occasionally, women) who tried for the brass ring in primary season were second rate pols, who often stayed in cheap hotels, ate cheap food, and felt free to disregard the security protocols.

And even within this motley crew there was a hierarchy. The two or three candidates believed to have a realistic chance at their party's nomination got the best of the available agents, while the others got whoever was left.

Which is how Masterson, after nine years in the U.S. Secret Service, found himself assigned to Senator Howard Stark, the darkest of this season's dark horses.

Unlike most of the agents assigned to this Ninth Circle of Secret Service Hell, Masterson wasn't a fuck-up. He wasn't lazy, sloppy, careless, or a drinker. He never blabbed to the press (or to anybody else) about any protectee's life, either personal or political.

All he had done to get himself in the shit was to politely decline a drunken sexual proposition from a President's teenage daughter, late one night at Camp David, just over three years ago.

The next morning the young lady, who in Masterson's opinion was mean and petty even when she *wasn't* hung over, had told Daddy that Masterson had propositioned *her*. Questioned by his boss, Masterson had told the truth. Since there'd been no witnesses, that made it one of those 'he said, she said' situations. But you can imagine that 'she' was believed in places where it counted. Since the White House wanted to avoid any whiff of scandal, Masterson had not been fired. As a civil servant, he'd have the right to a formal hearing if they tried to kick him out, and who knows what might get put into a transcript somewhere?

So instead of being discharged, Masterson was pulled from the White House detail and given the crappiest jobs available within the Executive Protection Service, in the hope that he would quit in disgust. But he had stubbornly refused to give them the satisfaction. So here he was in the boonies, for the famed Iowa Caucuses – the first formal test of the presidential candidates' popularity, even if only a handful of delegates were at stake – helping to protect Senator Howard Stark, in the unlikely event that someone thought him important enough to assassinate.

Stark's entourage was small (in Masterson's view, a reflection of the guy's slim chances for going all the way), which at least meant there were fewer people to keep track of. Fernando Garrett had signed on as campaign manager, probably attracted more by the depths of Stark's pockets than any realistic expectations of his success. Garrett had been a big wheel in John McCain's campaign a few years back, but had quietly bailed after spending fifteen minutes with McCain's hastily-chosen running mate. Masterson figured Garrett would also abandon Stark's ship once it was clearly sinking, a condition that would probably develop the morning after Super Tuesday – the day in February when twelve state primary elections were scheduled.

Martin Kane had signed on as Stark's domestic policy advisor. Kane, a thin guy who wore bow ties and seemed perpetually constipated, was supposed to be a big deal in the Poli Sci department at Ohio State. Masterson figured the professor was planning to get a book out of his campaign experience, however long it might last.

And Stark had managed to lure Gwen Galindo as foreign policy advisor. She was a hard right-winger who'd been U.S. representative at the U.N. three administrations ago, and never let anyone forget it. It was Masterson's conviction that she could not get out three consecutive sentences without one of them beginning "When I was at the U.N..." She was brilliant, hard-working, and had the personal charm of a rabid pit bull. It was a running joke among the Secret Service detail that Dr. Galindo (as she insisted on being called) would be incapable of ordering lunch at Burger King without finding a way to piss somebody off.

Before leaving his room, Masterson pressed a small button and spoke into the radio clipped to his lapel.

"This is Bat. Is Kingfish still in his room?" Masterson had suggested the Senator's code name to the rest of the detail. Several of the other agents had read *All the King's Men* in college, and agreed that the designation was appropriate, so it stuck.

A voice in his earpiece replied almost immediately. "Affirmative. Attila is with him."

'Attila' was short for 'Attila the Nun,' the agents' radio code for Mary Margaret Doyle. The Secret Service seemed to have an inordinate number of Catholic School graduates – or 'survivors,' as Masterson called them.

Masterson's own private name for her was 'Schoolgirl.' He had silently bestowed it the day he had followed Ms. Doyle into her room, during one of the Senator's periodic visits to New Hampshire. She'd been talking to him about security for the next day's scheduled speech, and hadn't stopped as she unlocked the door and went inside. Masterson had figured it would be rude to stand in the hall and let the door close on him, so he'd gone into the room behind her.

He was paying attention to what Ms. Doyle was saying (her tone implied there might be a quiz later), but Masterson was also trained in observation. A glance to the right took in the bed, and Ms. Doyle's suitcase, which lay open, its contents strewn across the bedspread. The same glance allowed Masterson to notice the black garter belt with matching stockings that had been laid out for Ms. Doyle's use, along with one other item of interest.

Masterson had amused himself once or twice by flipping through a Frederick's of Hollywood catalog, and he was pretty sure he knew a pair of crotchless pantyhose when he saw them.

Ms. Doyle had her back to Masterson while sorting through some papers, and by the time she turned to him his eyes were on her, his impassive face giving no hint of the titillating little display he had just seen.

He saw Mary Margaret Doyle's eyes flick toward the bed for an instant, but there was no break in the stream of instructions she was issuing. However, Masterson had thought that some color had appeared on her cheeks, and she had been even more abrupt than usual in dismissing him from her presence.

Being a professional (as well as a man who had already gotten in big trouble once by pissing off the wrong woman), Masterson had said nothing to the rest of the detail about his discovery. But from that point forward, the prim, proper, and ice-cold 'Attila' was always 'schoolgirl' for him. Although he'd never attended Catholic school himself, Masterson had enjoyed private schoolgirl fantasies since he was a teenager.

Crotchless pantyhose? Yowza!

Chapter 15

QUINCEY MORRIS DRANK the last of the water and put the glass down on his coffee table. His hands were not quite steady. That fact alone alarmed Libby Chastain almost as much as the account of the exorcism that Morris had just finished.

"What happened to the poor girl?" Libby asked.

Morris made a face. "She's in the psych ward at the nearest hospital."

"Psychiatry can't cure demonic possession. They won't be able to help her there."

"Yeah, tell me about it. But it was either that or jail. The cops couldn't just walk away from what... happened."

"Did they give you a hard time?"

"They thought about it. I spent hours under interrogation, until the lawyer the Jesuits hired showed up. But we had permission for the exorcism, and the parents backed us up on that. And the bottom line was that Susan hadn't been harmed – apart from some rope burns, which were clearly self-inflicted."

"The only one really hurt was your priest friend."

"Hannigan. Her fingers just destroyed his eyeballs. Went all the way through into the sockets."

Libby shuddered. "The poor man."

"Yeah. So now he's blind," Morris said, "and there isn't a damn thing they can do to fix it – I checked. Corneal transplants, sure. They do 'em all the time. But not the whole eyeball – too many nerve connections, or something."

"Quincey…" she began.

"On the plus side, I understand that the Bible was the first book ever put into Braille." Morris's voice was bitter. "So, at least Hannigan won't lack for reading material – once he learns the system, that is."

"Quincey, listen…"

"And if you're about to play some variation of that popular golden oldie, 'It's not your fault,' do us both a favor, Libby, and *don't*. Just fucking *don't*."

Since that is exactly what she'd intended, Libby Chastain sat silently, chewing her lower lip. She began to run through the options in her mind. You can't use magic (the white variety, anyway) to change what someone believes, especially if it's deep-seated. It is sometimes possible, to bring someone out of a deep depression using magical means. Several of Libby's sister witches were practicing psychotherapists, their patients never knowing the role that magic played in their recovery.

"And if you're thinking about using a little magic to 'help' me, don't you even fucking think about it – not if you want us to stay friends."

Well, shit. Her long personal history with Quincey Morris, and the closeness that had resulted from it, was often a source of comfort to Libby Chastain. But at the moment it was a major pain in the ass. Morris knew her so well, he could predict everything she was likely to do or say, and reject it out of hand before she could even speak or act.

Okay, then, Plan B. "All right, Quincey," she said. "I won't try to influence the way you feel about what happened. But given the events as you describe them, I'm having trouble understanding why it's all, or even mostly, your fault. But I'm willing to be convinced." She folded her arms across her chest. "So, convince me."

Morris looked at her, then looked away. "I don't reckon I have to convince you of shit, Libby. It's my life, and my decision. Why don't you just go home?"

"Not so fast, cowboy." Libby let some of the anger she was feeling come to the surface. "Do you know how much money our little partnership brings me every year? It varies, sure, but it's never so little that I'm not gonna miss it. A *lot*. You think I just wave my hands over the electric bill, mumble some Latin, and it pays itself? I *wish*."

All of which was true, even if it was pretty low on Libby's list of concerns right now. She paused, took a breath, and went on.

"And I won't even mention the fact that you're planning to deprive me of the chance to hang out with a guy I happen to like and admire, despite the fact that, at the moment, he seems to've thrown an elaborate pity party, with himself as guest of honor. If you're gonna take all that away from me, then you owe me a fucking explanation, Quincey Morris. So, go on – *explain*."

Morris snatched the empty water glass from the table and threw it against the far wall, where it shattered into a million pieces. Then he turned and looked at Libby again, and the expression on his face was one she had never seen before – at least, not directed at her. For the first time since they'd known each other, Libby was afraid of Quincey Morris.

She let none of it show.

I know he despises men who hit women, so he won't strike me. Probably.

But she still offered a quick prayer to the Goddess that Morris would maintain control, for reasons apart from the obvious one. *If he does whack me, things will never be the same between us, no matter how many heartfelt apologies follow. It will change everything.*

All of this went through Libby's mind in about two seconds, as Morris glared at her. Then he raised his right fist – and slammed the wooden back of the sofa, hard.

"*Fuck!*"

The fist came down again. "*Fuck!*"

And a third time. "*Mother fuck!*"

Libby was hoping that he hadn't broken any of the bones in his hand when he said to her, in a voice that shook a little, "If it was anyone else but you, Libby – anyone, damn it – they'd be lying on the fucking floor right now, bleeding."

Libby Chastain just nodded. She believed him.

Morris continued to look at her, but the redness of his face had begun to recede. He was breathing like a sprinter who had just run the 440.

Gradually the breathing slowed to something like normal, and his face resumed its usual hue. He looked down at the coffee table, where, Libby noticed, three flies were nosing around in a few drops of spilled tequila. All at once, Morris's hand was a blur as he swept across the little puddle and brought it up, closed into a fist.

He opened the hand slowly, and Libby could see a single fly crawling across his palm for a second, before it flew off.

"Well, Tex," she said, "you've still got the fastest hands in the West. That ought to count for something."

Morris looked at her, and the anger that had been in his face was replaced with a look of infinite sadness. "You don't get it, do you, Libby?" he said. "There once was a time when I'd have got all three."

Libby let a few seconds pass before she said, "So, are you going to talk to me, or what?"

FROM THE NEW YORK TIMES:

(Jan. 23) Ames, Iowa. Representative Francis 'Frank' Chesbro, considered one of the stronger contenders for the Republican party's presidential nomination, was found dead today in his hotel room, two days before the start of the Iowa Caucuses.

Mr. Chesbro's body was found by a member of his campaign staff not long after 11:00 last night. The aide called emergency services, but Mr. Chesbro was pronounced dead upon arrival at the Ames Medical Center. A time of death has not yet been released, nor has the cause of death been named by officials.

A member of the Medical Center's staff, who asked to be anonymous because she was not authorized to speak to the press, said that Mr. Chesbro apparently died from a self-inflicted gunshot wound.

In recent days the Chesbro campaign had been plagued by allegations that he had engaged in a homosexual affair while a young man. The flap began with an article in the National Tatler, *which was published on Monday and contained censored photos purporting to show a young Mr. Chesbro engaging in sex acts with another man. The Chesbro campaign vehemently denied the claims made in the* Tatler, *although the Congressman had refused to discuss them personally, either on or off the record.*

Mr. Chesbro was a member of the Mormon church, which considers homosexual activity to be abnormal and sinful. Last year, he voted against a bill that would have made it easier for gays and lesbians to adopt children. The bill was defeated.

Mr. Chesbro is survived by his wife, Evelyn, three grown children, and two grandchildren. Funeral arrangements have not yet been announced.

MARTIN FINLAY TOOK a sip of wine and looked across the kitchen table at the woman he loved. Five feet two, eyes of blue, as the old song went. Mind like a razor, which the song neglected to mention. And freckles. He had fallen in love with the freckles first. The rest had come soon after. "You make a nice dish of ravioli, Judith," he said. "Lovely sauce."

Judith Racine (never 'Judy,' a name she had hated since childhood) brushed a wing of black hair out of her eyes, took another bite, and swallowed. "It's a credit to my culinary skills, truly," she said. "Well, there was some help from Mr. Prego – if there *is* a Mr. Prego."

"Probably mythical, just like Mrs. Butterworth and Betty Crocker," he said. "Besides, *prego* is Italian for *you're welcome.*"

"You *would* know that. Oh, that's right – you studied in Rome for a while, didn't you?"

"Yep, two years at the Gregorian University, when I was in my twenties."

"Were you fluent in Italian by the time the two years was up?"

"Well, I learned *prego*, and that you're supposed to say it after somebody says *grazie*. Not too much

157

beyond that. My classes were in English, with a heavy sprinkling of Latin. And I lived with a bunch of other American and Canadian priests, so my exposure to the language mostly involved listening to cab drivers swear at each other."

She nodded, put her fork down, and pushed her plate away. "Something's bothering you. Care to tell me about it?"

He picked up his wine glass again, swirled the contents around a little, but did not drink. "I handed in my request to be released from my vows today."

"Did it go badly with what's-his-name, Voytek?"

"No it went better than I dared hope. He was very understanding, very compassionate."

"That's not what's bugging you, then. So, what is it? Second thoughts about leaving?"

"Uh-uh, no way. I've decided how I want to spend the rest of my life – and I'm going to spend it with you."

"Then I've run out of guesses, Marty. You'll just have to tell me."

"Voytek told me something I was unaware of. It seems that I'm the last exorcist the Order's got in North America. The last functioning one, anyway."

Her eyes never left his face. "Tell me he's not sending you on another one. Tell me that you're not leaving tomorrow to do battle with the forces of Hell, with no assurance that you'll be coming back – with your sanity intact, anyway. Tell me that, Marty – please."

"I'm not going anywhere, babe. Not tomorrow, or the day after."

She nodded. "Good. Although I'm pretty sure I sense a 'but' lurking back there somewhere."

"Like I said, I'm not being sent out on any exorcism. But all the other exorcists in the Order are either dead, dying, or retired – although Voytek's put in a call to Rome, through channels, for more. So, since I'm the last one… if something comes up, and the Jesuits can't handle it, or won't…" The remaining words came out in a rush. "I told him I'd take it, if they couldn't find someone else."

She struck the table with the flat of her hand, causing her wine glass to jump and almost topple over. "God *damn* it, Marty!" She got up swiftly and walked away from the table to the nearby window, where she stood, looking outward, and quivering.

"I wish you wouldn't swear like that, Judith," he said to her back.

"Why the fuck not?" She whirled to face him, and the expression on her face was not pretty. "I used to be a nun, remember? Everybody knows that behind the convent walls, all nuns swear like sailors, drink like fish, and have lesbian orgies every fucking Friday night."

Finlay decided to take a chance. "I asked you not to swear," he said mildly. "I never said anything about drinking or lesbian orgies."

She gaped at him, for a long two seconds – and then she started to laugh.

"Nothing like a nice lesbian orgy to start the weekend, I always say," he continued.

She was bent over with laughter now, and waved a hand toward him that meant 'Stop it, you're killing me.'

"I *am* a little surprised that the good sisters didn't give up the orgies during Lent, though. Or at least move them to Saturday."

Judith Racine was laughing so hard that tears streamed down her face. She took a couple of steps back and collapsed on the couch, where she remained until the spasms passed. She produced a handkerchief, wiped her eyes, and blew her nose. Then she stood up, slowly, as if uncertain of her legs' support, and returned to the dinner table.

She sat down and said, "I hope you're not going to be in the habit of doing that when we're married."

"What – mention lesbian orgies? You started it."

"No, I mean diverting my fury with humor. It hardly seems fair, somehow." She blew her nose again, and looked at him. "I have a right to be mad, Marty. You promised me that you were getting out of the exorcism business, for good."

"I know – and I did so in good faith, based on what I knew at the time. But, as I said to Voytek, I seem to be the last of the Mohicans – for the time being, anyway."

"Well, if you expect me to start calling you Chingatchgook, you'd better think again, dude."

"Maybe you can just do it on special occasions, like my birthday. Look, Judith, the last thing I want to do is let you down. But I don't want to let the Order down, either."

She drank the last of the Merlot in her glass. "I seem to recall a passage in scripture about serving two masters."

"'No man can serve two masters: for either he will hate the one, and love the other; or else he will hold to the one, and despise the other.' Matthew 6:24, I believe."

"Yeah, that one. Smartass. But that's your situation – what do you plan to do about it?"

Finlay lowered his head a little and looked at the checkered tablecloth. He held that posture long enough that Judith Racine figured he was either counting the squares or praying.

"They can't make me go," he said finally. "That's always been the case – the Church will not order a priest to perform a duty as extraordinary and spiritually hazardous as an exorcism. He has to *agree* to go."

He looked up then, and the strain she could see in his face squeezed her heart. "If an assignment comes during the time I have left – if I can possibly refuse, I will. There are other religious orders that do exorcisms, especially the Jesuits. The cavalry from Rome could arrive at any time, and people don't generally die from demonic possession, anyway. If I can decline in good conscience, then that's what I'll do. Is that enough?"

She reached across the table for one of his hands and squeezed it with all her strength. Looking into his face, seeing all the love that was there, she said, "I guess it will have to be."

Chapter 16

"OF COURSE IT'S my fault," Quincey Morris said. "I let go of her arm, and she, or *it*, used that arm to drive two fingers into poor Hannigan's eyes."

Libby Chastain sipped some of the coffee she had made them in Morris's kitchen and put her cup down. "Sounds to me like it's the demon's fault, if anyone's."

"Oh, don't play sophisticated games with me, Libby!" Morris snapped. "With demons, malign intent is something you take for granted. That's like saying that if I let a lion out of its cage and it eats somebody, then it's all the fucking lion's fault."

"'Your adversary, the devil, prowls around like a roaring lion, seeking someone to devour'," Libby quoted.

"Yeah, and you and Saint Peter can both go and –" Morris stopped himself, then turned his head away. "Aw, fuck it!"

Libby Chastain regarded that as a small, but hopeful sign. The Quincey Morris she knew was something of a gentleman, and would never have told her to go fuck herself, except possibly in jest. The fact that Morris was

162

making an effort to control his tongue meant that the old Quincey Morris might not be gone, after all.

Morris turned back to her. In a more normal tone he said, "I'm the guy opened the lion's cage, Libby. I let go of her arm. I'm responsible for what happened afterward."

"And you did that for your own amusement, of course," Libby said. Her tone was matter-of-fact.

"You *know* I didn't, dammit. But that doesn't mean I didn't *do* it."

"If not for your own amusement, then, why did you do it?"

"I already told you," Morris said. "It was that fucking burn scar on my neck. All of a sudden, it felt like I was getting burned all over again. Took me by surprise."

"It felt like being burned, you say."

"Exactly."

"You know," Libby said, "I read somewhere that burning is the most painful thing the human body can experience." Her expression turned grim. "That's why they used to burn witches, of course."

"Yeah, so?"

"So I'm trying to get a sense of what you were experiencing when you let go of the girl's arm. Had your burn scar pained you before? Since it healed, I mean."

Morris shrugged. "A couple of twinges, but nothing like that."

"And you believe the demon inside the girl had something to do with this particular attack?"

"I'm sure of it. I locked eyes with her – I know you're not supposed to do that, and I didn't mean to, it just happened. And as soon as her eyes met mine, I saw her – *it* – smile. And that's when the pain hit me."

"So, would it be fair to say that the discomfort you felt was the result of a demonic attack?"

"*Discomfort*? Jesus, Libby, it was like somebody pressed a red-hot iron against my neck. Discomfort, my ass!"

"Just an expression," Libby said. "Doctors use it all the time. So, you believe the demon caused this?"

"Absolutely. Maybe because the original burn was the result of hellfire – I don't know how that stuff works. Nobody does."

Libby nodded slowly. "Quincey, I'd like to ask you a hypothetical question, and I'd like you to consider it carefully before you answer. Will you do that?"

"If it'll get this over with faster, sure, whatever."

"All right then. Let's go back to that day. You've been under immense stress for hours. You're dead tired, physically and mentally. But you think the ordeal may be almost over. You're straining to hold down what is, in effect a creature from Hell, one of the foulest, most evil things imaginable. Fair description?"

"Yeah, I guess so."

"If, at that moment, someone had sneaked up behind you, holding an iron bar that's been heated in a fire until it's cherry-red – if that someone had laid that red hot metal against your neck, what would you have done?"

"Come on, Libby, can we stop playing –"

She held up a hand, palm out. "You said you would indulge me, Quincey. You promised you would answer. Thank about it for as long as you want."

"I don't have to think about it. I'd have yelled and put my hand up to my neck to protect it. Anybody would."

"That's all I wanted to know," Libby said. She stood, and picked up her bag. "Enjoy the rest of your life, Quincey, if you can. I'll show myself out."

She walked briskly out of the room and had taken two steps down the hallway when she heard Morris's voice.

"*Libby – wait.*"

AT THE DOOR of the suite shared by the Senator and Mary Margaret Doyle (separate bedrooms, of course), 'Bat' Masterson traded places with Jerry Arkasian, the agent who'd worked the night shift.

"Quiet night?" Masterson asked.

"Aren't they all?" Arkasian stepped away from the door. "I'm heading over to Mickey Dee's for some breakfast. Want anything?"

Masterson shook his head. "Naw, I'm good. Thanks."

Arkasian nodded. "Hey – I noticed that new Kevin Spacey movie, the one you said you wanted to see, is on HBO tonight at 9:00. We oughta be back from the rally by then, and since I don't go on duty until midnight...."

"Yeah, that sounds good. Let's check it out – assuming no shit has hit the fan around here."

"Always assuming that. Okay, Bat – catch you later."

Masterson took up position next to the door and checked his watch: 6:04. The Senator had a speech at 10:00 with a couple of interviews to follow. The day's itinerary had them (including the full Secret Service detail) leaving the hotel at 9:30, so there was plenty of time.

Masterson nodded pleasantly at the families and couples who passed him in the hall on their way to eat breakfast or check out. He gave the two solitary males who went by a little more attention, but neither of them looked or acted like trouble.

Masterson snorted quietly after the second guy had gone past without so much as a glance. The Secret

Service had done a threat assessment on Stark, as they did for all the people under their protection. It was based on factors like how much hate mail the person received, and what kind, as well as phone threats and other forms of expressed discontent. According to the Service, the threat level calculated for Stark was roughly the same as the one assigned to Boots – the White House cat. You wouldn't think a cat would get hate mail, but apparently a couple of dog lovers had been pissed off about—

Masterson came to full alertness in the space of a heartbeat. He had heard something from inside the suite: a male voice, lower and rougher than Stark's smooth tenor, yelling something. It was followed a moment later by a female voice screaming. *What the fuck...*

Masterson was pounding on the door now. "Senator? Ms Doyle? Anything wrong?"

No answer. Masterson was sure that if the Senator had a visitor, Arkasian would have said something. They were on the fourth floor, so nobody could have got in through the windows – or could they?

Masterson fumbled through his wallet for the master key card, which he had obtained from the hotel manager when the party had checked in. He found it, pounded on the door once more, waited a couple of seconds, then inserted the card into the slot in the door. There was a faint click, a green light appeared above the lock, and Masterson had the door open.

He stepped inside the room, drawing his weapon with one smooth motion. He was in the suite's small living room. "Senator?"

The door to Stark's room opened. Masterson pivoted toward the sound, bringing his gun to bear – then immediately lowered it, as Stark stepped through the door, pulling it shut behind him. The Senator's face was flushed, the normally impeccable hair in disarray. He wore a white terrycloth robe, and he was pulling the belt tight as he said, "What is it? What's wrong?"

"That's what I wanted to ask you, sir," Masterson replied. "I heard a man's voice from in here, different from yours, then what sounded like a woman, screaming."

"Oh, *that*." Stark waved a dismissive hand. "I was watching an old horror movie on TV – I'm afraid I'm addicted to them. I meant to turn it off, but my thumb must have hit the volume control instead. I guess the actress being unconvincingly devoured by that monster sounded pretty loud, for a second. Sorry about that."

At that moment, a shower was turned on nearby. Masterson was pretty sure that it was the shower in Stark's room. He noted that Mary Margaret Doyle's bedroom door had remained closed throughout his incursion.

If Stark heard the shower start up, his expression gave no hint of it. But there was *something* happening with his eyes... no, they were fine. "Anything else, Agent... Masterson, is it?"

"Yes, sir, Masterson. No, nothing else, Senator. Please forgive the intrusion."

"Oh, that's all right. You're just doing your job. Better safe than sorry, I always say."

"Yes, sir. I'll be in the hall, as usual, if you need me."

Masterson turned away and got out of there. As he returned to his spot outside the door, he was frowning. Despite all the advances in broadcast technology in recent years, he was pretty sure he could distinguish between a voice on TV and that of a real person, even through the relatively thin walls of the Holiday Inn. What he'd heard sure didn't sound like something that came out of a speaker, no matter what the volume setting was. Stark was right about one thing, though – the first voice Masterson had heard through that wall sounded like nothing human.

Masterson gave a mental shrug. If the Senator was putting the boots to Mary Margaret Doyle, it wasn't much of a surprise. Not since Masterson had gotten a look at those sexy undies of hers.

But there was something about the Senator's story that bothered Masterson. He didn't realize he was still frowning as he thought, *note to self*: *check the local TV listings later. See what channel is playing scary movies at this hour of the morning, when the main audience for that stuff is in algebra class*. A few hours later, the Senator and his small entourage left for the day's politicking, and Masterson had other things to think about.

AFTER THE DEMON Sargatanas had slipped the chain on the door to prevent any more intrusions by over-zealous Secret Service fools, he returned to his bedroom, where Mary Margaret Doyle, fresh out of the shower, was drying herself.

With a smile, she started to say something. But the words died in her throat when Sargatanas slapped her across the face.

Mary Margaret Doyle's eyes went wide with surprise and the shock of the blow. As with everything else Sargatanas did to her, it was carefully calculated – hard enough to show his displeasure, but not so hard as to leave a mark that might be seen, and wondered about, later.

"You worthless cunt!" His voice was not loud enough to carry outside the room, but the anger in it still rang clear as a bell. "Starting the shower while I was reassuring Officer Bat Man. If he had any doubts about the nature of our 'relationship,' they have now been dispelled."

"D-does it really matter?" Seeing his glare she hurried on. "I mean, they've probably suspected it all along, since we share a suite whenever we travel. The Secret Service types don't talk about such things. They'd lose their jobs, if they did."

He stared at her in silence for a few seconds. "You may be right, although do not think you will escape punishment for your carelessness. We can afford no mistakes. *None.* Republican politicians, even widowed ones, don't fuck the help. It could cost votes among the Bible-thumping crowd. They leave that to the Democrats. The Master we both serve will not show mercy if we fail him."

He ran his gaze slowly over her naked, still dripping body. "Any more than I will show mercy to you now."

Chapter 17

"IT WAS BLACK magic," Colleen O'Donnell said. "The smell of it was all over her."

Special Agent Dale Fenton nodded slowly. "I guess you'd know, if anyone would."

Fenton and O'Donnell had been partners in the Behavioral Science Unit for nearly three years. Although the unit's brief covered criminal psychopaths who crossed state lines, there were some cases that transcended psychology and edged into the territory of the occult. Within the unit, these cases were collectively known as 'the weird shit.' Ever since budget cuts five years ago had forced the elimination of the semi-secret department known as Shadow Unit, all investigation of 'the weird shit' fell to a small group of agents within Behavioral Science. At present, that group consisted of O'Donnell and Fenton.

Colleen O'Donnell, being a white witch, was uniquely suited to investigate such cases, but Fenton was the only person in the Bureau who knew of her special abilities.

They were sitting across from Gate 34 at Reagan National, where a Delta Airlines clerk had just announced that their flight to Indianapolis was being postponed 45 minutes, due to bad weather in the Midwest.

"I didn't know what to think," Colleen said. "At first, I wondered if Mel had actually gone over to the, uh –"

"Dark side?" Fenton smiled, his very white teeth standing out in contrast to his black face.

"Yeah, them. But I realized that the psychic odor wasn't strong enough to be coming from her directly. She'd picked it up by being around a person who used it, or a place where it was used."

"Her partner – what's his name – Garvin? Could it be him?"

"Doubtful. I ran into him at the federal courthouse in Baltimore last month. We were both giving depositions, but in different cases. We chatted in the hall for a couple of minutes, and there wasn't a whiff of black magic on him then."

"So it must've come from somebody else. Or some *place* else."

"And that's why I got a funny feeling when she told me about the last case she'd been on – not even a case, really, just one of those make-work deals that the bureaucrats come up with."

"Bullshit Federal regulations are as thick as fleas on an old dog. Which particular flea we talkin' about here?"

"The one that says when a member of Congress croaks, the Bureau has to make sure that the death wasn't suspicious."

"Even if he dies in a hospital? Seems like the COD would be pretty obvious there."

"No, that's the exception," she said. "And I expect most of them *do* die in hospitals – either of illness or iatrogenic medicine."

Fenton shook his head a couple of times. "You're using big words again. You know that just confuse us poor black folk."

"You're a riot, Dale. I bet that routine went over really well at – where'd you go, Yale?"

"University of Virginia – the 'Harvard of the South,' if that's not a contradiction in terms, and it probably is. I was in the same class as the chick who joined the Bureau and later shot that serial killer, Buffalo Billy. Clara Something."

"Sterling, I think it was. Damn, I'd have liked to meet her. What was she like – at UVA?"

"Didn't really know her," Fenton said. "Just to say 'Hi.' I was in a couple of classes with her, though – sharp lady. Very focused. I bet she'd have known that iatrogenic medical treatment is the kind that kills you, instead of making you better."

She gave him a look. "Yeah, well, Mel's guy died at home, in some kind of freak accident."

"Do tell."

"Apparently he got up during the night and went into the bathroom. There was some water on the floor, and he was standing in it when he flicked the light switch. Got electrocuted. Pronounced dead at the scene."

Fenton frowned. "That's not supposed to happen. That's why they make the damn switches out of plastic."

"Yeah, I know. Mel said the light switch was all melted. She's thinking manufacturer's defect, or something. Accidental death, anyway – open and shut."

"Except…"

"Yeah, except she may have picked up traces of black magic at the scene. And that means the accidental death…"

"Wasn't so damn accidental."

Fenton scratched his nose a couple of times. "Why would somebody use black magic to kill a Congressman? Which one was it, by the way? You didn't say."

"Ronald Brooks, Republican, New York 23rd."

"That name rings a bell. Is he Chairman of Appropriations, or something?"

"No, but he is – was – running for President."

"That's right, seen him on the news – I remember now. So why would somebody use black magic to take out a dude who's running for President?"

Colleen O'Donnell looked up at the closest Departures board, which was still showing their flight would be delayed. "Maybe they want somebody else to win," she said softly.

Fenton was quiet for a while before saying, "Look, we're getting ahead of ourselves, here. This whole thing is predicated on the assumption that your buddy picked up that black magic at the Congressman's place. And you know what they taught us at the Academy about assumptions."

"'When you assume, you make an ass out of you and me'," she quoted. "Yeah, yeah. That was probably clever as hell back in 1920, when somebody came up with it."

"But you know I'm right," Fenton said. "Without the established fact that Brooks's house is where the black magic came from, whatever you're thinking is nothing but smoke."

She nodded slowly. "Then I guess we'd better see if that fact can be established."

He looked at her. "Colleen."

"What?"

"I know what you're thinking."

"I bet you don't."

"I sure as hell do – you want to go to the Brooks house and sniff around, literally. I understand the impulse, but we need to catch this plane, Colleen. We have *got* to be in Indiana tonight."

According to the Indianapolis field office, local police had found the body of a female murder victim, strangled, with upside-down crosses carved, post-mortem, into her flesh in three places. That M.O. was the trademark of a serial killer dubbed 'The Reverend' who, over the last eight months, had left similarly mutilated corpses in Pennsylvania and Michigan. Fenton and O'Donnell had been working the case for Behavioral Science, and when word of the latest depredation came in, they had been ordered to get their asses over to Indianapolis, 'soonest.'

"I know that," Colleen O'Donnell said.

"We stepped in enough shit over that Idaho business to sink anybody's career, and it's only because the Office of Professional Responsibility couldn't prove any of the –" Fenton stopped talking and blinked a couple of times. "What do you mean 'I know that?'"

"I mean just what I said, Dale. Sure, I'd love to be on my way to Georgetown right this minute, but I realize that one more fuck-up could cost us our jobs. And not getting to Indy tonight would qualify as a *major* fuck-up."

"So, you're planning on doing what, then?"

"Something brilliant," of course." She sighed. "I just don't know what it is, yet."

"I HAD A flash of insight," Quincey Morris said, "or maybe you could call it a revelation."

"That sounds promising," Libby Chastain said. She and Morris had stayed up late, talking, and Libby

174

had spent the remainder of the night in Morris's guest bedroom. This morning she had made tea, and they sat in the kitchen drinking it, the pale winter sun coming in through the window. The cottonwood branches it passed through caused the light to form ever-changing chiaroscuro patterns on the table where the two mugs sat, side by side like old friends.

"It occurred during the four or five seconds it took you to walk from my couch and out through the door of the living room."

Libby nodded, saying only "Um-hmm." It was a technique she'd learned from her therapist, a sister-witch who had a thriving practice in Manhattan. Libby had been doing therapy off and on for three years. Witches have problems, too.

"I realized that only one part of my 'decision' to quit the business" – Morris had put air quotes around the word with his fingers, which gladdened Libby's heart – "was due to the guilt I felt over poor Hannigan."

Another "Um-hmm." Libby knew that Morris's head was feeling better. The tea had a lot to do with that, especially because Libby had added a pinch of something from her purse and muttered a few words over the pot while Morris was out of the room. If Morris knew she had used a little magic to help him feel better, he might be angry with her; ergo, she decided not to tell him. Sometimes white witches tell white lies.

"The rest of it," Morris went on, "was fear."

"But you've encountered fear before, Quincey," she said. "We both have. I remember you saying that anybody who dealt with the stuff we do who *wasn't* afraid was probably crazy. And I agree."

"Yeah, but that's not the kind of fear I mean."

"What, then?"

"It's being scared shitless that the next time the crunch comes, it'll happen again – I'll fold, like a bad poker hand. And somebody else will get hurt, or killed, because I let them down."

"But what you described as happening during that exorcism wasn't a failure of nerve, Quincey." She covered his hand with one of her own. "It was an involuntary reaction to sudden, excruciating pain. And I think the operative word there is 'sudden.' It came out of nowhere, you said. And it had never happened before, not since you got the scar months ago. Am I correct?"

"You know you are. So?"

"So, something can only take you by surprise once. You're aware the potential exists now, and you'll be ready for it if it happens again."

"You think that'll make a difference?"

She looked at him for several seconds before speaking. "I know that it must. Therefore, I believe it will."

"I reckon that'll have to be good enough."

Libby stared into her mug, as if seeking inspiration there. She may have found some, because she looked up and said, "I don't usually invite myself to be somebody's houseguest, but how about if I hang out here with you for a while? After a spurt of activity in the witch business, things have gone kind of slow. I only have one appointment scheduled for this week, and I can easily postpone it."

Morris gave her a lopsided grin. "You think I need a nursemaid?"

"Not a nursemaid, but maybe you could use a friend. I can help you put this place back together, and maybe we can do some meditation exercises to see if we can loosen up a few of those knots in your psyche."

Morris nodded thoughtfully. "I don't think I ever asked you, Libby," he said. "Do you play Scrabble?"

"I *love* Scrabble."

"In that case," Morris said, "you can stay as long as you like."

SUITE 501 AT the Hay-Adams hotel had a view of the White House and, beyond it, the phallic majesty of the Washington Monument. But Malachi Peters had not been interested in the scenery after one brief glance out the window. He spent most of his time staring at the screen of the Dell laptop he'd bought at Costco a couple of days earlier.

He was still having trouble getting used to the idea that you could have access to such an immense amount of information without even getting up from your chair. Peters had been prepared to spend long hours at the Library of Congress, finding out everything he could about Stark, as well as the current presidential race. Then he had planned to hit News World, the greatest newsstand that ever was, and buy the current issue of every U.S. newspaper they had, along with every magazine that covered politics.

Peters had recalled that in the early 1980s, a 24-hour news channel had started broadcasting, and some people had said it was going to be the next big thing in TV. He'd hoped that the CNN channel was still in business; it would save him from having to wait until 6:30 every evening to catch the network news.

Home computers had been on the market the last time Peters had walked the earth, but he remembered them as being expensive novelty items, good for playing games and maybe writing your novel, and little else.

Peters had been amazed by the power and variety of the personal computers you could get today, often for very little money. And soon thereafter, he had discovered the Internet.

He'd been prepared for a certain amount of technological advancement while he'd been gone, but he hadn't expected changes so drastic. He'd been utterly unprepared for the digital revolution, and it had just about blown his mind. That had lasted two hours. Then he had decided that he fucking *loved* it.

Which didn't mean that learning to use this new technology had been easy. His new computer sat on the oak desk the Hay-Adams provided for its guests, and next to it were piled *The Idiot's Guide to the Internet*, *PCs for Dummies*, and several other books with insulting titles that promised to teach you the basics – just in case you were from Mars, or had spent the last thirty years in Hell, or something.

There had been many times over the last three days when Peters felt like screaming in frustration, books or no books. But he was starting to get the hang of it now. Then, late on the third day, he discovered Internet porn.

Things really *had* changed since the Reagan era.

He shouldn't have been surprised. His memory was largely restored now, and he recalled reading somewhere that every new development in communications technology had always been immediately co-opted for three purposes: politics, commercial advertising, and pornography – not necessarily in that order.

Once Peters learned how to use Google, he found that the stuff was *everywhere*. You were supposed to pay for it, of course, that was the whole point of companies putting it up there. But there were plenty of sites where porn was available for free, as long as you were willing to put up with the numerous flashing annoyances that Peters learned were called pop-up ads.

Peters found online porn fascinating; he was, after all, male. The only thing that kept him from wasting hours looking at the stuff was the knowledge that eventually Astaroth would consider him to be slacking off, and Peters had no wish to find himself back in Hell. He was not unaware of the irony involved in worrying about whether a demon would get pissed off because some human was looking at pornography.

Chapter 18

THE PRESIDENTIAL PRIMARY season dragged on. January gave way to February, and the snows of Iowa were replaced by the even deeper snows of Maine.

In between had been New Hampshire – the first political test of the year in which actual delegates were at stake. In terms of getting a candidate closer to the nomination, the Iowa Caucuses were meaningless. But, because they represented the first chance that voters in this election cycle had to express a preference, the media had decided that they were important; therefore, they were.

Stark had come in fifth in Iowa. It might well have been sixth but for Chesbro's tragic suicide, a few days before voting was to take place. This untimely death of a dedicated public servant had shocked and saddened his political rivals – in public, at least.

But last place was still last place, and some of the pundits had already begun to compose Howard Stark's political obituary. New Hampshire should have been the last nail in the Senator from Ohio's political coffin, except that it wasn't – quite.

Stark had managed fourth place in New Hampshire, ahead of New Mexico's Senator Ramon Martinez. This was unsurprising to many, since the Latino population of the Granite State wouldn't have filled the bleachers at a Little League baseball game. Martinez was expected to do much better as the primary season moved south and west. But fourth place was still an improvement over fifth and, as they say in Peru, better than even a small earthquake.

Fernando Garrett, Stark's campaign manager, was not known in political circles as 'Doctor Spin' for nothing. On the night of the New Hampshire primary, once all the votes had been counted Garrett had explained what it meant, to any journalist who would listen or put him in front of a camera.

"We're actually quite pleased with the result," he would say earnestly. "Of course, we didn't do as well as we had hoped, that goes without saying. But we find this result encouraging, for several reasons. First of all, it represents progress. Fourth place may not be great, but fourth beats fifth in any race I ever heard of – and don't forget, Senator Martinez was predicted to do very well here." Who, apart from Martinez's own camp, had made such a prediction, Garrett didn't bother to mention. Like most people in politics, he refused to be hindered by inconvenient facts.

"Secondly, I think it's important to remember that candidates from the Midwest, like Senator Stark, have traditionally not done well in New Hampshire, which may help to explain why Governor Lunsford was able to capture First Place." Although it was true that Lunsford was from Massachusetts, it was also true that in three out of the last five elections, at least one Midwesterner, either Democrat or Republican, had taken First in New Hampshire. Another inconvenient fact, easily ignored.

"And finally, I'd like to point out that donations to the Senator's campaign prior to this primary are four times what they were as we were heading into the Iowa Caucuses just a few weeks ago. I think that demonstrates clearly that Senator Stark's message is getting out to the American people, and that many of them are responding by making contributions, small and large, to his effort to restore real leadership to this country. No, I don't have the precise figures, but the campaign will be releasing its financial disclosure forms in due time." Garrett was telling the truth, technically, since Stark's Iowa campaign had been financed almost entirely by the Senator's own fortune (his family had once owned more than half the ships transporting iron ore across the Great Lakes). Consequently, the $11,400 in contributions the campaign had received between Iowa and New Hampshire represented a significant gain – in percentage, if not in actual dollars.

And now the political battleground had moved deeper into New England. Voting in the Republican Party's Maine Municipal Caucuses would begin the day after tomorrow, and the GOP's Presidential contenders were giving speeches at every venue that would have them. None of the candidates had yet stood up to orate during the breakfast rush at the Derry IHOP, but Bat Masterson figured it was just a matter of time before one of them started promising that under his administration, French toast would be renamed American fried bread.

Senator Stark had managed to draw a pretty fair crowd at Bannerman High School's auditorium in Castle Rock this evening. With five Republicans going at it, and the Democrats due in for their own shindig in just ten days, you'd think the people of Maine would be speeched-out by now. But apparently their appetite for political oratory was nearly endless.

Either that, or Stark was starting to catch fire.

And maybe he was. One thing was clear to Masterson: over the last few months, Stark had made substantial improvement as a public speaker.

Once he found out that he was being assigned to Stark's protection detail, Masterson had tracked down and watched the only available footage (courtesy of C-SPAN) of Stark giving a speech – one he'd done for some Christian Right group in Boston last October. Masterson didn't give a damn about the oratory – he was interested in the crowd. He was looking for someone in the audience acting hinky. If he'd found something, Masterson would have made a screen capture of the image. It would then be enlarged, examined, identified if possible, and kept in the Secret Service 'potential threat' file – just in case. But as far as he could tell, the Bible thumpers had liked Stark just fine.

Stark had gone over well with the fundies because he'd told them what they wanted to hear. The speech itself earned a 'B-minus' in Masterson's opinion – adequate for a U.S. Senator, but nothing destined for the history books, or the White House, either. Among other problems, Masterson had thought Stark to be afflicted by what he privately thought of as 'Ted Kennedy Disease': a tendency to shout your way through an entire speech, so that every idea, from the mundane to the exceptional, was given the same frantic emphasis, which amounted to no emphasis at all.

But it seemed that Stark had got himself some lessons. His gestures were now compelling without seeming stagy, his eye contact with the audience was much improved, and he was finding nuances within the spoken words that had apparently escaped him completely just three or four months ago.

I don't know who the Kingfish's new speech coach is, but the sumbitch is good, Masterson thought. *This guy might just have a shot at the brass ring, after all.*

The speech concluded a few minutes later. Stark remained at the podium a little while to accept the applause, then he left the stage to shake hands with people in the audience. The media had covered several of Stark's events earlier in the day, but they were apparently elsewhere this evening. Masterson noted the absence of network video cameras, and he didn't see any of the print journalists or bloggers whose faces had become familiar to him.

What Stark was doing gave security people ulcers on their ulcers. Protecting somebody in a crowd situation like this was a nightmare for the Secret Service agents, and there wasn't a damn thing they could do to prevent it. Politicians like to press the flesh, because personal contact means votes, and the people charged with keeping them safe would just have to lump it. As usual.

One agent went down the rope line about twenty feet ahead of the candidate. "Can you just put your hands out, folks, just like you were about to shake hands with the Senator. That's it. Now please keep 'em up like that if you would – you won't have to wait long."

The hand you can't see may be the hand clutching a weapon. Obviously, a bad guy could have a weapon in his other hand, but asking people to stand for two or three minutes with both hands out in front of them was unreasonable. In the Secret Service, you take what you can get, and one hand in view was better than none.

They moved slowly down the rope line, the agents stepping sideways, so that they were facing the crowd at all times. After the advance guy, who got peoples' hands up, were two more agents, who geared their rate of lateral movement to the speed the protectee (in this case, Stark) was moving. Then the Man himself, followed by two more agents, in case somebody had the idea of shooting Stark in the back after he passed. Masterson had placed himself second from the end, which put him a few feet to Stark's left.

When he worked a crowd or a rope line, the same refrain always ran through Masterson's mind like a mantra, replete with names of infamous security failures of the past.

Watch the hands of the ones close up, watch the faces of those farther away, John Hinckley, watch the hands, keep The Man moving, watch their hands, check the faces for the guy who isn't smiling, Lee Harvey Oswald, don't let him stay in one place more than a few seconds, keep him moving, watch their hands, Arthur Brenner, don't over-react – shoot some civilian who's reaching for a breath mint and your career's over, Sirhan Sirhan, watch their faces, look ahead, anticipate, John Wilkes fucking Booth, the hands, watch their hands…

When trouble came, it appeared out of nowhere, as it always does. They had almost reached the auditorium doors when Stark suddenly recoiled from someone, or something, in the crowd.

It was a tribute to the professionalism of the Secret Service agents that nobody yelled "Gun!" That word would have galvanized the entire detail, sending the agents into a series of precise and coordinated actions as carefully planned and practiced as any play called by an NFL quarterback. But none of them had seen a weapon or a muzzle flash, or heard a shot, and so they refrained, even though they knew that *something* was wrong.

That was enough for Masterson to call a Class 2 Security Alert. Two agents surrounded Stark and got him quietly but firmly away from the people and out the door, no drama, while the other agents went the other way, wading into the crowd near the spot where Stark had been a few moments earlier. Their attentions focused on a thin, middle-aged man in a Navy blue sweater. The man didn't pull a weapon, or fight, or try to run. In fact, he seemed confused by the questions being shouted at him by several large men in suits.

The Secret Service had commandeered an office just off the auditorium for use as a staging area, and it was there that they brought the man in the blue sweater, who was now looking both bewildered and scared.

They hadn't read the man his rights yet – it wasn't clear at the moment what they would charge him with, if anything, and the paperwork involved in filing an arrest report with Washington was a major pain in the butt. Better to find out what they were dealing with, first.

The initial order of business was a thorough frisk, which gave absolutely no consideration to the man's dignity or privacy. In a few minutes, it was clear that he carried nothing that could conceivably be called a weapon.

The contents of the man's pockets were arrayed on a nearby desk, and Masterson looked them over with a practiced eye. He picked up a slim book bound in black leather. Hanging from the bottom were several thin ribbons in different colors, each about the width of a shoelace.

Masterson tugged one of the bits of cloth, and the book opened in his hand. He saw now that it was a bookmark that ran from the top of the spine all the way down the page.

Funny way to keep your place – and why would you need five of them?

Then he realized that the pages open before him were in a foreign language. He wasn't Catholic, but Masterson recognized Latin when he saw it.

He turned to the man in the blue sweater, who now sat in a chair, hands in his lap. "You're a Godly man, are you, Mr…?" *Maybe he's a religious nut? That might help explain a few things.*

"Bowles," the man said. "Joseph Robert Bowles. He assayed a small, nervous smile, then said, "Yes, I like to think of myself as Godly. I do my best, anyway."

Rex Cummings, one of the other agents, had started going through the man's cheap-looking wallet. "Yeah, I'd say he was Godly, all right," he said, handing the open wallet to Masterson. "Take a look at *this*."

Masterson took it and saw a laminated ID card. It had the man's photo, confirmed that his name was Joseph R. Bowles, and contained a bunch of other information. Stamped across the whole thing, in big letters, was 'CLERGY.'

Oh, sweet fucking Jesus. That's all I need.

THERE WAS NO standing in line this time. The package was just a manila envelope, so thin that when folded lengthwise that it actually fit into Nestor Greene's Post Office box. He waited until he was back in his car to open it.

The return address was another P.O. box, although he knew that to be fictitious. Greene knew who had sent the envelope; he recognized the spider-thin handwriting, including where it said 'Do not bend!' He shook his head in disgust. Even though the admonition on the envelope had been ignored by the postal service nitwits, he saw that the contents of the envelope had not been adversely affected by being bent and crammed into his mailbox.

Green frowned as he examined the materials. He was not being given a lot to work with, this time around. There were no juicy photos to pass on to the tabloid press. Well, at least he wouldn't have to meet with that macho idiot Mundenar again.

The manila envelope contained a single sheet of paper that, he knew, would bear his instructions from Mary Margaret Doyle, and two sets of paper-clipped documents. One consisted of a series of photocopies of what looked like pages from a book. The other was made up of some sort of typed material, the pages crinkly and a bit faded with age. Greene frowned and decided that he'd best wait until he was home to examine these latest treasures.

Twenty-five minutes later found Nestor Greene seated behind the desk in his study, an icy glass of Stolichnaya Elit sharing space with the envelope from Mary Margaret Doyle. He grasped the envelope at the bottom and tilted it, allowing its contents to slide onto the polished teak surface.

He put the single sheet of instructions off to the side. No sense in spoiling the surprise. Greene enjoyed the challenge of figuring out just who was about to get royally fucked, and in what precise way.

He decided to let the photocopied material wait and picked up the other sheaf of papers, noticing the slightly musty small they gave off. He removed the paper clip and peered at the first page, which was apparently some kind of cover sheet. At the top was typed, in all caps: SHOWDOWN AT CREDIBILITY GAP: PARAMETERS OF DECEPTION IN THE ADMINISTRATION OF LYNDON BAYNES JOHNSON.

Hmmm. Rather clever, in a puerile sort of way. The words on the page, he saw, were the product of a real typewriter, not a printer from some computer. *How quaint.* That meant that the document was practically antediluvian.

In the middle of the page, centered, was:

A Senior Thesis
Department of Political Science
Amherst College
In partial fulfillment for the degree
Bachelor of Arts

And down near the bottom was typed:

by
Randall R. Lunsford
May, 1977

Greene frowned. Randall Lunsford was the name of one of the stronger Republican candidates for the presidential nomination this year – but why the hell should anybody, including Nestor Greene, give a rat's ass about his senior thesis, written thirty-some years ago?

Greene checked the number of the last page – Mother Mary, the thing ran to 87 pages. Was he going to have to read all of it? Greene used his thumb to flip through the pages, and that's when something caught his eye. He stopped, and looked closer. Part of page 9 was highlighted with that yellow ink that students use to mark up their textbooks. Unlike the typed words on the page, the yellow stuff seemed fresh, as if applied much more recently. Greene read the passage thus indicated, and found it unremarkable. *Yeah, yeah. LBJ was a lying bastard. Tell me something I don't already know, kid.* He flipped some more pages, and found the yellow markings on two, three, four... seventeen pages, in total.

Greene scratched his cheek. His attention was clearly being directed to certain specific parts of this piece of ancient history, but what this had to do with destroying some politico's career today...

He turned to the collection of photocopies. The top sheet looked like the title page from a book: *Johnson and His Critics: Lies, Damn Lies, and Statistics* by one Adam H. Quiller. The book had been published by some obscure university press in 1975.

I think I'm starting to see where we're going here, Greene thought. *But is this journey really necessary?*

The second page had a paragraph that had been marked by the yellow highlighter.

"'When Johnson ordered the Navy to bomb the North Vietnamese radar installations – the first time the North was targeted for aerial bombardment – in retaliation for the attacks on the *Maddox* and *Turner Joy* by PT boats in the Gulf of Tonkin, he was already aware that the officers commanding the U.S. vessels were expressing doubts that such an attack had ever occurred.'"

Greene was pretty sure he recognized the passage. He went back to the senior thesis and began turning pages rapidly – until he came to page 32.

When Johnson ordered the Navy to bomb the North Vietnamese radar installations…

Green looked for quotation marks around this passage. There were none. He looked for a footnote number. None. He looked for anything that would tell the reader of the senior thesis that these words were anything but the product of the undergraduate brain of one Randall Lunsford. There was nothing.

Greene didn't bother to match up the other marked sections of the two documents. He already knew what he would find.

He sat back in his chair, reached for the glass of vodka, and took a long sip.

Okay, fine. What we have here is conclusive proof that Randy Lunsford, current Governor of the Commonwealth of Massachusetts and candidate for the office of President of the United States, had committed blatant plagiarism in writing his senior thesis at Amherst, all those years ago. Since the thesis was certainly a prerequisite for his Bachelor's degree, the degree was probably granted fraudulently, and could even be revoked, if the folks at Amherst are willing to take the chance of making a mortal enemy of their governor who has, I believe, two more years left in his term.

Greene took another pull at his drink, and set the glass down.

Big fucking hairy deal.

This kind of revelation was not unknown in American politics. It was a blow to Lunsford's candidacy, but not necessarily a fatal one. Just off the top of his head, Greene could think of three potential lines of defense: 'I Was Young and Stupid,' 'I Was Young and (Temporarily) Having Emotional Problems,' and 'This Is a Smear Campaign by My Enemies.'

It would be a nine day's wonder that wouldn't even last nine days. The late-night comics would get some good jokes out of it (*Did you hear that Governor Lunsford's campaign has released an advance copy of his newest campaign speech? It begins 'Four score and seven years ago...'*), a few reporters would ask questions and receive carefully-scripted, well-rehearsed answers, and it would all blow over. Probably.

As a political weapon, it sure couldn't compete with photos of a guy sucking cock.

If this was the best Mary Margaret Doyle could come up with to deal with one of Stark's competitors... It occurred to Greene that he ought to read her accompanying memo.

No salutation, of course. Gets right to the point, does our Ms. Doyle.

Compare the video footage of Lunsford's speech announcing his candidacy with a speech by Glenda Jackson (yes, the former actress) given when announcing her decision to run for Parliament in 1992. The similarities between the two are far too numerous to be chance, or even honest paraphrase. It is possible, of course, to overcome this kind of error. Joe Biden was caught in 1987 lifting parts of a speech by Brit M.P. Neil Kinnock, and his career in politics was not over – but he didn't get to be President, either. When Lunsford's lapse is combined with the clear evidence of earlier plagiarism, a pattern would seem to emerge – a pattern of extreme carelessness at best, or of repeated, deliberate deception at worst, etc. You know how to get the story out there. Do it ASAP, and try not to fuck it up.

Nestor Greene muttered several unkind, and anatomically impossible, things about Mary Margaret Doyle. Then he turned on his computer and tried to remember whom he might know at the BBC that could be either bribed, begged, or blackmailed into doing him a favor.

Chapter 19

IN ORDER TO avoid being summarily returned to Hell for goofing off on the job, Malachi Peters put in a lot of hours doing research on Senator Stark, interrupted only occasionally by brief forays into the Wonderland of Internet porn. He had been doing it that way for three days now, and it must not have pissed Astaroth off, since Peters was still here.

Assassinating Stark was going to be a complex problem. Peters had spent six years in Europe, killing people who had been deemed threats to U.S. national security. But a hit was a hit (although Peters' immediate superior, an enigmatic man known only as Mac, always referred to it as a 'touch'), regardless of where you were, and the relevant factors were always the same: access, termination, and egress. Or as his instructors at The Farm in Virginia liked to call it, "Getting in, getting it done, and getting out."

To Peters, it seemed like the third stage was going to be the hardest. It usually was – for the first two, you had surprise on your side. But by the time you got to egress, if you lived that long, everybody was after your ass.

Peters had every intention of reaching the third phase, and getting away clean. If he were killed, that was probably an express ticket back to Hades; if he got caught, that would mean either execution for murder, or the rest of his life spent in prison, enduring one kind of hell while waiting for the real thing. Or, if captured, he could always just tell the authorities the complete truth about who he was and how he'd gotten here – the result being his incarceration in a high-security mental hospital for life.

And if he *were* locked up somewhere, it would be just like that bastard Astaroth to grant him a long, long life.

Even the first two steps of the assassination sequence were probably more difficult than they used to be. It must be a security nightmare these days – guarding against an assassin who doesn't care if he dies, who even *wants* to die, for the greater glory of Allah.

Welcome to the 21st Century, Mr. Peters. We have good news and bad news. The good: your country's nemesis, the Soviet Union, is no more. Communism there is a thing of the past, and relations between Russia and America are, if not warm, at least cordial.

Now for the bad news...

Peters had known about the 9/11 attacks even before his return to Earth. He'd been near the intake area of Hell on that fateful day, and had been present when the souls of some of the dead from the Twin Towers arrived. They were accompanied by the spirits of the hijackers, and didn't *they* look surprised.

Sorry, boys – no 72 virgins apiece. Virgins are pretty scarce around these parts, anyway, and if anybody's going to spend eternity getting fucked, it's gonna be YOU.

Peters sat back and rubbed his tired eyes. Knowing where Stark was going to be on any given day over the next four months was easy. The primary schedule was online, and Peters had already printed it out.

And there was always the Republican convention, which was being held in New York this time around. Even if Stark didn't get the nomination, he'd almost certainly be there; such things were expected of politicos.

The downside of waiting until then was that security at the convention would be both wide and deep. But there was an upside, too. With that many people, and that much chaos, it might be possible to nail Stark and then disappear into the crowd – which might even panic and stampede when Stark went down, depending on how it was done.

Peters had a New York State driver's license, made current again by the power of Astaroth. The state gun laws hadn't changed much – they were still the toughest in the country. To buy a pistol legally you needed a permit, and New York permits required lots of paperwork, persistence, and patience. He'd also read that the gun dealers were now required to do a background check before they could sell you a handgun. Peters wondered what the clerk at some gun store would say if the background check on him came back marked 'Deceased.'

Rifles and shotguns had always been easier to get, and that hadn't changed. All you needed was proof that you were over eighteen. A long gun might be his best bet, anyway. Getting close enough to nail somebody with a pistol meant giving his bodyguards the chance to nail *you* right back.

He got up from the desk, hearing his vertebrae snap and pop. He'd found that his libido had returned with his memory, and his little 'porn breaks' had only strengthened a need that masturbation couldn't satisfy. It had been a very long time since he'd been with a woman. Peters tried not to think about what passed for sex in Hell.

Feeling nervous and ridiculous in equal measure, Peters cleared his throat and addressed the empty room.

"I don't know if you can hear me, my Lord Astaroth. I'm assuming you can. So, here's the thing: I've done all I can think of to do for you today, and I'm tired."

He paused for a second, then went on. "I'm also horny, and I want to get laid. I'm hoping you won't see that as neglecting my work – but if you do, let me know now, and I won't go through with it. I'd rather not get dragged back to Hell yet, and I expect you'd prefer to have me here doing the job you sent me to do. So, if you've got a problem with me hiring a hooker and doing some sex, please let me know now."

Peters then stood there for a full minute, noticing for the first time the faint hum of traffic five floors below on Pennsylvania Avenue, hearing a faint clanking sound from the hall that he assumed was somebody's room service dinner being wheeled past his door.

Then, with an audible sigh of relief, he went to sit on the bed and picked up the D.C. Yellow Pages. He'd checked yesterday, while still nerving himself up to risk Astaroth's anger, and found that escort services continued to advertise in phone book. Some things, it seemed, didn't change.

He flipped to the 'E' listings. There were eight pages devoted to escort services, with ads ranging in size from a full page to about half the size of a playing card.

With the money and credit he had to work with, Peters figured he didn't need to settle for some gum-chewing teenager with cheap perfume and a nose that was perpetually runny from her coke habit. He could afford the best,

He finally decided on a place in Bethesda that called itself 'Elegant Evenings.' Their ad, at least, looked classy. He'd have to see if their employees came up to the same high standard.

Making note of the number, Peters was just reaching for the phone to order himself some high-class pussy when there was a knock on the door.

THE SECRET SERVICE detail protecting Senator Howard Stark had brought three cars with them to Bannerman High School Auditorium for the occasion of the Senator's speech. One car had left with the Senator an hour ago, as per procedure. Another was still in the parking lot behind the main school building. Masterson stood in the doorway of the auditorium and watched the third car drive off. One of his agents was giving Joseph Robert Bowles a lift home. Bowles had been released from Secret Service custody a few minutes ago, with apologies and a handshake. Fortunately, he didn't seem inclined to sue anybody over tonight's 'misunderstanding.' Masterson doubted the man would have won in court – the agents had acted in good faith, and for sound reasons – but the nuisance factor of such legal actions was always substantial.

He pulled out his radio. "Three-six, this is one-six. Do you copy? Over." Three-six was one of the two agents who had taken Stark to the hospital to be checked out, and treated if necessary.

A couple of seconds later, he heard a familiar voice in his ear. Bryan Knapp was the newest agent on the detail, having finished training about six months earlier. "This is three-six. Got you loud and clear. Over."

"What's your twenty? Over."

There was a brief pause. "We're back at the hotel. Over."

Masterson frowned. Stark must have been gotten through the hospital ER in record time, even for a U.S. Senator. "You've got Kingfish? Over."

"Uh, affirmative," Knapp said. "Attila, also. Over."

"What's Kingfish's condition? Over." Masterson asked.

"I would, uh, assess that as a '9.' Over." In Service code, '10' meant 'in perfect health,' and 'zero' was a number no agent ever wanted to have to report.

"What's the ER situation? Was Kingfish not injured, or was he treated and released, or what? Over." Masterson was starting to get impatient with the newbie.

"Negative, one-six. He, uh, refused to go. Over."

"Say again? Over." Masterson was hoping he had misheard.

"Kingfish refused to let us take him to the hospital. He insisted we bring him back here. Over."

Masterson struggled to keep his voice even. "That's not his decision to make, three-six. You *are* familiar with the SOP following any kind of security incident? Over."

Masterson thought he could hear Knapp swallow. "That's affirmative, one-six. I know the procedure. Over."

Masterson took a couple of deep breaths. Yelling over the radio was considered unprofessional.

"All right, three-six. We'll be returning to the hotel shortly. When I get there, you and me and your partner going to have us a conversation. Over."

"Roger that," Knapp said miserably. "Three-six out."

Masterson broke contact and turned to the other three agents, who were dismantling the temporary command post. "Get this shit packed up and in the car! I wanna be at the fucking hotel five minutes ago. Move it!"

* * *

From the *Wall Street Journal* editorial page:

It is troubling to consider the apparent ethical lapses attributed to Massachusetts Governor Randall Lunsford, which have recently come to light. The earlier incident – a clear case of academic plagiarism, which is just another word for stealing – might be passed off as the poor judgment of an immature, 22-year-old college student. But the second case is much more recent, and consequently of greater concern to those of us who have heretofore viewed Governor Lunsford as a viable candidate for the highest office in the land.

The Governor's admission that dishonesty was committed in the earlier case is welcome. He has taken full responsibility for his ethical lapse as an Amherst undergraduate, although some members of his campaign have been using phrases like 'ancient history' when referring to the matter off the record.

But Governor Lunsford's claim that the reason his announcement speech last summer contained several passages identical (or nearly so) with one given years ago by British Liberal M.P. (and former actress) Glenda Jackson is due to the careless work of a staffer do not hold water, and are unworthy of him.

In an interview with Newsweek *magazine last December, the question of who is responsible for his speeches was asked – and answered unequivocally. "I write all my own*

200

stuff," the Governor is quoted as saying. "Sure, I run ideas past members of my staff, and I often invite their comments on early drafts, but I don't have a speechwriter. I'm my own speechwriter, for better or worse."

It is perhaps worth mentioning that in the weeks since the Newsweek *interview appeared, neither Governor Lunsford nor any member of his staff has raised any concerns about its accuracy.*

The Governor is a man of high intellect and undeniable ability as a public servant. Neither of these has been called into question by recent events. But the issue of character cannot be ignored, especially when one is choosing a Chief Executive, and it is in this respect that the Governor may have been found wanting. Those who have supported Governor Lunsford's candidacy may well have to consider…

Chapter 20

PETERS FROZE, STARING at the door as his heart rate accelerated.

He hadn't ordered anything from room service. The valet service wasn't dropping off any dry cleaning. He hadn't called Housekeeping for extra towels. And he sure hadn't called for the girl yet. There was no reason for anybody to be knocking on his door, he thought, just as the knock came again. Peters felt sweat began to bead on his forehead.

Come on, time to get real. If it's Astaroth, come to drag my sorry ass back to the Bad Place for disobedience, he wouldn't bother to knock. Hell, he wouldn't even use the door – just appear out of nowhere and scare the shit out of me. He likes stuff like that.

Peters' brain could find no fault with the logic. He just wished his central nervous system would get the message and calm the fuck down.

Might as well get it over with, one way or another.

Peters got up and walked to the door on legs that were not quite steady.

He looked through the peephole's fisheye lens, which gave him a view, slightly distorted, of the whole corridor.

A woman. Young. Pretty. Not wearing a maid's outfit, or any other kind of hotel uniform. Somebody got the wrong room?

Feeling his body relax a little, Peters pulled the door open. "Hi, can I help you?"

She tilted her head slightly and looked at him through gray eyes that seemed amused. "Actually, I was thinking that I might be able to help *you*." Her voice reminded him of the young Kathleen Turner.

What the fuck is this? Jehovah's Witness, or something? They don't work hotels, do they? She's not carrying any Watchtowers, either.

Peters shook his head slightly. "I'm sorry, I don't understand. Are you sure you've got the right room?"

She gave him a half-smile. Her voice contained the slightest hint of mockery as she said, "I'm reasonably certain, Mr. Peters. Didn't you say you were interested in some… company this evening?"

Peters stared at her.

Did I call the escort service already and fucking forget? How is that possible? Could I have called them and then fallen asleep, or something? Or am I just losing my fucking mind?

"Uh, yeah. Right. I mean – come in."

He stepped back to give her room. Whatever was going on, it wasn't some pissed-off demon lord sent to drag him back to Hell, so how bad could it possibly be?

She wore a tan, double-breasted topcoat, unbuttoned. It looked like a trench coat, but without the trademark belt made famous in a hundred private eye movies.

"Uh, can I take your coat?" Part of Peters's mind realized that he sounded like a high school nerd trying to make

203

witty conversation with the prom queen, but he couldn't seem to get his bearings. What was she *doing* here?

"Why, yes, thank you." She carried a large black leather bag which she set gently on the floor before slipping the coat off with one graceful motion and handing it to him.

As he hung the garment up in his closet, Peters noticed the distinctive plaid lining that meant Burberry – and *that* meant expensive.

He gestured for her to go first, and she walked before him into the living room of the suite. The woman let her gaze wander the room briefly, then nodded her approval. "Nice place you've got here," she said. "I've always liked the Hay-Adams. They know how to do elegance without being heavy-handed about it."

"Yeah, I know what you mean," he said, as if he had any idea what she was talking about. Now that she was out of the hall and into the well-lit room, Peters took a moment to study her. She was thirty, maybe, and tall. He glanced at her simple black pumps, saw two-inch heels, and calculated her real height as about 5'9". He had always liked tall women, maybe because he was 6'2" himself. Her hair was ash blonde, a color he'd always found attractive, and she wore it in an off-the-shoulder style that he bet every woman in town would be asking their hairdressers for, six months from now.

Her simple black dress came down to mid-thigh to reveal dark hose that encased superb legs. Around her throat she wore a single strand of pearls.

It occurred to Peters that if he had been offered the chance to design the perfect female for himself, the result would look something very like the woman who stood before him now, one hand on a slim hip, the other holding the straps of that huge leather bag.

"It seems you know my name," he said, "but I don't know yours."

"You can call me Ashley," she said. Then she parted those red lips and gave him a full wattage smile that Julia Roberts would have traded her soul for. Peters's heart was beating fast again, but for a different reason this time.

"Is that your real name?"

"It might be," she said. "Does it matter?"

"No, I guess it doesn't, but here's something that *does* matter: what are you doing here, Ashley? Unless I'm having blackouts without the booze, I don't remember calling for female company – although if I had, I could hardly have asked for someone more attractive than you."

Another smile. "Awww, flattery." She tossed the bag on his bed, then kicked off her shoes. "It may not get you everywhere, but it could take you a long way. At least, on this occasion."

She walked slowly over to him, not making a big production of it, but he thought she moved like a panther. Maybe it was the black outfit that gave that impression – but maybe not.

She reached up and slowly put her arms around his neck. That put her face about six inches from his. Her perfume smelled of sandalwood.

"You did ask for me, you know," she said, her voice barely above a whisper. "It's true you didn't get to call the Elegant Evenings escort service…"

Peter's felt a chill run down his spine, as if she'd just slipped an ice cube down the back of his shirt.

She leaned forward and kissed him, once, briefly, a promise of bliss to come. Then she brought her head back a little, and the large, gray eyes were looking directly into his as she said, "But you *did* tell Astaroth."

* * *

"I STILL THINK you should go to the hospital, Senator," Bat Masterson said. "Chemical burns are nothing to fool around with."

"It's completely unnecessary," Stark told him. "I'm sure I overreacted – I was startled, rather than hurt. See for yourself."

Standard Operating Procedure for an attack of any sort was go get the protectee to the nearest hospital, fast. The agents who had hustled Stark out of the auditorium and into the car were in the process of doing that very thing when Stark had overruled them – in the strongest possible terms.

As it happened, the guys who were with Stark in the car were the least experienced of the whole detail – Porter had been on the job for just over a year, Knapp for six months. They apparently hadn't yet grasped the idea that in cases like this, the protectee's wishes were of no accord. They should have taken him to the hospital anyway. But Stark, with the able insistence of Ms. Doyle, had bullied them into returning to the hotel, instead.

There, Ms. Doyle had displayed a well-equipped first aid kit, and claimed that she'd had training in its use. She had accompanied Stark into his room, and locked the door behind them, leaving the two young agents in the sitting room, looking at each other in confusion.

Masterson had learned this from Porter and Knapp themselves. Arriving back at the hotel, he had assigned two other agents to the Senator and Mary Margaret Doyle. Then he had taken Porter and Knapp into a quiet room and debriefed them.

In this case, 'debriefed' was a synonym for 'cutting them each a brand new asshole.' Leaving the two young agents to contemplate their futures, Masterson had gone to see the Senator. The conversation with the protectee was not going the way he had intended.

Mary Margaret Doyle was unwrapping the gauze bandage with which she had encased the Senator's right hand.

"Let me be sure I understand what happened," Masterson said. "You were working the crowd, shaking hands. Then you felt something burning your hand? That's why you jumped back?"

"Exactly," Stark said. "I didn't know what was causing it, but I knew it wasn't a sensation I should be having, under those circumstances. Who knew what some nut might be trying to do? So I recoiled, automatically."

Mary Margaret Doyle was taking her time, but the last of the long bandage was almost unraveled.

"It may be that I responded too dramatically," Stark said, with a self-deprecating smile. "In any case, no harm was done. Ms. Doyle's magic salve seems to have done the trick."

The last of the gauze bandage dropped to the floor, and Stark turned his hand so that the open palm faced outward.

Masterson blinked. There was nothing there.

"See Agent Masterson? There was some skin irritation, but that's just about cleared up. A visit to the local hospital's emergency room would just have diverted the staff's attention from people who desperately needed care. Not to mention the distraction that would have been caused by the media people, who'd probably show up, hoping for some melodrama to report on."

The skin covering Stark's palm and fingers was a little pinker than was probably normal, but that was the only sign Masterson could discern that anything might have been amiss. He looked from the hand back to Stark's face. "Any pain when you open and close it?"

Stark flexed his fingers a couple of times. "None at all. In fact, I don't think I even need the bandage any more, do you?"

He turned to Mary Margaret Doyle, who was hovering. "An excellent job of first aid, M.M. Thank you. Get me something to wipe this gunk off with, will you?"

Turning back, Stark said, "See, Agent Masterson? No cause for concern after all."

"Yes, sir, it would seem so. Glad to see you're okay." Masterson cleared his throat. "But we have to get something straight between us, Senator. For your own safety, you *have* to follow the security procedures. It may be a nuisance at times, but it's the price that comes with presidential politics – and with Secret Service protection."

Stark nodded gravely. Mary Margaret Doyle returned with a hand towel from the bathroom, and as he wiped his hand off, Stark said, "I understand completely. In future, I will defer to your judgment, or that of the other agents, no matter what my own views of the situation may be. Fair enough?"

Masterson returned the nod with one of his own. "Yes, sir, thank you. It's for the best, believe me."

His palm clean of what he had called the magic salve, Stark handed the towel back to Ms. Doyle. "What happened, anyway – was it just some idiot's idea of a prank? Have you arrested anybody?"

"We did, sir, but we've released him."

Stark gave Masterson raised eyebrows. "Indeed?"

"The agent who was closest to you when the, um incident occurred took a man into custody, believing him to be the perpetrator of... whatever it was that took place."

Stark exchanged glances with Mary Margaret Doyle. "But now you believe otherwise?" he said.

"We had no evidence on which to hold him, Senator. He carried no weapon of any kind, nor was there any trace of a corrosive agent that might have caused your... injury. We questioned him thoroughly, of course."

"I'm sure you did. What was his story?"

"Nothing all that remarkable. He saw in the paper you were going to be speaking at the high school, and wanted to see you in person. He thinks you make a lot of sense, he said."

Stark gave a twitch of a smile. "I've lost his vote now, I suppose."

"I wouldn't know, sir. But we checked his ID, and it was legitimate. He willingly let us have his prints, and we ran them through NCIC. Both the name and the prints were negative."

Mary Margaret Doyle joined the conversation for the first time. "NCIC? Isn't that some awful television show?"

Masterson looked at her. "I believe you're thinking of NCIS, ma'am, which is the Naval Criminal Investigation Service. I was referring to the National Crime Information Center, which is a database run by the FBI. A lot of agencies use it."

"So, you found nothing when you sent them this man's name and fingerprints," Stark said. "What *is* his name, anyway?"

"Bowles, sir. Joseph Robert Bowles."

Stark looked a question at Mary Margaret Doyle, who thought briefly, then shook her head.

"And you believe," Stark said to Masterson, "that Mr. Bowles is innocent of whatever —" he held up his apparently uninjured hand "— *inconvenience* I experienced?"

Masterson nodded, and got to his feet. "Yes, sir. I've got someone in Washington doing a double-check, but I'm inclined to believe his story."

"Simply because you can't prove otherwise?" Stark was frowning like Masterson's high school principal used to.

"Yes, sir. That and the fact that Bowles is a Catholic priest."

Chapter 21

WHEN HE HEARD Ashley say 'Astaroth,' every muscle in Malachi Peters' body went rigid. He gazed into the beautiful face a few inches from his own and wondered if it were the last sight he were going to see before being returned to the fires of Hell.

His throat felt as constricted as if he were being choked, but he finally managed to force words out of it. "Have you come to... take me back?"

She kissed him again, gently, a mere peck on his lips. "No, sweetheart, I'm here to get you off. That's what you wanted, isn't it?"

She withdrew her arms from around his neck and turned, presenting her back to him. "Would you unzip me?"

Questions flew through Peters' mind like a flock of frightened sparrows. He tried to speak again, to demand to know what was going on, but no words came out.

The tab of the black dress's zipper lay there in front of him. He reached out with a hand that was not quite steady, grasped the little rectangle with thumb and forefinger, and slowly pulled it down. The back of the dress parted, revealing flawless skin and the strap of a black bra.

In a moment, the garment was a shadow pooled around her feet. She bent and picked it up, folded it quickly, and placed it over the back of a nearby chair. She took her time; she knew he was looking at her.

She turned toward him and spread her arms wide, displaying herself. With the bra she wore matching panties that looked like they might be silk. Instead of pantyhose, she wore thigh-high stockings, the tops of which stopped just short of her groin. Those were popular now, according to the porn sites Peters had been visiting.

Ashley reached behind her back for a moment, then the bra was sliding down her arms. She caught it before it fell and placed it atop the dress. Her breasts were beautiful. Peters had never belonged to the 'more is better school' of ta-ta appreciation, and he thought that her moderately sized but perky endowment was perfect for her slim frame.

She let him look for a few more seconds, then reached down and hooked her thumbs into the waistband of the black silk panties. With all the teasing deliberation of a stripper, she slowly pulled them down and off. Peters saw that she had followed the trend popular in porn these days and shaved herself bare, apart from a four inch long 'landing strip' just above the essential area.

She let him take in the view for a bit, then walked slowly back to him, stopping where she had stood before, inches away. He thought she might kiss him again, but instead she said softly, "You've unzipped me – the least I can do is return the favor" and dropped to her knees. Soon there was the sly sound of a zipper in descent. Then the room was quiet for a while, except for the hum of the heating unit, the wet sounds that Ashley was making, and the soft moans that escaped Peters' lips.

Then she stopped what she was doing, and stood, effortlessly. She took Peters' face in her hands and kissed him again, and this time it was the real deal. When she finally withdrew her tongue from his mouth, he said "Listen, I –"

She stopped him with a finger to his lips. "Do you remember a country song called 'Shut Up and Kiss Me'?"

Peters shook his head.

"Oh, that's right – it was popular for a while when you were away."

He blinked a couple of times. "You... know about that?"

"I know everything I need to know. And the lady who wrote that song had a pretty good idea. She just didn't take it far enough. No questions, Peters. Just shut up and fuck me. Okay?"

She took him gently by the hand and led him toward the suite's bedroom. She seemed to know the way.

"WHAT WAS THAT you put on my hand before you bandaged it – that greasy substance?" Sargatanas asked.

"Just Vaseline petroleum jelly," Mary Margaret Doyle said. "It's often used to treat burns, although usually minor ones. You said you were going to heal yourself, but I thought it might add some verisimilitude, if we needed it."

"As we did," he said. "That was good thinking on your part. For a human, you are sometimes quite intelligent."

213

Mary Margaret Doyle actually blushed. She looked at the floor and said nothing.

"And now we have work to do. Important work."

"What do you have in mind?" she asked.

"This *priest*. Bowles. Why was he there tonight? Why did he wish to touch me?"

She considered. "It could be just what Masterson said. Priests vote, too. He may have gone to hear the Great Man's speech, and shake his hand."

"You believe that was all?"

"I'm just saying it's not inconceivable."

"Well, perhaps that was the reason. But it could have been something else – a test."

"To see if you were…"

"One of demonkind, yes. And if it *was* a test, then now he knows something. He may not understand it yet, but he *knows*. And something else concerns me, as well."

"What's that?"

"The possibility that this priest did not come on his own initiative. Rather, that he may have been *sent*."

"Sent?" Deep worry lines appeared just above her nose. "By whom?"

Sargatanas made a fist and stared at it, as if he were squeezing some small creature to death in his palm. "There are any number of possibilities. Your world contains no shortage of dilettantes who know far too much about the netherworld than is good for them. Any of them might have put the priest up to it."

"Which means, whatever the priest knows, they now know."

"Yes, or they will soon." Sargatanas shook his head slowly. "Too many unknowns. Too much potential for something to go wrong, later. Such a situation cannot be tolerated. That is why you are going to pay a call on the priest."

"*Me!* Are you –" She stopped herself in time. "Yes, of course. Forgive me. I assume you have a… plan for me to follow. And perhaps some magic for me to use?"

"I have both. Come here."

She walked over to where he sat tentatively – unsure whether he was going to punish her for her verbal slip earlier, or use her sexually before sending her out to find the priest, or… something else.

When she stood before him he said, "Bend over."

She frowned in puzzlement. She had been given that command before, but always when her back was to him.

As she bent forward, he took her face in his hands in a grip that was not quite painful. "Be still," he said, and began to recite something in a language she didn't recognize. After a few moments, Mary Margaret Doyle closed her eyes. Staring into the demon's eyes at that distance was more than even she could bear. After perhaps twenty seconds, he released her.

"Now, then," he said, once she had straightened up, "This is for you."

He handed her a leather folder like the one the Secret Service agents used to hold their credentials. She flipped it open and saw that it contained the badge and ID card of Ronald J. Porter, one of the agents who had tried to rush them to the hospital earlier.

"This will gain you access to the priest," he said. "Tell him that additional questions have arisen about tonight's *incident* and that he must accompany you to the local FBI office – but in fact, you will take him elsewhere."

She stared at him for a few moments. When she finally spoke, it was clear that she was choosing her words carefully. "I'm sure that there is something here that I do not understand. Will you explain it to me, please?"

"I will do better than that," he said with a grin. "Go to the mirror."

She took a couple of steps sideways, until she stood in front of the room's full-length mirror. Then she gasped in shock.

Looking back at her was a blond man in his late twenties, his big shoulders encased in a dark suit of dubious quality.

It was Ronald J. Porter, Special Agent of the U.S. Secret Service.

Mary Margaret gaped, looking her 'self' up and down. She touched her head; Porter's mirror image touched his. She wrinkled her nose; the reflection did the same.

"I've placed a 'glamour' on you," Sargatanas said. "Anyone who looks at you will see Porter – until I take it off, that is – upon successful completion of your mission."

She turned reluctantly away from the mirror and faced him. "I'm still not completely certain what the mission is."

"I've already told you most of it, idiot! You take the priest into custody, using your new appearance and identification. Tell him you're bringing him to FBI headquarters in the Government Center to be questioned further."

"What am I doing with him, instead?"

"Look here," he said, and turned to an open laptop computer. He touched a couple of keys, and a topographic image appeared, like the kind produced by Google Earth.

Sargatanas picked up a pen and touched the screen with it. "You take him here."

She leaned forward and squinted. He was pointing at what looked like a long, rectangular structure a little distance outside town. No other buildings stood nearby.

"It's an old strip mall that closed last year. All the stores are empty, and nobody goes there anymore. It should be the perfect place for you and Father Bowles to have a little chat."

"All that glass, facing the road." She was frowning as she stared at the screen. "If I show any kind of light at all in there, it might be seen by a passing cop. A real one."

"That has been considered."

"And the temperature's already close to zero outside. That place will be an icebox." She held up a hasty hand. "Not that my own comfort matters, in the face of such an important task. But it will be difficult for me to concentrate on the work if I'm freezing half to death."

He nodded. "That, also, has been considered – and accounted for."

She shook her head. "I don't understand."

He tapped a few keys, and the abandoned strip mall came into closer view. "Each of those seven stores has a stockroom in the rear, along with a back door for deliveries. You can take him to one of them."

"Yes, all right, but —"

"And there is an important fact, of which you are unaware," he said. "The power is still on in that structure. The electric company never got around to turning it off, and since none is ever used, their meters never remind them."

"Oh." She blinked a couple of times. "I see"

"You will have all the light you would wish, and it will not be visible from the front of the place. And you can turn on the heat when you get there. Soon, you will be able to interrogate the good Father in comfort. Yours, if not his."

"If I may ask, how did you learn all that from here? I wouldn't even know where to begin looking online, to find that information."

"I have access to sources that you do not. That is all that you need to know."

He reached into a pocket and produced a pair of handcuffs. "Here," he said, and tossed them to her. "You may find these useful. Be sure to bring them back, though. Agent Porter will miss them eventually, although he won't be concerned with them tonight."

"More 'glamour'?" she asked.

"Precisely."

"It seems you've thought of everything." She did not sound overjoyed at this fact.

"Everything including the brief stop you're going to make before you fetch the priest. Try a hardware store, if you can find one open. Although a big drugstore will serve, I expect."

She shook her head. "I'm sorry, I'm not trying to be dense, really I'm not. It's just that I've had a lot to absorb, in a very short time. What is it you want me to pick up?"

"Tools, of course. Materials to assure the cooperation of Father Bowles." The grin he gave her was something terrible to behold. "I would recommend a pair of pliers and a blowtorch. Perhaps a bottle of rubbing alcohol, too – you'll be amazed at the effect that has on freshly burned flesh. But use your own judgment."

"How LONG WERE you and Senator Martinez... *intimate*, Ms. Sorensen?" The big room was noisy from conversations in two languages, and the smell of

Mexican cooking was overpowering – or it may have just been that Nestor Greene was unused to it.

The woman tossed blonde hair out of her eyes and gave Nestor Greene a crooked grin. "You mean, how many times did we fuck? It's hard to say, honey – I'd have to check my diary."

Greene leaned forward a little – whether out of sudden interest, or an increased desire to keep their conversation private wasn't immediately clear.

"You had a diary back then? And you've kept it?" Greene kept the eagerness out of his voice – there was no point in driving the price up. As it was, this bimbo was probably going to end up costing him a substantial chunk of Mary Margaret Doyle's money. But she might well be worth every cent. Especially if there was a diary.

"Sure I did," she said, as if asked whether the sun will rise tomorrow. "A girl has to look out for her future, ya know."

At this point in her life, the word 'girl' could accurately be applied to Ina Sorensen only in its broadest sense. She would see neither forty nor a size 6 again, and the years along the way had not always been kind – nor had her use of tobacco, alcohol, and, doubtless, other substances, softened the blows of Father Time. Judging by the old photos he'd seen of her, she had tried to compensate at some point by having her breast implants replaced by larger ones, but Greene found the total effect less erotic than pathetic.

"What I was asking," Greene said, "was over what period of time were you Senator Martinez's mistress?"

She gave a snort of laughter. "*Mistress*? People still say that?"

Greene shrugged. "Some do. The *Washington Post*, for one. So – how long were you fucking the Senator?"

219

"See? I knew you could speak English, if you put your mind to it," she said. "He wasn't Senator then, though. Just a State Rep."

"I'm aware of that. It doesn't matter."

Her brows furrowed in concentration. "Well, I worked for his office for just over three years, and I'd been bangin' him pretty regular for about six months before that. So, what's that, three-and-a-half years?"

"Just about. When you worked for him, what was your function?"

"My function?" She gave Nestor Greene a look that village idiots everywhere must get very tired of. "My 'function' was to fuck him, suck his cock, and let him do me up the ass when he was in the mood. Fortunately, he wasn't in the mood for anal too often." She leered at him for a moment. "He's a pretty big boy, Ramon is – know what I mean?"

Greene nodded. "I meant, what was your function in his office?" he asked. Greene worked in Washington, D.C., after all – he was used to dealing with whores of all kinds.

"I just *told* you that, honey. Well, we did it in his office once or twice a week, anyway. Ramon seemed to get a real charge out of screwing me on top of his desk. After everybody went home, I mean."

"What was your *job description*?" Even Nestor Greene's storied patience could fray at the edges.

"No need to get snippy," she said. "My job title was 'Secretary II,' I think. They didn't have a name for what my real job was. Not in the civil service manual, anyway."

"Did you perform any... regular work there at all?"

"Nope. I can't type, and I don't know how to file. Only time I was there was after hours, when Ramon wanted to play 'Boss and Horny Secretary' in his private office."

"Where did you usually have sex, apart from his office?"

"My place. I had a nice little apartment, just off Tenth St."

"Martinez paid the rent?"

"You bet he did. Santa Fe ain't a cheap place to live."

"Did he just give you the money, or pay the landlord directly?"

"He used to write checks, payable to the company that owned the building. Couple of times, he wrote out a check and left it with me, and I'd drop it off at the realty office the next day."

"You don't happen to remember which bank the checks were drawn on, do you?"

She shook her head. "Nope, sorry. I can't remember stuff like that. Not back that far."

"No, I imagine not." *I bet you remember the serial number of the first hundred-dollar bill a man ever gave you, you greedy cunt.*

"But I made Xerox copies of them, before I paid the landlord." Ina Sorensen shrugged. "Like I said, a girl's gotta think about her future."

Chapter 22

"It may be a while before I actually *get* another job," Morris said, changing lanes to pass a tractor trailer. "Word's probably been getting around that I've 'retired.'"

"You've been turning down work?" Libby said. "What a great day for the Forces of Evil." She smiled as she said it, but only a little.

"I've tried to farm out as much as I could. Refer clients to some folks I trust."

"Really? I don't you recall sending any to *me*," she said, with a touch of mock indignation.

"Yeah, I know. Sorry about that. Nothing came along that I thought might be in your line, really. And, besides…" Morris made a face. "I guess I couldn't stand the idea of you working with anybody else but me."

"Awww." Libby laid a gentle hand along the side of Morris's face for a second. "So, if not me, then who have you been giving referrals to?"

"Well, there's Anita. I sent a couple of people her way."

"Oh. *Her*."

Morris gave a snort of laughter. "You said that the way I bet Dracula used to say 'Van Helsing.'"

"Not for the same reason."

"She's good at what she does, Libby."

"Well she *used* to be. But from what I hear lately, she's more interested in *who* she does than *what*, if you know what I mean."

Morris grinned at her. "Moral judgments, Ms. Chastain?"

"I'm not a prude, Quincey, you know that. But if the stories are true…" She shook her head.

"Different strokes. In Anita's case, I grant, *very* different. And lots of them. But she's not the only option. A few months ago I came across a lady in the business who I hadn't been aware of. And I thought I knew everybody."

"Really?"

"Name's Jill Kismet. Lives in New Mexico. Superbly trained, and tough as nails – toward the bad guys, anyway."

"I'd like to meet her, sometime. She sounds a little like our old friend Hannah Widmark, rest her soul."

Morris bit his lip for a moment. "Um, yeah, about that."

Libby turned and looked at him closely. "What?"

"I meant to tell you, but with all the drama since you got here – which is my fault, entirely – I clean forgot. Thing is, I got kind of a funny card, last Christmas."

"Funny ha-ha, or funny strange?"

"Definitely on the strange side," he said. "Paris postmark. On the outside of the card, it just said *Peace,* with a little image of the Eastern star underneath. Inside, it was blank, except where somebody'd written, *S. Clemens was right about those rumors.* And it was just signed *H.*"

There was silence in the car. Then Libby said, "Samuel Clemens was the real name of Mark Twain. And Mark Twain once said – or wrote, I forget which – 'Rumors of my death have been greatly exaggerated.'"

"Yep, he surely did."

"Dear Goddess," Libby said softly. "Hannah's *alive*? How can that be possible?"

"Well, her body was never positively identified, we knew that. Everybody – every *thing* – in Grobius's compound was pretty much burned to a crisp. And nobody could find any dental records on Hannah to make an ID that way. Maybe she had perfect teeth, and never needed a dentist."

"But, as you just said, everything there was incinerated. You barely escaped yourself."

"Yeah, and even I got a little souvenir on my neck to remind me of the experience."

"I wish I could do more to help you with that, Quincey, I really do. But burns are really hard to treat, even with magic. It's specialist work, and even then it doesn't always succeed. In fact –" Libby stopped speaking suddenly.

"What's wrong?" Morris asked.

"I was just about to say that the Sisterhood has a medical facility that has been doing some good work in developing treatments for burn victims." She looked at Morris. 'It's just outside Paris."

"Well, now. I just wonder…"

"Hannah knows the Sisterhood pretty well, after Idaho," Libby said. "And vice-versa."

Morris rubbed his chin for a second. "I reckon if Hannah *is* alive and wants to get in touch again, she will. Maybe she doesn't want any visitors. Could be she was scarred a lot worse than I was."

"Well, I think I'll start sending a few prayers in the general direction of Paris every night. Couldn't do any harm," Libby said.

"I think I'll say a few myself." Morris tapped the fingers of one hand on the steering wheel. "Actually, I suppose it's possible I could have some work in the offing. Remains to be seen."

"Really? Do tell."

"Before we left, I got a call from a guy I know named Masterson. His first name's Hugh, I think, but everybody calls him Bat."

"Like the Old West lawman?"

"Exactly. This one's a lawman, too. I first met him when he was a cop in Ohio, but these days he works for the U.S. Secret Service."

"What does he want you to do," Libby said, "help him protect the President?"

"He's not guarding the President these days. They've got him protecting some Senator who's *running* for President.

"So, what does he want you for? To help keep an eye on this Senator?"

"He didn't say. He did tell me that he's come across something that's 'really fucking weird,' to use his words, and he wants to talk about it. He's flying in tomorrow."

Libby was quiet for a few seconds before saying, "Are you sure you're ready to go back to work, Quincey? Emotionally, I mean."

"I think so, since you've helped pull me out of that downward spiral I was in. It was a good week, Libby. Thank you."

"You're quite welcome. You're pretty good at Scrabble."

"Not as good as you."

"Nobody is," she said. "In the absence of Scrabble, try to keep up with the meditation – it's a far better stress reliever than booze, drugs, or sex."

"I hear you. Anyway, Bat coming out doesn't mean I have to jump back into work, if I don't think I'm ready. The guy just wants to talk. I mean, how bad can it be?"

AN HOUR OR so later, as they lay in a tangle of sweaty sheets and scattered pillows, Ashley said lazily, "You don't smoke, do you?"

"No, I don't." Peters glanced at her. "Does that mean you do?"

"Not really," she said. "But the image of the two of us lying here smoking just seems so cinematically perfect. Very French New Wave."

"I don't know how a cigarette, or anything else, would make what just happened more perfect than it was."

She rubbed his bare leg. "More flattery. I love it. You show promise, Peters."

"So, what's the deal?" he asked her. "Does Astaroth run an escort service as a sideline?"

She laughed lightly. "Not quite – although I *am* here at his bidding."

"Did he, um, hire you? Are you a professional escort?"

"No, honey. In that regard, I retain my amateur status. I'm here more in the nature of a favor."

"Oh." Peters thought for a while. "So, you do favors for Astaroth? Have you… known him long?"

Her voice was suddenly cold and bleak as she said, "I've known him a very, very long time."

Peters wasn't sure what he ought to say to that. Before he could come up with something appropriate, she said, in a more normal tone, "He didn't explain his motives

226

to me all that clearly, but it is unlike Astaroth to have one simple reason for doing anything."

"Yeah, I have no trouble believing *that*," he said.

"One purpose of my little visit is pretty obvious, I think. I'm here as a reward. You've been working quite diligently on this little assassination project, I understand, and Astaroth decided some recreation was allowed. I trust you will agree that I am *first-class* recreation."

Peters was shaking his head. "Nope, I'm not buying it. I know enough to understand that the words 'gratitude' and 'demon' don't go together. Not ever."

"I'm not suggesting that Astaroth is motivated by benevolence. That *would* be a stretch, wouldn't it? No, it's just that he considers himself something of a behaviorist."

Peters closed his eyes for a moment. "Now you've really lost me."

"Motivation, sweetie. Stimulus-response. Fear is a fine motivator, but Astaroth believes the stick is more effective when combined with a carrot, and furthermore – why are you laughing?"

Peters clamped down on the laughter, which threatened to rise into something very like hysteria. "Sorry. I was just having trouble viewing you as a root vegetable."

"Oh, you'll find that both are good for you, if eaten on a regular basis."

"So, that's it? You were sent to give me the best sex of my life because I've been a good boy?"

"Well, there *is* your little porn problem."

"Hold it – Astaroth's cool with that. He *must* be."

She turned her head on the pillow and gave him one raised eyebrow. "Because he hasn't dragged you back to Hell for the time you've spent at *Lesbian Schoolgirls dot com*?"

With everything that had happened to him, on Earth and in Hell, Peters wouldn't have thought himself capable of blushing. He would have been wrong.

Her laughter was gentle. "Oh, don't feel bad about it, honey. It's very well done, for that kind of niche porn. Really quite arousing."

Peters looked at her. "You, uh, like girls?"

With mild exasperation she said, "I'm the woman of your dreams, am I not? Everything you've ever wanted in a female?"

"Yeah, I guess so."

She gave his thigh a stinging slap. "Wrong answer."

"Ouch! Yeah, okay, you're the woman of my dreams."

"And does the woman of your dreams like girls?"

"Well... yeah."

"Then, Q.E.D., I like girls."

"Q.E.D.?"

"*Quod erat demonstrandum*. The Latin equivalent of *Duh!*"

"Sorry," Peters said. "Don't mean to be dense."

"It's all right. In fact, if you work really hard, like a good little assassin..." She slowly ran one index finger lightly along his thigh where she had slapped him, with a very different result. "... some night we can actually call Elegant Evening Escorts. We'll have them send over one of their girls who does couples, and have ourselves a nice threeway."

She might have been discussing a recipe for pot roast.

"Or," she continued, "you can just watch me with her, if that turns you on – oh, right, you're male. Of *course* it turns you on."

"*Quod erat demonstrandum?*"

Another tinkle of laughter. "Touché, Peters. Touché. We may make a wit of you yet."

228

"Wait – *some night*? You mean, this isn't just a one-shot?"

"Afraid not, sweetie. I'm assigned to you for the duration. I hope you don't snore."

"You're *assigned* to me – assigned to do *what*?"

She ticked the points off on her fingers. "One, to lend my not inconsiderable intelligence to any problem that may arise which you can't solve yourself; two, to keep you focused on your work and away from ten-minute 'porn breaks' by keeping you so sexually satiated you will consider porn a waste of your time; and three, to provide my assistance, as needed, in carrying out the assassination of Senator Howard Stark and sending that importunate bastard Sargatanas back to Hell where he belongs."

Peters looked at the ceiling for a few seconds. "And, four, to take me back to Hell when the assignment's over?"

She shrugged her elegant shoulders. "I don't have orders on that yet. We'll have to see what develops."

More silence, until he said, "And if you already had instructions to drag me back with you, you'd lie about it, wouldn't you?"

"Naturally. Would you expect anything else?"

"So, I won't know if you're taking me back until it's all over, one way or the other?"

"I'm afraid so, sweetie."

"Well, it's not like I have any choice, is it?"

"Nope – none at all."

"What are you, anyway – a succubus?"

This time, her laughter held derision. "Those simple little fucktoys? Not hardly, my dear man. Not hardly."

"Then what –"

"I am a demon of the fourth rank, three choirs down

229

from Astaroth. He is one of those just below my Lord Lucifer, of course."

"Wait a minute – Astaroth told me he can stay here for only twenty-four hours at a time."

"He spoke truly – unusual for him, when addressing a human."

"He has to go back to Hell, but you can stay? That doesn't make sense."

"It does, in a perverse way. Astaroth, as I said, is a demon of the first order. He had once been high among the ranks of angels, and was one of Lucifer's generals during the Late Unpleasantness."

"Yeah, I guess I heard about that... back there."

"Having been so favored by, um, you know, his defection was that much more of an offense. To the greater offense goes the greater punishment. Astaroth's suffering is thus more severe than mine in every respect, including the amount of time he can spend in this plane of existence."

Peters lay there for a full minute, trying to wrap his mind around these cosmic truths that were being revealed to him – in bed, by a hot, naked woman who wasn't really a woman at all.

Finally he said, "Since telling the truth isn't part of your job description, I'm guessing that the name you gave me earlier isn't true."

"No, but it's close enough. I am known in Hades as Ashur Badaktu."

She leaned over and gently brushed her lips against his. "But you may just call me Ashley."

After that, Peters could not think of any more questions. For a while.

*   *   *

LIBBY CHASTAIN'S FLIGHT into JFK had benefited from a tailwind and actually touched down five minutes early. She rescued her suitcase from the baggage return and grabbed a cab that let her off in front of her building a few minutes before 9:00 in the evening. She paid the driver and stepped out into a cold wind that was in marked contrast to the mild temperature of Austin.

Libby was glad she'd made the trip. Quincey Morris had not been quite his old self when he'd dropped her off at Stephen F. Austin, but he seemed to be well on the way. She hoped his Secret Service buddy might have something for him, as long as it wasn't too strenuous or harrowing. He needed to prove to himself that he was still good at what he called the 'ghostbusting' business. Even better would be a case the two of them could take on together.

In the lobby, the elevator was about to close in her face when a man's arm came between the doors and made them reopen. Libby stepped inside and found that the arm's owner was a quiet man in his forties who, she knew, lived on the floor above her condo. She saw that the man, whose name she thought might be Victor, was accompanied by an attractive redhead a little younger than he, whom Libby had also seen around the building.

"Thank you so much," she said to the man, although she let her smile take in the woman, too. "This elevator's so slow, I might've had a long wait until it came back down."

"No trouble at all," the man said. "You're on nine, aren't you?"

"Yes, thanks," Libby said and watched him press '9,' followed by '10.'

She knew the trip would take a while. Might as well be friendly. "I've seen both of you in the building, but we've never met." She put out her hand to the man. "I'm Libby Chastain."

The man shook hands and smiling said, "I'm Vince Cook. And this is my wife, Donna."

"Libby shook the woman's hand, too. It was warm, as if her body temperature might be a little higher than average.

Vince nodded toward Libby's suitcase. "Looks you've been away," he said. "Someplace warm, I hope."

"Actually, I was," she said. "Not the tropics, exactly, but I've been in Texas visiting a friend. It's brutal down there in summer, but very nice this time of year. Quite a contrast with New York right now."

"I hate the cold," Donna told her. "We try to get away for a couple of weeks every winter. We adore Jamaica – such gorgeous beaches."

"I've only seen it in the movies, but it looks fantastic," Libby said.

"There's a resort we stay at every year," Vince said. Libby detected a very slight change in his tone as he said, "It's called Hedonism Two."

Libby nodded. That name rang a bell, although she wasn't sure why. Something she had read somewhere.

"We're leaving a week Sunday,' Donna said. "I can't *wait*."

The elevator was just passing the fourth floor. As she glanced at the floor indicator, Libby said, just to be saying something, "You must have your bathing suit already packed."

She caught the quick look the two gave each other, along with the small smile of a shared secret.

"Well, no, not really," Donna said casually. A pause. "You don't need a bathing suit at Hedo. Nobody wears them."

232

Libby nodded and said "Oh," as if it all made perfect sense to her. A moment later, it did. She remembered what she had seen in a magazine article once. Hedonism Two was a swingers' resort. Libby had never been to such a place, and would probably never want to go, but still, it sounded... interesting.

She looked at the floor indicator again, and saw that the elevator hadn't made much progress. From the corner of her eye she saw Vince and Donna look at each other again, and thought she saw a small nod from Vince.

"Now that we've met, Libby," he said, "why don't you come up for a drink – once you've had a chance to unpack and freshen up, I mean."

"Yes, please do," Donna said. "We'd *love* to get to know you better." Her voice was pleasant, no more, but Libby thought she detected a hint of something else.

Libby looked at the attractive, middle-aged couple for a moment before responding. She thought she knew what was being offered, and it was more than a drink and casual conversation. This was something Libby had heard about, but not tried. Yet. She could always plead fatigue or a headache, and say she was going to bed, alone.

What came out of her mouth was, "Thanks, I'd love –" and that's when her phone began to fill the small space with a light, bouncy piece of music.

"Excuse me," Libby said. She pulled out her phone and looked at the caller ID: *C. O'Donnell*. She pressed 'Answer' at once.

"Hi, Colleen."

"Hey, Libby," Colleen's voice said in her ear. "Listen, I need to talk to you about something pretty important. Can you spare some time?"

Libby knew when FBI Special Agent and Sister Witch Colleen O'Donnell said something was important, she wasn't talking about a recipe for lamb stew.

"I'm in the elevator in my building," she said, "heading up to my place. Can I call you back – say, in ten minutes?"

"That'll be fine, Libby. Thank you."

"Talk to you soon," Libby said, and ended the call. She looked at the Cooks, who seemed disappointed. So was Libby – at least, she thought she was.

"I'm sorry," she said, "but this is pretty important. Work stuff. How about a rain check – on the drink, I mean?"

"Of course, absolutely," Donna Cook said, pleasantly, and her husband nodded.

"Stop by any time," he said.

As the elevator finally reached Libby's floor, Vince Cook said, "Your ring tone sounded kind of familiar, Libby, but I can't place it."

"I heard it somewhere, too, years ago," his wife said. "It's from some old TV show, right?"

"Right," Libby said. "A relic from the Sixties, but I kind of like it." She stepped out onto her floor, pulling the suitcase behind her. Looking back at the Cooks as the door closed, she winked and said, "*Bewitched.*"

Chapter 23

"IT WAS JUST by the weirdest fluke that he was found at all, let alone so soon after... after he was killed." Bat Masterson shuddered, despite himself.

The Maine State Police had sent him a copy of their case file pertaining to the unlawful death of Joseph R. Bowles. It had included the autopsy report, as well as all the photos taken at the crime scene. Masterson didn't investigate homicides. His job was to prevent murder, not look at it. He had been a street cop for several years before joining the Secret Service, but even that had given him exactly zero experience with the kind of hell depicted between the covers of that manila folder.

Masterson hoped he'd live long enough for those images to fade from his memory.

"Whoever killed him chose the location well, then," Quincey Morris said. "Apart from the effects of random chance, that is."

"Oh, sure. Deserted strip mall, closed for a couple of years, no houses nearby." He snorted his disgust. "As a place to torture somebody to death in privacy, it was just about perfect."

There was intermittent banging coming from down the hall, and a couple of male voices talking loudly. Morris got up from his desk and closed the office door.

"Sorry if I came at a bad time, Quincey."

"You didn't," Morris told him. "I'm just having some renovations done on the living room. I figured it was time for a change."

Morris sat down again. "So, how was this perfectly private torture chamber discovered so fast?"

"Maine Power and Light's computer alerted them that there'd been some power usage from a source that wasn't supposed to be using any."

"The deserted shopping center."

"Bingo. So they reported it to the realty company that owns the place, who figured it was maybe some homeless folks squatting on the property. The realtor called the local P.D. and reported possible trespassers. The Castle Rock police sent a car over and found – what I told you about."

"Wait – you said *Castle Rock*. That's where it happened? Castle Rock, Maine?"

"Yeah. So?"

"So nothing – probably. But some weird shit has been reported in and around that place over the years. It's almost like it is a nexus for..."

"For what?"

"Never mind. It doesn't matter."

"You were about to say evil, or dark forces, or something like that, right?"

"Yeah, something like that."

"Well you can say it all you want around me, Quincey. This is the Bat, remember? Just because I never talk about it around the guys in the Service doesn't mean I forgot what happened in '02, back in Toledo."

"I know, Bat. It was just force of habit. I've learned to be cautious about what I say around law enforcement types. Even when the cops are the ones called me in, like they did that time in Toledo, most of 'em are one step away from labeling me a fraud and ignoring anything I say."

"Can't hardly blame them, man. Cops deal with the evil that men do every fucking day. They're not real inclined to worry about the supernatural kind."

"You were pretty open-minded, though, for a Patrolman Second Grade."

"One of the kids who went missing was my nephew, remember?"

"Yes, I do. A real shame."

"By the time you arrived, I was willing to do anything it took to find who killed him – *what* killed him, it turned out."

"Even willing to volunteer to escort the ghostbuster, as they called him, around town and keep him out of trouble."

Masterson gave a snort of laughter. "Yeah, that last part didn't work out too well, did it? I'll never forget what we saw that night. Or what I had to help you do."

"And you figure there's more of the same operating in Castle Rock?"

Masterson leaned forward, elbows on knees, and looked at the floor. "That's the most fucked-up thing about this whole mess, Quincey. I've been that thinking maybe whoever did it wasn't *from* Castle Rock. It might've been a visitor."

"A visitor?"

"Yeah, somebody passing through town." Masterson looked up then, and Morris could see the fear stamped on his face. "Just long enough to give a couple of campaign speeches."

LIBBY CHASTAIN, IN a sky-blue corduroy robe, hair damp from a quick shower, pressed a button on her phone and waited a few seconds. "Hi, Colleen – it's me."

"Hi, Libby. Thanks for getting back to me so fast."

Libby wandered over to one of the condo's windows and looked out. "It's no problem. You gave me a reason to pass up an opportunity I'm not sure I should have taken."

"Excuse me?"

"Never mind, Colleen, I'm blathering. You said 'important' earlier."

"Yes, and so it is, at least potentially."

"You've teased me enough, sweetie. Out with it."

Colleen ran it all down for her: the meeting with Melanie Blaise, the unmistakable scent of recent black magic clinging to her friend and fellow agent, her casual questioning to find out what Melanie had been up to lately.

When Colleen finished speaking, there was silence on the line. "Libby? Still there?"

"Right here. I'm trying to get my mind around this. You're saying that someone may have used black magic to create a 'freak' accident that killed this Congressman."

"That's my fear, yes."

"Putting the means aside for a moment, let's look at it as a simple murder. We have to ask the question that comes up in those mystery novels Quincey is always lending me: *qui bono?*"

"Who benefits?" Colleen translated without hesitation. Everyone with law enforcement training knew the phrase.

"Right. Why would someone want to take out this Congressman, uh –"

"Brooks. Ron Brooks."

"Right. Why would someone kill Ron Brooks, irrespective of the method used?"

"In almost any homicide," Colleen said, "the circle of suspects starts with the immediate family and moves outward."

"So that makes Mrs. Brooks a prime suspect."

"In a homicide investigation, yes. If you don't consider the black magic angle."

"Or even if you do, maybe," Libby said.

"I don't follow you."

"I mean, who's to say that Mrs. Brooks hasn't taken a journey down the Left Hand Path? She wanted to get rid of her husband, for one of the usual reasons, and cast a spell to make it look like an accident."

"I hadn't considered that," Colleen said. "I suppose it's possible. The Sisterhood tries to keep track of black magicians, but I'm sure we don't know them all."

"Or," Libby said, "she could have hired it out to someone. There are black magicians who do their wickedness for money."

"Yes, that's another possibility."

"Did your friend talk to Mrs. Brooks personally?"

"No – she and her partner just went through the house, she said."

"Then maybe it's time someone did."

Partial transcript of the March 6th broadcast of Meet the Nation.
Interviewer: David Huntley
Guest: Senator Ramon Martinez (R-NM)

Huntley: Senator, you have been positioning yourself to become the first Latino Presidential nominee from either of the major parties. But as you know, there have been recent allegations in the news concerning your personal life, dating back to when you were a member of the New Mexico state legislature. They originated in the tabloid press, but more recently they've been appearing in many of the mainstream media news sources.

Martinez: Yes, David, I've been made aware of these so-called news stories.

Huntley: They claim that you, a married man, had an ongoing relationship, a sexual relationship, with a woman that lasted almost three years. The woman in question, a sometime cabaret singer named Ina Sorensen, recently came forward with these accusations.

Martinez: As I understand it, David, she came forward in the pages of the *National Tatler* – a newspaper, if I may call it that, which is rarely compared with the *New York Times*. And that paper admits that they paid her $20,000 for her story, something that legitimate journalists would never do.

Huntley: I agree, the circumstances surrounding these accusations are sleazy, to say the least. But that does not, in itself, mean the story is untrue. As you know, there have been cases in recent years where something that originated in one of the tabloids was found to have a factual basis and later received coverage by the mainstream news media.

Martinez: Yes, among the many hundreds of times when their stories were found to have been exaggerated, distorted, or completely fabricated.

Huntley: You believe the recent stories about you to be one of those things? If so, which one?

Martinez: David, the story is a complete fabrication. It appears to be the co-creation of a woman who is desperate for money, and a trashy newspaper desperate to sell papers.

Huntley: So, you deny all of Ms. Sorensen's allegations?

Martinez: I deny them categorically. I did not have sex with that woman.

Huntley: She claims to have been on the payroll of your office when you were a state legislator.

Martinez: That's entirely possible. In the twelve years I served as a state representative, I employed a good many people, at one time or another. This woman may have been one of them. That was fifteen or so years ago, and I'm afraid I can't remember the names of every secretary or aide who worked in my office for a while. But I never had an affair with any of them, and I am insulted that anyone of integrity would take such allegations seriously.

Huntley: Ms. Sorensen alleges that, although she drew a salary for three years, she never actually worked in your office. She's quoted as saying: "I can't file. I can't even type."

Martinez: This is nonsense, David. Anyone who has ever been employed by me, then or now, performs a legitimate administrative or political function. These are dedicated public servants, and they deserve better than to be slandered by malicious gossip.

Huntley: Senator, *The National Tatler* is published every Tuesday, but we've been able to obtain an advance copy of this coming week's edition. In it, Ms. Sorensen claims to have kept a diary dating back to the period in question. Supposedly, she kept a record of every occasion, I should say alleged occasion, when the two of you were intimate.

Martinez: David, this business is moving from the ridiculous to the absurd. Anybody can write something down in a diary – that doesn't mean it really happened. I understand that some teenage girls put in their diaries accounts of their affairs with rock stars – something that would amaze the objects of their obsession, if they were to ever read it.

Huntley: That's certainly a valid point. But Ms. Sorensen also alleges in this issue of the *Tatler* that you paid the rent on an apartment for her where the alleged trysts took place.

Martinez: Ridiculous. And quite possibly libelous.

Huntley: Ms. Sorensen also claims to have photocopies of several checks that you wrote and gave to her to cover the monthly rent.

Martinez: [Inaudible]

Huntley: Senator?

Martinez: David, all I can say is, if such documents exist, they are malicious forgeries that have been concocted to smear my reputation. And, as far as I'm concerned, we've spent quite enough time this morning discussing such nonsense.

Huntley: We'll be back, right after these messages.

II

INTERVENTION

Chapter 24

MORRIS HAD MADE tea for both of them. It lacked whatever magic ingredients Libby Chastain had used, but he still had faith in its restorative powers. He handed Masterson a mug then sat back down behind his desk.

"All right, Bat. Since I know you're not crazy – at least, you didn't use to be – you'd better explain to me why you think a U.S. Senator would take the risk of murdering a Catholic priest. Notice I didn't say 'is capable of' – there isn't much I'd put beyond some of those fellas. But most of them are smart enough not to put their dicks in a wringer by killing somebody."

"The evidence is all circumstantial, I admit that," Masterson said. "In fact, I'm not even saying Stark did it personally, if he was involved at all. He might have even sent Attila to do it."

"Attila? As in the Hun? I could be wrong – maybe you *are* delusional."

"'Attila' is our code name for Mary Margaret Doyle, Stark's Chief of Staff and campaign manager. She was educated by nuns and looks it, although I happen to know that she's not quite the proper little tightass she seems."

"For now, give me the short version of why you think either Stark or this Doyle lady might've done what you just described to a Catholic priest."

"The shortest version is: because the priest, Bowles, burned Stark. Burned his hand."

"How'd he do that?"

"By touching him."

There was silence in the room, broken only by the faint sounds of hammering from another part of the house.

Finally, Morris said, "Maybe you'd better give me the long version, podner."

Masterson told Morris about Stark's speech, the gladhanding afterwards, the agents' response to a perceived attack, the searching and questioning of Father Bowles along with the negative background check, the rush to the hospital that was never completed, and the injury that seemed to have healed itself.

"You're sure Stark's burned hand was pretty bad, at the outset?" Morris asked.

"I talked to the agents who were in the car with him. One of them got a pretty good look at the hand before Stark got it out of sight. My guy says that Stark's palm and fingers were showing second-degree burns."

Morris tilted his desk chair back and used one hand to massage the bridge of his nose. "Jesus, Bat."

Masterson nodded glumly. "Yeah, I know."

After a few seconds, Morris leaned his chair forward again. "Do they have a time of death established for the priest?"

"You know how coroners are about stuff like that," Masterson said. "Tuesday night is the best they can come up with. I can narrow it down a little, though."

"Oh? How?"

"I had one of my guys give him a ride back to the rectory at St. John's. Dropped him off a little after nine. And I understand he was scheduled to say mass at 6:00 the next morning. He never showed."

"Between 9:00 and 6:00, then. Where were the Senator and his henchwoman during that time?"

"Well, I had a talk with them when I got back to the hotel, for all the good *that* did. Although, I did get a look at his hand while I was there."

"Condition?" Morris asked.

"Smooth and pink as a toddler's butt. Ms. Doyle said she had put some magic salve on it, but I never heard of any fucking ointment that can turn second-degree burns into a light sunburn in the space of a couple of hours."

"Nor have I, amigo," Morris said. "Nor have I. Were the Senator and Ms. Doyle's movements accounted for over the rest of the night?"

"Put it this way," Masterson said. "Nobody saw either of them leave the suite. I just assumed they were in there, fucking their brains out."

"Oh? They've been doing that, have they?"

"I'm almost positive, and that brings me to another little anomaly I wanted to tell you about."

"Go on."

"I was on station outside the Senator's suite one morning, a few weeks back. Everything's quiet, then I hear these voices, right through the walls behind me. There's a woman's voice, kind of screaming, but the one that really gets my attention is what sounds like a man's voice, yet it isn't. It sounded kind of like a lion roaring, if the lion could say words. One thing it did *not* sound like is Senator Howard Stark."

"It was like a man's voice combined with an animal's roar?" Morris said.

"Yeah, that's about right," Masterson said. "Sounds pretty fucking whacked, huh?"

"Not as much as you might think. Keep talking."

"So I'm banging on the door, and not getting any answer. I use my master to unlock the door, which brings me into the living room, or whatever they call it, of the suite. There's nobody there, and I turn toward the Senator's room just as the door opens and he comes out, wearing a bathrobe. So I ask, is everything okay, I thought I heard yelling."

"Did you notice anything different about him when he came out? Physically, I mean."

"No, not that I remember. Of course, I was pretty focused on looking for Lee Harvey Oswald right there in the suite, if you know what I mean."

"Yeah, okay. So what did he say to you?"

"He gives me everything's fine, nothing to be concerned about, blah, blah. I tell him I thought I heard yelling, and he says that he'd been watching some horror movie on TV. He meant to turn it off, but hit the volume control, and cranked up the sound for a second. That must've been what I heard, he says."

"It sounds plausible, Bat," Morris said.

"Just wait. After I find out that everything's cool with him, I'm about to ask him if I should check on Ms. Doyle. She's got the other bedroom, opposite side of the living room from Stark. But then the shower in his room starts going. That can't be anything but Mary Margaret Doyle, all naked and wet in his bathroom, as if I care. I don't say anything, and neither does he. His expression doesn't change either, but just for a half-second I'd swear that his eyes had like a red glow about them. It happened so fast, I wasn't sure if I imagined it. I'm still not sure. Anyway, I got out of there and went back to my post in the hall. Then I got thinking, what station shows gory horror movies at that hour of the morning, when school's in session? Wouldn't be much of an audience, I figure."

"I wouldn't have thought of that," Morris said, "but you could be right."

"Pretty soon it was time to get ready for the Senator to leave for his first campaign stop, and I forgot all about it – for two days. Then I remembered to check."

"I think I can see where this is going," Morris said.

"You'd be right, too," Masterson told him. "First thing I do is check my own room's TV, to see what channels the hotel is providing its guests. Then I get online. It takes a while to find the TV program listing from two days earlier, but I finally track it down. I'm looking to find out what was on TV at the time Stark was supposedly watching his horror movie. His *loud* horror movie."

"I'm assuming that nobody was running a George Romero film festival, that hour of the morning."

"Nothing even close. Scariest movie on TV during that time was *Pee Wee's Big Adventure*, and I only mention it because that Pee Wee Herman dude creeps me out."

"So Stark lied to you about the source of those voices you heard."

"He sure as hell did," Masterson said. "The woman's voice, well I figure that was Mary Margaret achieving what people used to call one hell of a climax."

"Nowadays, I think it's called 'coming your brains out,'" Morris said.

"Yeah, that's a pretty fair description," Masterson said. "But that other one, I call it a man's voice for lack of anything better, but, Quincey… it wasn't anything human."

*   *   *

"I'M SORRY TO have to intrude on your grief," Libby Chastain said. "But this shouldn't take very long."

"It's all right, Miss –" the woman glanced down at the business card she'd just been given. "– Widmark. I've talked to so many insurance adjustors, one more doesn't make any difference. But I thought I had spoken to them all, by now." Evelyn Brooks looked to be in her mid-fifties. Libby saw iron-gray hair, severe-looking glasses, and, even now, the black dress of widowhood.

"Yes, ma'am, I'm sorry it's taken me so long to contact you. Our computer system at the office has been giving us a lot of trouble – we're getting a new one in April, thank heaven – and notice of your husband's... passing didn't reach the Claims Adjustment Department nearly as soon as it should have."

"The odd thing is, after you called yesterday, I went through all of Ron's policies. I thought I had every one set aside, but didn't find one for –" She looked at the card again. "– Massachusetts Mutual. I hope that isn't going to mean you came over here for nothing."

"Not at all, Mrs. Brooks. I imagine the policy will turn up eventually. When it does, I'd be obliged if you'd tear off the last page, fill it in, and mail it to us. But it doesn't really matter. We have a copy of your husband's policy, and we wouldn't dream of denying the claim just because you can't produce yours at the moment. That's not the way we do business. We'll have a check for $20,000 in the mail to you in a few days. I just need to get your signature on a few things. You know how the bureaucracy works."

Evelyn Brooks smiled sadly, and nodded. "Ron was in politics for twenty-two years. I know all there is to know about bureaucracy."

Libby took the clipboard she'd brought with her over to Mrs. Brooks, and squatted next to her chair. "I'll need you to sign and date here, and here, and two places on this one – up here and at the bottom. Oh, and I'll need to see the, um, scene of the accident, if you don't mind."

The older woman's face furrowed in confusion. "The... scene of the accident? You mean the *bathroom*?"

Libby thumbed through the forms, stopped at the third one and seemed to scan it for a moment. "Yes, ma'am, that would be the bathroom."

"What on earth *for*? The police were done with it last week. The contractor sent a man over, day before yesterday. He replaced the light switch and put up the new wallpaper that I picked out. To look at it, you'd never know that Ron..." Her face crumpled for a moment, but she held back the tears and regained control.

Waiting until I leave. Libby thought. *Doesn't want to break down in front of a stranger. Good for her.*

"I understand what you mean, Mrs. Brooks. It doesn't make a lot of sense, does it? But I just do what they tell me, until five o'clock, and I have to be able to say that I observed the location in question. I'll also take a few pictures with my camera phone. It won't take more than a couple of minutes, I promise."

"Well, you have to do what you have to do," she said with a shrug. "Would you mind... going up by yourself? It's the second floor, at the end of the hall. I've been using the powder room down here. I'm... not ready to go in there, just yet."

Libby stood. "Of course, it's no problem at all. In

fact, would you mind if I took a minute to freshen up, while I'm there?"

"Of course, honey. You take as much time as you want."

The 'freshening up' would give Libby a few extra plausible minutes upstairs, if she needed them. And it would give Mrs. Brooks a chance to weep down here in private, if that's what she needed to do.

Two minutes later, Libby was in the bright, cheerful bathroom, door closed and locked behind her. She stood in what she estimated was the center of the room, turned to face east, and spread her arms out wide.

Such theatrics were probably unnecessary, but it had been ten days since Brooks's death, and Libby wanted to be sure that she didn't miss any lingering taint of—

And there it is.

To the trained sensitive, black magic has a psychic odor that is like nothing else. For Libby, it was like the faint but recognizable smell of cigarette smoke you find in a room hours after the smoker has left. Except this stuff smelled less like tobacco than it did a rotting corpse.

So. There are traces of black magic at the place where a man died, under circumstances that are looking increasingly more suspicious. The man was a senior member of the U.S. House of Representatives. The man was running for the office of President of the United States.

What is wrong with this picture? Only everything.

As Evelyn Brooks saw her to the door, Libby Chastain said, "Please let me offer my condolences once again. I think I know how awful this must be for you."

As she spoke, Libby placed her right hand on Mrs. Brooks's shoulder in a compassionate gesture. Then she unobtrusively moved the hand to rest gently on the back of the older woman's neck.

"*I think it would be best if you forgot I was ever here,*" Libby said, using magic to give a little *push* along with the words. "*Can you do that for me?*"

"Why of course," Mrs. Brooks said. "You called, I remember, but never showed up. I was quite annoyed."

Keeping her hand in place, Libby began to move it in small, slow circles. "*The burden of your grief will start to ease soon. Every day, your sorrow will be a little less. In three more weeks, it will be gone completely. Do you understand me?*"

Mrs. Brooks nodded. "Yes, I understand."

"*You will never forget the love you had for Ron, or the time you shared together. But starting in a short while, thinking of it will no longer make you want to cry. Does that sound like a good idea, Evelyn?*"

"Oh, yes, that sounds fine. Just fine."

ANOTHER PRIMARY, THIS one in Pennsylvania. Mary Margaret Doyle sat on the hotel suite's couch with the *Wall Street Journal* while Sargatanas slouched in a chair across from her with his laptop. They had finished a bout of vigorous sex fifteen minutes earlier.

Without looking up, Sargatanas asked, "So – feeling pretty good?"

"You know I am," she lowered the paper and grinned at him.

"Pity that I am about to spoil it."

"What did you say?" Her smile fled like a frightened deer.

"They've found the priest's body."

She began shaking her head slowly. "No – no, that's not possible! I did everything you said, took every precaution, I never –"

"Stop! If I thought you were at fault, your punishment would have already begun. But with the priest, you did exactly as instructed, thus demonstrating the truth of Hell's First Law."

"What's that?"

"'You can do everything right, and still lose.'"

She thought about that for a second then said, "So if I did everything right, how *did* we lose?"

"Before I answer that, keep in mind that *lose* is a relative term in this case. It would have been better to have the priest simply disappear, but the stupid police have no evidence to connect his death to you."

"How do you know that?"

"Everything is digitized now, including the reports filed by law enforcement agencies. That which resides in one computer can be retrieved via another, if the user possesses the necessary knowledge and skill. Needless to say, I *do* possess them. A touch of black magic is also sometimes useful."

"I assume those same reports reveal why we were discovered so quickly," she said.

"It seems a computer at the power company made note of the small electricity usage coming from the shopping mall that night, since there was supposed to be none at all. The next day, the police were sent to determine the cause. Some vagrant keeping himself warm must not be allowed to interfere with corporate profits, after all – even in a small way."

"So they found what I... left behind." Her eyes narrowed in concentration as she said, "They won't have much to work with. I had gloves on the whole time, because of the cold, so there are no fingerprints. I took my tools with me and dropped them off a bridge into whatever that river is they have there."

"The Penobscot."

"Whatever. And, thanks to your glamour, I was not recognized by anyone."

"So we are, as they say, in the clear." He looked at her for a moment. "You liked it, didn't you?"

"Liked – liked what?"

"Everything you did to the priest. Admit that you liked it."

"*Liked* it? I found it *appalling*. I only did it because you ordered me to! You said it was essential to the plan!"

"I see. You were only following orders."

"Yes, exactly."

"That excuse didn't play too well at the Nuremburg Tribunals, if I remember correctly."

"At the what?"

"Ah, my roommate Senator Stark was right – there *are* some gaps in that Vassar education of yours."

"I might not know about that Nuremburg thing, but I know I did *not* enjoy what you made me do! I didn't"

"I must have been mistaken, then. After all, anyone who could do that to a fellow human would be something less than human, herself. She would be a monster, don't you think?"

"I am *not* a monster!"

"Of course you're not. Now – what does today's *Journal* say about Senator Stark and his candidacy?"

Chapter 25

LIBBY CHASTAIN STOOD near the front-facing window of her hotel room, which seemed to give her the clearest reception. You'd think a place like Washington D.C. would have cell towers everywhere. Maybe that was the problem – all the bullshit floating through the air was interfering with the electronics.

Then Colleen O'Donnell's voice was in her ear. "Hey, Libby."

"Hi, Colleen. Before the days of caller ID, I would have been inclined to credit you with precognition."

"Caller ID? What's that?" Libby could hear the smile in her friend's voice and regretted that she was about to wipe it away.

"I went to Congressman Brooks's house," she said. "Did a little song and dance for the widow and got into the bathroom where he died. You were right, Colleen."

"Black magic." As Libby had expected, all levity was gone now.

"Faint, but distinct. I'd know it anywhere."

There was a silence that went on long enough to make Libby wonder if the call had been dropped. "Colleen?"

"Sorry. I was trying to think about two things at once."

"Which were?"

"One is, why would someone use black magic to kill this guy?"

"To make it look like an accident? If so, it worked pretty well."

"Yeah, okay, let me rephrase. Why would someone want to murder Congressman Brooks and make it look like an accident?"

"When you put it that way, it *is* a pretty good question."

"And my second problem is, what are we going to do about it?"

"What you mean *we*, kimosabe?" The comeback was automatic, since Libby didn't see anything funny in what they were talking about.

"I meant the Sisterhood," Colleen said. "Although, now that you mention it…"

I didn't need precognition to see THAT coming, Libby thought, but all she said was "Yes?"

"Fenton and I can't just fly back to D.C. and look into this, Libby, much though I want to. We've got some good leads on this serial killer, and we have to run them down. Anyway, we're on pretty thin ice with the Bureau these days."

"After Iowa, you mean."

"Idaho."

"Right – I'm always getting those confused."

"Point is, we've got to be good little Special Agents for a while, instead of chasing down the forces of darkness as the whim strikes us."

"I thought your boss was *simpatico*," Libby said.

"She is, but *her* boss isn't, and *his* boss even less so."

Libby sighed. "Say what's on your mind, Colleen."

"I want you to look into this, Libby. For the Sisterhood."

"I'm not refusing, but I wouldn't even know where to begin. I didn't go to the FBI Academy, remember? I'm not an investigator."

"No, but you've got a buddy who is."

"You mean Quincey."

"I do, indeed."

Libby chewed her lower lip for a few seconds. "That's not a terrible idea, Colleen. But money's an issue."

"It is?"

"I'll do it *pro bono*, since it's for the Sisterhood. But Quincey does this stuff for a living, and I happen to know he hasn't worked in a while. He'd probably take it on as a favor to me, but I'm reluctant to ask. I owe him enough, as it is."

"You mean your life, and all that."

"That's exactly what I mean."

"Um. What do you think Quincey would charge for a job like this?"

Libby told her.

"Well, that's not unreasonable, considering he's a specialist. Look, let me talk to Rachel. The Sisterhood has a fund for emergencies, and this may well qualify, considering the possible implications."

"There's a fund? Where did *that* come from? We don't pay dues, or anything. At least *I* don't."

"Me, neither. But quite a few of the Sisters have successful careers, and they've been generous, over the years. I don't know how much is in there, but there certainly ought to be enough to pay Quincey's fees and expenses. Your expenses, too, for that matter."

"So, I should talk to Rachel?"

"No, I'll do it, since I'm the one proposing that we hire your boyfriend."

"He's not my boyfriend, Colleen. You know that."

"Just an expression. I should have an answer for you later this evening, then you can get in touch with Quincey. Sound good?"

"All right, Colleen. I'll talk to you later."

Libby's flight back to New York didn't leave until morning. As she unpacked her suitcase, she hummed quietly to herself. Any fan of old cowboy music would have recognized the tune as 'Back in the Saddle Again.'

QUINCEY MORRIS LEANED back and looked at his old friend.

"So, okay," he said to Masterson. "Let's see what we know. We've got a member of the U.S. Senate, who also happens to be one of the strongest contenders to become the Republican Party's candidate for President –"

"Yeah, about that," Masterson said.

Morris looked at him. "What?"

"I don't know how much attention you've been paying to the campaign so far –"

"Not much. I've had other stuff on my mind."

"All right, but you might want to take a good, hard look at how Stark got to *be* somebody with a real shot at the nomination."

"There's only one way, isn't there?" Morris said, frowning. "You run in the various state primaries and pick up delegates for the national convention. The guy with the most delegates at the convention is the nominee. End of story."

"Yeah, except when this particular story started, Stark was at the back of the pack."

"'The Un-Magnificent Seven', right?"

"Uh-huh. And if you were going to rank their chances, Howard fucking Stark was the consensus choice for number seven."

"Seriously?"

"A year or so ago, there's seven of them, with Stark as ass-end Charlie. Then what's-his-name, Brooks, gets electrocuted in his house, and suddenly there's six."

"I don't remember anybody claiming there was something hinky about the guy's death. It was supposed to be some kind of freak accident, right?"

"That's what everybody says. Leaky pipe, water on the floor, defective light switch and *bzzzz* – Ron Brooks is off to that great quorum call in the sky."

"And you figure he had some help along the way. Based on what evidence?"

"Bear with me, Quincey. It only makes sense if you look at the whole picture."

"Okay, then." Morris spread his hands. "Paint me a picture."

"So Brooks is an accidental death, and the seven becomes six. Then Frank Chesbro blows his brains out, just before the the Iowa caucuses."

"Really? I don't remember that."

"You don't? Jesus, Quincey, it was all over the news."

"This was in January?"

At Masterson's nod, Morris said, "That explains it. I had some other stuff going on then. Took up all of my attention, for a while. Why'd this fella do himself in – anybody know?"

"Well, I'm pretty sure the photos of him sucking dick had something to do with it."

"Dear God," Morris said. "Yeah, I reckon that'll do it, all right."

"Happened when he was in college. I don't know if Chesbro was gay, or just trying it out back then. But he was unwise enough to let somebody take pictures."

"*Unwise* is right."

"Person or persons unknown dug up those photos and provided them to that piece-of-shit rag *The National Tatler*. They put little black bars over the naughty bits when they published, but pretty soon the original photos were all over the Internet, and the black bars disappeared."

"Destroyed the poor bastard, and his family too, I reckon."

"That's for sure. I mean, there's stuff you can do when you're young and maybe explain away later – like DWI, or smokin' some weed."

"Especially if you don't inhale."

"Especially that. But you can't get caught with another dude's cock in your mouth, even if it was forty years ago, and expect to be President. Not yet, anyway."

"I think I'm starting to see where you're going with all this," Morris said. "Okay, so Chesbro's dead, and that leaves five, including Stark."

"Two more of them are alive, physically, but in serious trouble politically. In Lunsford's case, somebody dug up evidence –"

"Person or persons unknown, again?"

"The very same – or, at least, I'm betting it is. Anyway, Lunsford's apparently got a history of plagiarism."

"That sounds like something else from college days," Morris said. "Ancient history."

"Some of it is, some isn't. True, he seems to have lifted parts of his senior thesis out of some guy's book. But the other instance is a lot more recent – like last year."

"Even so, I wouldn't think too many people outside of academia give much of a damn about plagiarism, Bat."

"They do when it's in the speech announcing that you're gonna run for President."

"Guess I can see how that *would* make a difference."

"Apparently, big chunks of his speech are identical to one that was given by Glenda Jackson."

"The actress? *Elizabeth R*, and all that?"

"That's the one. She quit acting and ran for Parliament about twenty years ago. Been there ever since."

"Yeah, I guess if you're going to rip off somebody's speech, it would be better to use one from another country, especially an old speech. Folks over here probably wouldn't even notice."

"Except for 'person or persons unknown.'"

"He does get around, doesn't he? Or they do."

"All the way down to New Mexico, too. Looks like he found some bimbo who used to bang Ramon Martinez on a regular basis, back when he was a state rep."

"That's right, I saw something on TV last week," Morris said. "Slipped my mind completely. I'm trying to think – there's some kind of smoking gun, isn't there?"

Masterson nodded. "Looks like Martinez was paying her rent for a while, and a couple of times he wrote out checks. The bimbo made photocopies."

"Did she? And kept them all this time? My, my. Well, it's not quite as good as having the guy's jism on a dress hanging in your closet, but it ain't bad, either – unless you're Ramon Martinez, that is."

"Martinez isn't dead yet, and neither is Lunsford – politically, I mean. But they've both dropped in the polls, big time. And guess whose numbers have been looking better and better?"

"Wouldn't be Howard fucking Stark, by any chance, would it?"

Masterson nodded slowly. "You got it in one."

"Okay, Bat, I admit it looks like a pattern. But apart from the first guy, who might have just been a freak accident, it looks like nothing but old-fashioned dirty politics. You don't need the Forces of Darkness for that. Or if you do, then they've been at it for a hell of a long time, no pun intended."

"Yes and no. Sure, coming up with dirt on political opponents probably goes back to ancient Greece, if not farther. But where did *this* particular dirt come from? All these guys have been in politics a long time, which means they've made a lot of enemies. But nobody has found this shit, until now. *Nobody.*"

Morris sat there, staring at his now-empty tea mug without really seeing it. Finally, he said, "All right, let's say that this pattern of nastiness is so unlikely that we'll put a question mark on it. We'll add it to the other things we know, which include a voice you overheard that didn't sound human, Stark's face undergoing a momentary change that may have been unnatural, Stark receiving an apparent burn from contact with the consecrated hands of a Catholic priest, the burn healing unnaturally fast and said priest dying shortly thereafter, in a particularly gruesome fashion. Is that a fair summary?"

"Yeah, more or less."

"Okay, then." Morris leaned back in his chair. "So, my question for you is, 'What do you want me to do about it?'"

THE DEMON CALLING herself Ashley leaned forward until she was looking over Peters' shoulder. The computer monitor in front of them contained the schedule of Republican primary elections for the next month.

"How're we going to do it, Peters?" She spoke in the same matter-of-fact tone she used when suggesting delightfully perverse sexual acts. "How do we off this cocksucker?"

Without taking his eyes off the screen Peters said, "How can somebody so beautiful also be so vulgar?"

She went over and flopped into a sitting position on the edge of the bed, the winter sunlight turning her hair golden. "I suppose you could say that I come by it honestly. And only in this stupid Puritanical culture are the two things considered mutually exclusive."

Ashley was dressed in tan yoga pants and a loose-fitting gray sweatshirt that said 'All Souls Parish Choir' on the front.

"No argument from me," he said, scrolling down the page in front of him.

"But my question remains – how do we do it?"

"Better question: how do we get away with it?"

"Well, yes, that too."

"'That, too'," he repeated. "Easy for you to say. You can probably discorporate at will, leaving me to face the guns of the U.S. Secret Service alone."

"Peters, listen to me," she said. Some exasperation had crept into her tone. "This body I have created is solid flesh and blood, as you have reason to know. If somebody shoots me in the right spot, the body will die, and my essence will be returned summarily to Hell, a journey I am in *no hurry* to make."

He held up a pacifying hand. "Okay, no offense, I didn't know."

"Well now you do, and you'd better know this, too: the same thing is true for you."

"Yeah, I figured that."

"So, if we don't succeed in this little mission of ours, getting shot dead by the Secret Service is going to be the very *least* of our worries."

"It's not like I need any more motivation, Ashley," he said. "Astaroth gave me all I could ever want, my first night back on Earth. But can we agree it would be a very good thing if we could assassinate Stark, *and* not get killed ourselves, *and* not get sent to prison for 99 years? Sound reasonable?"

"Of course it does, sweetie – which is why I keep asking how best it can be done. How would you have managed it back in the old days, when you were the CIA's answer to 007?"

"Not me, I was never that suave. And I never was assigned a target anywhere near as important as Stark is over here, or as well-protected."

"How about a bomb?" she said. "It shouldn't be hard to determine where's he's going to be speaking a few days in advance. His PR people would probably be happy to tell us. A couple of pounds of Semtex, in a shaped charge, maybe. The technology they have these days, we could set it off from a half mile away, and then go out to lunch. You're buying, since you've got the magic wallet."

Peters was shaking his head before she'd finished speaking. "No – no bomb."

She looked at him, one elegant eyebrow raised.

"Two reasons," he said. "One is, they've got dogs that can sniff out explosives, and if those poochies aren't trained to recognize Semtex, then somebody's not doing his job."

She made a face. "I hadn't thought of that." Then she brightened a little. "See? That's why Astaroth picked you for the job. What's the other reason a bomb's no good, by the way?"

"I was sent here to kill Stark. Fair enough – Stark isn't even human anymore, not really. And if he gets into the White House, some real bad shit's going to happen. But a bomb will most likely take out a bunch of innocent people, and I'm just not gonna do that."

"You're serious," she said, as if she didn't believe he was. Or maybe she just didn't want to.

"Damn right, so to speak."

"Peters, you and I have both been in Hell. And if there's anything we should both know down to the marrow of our borrowed bones, it's that there *are* no innocent people."

"You can split semantic hairs any way you want, Ashley. I don't know what role I'm supposed to play, in the ongoing battle between Heaven and Hell. Astaroth says I'm here to do Hell's bidding – well, the bidding of one faction. But he's a demon, and I hear they lie a lot, no offense to present company. Or, could be that's what he *thinks* is going on, but it's more complicated than that. Maybe I'm not here on Hell's business, after all – or not exclusively. Maybe I've actually got a chance at, forgive the expression, redemption."

The look she gave him was pitying – or would have been, were she capable of pity. "Peters, we're both damned souls, each in our own way. Redemption just isn't an option for us, sweetie. Get it out of your head. That train left the fucking station for both of us, a long time ago – years for you, millennia for me, but the fact is that it's *gone*."

"Maybe the thing that puts it out of reach is our belief that it's no longer possible. You ever think about that?"

She rubbed her forehead with the fingertips of one hand. "I never thought that there was a human, alive or dead, who could confuse me. But I think you may have just managed it."

"Then let's break it down to the essential facts. One: I'm gonna kill Stark, because that's what I was sent here to do. Two: If I can help it, I'm not gonna kill anybody else – and I'm pretty sure I can help it."

She looked at him with open curiosity. "You are one piece of work, I'll say that – although what precise kind I'm not really sure. I don't know if I want to break your neck, or give you a blowjob."

"How about you forgo the first one, postpone the second and instead help me figure out a couple of things."

"Such as?"

"Where I can get the kind of rifle I think I might need – and a silencer to go with it."

"A rifle – now you're talking," Ashley said. "Did I ever tell you that I met Lee Harvey Oswald in Hell?"

"No you didn't," Peters said. "But I can't say that I'm surprised."

Chapter 26

"WHAT THEN, BAT?" Quincey Morris asked. "That's the question before this house."

"House? What fucking house're you talking about?"

"Just an expression. Assume everything you've told me is God's gospel truth. Let's posit that all your suspicions, your worst fears, are all as true as the fact that the sun's gonna rise tomorrow. What do you want me to do about it?"

"Jesus, Quincey, I..." Masterson ran his hand through his hair, something, Morris knew, that he did when frustrated. Morris understood, even sympathized. But that didn't change anything.

"I understand your concern. I know you from the old days, podner, and I'm well aware you're not given to flights of fancy. And in your situation, I'd be pretty worried, too."

"They why are you giving me a bunch of shit, all of a sudden?"

"I'm giving you shit, if you want to call it that, because I'm thinking ahead. That's something my dad taught me, and that he learned from *his* old man. I never knew my granddad – we Morrises tend not to live to a ripe old age. But either one of them would tell me that when you're dealing with what may be supernatural forces, it pays to think ahead, and plan ahead."

"That's just good sense in any job, including mine," Masterson said.

"Maybe, but in my profession the stakes can be real high – higher even than the ones in yours. So, if some fella tells me he thinks he's got vampires in his basement, I don't just drop by his place some night with a flashlight and a crucifix and ask where the basement door is. There's a word for occult investigators who do stuff like that, and the word is 'deceased'. If not worse."

"Christ, what's worse than 'deceased?'"

"'Undead', for one. 'Damned' might be another."

"I'm not *asking* you to do anything reckless, goddammit. I'm just saying that something pretty fucking weird is going on, and investigating weird shit is what you do – as I have reason to know."

"Okay, look – let's take the worst-case scenario. You've got a guy who sometimes talks in a voice that doesn't sound human, whose eyes change color when he's pissed off, who apparently received a burn from physical contact with a Catholic priest, a burn that then healed faster than any burn is supposed to, and let's not forget what happened to that poor priest."

"That's Stark, all right."

"At the risk of a stupid question, I'll ask you this: Stark's been seen in sunlight, right? With no ill effects?"

Masterson shrugged. "Sure – lots of times. Why?"

"I was hoping against hope that it was something simple, like vampirism, but it's hard to believe that a Presidential candidate could conceal that for very long."

"No, this bastard's no bloodsucker," Masterson said. "I'd have staked him myself if he was."

"Thing is, absent vampirism, there's only one other plausible explanation, and I bet you were thinking of it long before you got here: demonic possession, or some other kind of demonic manifestation."

"Yeah," Masterson said after a moment. "I haven't been able to say it out loud up 'til now, but – yeah."

"So – and I hate to keep coming back to this, Bat – what is it you want me to do?"

Masterson wiped a hand across his face. "Confirm it for me. Prove that the voice wasn't really a horror movie, that the burn wasn't just a skin condition, and that some former altar boy with a grudge didn't do all that awful shit to Father Bowles."

The workmen down the hall had apparently called it quits for the day – there was no noise in the house now. The ticking of the battery-powered clock in Morris's office seemed loud in the silence.

"Say I manage to confirm it – me, or a friend of mine named Libby, who's good at this stuff. So, next week, or the week after, I sit you down and say, 'You were right, my friend. The Presidential candidate you're guarding is actually a demon from Hell.' Then what?"

"Then maybe I get the chance to make up for some stuff in my past," he said bleakly. "I've done a lot of bad shit in my time, Quincey. You don't need to know about it. And I'm not sure if anybody up there is keeping score, but it seems to me that I probably could – what's the word – *atone* for quite a few of my many sins by drawing my weapon and putting two rounds into the head of Howard W. Stark – or whoever the fuck he really is."

*   *   *

LIBBY CHASTAIN LAY on the hotel bed watching a movie in which Hugh Jackman was supposed to be a guy named Van Helsing, but he was behaving a heck of a lot more like Indiana Jones. *At least they called him Gabriel, not Abraham, so maybe the old man isn't turning over in his grave – much.*

She was about to change the channel when the theme from *Bewitched* began playing. Libby clicked off the TV and picked up her phone. The caller ID showed that it was Colleen again.

"Hey, girlfriend."

"Hey, Libby. I talked to Rachel, and she'll pay Quincey's *per diem* and expenses to look into this black magic thing. Assuming you guys are going to work together again, she says she'll also pay your expenses. Your *pro bono* services, she says, will earn the Sisterhood's gratitude."

"The Sisterhood helped save my life not all that long ago," Libby said. "So how about I do this job, and we call it even? I'm kidding, of course – I'd need to do a lot more than this to pay off that particular debt."

"It's not a debt, Libby. The Sisterhood takes care of its own."

"I know – but I still welcome the opportunity to do something useful. Speaking of which, I better ask you the question that I know Quincey is going to ask me."

"Ask away."

"What exactly is it you want us to do? Quincey likes to be precise about these things, and I can't say that I blame him."

"As it happens, I asked Rachel the same question."

"Now there's a *smart* little FBI agent."

"Rachel says she wants you to identify the source of the black magic that was lingering at the death scene. I

270

assume none of us is naïve enough to think the two are unrelated."

"You assume correctly, kiddo. I don't figure whoever left the traces in that bathroom just stopped by to admire the wallpaper."

"So, okay: locate the source. If you're able to determine a motive, all the better – but it's not absolutely required."

"Well, that certainly seems clear enough. But what's Rachel going to do about it, assuming we're successful?"

"She didn't say, and I didn't ask. But the Sisterhood can't just stand by and let somebody get away with murder – not murder by black magic, anyway."

"No, I suppose not."

"You'll recognize this particular strain if you get close to it, won't you?"

"Oh, sure. It's in my sense memory. I'll know it if I smell it again."

"So, how do you plan to proceed? Rachel didn't tell me to ask – I'm just nosy."

"If you left it up to me, I wouldn't know where to begin. Fortunately, Quincey does this kind of stuff all the time. I'm sure he'll have some ideas."

"Then we'd both better hope he's not busy doing something else."

MALACHI PETERS, HAIR still damp from his recent shower, was on the Internet trying to determine the right kind of gun for his task.

"It's got to be a rifle," he'd told Ashley. "Even though Astaroth thoughtfully supplied me with a 9 mm Berretta and a silencer, getting close enough to do the job with a pistol would be suicide."

"If I had to guess," she said, "I'd say he provided them as props, to remind you of your former profession. He doesn't care how you kill Stark, as long as it gets done."

"The right kind of hunting rifle will probably do the job," Peters said. "I shouldn't have to work so far out that only a sniper rifle would have the range. Stark's Secret Service detail isn't that big, yet. Their perimeter won't extend more than a block or two."

"So we're going shopping? Oh, good – I hear that women *love* shopping."

"I don't think they're usually looking for lethal weapons when they go," he said.

"More fools, they," Ashley said.

"The hard part is going to be getting a silencer for the rifle."

"Is that essential?"

"I think so. We might get lucky enough to fire from someplace where there are no people close by, but I wouldn't count on it. And if I fire off an unsilenced rifle inside a building, everybody else in there is going to know about it. Getting away would be hard; getting away without a whole bunch of witnesses would be practically impossible."

She shrugged. "Then buy a silencer."

"Hard to do. They're much more tightly controlled than rifles. I've been researching it online – you need a Federal Firearms License, which costs five hundred bucks, takes forever to process, and requires a *very* detailed background check."

"I begin to see the problem."

"Yeah. The money's easy, but we haven't got months to wait – and as for the background check..."

"'This dude's been dead for almost thirty years.' Might cause them to look at you kind of funny."

"Yeah, right before they call the cops. It's a pity I can't just ask the CIA…"

Peters had stopped talking, and was staring into space. After watching him for a few seconds Ashley softly asked, "Something?"

Peters ran one of his big hands over his face, as if washing it.

"Maybe. There was a guy I used to know in the Company, Charlie Dedrich. We called him 'the Armorer.' Anything special we needed for a mission, he'd get it for us."

"At the risk of pointing out the obvious…"

"Yeah, I know – I'm not with CIA any longer. But I bet Charlie isn't, either."

"No," she said, "he's probably dead by now."

"Maybe not. He was a young guy back then, mid-thirties. And here's the thing: he always talked about taking early retirement and going back home to open his own gun store. Doesn't sound like a big deal to me, but it was his dream, for some reason."

Ashley was watching him closely. "And where was home for this young firearms fiend?"

"I can't remember the town. I've been trying these last couple minutes, but it's a complete blank."

She threw up her hands in exasperation. "Then what the fuck *good* –"

"But I do remember the state," Peters said, grinning at her. "It was Virginia."

Chapter 27

Stark had come in third in Maine, despite the distractions stemming from the candidate's encounter with Rev. Joseph Bowles, now lamentably deceased. Then, two weeks later, he had to face Super Tuesday.

The media had come up with the name years earlier – manifesting, as usual, its collective obsession with the 'horse race' aspects of the campaign and virtually ignoring anything that had to do with the issues. A candidate's views on health care, gun control or taxation were often complex and therefore dull, of interest to only a few 'hot button' voters. But who was ahead, who was behind, who had just made an embarrassing gaffe that could cost him victory – *that* was understandable and hence interesting.

Thus the designation Super Tuesday, referring to the day when a large number of state primaries took place simultaneously. For the Democrats, it was a day of immense importance; twenty-one states, ranging from Alaska to Utah were holding either binding elections or caucuses. Republicans seeking the Presidency faced a challenge that was less imposing, but only slightly less so, with fourteen states on the line. For both sides, California was the big prize, with 370 delegates on the line for Democrats (causing some political pros to call it 'the Big Enchilada' or 'the Widowmaker') and 173 for the GOP (which had prompted no cutsey nicknames whatsoever).

On the night of Super Tuesday, once all the votes had been cast and counted, Senator Howard Stark spoke to supporters gathered in the ballroom of the Westin Bonaventure Hotel, his words carried live to smaller crowds at Stark campaign headquarters in the other thirteen states that had been in play for his party that day.

Stark stood at the podium, gently motioning the crowd of volunteers, campaign staff, and hangers-on to quiet down. Over his left shoulder could be seen Mary Margaret Doyle, her severe Mother Superior face split in a grin that was rarely seen there in public.

Those assembled in the packed ballroom – excited, exhausted, and, in many cases, at least half-drunk – did not quiet down fully, despite their leader's calming gestures. Stark began speaking anyway, reasoning that silence would quickly follow. He was right.

"First of all, I want to thank all of those good people, in California and in other states across this great country, for taking time out of their busy lives to come out and vote today." *Pause two beats, then continue, deadpan.* "I especially want to thank all those who had the kindness." *Pause one beat.* "And the good sense" *Pause for laughter.* "to vote for me!" *Pause for sustained applause, looking both happy and humbled, if possible.*

"When I first announced, just nine short months ago, my intention to seek the highest office in the land, there were those in the media who called me 'Howard Who?'" *Smile, and pause for good-natured booing.* "There were even some so-called political 'experts' who considered my candidacy a joke." *Pause for sustained booing, careful not to look serious, but not angry.* "However, I think it is fair to say that on this occasion, thanks to your efforts, and those of many good people across this great land of ours, that everyone knows who Howard Stark is, and nobody is laughing now!" *Pause for sustained applause and cheering. More of the happy and humbled, with a touch of righteous satisfaction.*

The rest of it was boilerplate derived from several of the standard Stark campaign speeches – red meat to his followers, of little interest to anyone else. Even Mary Margaret Doyle had to clench her jaws to keep from yawning – although, it must be admitted, she had not had much sleep the past two days.

It was left to Fernando Garrett, speaking off the record to reporters in the hotel bar, to put it in perspective.

"California is our only first place finish so far, but it's a big one. For the electoral votes, sure, but it means a lot more than that. And don't forget – we did no worse than third in the other states, and came in a close second in five of them. This shows that Senator Stark's candidacy must be taken seriously – that he has a very real chance to go all the way. And not just to the nomination in August. I'm talking about all the way to 1600 Pennsylvania Avenue.

"Success breeds success – you guys know that as well as I do. More money is going to come in now, from donors large and small. The Senator can put his checkbook away, and let the American people, through their donations, fund this campaign. We'll be getting a lot more media coverage – at least, I sure as Hell *hope* we will, which means more of the public will learn about our message, in addition to the paid media which the increased donations will allow us to increase exponentially."

While Garrett and other members of his growing entourage were spinning the press for all they were worth, the subject of their earnest advocacy was on the way to bed. As their party approached the Senator's suite on the 16th floor, Mary Margaret Doyle idly said to Special Agent Jerry Arkasian, "Where's Agent Masterson? I don't think I've seen him all day."

"He had to take a couple days' leave, ma'am. I understand his Mom's real sick."

"Oh, I see." She nodded her acknowledgment, but a pair of frown lines appeared on her forehead.

Five minutes later, she walked across the suite's living room and through the open door of Stark's room.

Sargatanas was still dressed and reading something on the screen of his laptop. He glanced up when she came in and said, "I'm busy."

"I just thought you'd like to know something I learned from one of the Secret Service dolts."

Without looking up from the computer, Sargatanas said, "I'm listening.

"I realized that I hadn't seen Masterson around lately, so I asked one of them. He told me that Masterson had taken leave to see his mother, who's seriously ill."

"What do you want me to do – send the old bitch flowers?"

"Of course not. It's just that I once heard Masterson say that he'd grown up in an orphanage."

He was looking at her now, and she could tell that he was thinking. "Could be that he's just got some pussy waiting somewhere, and used the mommy excuse to get away and get laid."

"Yes, that could… could be it, I suppose."

"Confront him with the orphanage thing, when he gets back. See what he says."

"Yes, of course. I'll take care of it."

"Now get out of my sight."

AN HOUR AFTER Bat Masterson had left to rejoin the Stark campaign, Quincey Morris was back behind his desk. This time, his laptop open in front of him, he was staring at the screen with a sour expression.

There was no shortage of video clips of Howard Stark to be found online. YouTube boasted half a dozen, presumably posted by fans of the Senator. There were more to be found at the websites for the big news organizations: CNN, MSNBC, and Fox News, not to mention the network news operations. Even the Stark's campaign website provided some footage of the candidate out committing rhetoric. Morris was scowling because Stark seemed so… *ordinary*. Just another specimen of *politicos Americanus*, genus *moderato rightus-wingus*. He was perhaps a little smoother than the usual presidential candidate, a touch more articulate – but there was certainly nothing about him that would cause you to point your finger and scream 'Spawn of Satan!'

Morris shook his head over his own optimism. *What did you expect – horns? A pointed tail protruding from the back of those expensive suits? Maybe a little hellfire scorching the podium?*

The thought of hellfire prompted Morris to scratch the burn scar on his neck, although it wasn't itching.

He was about to go back to his background research on Stark when his phone, which had a separate ringtone programmed for each person on his call list, began to play Billy Joel's 'Uptown Girl.'

Morris smiled as he picked up the phone. "Hi, Libby."

"Hi, Quincey. I hope I'm not calling at a bad time."

"Nope, not at all. My coke dealer left twenty minutes ago, and the hookers won't be here until 6:30."

There was silence on the line.

"That was intended as humor, Libby," Morris said gently. "In poor taste, maybe, but humor nonetheless. It's okay to laugh."

To her credit, Libby Chastain managed something that sounded reasonably like laughter, before saying, "I wasn't calling to play Big Sister. Really."

"Just as well. For one thing, I'm older."

"Like *that* would matter. No, I've got some work for you – for *us* – if you're interested."

It was Morris's turn for silence.

"Quincey?"

"Sorry. I was just thinking that when it rains, it really does pour. Oh, wait – that only refers to bad stuff, doesn't it?"

"I haven't the faintest. What's been raining on you?"

"What I meant was, I just took a job. Sort of."

"Well, that's good news, but why 'sort of'?"

"I don't know if I'll ever get paid for it, so I guess that makes it more of a favor than a job. Remember Bat Masterson, who I told you about before you left?"

"The Secret Service guy?"

"That's him. He's heading the detail that's guarding Senator Howard Stark this primary season. You know who that is, right?"

"He's the one with the hair."

279

Morris snorted laughter. "Yeah, that's him. Thing is, Bat's come across some stuff that's got him... concerned."

"Concerned? About what?"

"He's seen and heard some things that have him kind of spooked. And I can't say I blame him."

He summarized for her everything that Masterson had told him, adding his own observations and conclusions along the way. When he was done she said, pensively, "Black magic has its roots in the demonic."

"Yeah."

"The practice of black magic is really nothing more than the invoking of demonic power, then channeling it – almost always for evil purposes."

"You're, uh, not telling me anything I don't already know, Libby."

"Then let me see if I can change that. You ever hear of a Congressman from New York named Ron Brooks?"

"Don't think so – should I?"

Libby told Morris what she knew about the death of Ron Brooks – as well as what she, and others, suspected. When she was done, Morris said, "When you first mentioned his name, it rang a bell but I couldn't say from where. So while you've been talking, I Googled the guy. Says here he was running for President."

"That's right, Colleen said something about that. Maybe you and I should both start paying more attention to what's going on in the political world."

"If the Forces of Darkness ever give us a break, maybe we'll have the time." Whenever they used that term with each other, Morris and Libby always gave the words a light coat or irony. But that didn't mean either of them denied the very real nature of what they had fought against so many times.

"And speaking of the Forces of Darkness," Morris went on, "Ron Brooks's name was familiar because Masterson mentioned it when he was giving me a rundown of some of the weird things that have happened to Stark's political opponents."

"I have the impression that a fair number of people try for the major parties' presidential slot every four years," Libby said. "Was Brooks a serious contender, or just one of the attention hogs?"

"According to his obit in the *New York Times*, which I have in front of me, he had a definite shot at it. The House of Representatives isn't usually considered a prime launching pad for the White House, but I guess Brooks made a name for himself last year, when he chaired those hearings looking into right-wing extremism in America. He exposed some very nasty groups that like to stay below the radar."

"Sounds like something that conservatives and liberals would both agree with, which makes it something of a minor miracle."

"Yeah, and that's probably why he decided to make a grab for the brass ring. And it cost him his life, poor bastard."

"You believe that was the reason? To get him out of the way?"

"Based on what we know, I'd say it's a good working hypothesis. It sure fits Occam's Razor."

"'The simplest explanation that fits the known facts is probably true'" Libby quoted.

"Uh-huh. I reckon that it's time we got a closer look at Howard Stark," Morris said. "Especially you."

"I don't disagree, but why me in particular?"

"Because you're the one who can smell black magic."

Chapter 28

THERE WERE PLENTY of open parking spaces at Dedrich's Guns & Ammo in Newport News this time of day, so Peters was able to park the rented Toyota Camry within fifty feet of the front door.

"Think this will work?" Ashley asked.

"If Charlie's in the store, it might. Their web page says he's the proprietor, but that could mean anything. Maybe he runs the place from a condo in Miami Beach. But it's our best chance to get what I need."

"And you don't want me to do anything?"

"Just be your usual charming self. I told you that you didn't have to come down here with me."

"Uh-uh. Where you go, I go — at least until this is over. Besides, if you left me alone in that hotel room for several hours, I might get bored. Then who *knows* what might happen."

"As I was saying, thanks for coming along, Ashley."

"My pleasure, Peters. Now let go get us some ordinance."

Two clerks stood behind the long rectangular counter. One was talking to a burly man in a camo jacket, but the other was idly thumbing through a copy of *Shotgun News*. He was in his forties, had a round face and brown hair that receded in a pronounced widow's peak. He looked up as Peters and Ashley approached.

"Afternoon," he said with a professional smile. "How can I help you folks today?" His name tag read 'Vince.'

"Howdy, Vince. I'm Mal, and this is Ashley."

Vince looked at Ashley longer than he needed to, but he was, after all, human, and male.

"Pleased to meet y'all," he said finally. "Were you interested in some –"

"You'd be Charlie Dedrick's son, right?"

Vince looked at Peters for a second. "That's right. You know my Dad?"

"Not personally, but my old man used to talk about him quite a bit. They used to work for the same... Company."

"'Company' was spook lingo for the CIA, and this was an easy way to find out if Charlie Dedrick had told his son the truth about his past.

"That right?" Vince said. "And when would that be?"

"Late Seventies, early Eighties. Your dad was based in England. Mine used to... travel around a lot. But Pop said he could always count on your dad for the right machinery when he needed it."

Vince was smiling again, and this time it reached his eyes. "Well, now, don't that beat all?"

"We're just down on vacation," Ashley said, "but as soon as we passed this place and saw the sign, he just had to come in and see if it was the same Dedrick his daddy used to know."

"Well, my daddy's in the back, in the office. I'm sure he'd like to meet you folks. What'd you say your last name was, Mal?"

"Peters. Mal Peters."

And that was how, forty minutes later, Peters and Ashley walked out of Dedrick's Guns & Ammo the proud possessors of a Remington Model 7 .300 Ultra-Mag, two boxes of Savage 99 180-grain cartridges, a Leupold 3-9x 40mm scope, a steel rifle case with a handle and two locks, the address of a local gun club that sold day passes to its rifle range – and a SWR Omega 300 rifle silencer.

NESTOR GREENE STOOD resignedly in the slow-moving line, holding the smudged white card notifying him that he had once again received something too big to fit within the 4x4-inch dimensions of the box provided him by the U.S. Postal Service. He had figured he was due for one more little package from Mary Margaret Doyle. Thanks to his efforts (and, unbeknownst to him, a touch of black magic), all but one of Howard Stark's competitors for the Republican nomination had encountered serious problems – in Chesbro's case, a fatal one.

He had lost precisely zero sleep over Senator Chesbro's suicide. As the result of a long career in politics, Nestor Greene had developed the mental capacity to rationalize pretty much anything. *I'm not the one who told him to suck dick back in his college days, and it wasn't my bright idea to take pictures of it, either. He brought it on himself, the fucking faggot.*

Greene had experienced homosexuality himself, at the Catholic boarding school where he spent his formative years. The older boys had given him no choice in the matter. As a result, Greene could not now imagine why any man would suck cock of his own free will. Women, well that was different. That was *natural*.

284

Greene finally reached the head of the line and handed over his card to the bored-looking clerk. Two minutes later, he was in the Jaguar with a small package, wrapped in plain brown paper and about half the size of a shoe box.

Greene had anticipated a final dose of political poison, freshly brewed in Ms. Doyle's cauldron, because there was one serious contender remaining between Howard Stark and the GOP presidential nomination. Florida Governor Bob Leffingwell was a former Congressman, decorated Vietnam veteran, and author of two well-received books on fiscal policy. He was also, apparently, clean as the driven snow. Nestor Greene hated him.

He had done some preliminary research on Leffingwell, hoping to impress Mary Margaret Doyle with his initiative – just as he had done with Ramon Martinez and his bimbo, a revelation that had proved to be a thorn in the Senator's side roughly the size of a harpoon. But Leffingwell had apparently lived a virtuous life, damn him. War hero, Harvard Law grad, eight years in Congress, governor of one of the few states not running huge budget deficits caused by the recession. Married to the same woman for thirty-two years, father of three adoring, now-grown children, not one of whom had ever gotten into serious trouble. Robert Leffingwell might have stolen a candy bar from his local Rexall when he was ten, but if so, there was no evidence of it.

But now Mary Margaret Doyle had found something, it looked like. She had a genius for digging up dirt that was positively diabolical.

Greene looked at the small parcel on the seat next to him. The shape meant it didn't contain documents this time. Letters, maybe? More naughty photos, perhaps of a young Bob Leffingwell buggering a goat at a fraternity party? He decided to wait until he was home to find out. No one would ever accuse Nestor Greene of undue sensitivity, but there was something about the box that made him... uneasy. He would examine its dark treasures soon enough.

Sitting behind the desk in his study, Greene found that his little premonition had been well and truly justified. The box had contained no letters or indiscrete photos. In fact, the contents had nothing to do with Bob Leffingwell's life at all – but they might well play a role in his death.

Not political poison, after all – the witch sent the real thing.

Mary Margaret Doyle's little care package had contained four objects. Greene had them lined up on the desk in front of him, like soldiers in a firing squad.

The bottle of clear liquid was squat, with a stamped-on metal lid that had a small circle in the middle made of some semi-porous material. It was the kind of bottle you see in doctors' offices and hospitals all the time. Insert the point of a hypo through the little round membrane, and draw out the drug you were planning to inject into the patient.

Even if Greene had failed to recognize the bottle's nature, Mary Margaret Doyle had cleared up any ambiguity by including a small hypodermic needle, bubble wrap protecting its glass middle from any danger of breakage. The sharp tip gleamed wickedly under the bright light of Greene's desk lamp.

And then there was the money – a thick stack of hundred dollar bills that had added up to $50,000 every time Greene had counted it.

The fourth object was a folded square of paper that contained Mary Margaret Doyle's macabre instructions.

Three drops of the liquid in any beverage, hot or cold, will induce cardiac arrest, even in a healthy individual, within twelve hours. It is not expected that you will undertake the assignment yourself – there is enough money provided herewith to hire someone reliable. Any money left after you pay the subcontractor is yours to keep. Following the successful completion of the assignment, you will receive an additional $50,000.

It is vital that the assignment be carried out no later than 10 March. Refusal is not one of your options. Just as success will bring rewards, failure will have adverse consequences. They will be severe.

Nestor Greene read through the page twice. Then, as he sat there thinking hard, still holding the sheet of paper – it burst into flame. He dropped it onto the desk just in time to avoid scorching his fingers. Transfixed, he sat and watched as, within seconds, the paper burned to nothing – no ash, no residue of any kind. Soon the only evidence that it had ever existed was a faint odor of sulphur and a discoloration on his Danish teak desk, the size of a half-dollar, that would probably never come out.

That crazy bitch! How the fuck did she do that – and why?

The answer to 'how' continued to elude him, but after a while Greene thought he could discern several reasons behind 'why.'

The destruction of the paper eliminated any evidence that Greene had just been ordered to arrange for a political assassination. He didn't know if it was possible to trace a computer-printed document back to its source the way the cops could do with a typewriter, but the point was certainly moot now.

And the unexpected combustion was probably intended to serve as a warning, as well. Mary Margaret Doyle was reminding him that she could reach him anytime she wanted. If he failed to carry out his instructions by the deadline, she seemed to be saying, the next thing to catch fire could be him.

Greene regarded this latest assignment as outside his job description. He had destroyed many a reputation in his career, and sometimes the work resulted in collateral damage – Chesbro's suicide being the most recent example. But he had never gotten involved in something that could end with Nestor Greene strapped to a gurney, watching as a prison doctor inserted a needle into his arm. He hadn't signed on for anything like this, and he didn't have to do it. He could go to the FBI, or the Secret Service. He could tell them… what?

Let me see if I understand you correctly, Mr. Greene. You were ordered to arrange the assassination of Governor Leffingwell by Senator Stark's Chief of Staff, Mary Margaret Doyle. You've got a bottle of some drug, a hypo, and a big pile of hundred dollar bills as your only evidence of this conspiracy. No one has ever seen you with Ms. Doyle, phone records show no contact between you, and she denies even knowing who the hell you are. And the piece of paper on which she wrote your instructions for taking part in this conspiracy spontaneously burst into flame shortly after you read it. Have I got that right?

Suddenly, Greene sat up very straight. The package had been hand-addressed, in what Greene knew was Mary Margaret Doyle's perfect Palmer method handwriting. Even if there were no fingerprints (and he was betting there weren't), the handwriting would prove a connection between her and the package.

Greene reached out for the brown paper that had wrapped the little box of death. That, at least, hadn't burned up, and he could—

The wrapping was blank.

Where Mary Margaret Doyle had written his name and P.O. box information, and a fictitious return address, was nothing but unblemished brown paper. Greene tried to wrap his mind around what he was seeing. *Okay, so she used disappearing ink. Any kid with a book on magic tricks can do that. Big fucking deal.*

But then he thought some more. *That package was sitting in the post office God knows how long – a day, two days, three? Not counting transit time from wherever she mailed it. How does the ink know enough to disappear only after I've opened the package?*

Nestor Greene was beginning to think that maybe the FBI wasn't such a good idea, after all. In fact, he was rapidly coming to the conclusion that the best chance for his continued good health was to do exactly what Mary Margaret Doyle had told him to do – and the sooner, the better.

Greene had no idea how or where to find a professional assassin. But it might just be that he knew somebody who did.

He reached across his desk, grabbed his huge rolodex, and pulled it closer. Everything was computerized these days, but in some ways Greene was old school. He liked the feel of the cards under his fingers as he searched through them.

He put on the glasses he used for reading and started looking.

*　　*　　*

ANOTHER CITY, ANOTHER hotel suite. Mary Margaret Doyle sometimes had trouble remembering what state she was in. But it didn't matter, much. Stark had plenty of people who would keep track of that sort of thing. As his performance in the primaries had improved, everything else about the campaign also got better – or, at least, bigger.

Stark's entourage had grown. It now included a media relations specialist who was supposed to ensure that the journalists who followed them around like sheep knew everything that Stark's campaign manager wanted them to know – and nothing more. A retired Marine Corps general had come on board as foreign policy/military affairs advisor. He was quite knowledgeable, but Mary Margaret Doyle had assigned one of the campaign's flunkies to keep a special eye on him. The General liked to take a drink or two in the evening, and he had an eye for the ladies. There were three others who had joined the team – two men and a woman – but she kept confusing their names and was only vaguely aware of their function, if any.

She had once asked Sargatanas if the campaign needed all these people. "Garret says we do," he had said, "and I agree with him. I don't have much to learn from any of them, but their very presence testifies to my significance as a candidate."

"Yes," she'd said, "I suppose it does."

"Garrett says that in Hollywood it is axiomatic: the bigger the star, the larger the entourage. The same is true in politics which, to paraphrase my old friend von Clauswitz, is merely entertainment carried out by other means."

Stark was huddled with some of the entourage now, giving the illusion that he cared about their opinions. Mary Margaret Doyle glanced at her watch. They should be done soon. Her Lord and Master ran a tight meeting.

True to her prediction, two minutes later she heard the door buzz as someone inserted a key into the lock from the hall. That would not be Stark, she knew. One of the Secret Service apes would come in first, to make sure that no terrorists were hiding in the bathroom with AK-47s.

It was the one named Thorwald, whose blond good looks and earnest manner reminded her of the Cummings poem about a fool named Olaf: 'more brave than me, more blond than you.'

"Good evening, ma'am," he said, unsurprised to find Mary Margaret Doyle in the suite's living room.

"Good evening Special Agent."

"Everything quiet?"

"As the grave." This produced a look of perplexity on the stolid face for a moment, but Thorwald said nothing else as he quickly checked Stark's bedroom, then hers. Opening the door to the hall, he said "Clear," to someone out of her sight and stepped back to allow entry.

The creature whom the world knew as Senator Howard Stark came in, accompanied by Fernando Garrett and two more Secret Service types. One of them was Masterson.

As Stark and Garrett talked about something to do with media buys in Virginia, Mary Margaret Doyle put a sympathetic expression on her face, stood up, and walked over to where the three Secret Service agents stood, chatting quietly. She put a hand on Masterson's arm, and when he turned to her said, "Welcome back, Agent Masterson."

He nodded stolidly. "Thank you, Ms. Doyle. It's good to be back."

"I understand that a member of your family has become ill?"

"Yes, ma'am – my mother." His face portrayed no emotion. "Liver cancer. They're doing what they can for her."

She nodded solemnly and said, "I'm very sorry to hear that. But one thing puzzles me." She knew his face would betray nothing, so she was watching his eyes.

"Ma'am?"

"I thought I remembered hearing you say once that you'd grown up in an orphanage."

He glanced down for a second and when he looked back at her the pupils of his eyes had contracted. "That's true, ma'am – until I was twelve, when the Mastersons adopted me. Pretty unusual for a kid that age to find a home, let alone a good one, but I guess I lucked out."

"So the woman... the poor woman with cancer, she isn't really your mother."

"She's the only mother I ever knew, ma'am," he said, a touch defensively. "She'll do just fine."

A few minutes later, Garrett and the Secret Service agents were gone, and she was alone with Sargatanas.

"When I return to Hell – in triumph, I trust – I will have a suggestion for My Lord Lucifer regarding a new variety of torment to inflict upon the damned," he said.

"Oh?"

"Meetings – lots and lots of meetings."

She laughed at the joke, but was careful not to overdo it. It would not be wise to give the impression that she was laughing at *him*.

"I wanted to tell you," she said, "that I spoke to Masterson, about his alleged sick mother."

"And?"

"He said that he had, in fact, been reared in an orphanage – until he was twelve, when a couple named Masterson adopted him. That's the woman he thinks of as his mother, he says."

"It makes sense, given the stupid sentimentality you humans are prone to."

"Yes, but as he spoke I was watching his eyes. These government apes don't reveal much with their faces – they're trained not to – but pupil dilation and contraction is what's called an autonomic response, outside of the control of the will. Like blushing."

"How interesting. I did not know that." His tone of voice meant that neither of those statements was true.

"When I mentioned the orphanage, *his pupils contracted*. He knew he'd been caught in a lie – although he recovered rather well, I will say that for him."

"I see."

"Now the question is – well, it's two questions: where was he really, and why did he lie about it?"

"No, that's not the question. The real question is, considering the immense importance of this undertaking, why did I have to be afflicted with an idiot for a minion?"

"*What*? I mean, I... um, I'm not sure what you mean."

"Pupil dilation and contraction doesn't measure deception, any more than a polygraph does. It measures changes in emotion. Correct?"

"Well, yes, of course. But I assumed –"

"Don't *assume* – *think*, you stupid cunt. When Masterson's pupils reacted, what were you and he talking about? Hmmm?

293

"Uh, the orphanage he grew up in."

"Do you suppose that his memories of that experience might have some *emotions* associated with them?"

"Yes, um, I suppose they would. Probably. Yes."

"So, is it possible that the pupil dilation you so alertly observed might have occurred in response to his memories of the orphanage, rather than any lie he was telling you about it?"

"Yes, quite possible," she said with a sigh. "Sorry."

"And if he was lying about where he went, he probably wanted to spend a few days getting laid. Men do that, I understand."

"Yes, they do. I didn't mean to waste your time. I apologize."

"Idiot," he said. Then, after a moment he added, "There *is* something you should do tomorrow. Just in case your original instincts about Masterson were correct. Are you listening?"

"Yes, of course."

"See if you can find out what flight Masterson took when he went on leave, and where it brought him. Just to be on the safe side. I'll show you how to get into the airlines' computer system – it's not difficult at all."

"Yes, all right. I'll take care of it tomorrow."

Chapter 29

"CAN YOU DO it?"

The Rialto Bar and Grille in Fairfax wasn't busy at this hour, so Nestor Greene was careful to keep his voice down. His companion had been doing the same.

The man sitting in the booth opposite Greene had lifeless brown hair, a quiet brown herringbone sport coat, and a blue button-down shirt open at the collar. He looked like somebody who'd be sitting in your living room trying to sell you car insurance. He certainly didn't look like a professional killer.

I guess that's sort of the point, Greene thought.

The contact who had put this meet together had told Greene that nobody seemed to know the brown-haired man's real name, or even what name to call him by, since he changed identities with every job he did. The contact had said that some in the underworld referred to the killer as 'The Grocer's Boy,' although nobody was sure why. One story had it that his father, or maybe foster father, had been in the business, too, using a small grocery store as a cover. He had supposedly trained the kid in every aspect of the killer's trade. The Grocer's

Boy, the story went, had killed his first man when he was fourteen years old.

On the table between them Greene had put a small paper bag, the kind people carry their lunches to work in. The killer opened it and looked inside at the plastic baggie in which Greene had put the vial of poison and the hypo, but didn't take it out of the bag.

"Does it have to be done this way?" the killer asked. "I'm not objecting, just asking."

"It has to look like a natural death, and you can bet there will be a damn thorough autopsy afterward."

"So any kind of natural death is acceptable?"

Greene thought a moment, then nodded. "I would say so. But if you use another method, it has to be foolproof. It can't look like a... a hit."

"I understand. Just checking to see what my options are." The killer paused for a small sip of the Scotch and water that was in front of him, only the second sip he had taken since sitting down. "The price is fifty thousand," he said.

Greene nodded glumly. So much for making a profit on the cash Mary Margaret Doyle had sent. Good thing more money was coming his way once the job was done.

He had been told that this man would charge fifty grand. And he had been warned not to haggle over the killer's fee.

"Half now, half when it's done?" Greene asked. "I understand that's customary."

"Not with me, it isn't. You pay me the whole fifty when the job's finished. If, for some reason, I can't get it done, you don't owe me a dime." He gave Greene a friendly-looking smile, as if he'd just agreed to buy the million-dollar whole life policy. "That isn't very likely, though."

Greene tried not to show his surprise. He had brought all of Mary Margaret Doyle's fifty thousand, in case the killer had demanded the full fee in advance. Greene had been prepared for that; he had not expected to pay nothing up front at all.

"You're thinking that it's stupid of me to trust you like that," the killer said.

"No, I wouldn't –"

"A guy tried to cheat me out of a fee, once. I killed him, and it was messy. There hasn't been any problem since. Nobody cheats me."

"Yes, I can imagine. Well, you don't have to worry about me making that kind of mistake."

"I'm not worried. Especially since you're going to give me a look at your driver's license."

"My – why the hell do you want to see that?"

"To determine your real identity, Mr. 'Smith.' Just in case you get an attack of the stupids between now and when it comes time to pay me. I want to know who to come visit."

"Well, I'm not sure I want to –"

"No license, no deal. But you're paying for my drink, either way."

Greene slowly reached for his wallet. He put it on the table, found his license, and handed it over.

The man they called The Grocer's Boy studied the license for a few moments, then held it up to the light and bent it back and forth a few times.

"What the hell are you doing?" Greene asked.

"Making sure it's genuine. There are ways you can tell, and this one looks legit." He handed the license back. "Thanks, Mr. Greene. Now all I need is a phone number where you can be reached."

"What do you want that for? You already know where I live."

"I want it so I call you when the job's done and tell you where to send my money," the killer said patiently.

"Very well." Greene pulled the cocktail napkin from under his glass and reached in his shirt pocket for a pen.

"No need to write it down. Just tell me. Twice."

Greene recited his cell phone number, then repeated it.

"Fine. Take care, Mr. Greene. I'll be in touch."

Then he slid out of the booth and was gone before Greene could come up with a clever exit line. Just as well. Nestor Greene wasn't feeling very clever at the moment.

QUINCEY MORRIS'S FLIGHT touched down at Virginia's Richmond International Airport a little before noon, and by 1:00 he was checked into his room at the Crowne Plaza, smack in the middle of downtown.

He wasted no time plugging his laptop into the room's Internet port and was reading his fourth story about the Stark campaign when someone knocked on his door. Morris peeked through the fisheye lens, then turned the knob to admit Libby Chastain.

"Good flight?" Morris asked after they had exchanged a quick hug.

"I'm beginning to think that may be an oxymoron," Libby said. "But, on the plus side, nobody hijacked the plane, they didn't lose my luggage, and I sat next to a cute guy who travels for IBM, but is based in Richmond. When we reached the terminal, he demonstrated that Southern gentility isn't dead yet, by saying something like 'Ah am honored to have had as a travelin' companion a lovely and charmin' lady, such as yourself.'"

"I've often felt the same way myself, Libby, but I was too shy to say so."

"I bet." She gave the room a quick scan. "This is a nice change from chain hotels. Good choice. My room's on 14, and has quite a lovely view of the city."

"I'm glad you like the accommodations, although I chose the Crowne Plaza because of its proximity to the Stark rally that's going to be held here, day after tomorrow. We could even watch it from that window, but I suspect we'd be a little too far away to do any good."

"And have you worked out some fiendish plan for getting me close to Senator Stark without getting gunned down by the Secret Service?"

Morris smiled at her. "Fiendish plan? No, that's the other side, remember? The team that Stark may be playing for, which is what we're here to determine."

"Why Richmond, anyway? You didn't say when you emailed my plane ticket."

"It was Masterson's idea. Stark's devoting all his energies to Virginia this week. The other primaries are in states like Montana and the Dakotas – more sheep and cattle than people, and not a heck of a lot of electoral votes. Masterson says the campaign's relying on TV ads for those."

Libby walked over to one of the beds and sat down. "That explains Virginia, not Richmond."

"According to Masterson, Stark's speech in Kanawha Plaza, which you can see from yonder window, by the way, is the only one this week where he's likely to be walking a rope line."

"Pressing the flesh as he goes, I assume."

"That's the whole point of having the rope line. There's no guarantee that *your* flesh will be among that

299

getting pressed, though. You said you don't have to touch him."

"I don't. Magic isn't an exact science – in fact, it isn't science at all, although math comes in handy sometimes. But if you can get me within, say, twenty feet, I should be able to tell if he's been anywhere near black magic."

Libby noticed that Morris was frowning. "What?" she said.

"As I was listening to you, a quote popped into my head, or part of a quote. 'When you look into the abyss, the abyss also looks into you.'"

"It's from Nietzsche," Libby said. "Um. Let me think a second." She closed her eyes, then recited, "'He who fights monsters should take care that he does not himself become a monster, for when you look into the abyss'... et cetera."

"I've always admired that memory of yours," Morris said. "So, within twenty feet or so, you'll know if Stark is playing for the bad guys. Question is, will he be able to tell that you're one of the good guys?"

"That hadn't occurred to me," Libby said pensively. "Yes, he probably will." She shrugged. "So what? It's not like he'll be able to do anything about it with all those people around, even if he were so inclined."

"Yeah, I guess," Morris said. He rubbed the burn scar on his neck. "But I'm leery about him knowing who you are. Once they get their mark on you..."

"I'm a big girl, Quincey, and a Witch of the White by choice. I'll take my chances – assuming there's a risk, which there probably isn't. I *am* a little surprised though that we're going to have only one chance to put ourselves near Stark. I thought getting up close and personal with the voters was what these guys lived for."

"It's our best chance this week," Morris said. "And considering what may be at stake, I figured we'd best not waste any time. Look here."

The screen of his laptop displayed the list of Stark's speaking engagements for the week, in various cities across Virginia. Each venue's name had comments typed under it.

"I put this together after talking to Masterson," Morris said. "Check it out – in Newport News, he's giving a speech at some big country club. Members only invited. He probably plans to hit them up for fat contributions. In Norfolk, he's speaking at the Lions Club breakfast, then the Rotary at lunch. Gotta be a member to get into either one."

"Couldn't Masterson get us in?"

"He says no. Apparently the Secret Service can only keep people out – known felons, cranks, people like that. The campaign decides who get in."

"How very cozy. So his only outdoor event is here in Richmond."

"Yep. And there's gonna be a rope line. If we get there early enough, we should be able to position ourselves in the front of the crowd, or at least pretty close. Well within twenty feet of Stark, I figure."

"And then we'll see," Libby said quietly.

"Then we'll see. We'll probably be standing for hours. I hope you brought comfortable shoes."

"So now that you're properly armed," Ashley said, "I assume it's time to go kill ourselves a Senator?"

"Looks like it. I bought that fancy rifle case to transport the weapon on a plane. But it looks like we can just drive to where we're going to pop him."

"Which would be where, exactly?"

"The Commonwealth of Virginia, which we visited just yesterday. Different part of it, though."

She looked over his shoulder at the computer screen. He tried not to let her soft breath on his neck distract him.

"Where are we going to do it?"

"Looks like it'll have to be Richmond. It's the only place where the son of a bitch is going to be speaking outdoors. He's got a rally planned for downtown in someplace called Kanawha Plaza. The rest of his schedule is all indoor stuff."

"Richmond it is, then. I assume we'll leave in the morning."

"You assume correctly. Stark speaks there the day after tomorrow. It'll be good to have an extra day to get ready."

"We'll need reservations." She signed theatrically. "I don't imagine there's anyplace nearly as nice as the Hay-Adams in Richmond."

"Don't be a snob. Richmond's a pretty nice town, as I remember. Besides – anywhere we stay, even the filthiest hovel, is a lot better than Hell, babe."

"Good point. Do you want me to find us a hotel in Richmond?"

"Already got one. No hovel, either. It's a nice place called the Crowne-with-an-e Plaza. And apart from what looks like pretty nice rooms, it offers another advantage."

"The suspense is killing me."

"It overlooks Kanawha Plaza – from a distance of about 500 yards."

"I just love it when you talk dirty!" She leaned over and kissed him, hard.

"We'll need reservations in a name other than Malachi Peters," he said, once her tongue was out of his mouth, "and a credit card in the new name for when we check in. Think you can help us out with that?"

"I don't see why not."

"One of the many things I love about the Internet is that a lot of hotels will not only let you make a reservation online – you can even reserve the room you want."

He clicked the mouse, and a diagram of the Crowne Plaza came up on the screen. Peters moved the cursor until it rested on one room. "Get this one – 1408. There's one floor above it, but it's all luxury suites, and they're booked for this week. I checked."

"You're looking to get high up."

"As high as I can, and the fourteenth floor should do just fine. Gives me a nice angle of fire. The trees are already budding down there, and I want to get above them. This'll do it."

She nodded approvingly. "So, if all goes well, we'll be able to put up the 'Mission Accomplished' banner the day after tomorrow."

"Yeah, I hope so." He turned in his chair and looked at her squarely. "And then what?"

"What do you mean?"

"Don't play dumb – you know what I mean. Do you drag me back to Hell as soon as the job's done?"

"I told you, Peters – I don't have any instructions about that."

"You also told me that if you did, you'd lie about it."

"Yeah, I did say that, didn't I?" She went over to the bed and flopped down on her back. "Let's assume, for the sake of discussion, that I really don't have any orders about what happens after."

303

"Okay – for the sake of discussion."

"But I might be able to make some educated guesses."

"Fine, let's hear those."

"I think Astaroth is going to have a lot on his plate, once certain high-level demons, including My Lord Satan Himself, see that Sargatanas is back in Hell, instead of in the White House, getting ready to blow up the world."

Peters nodded. "Yeah, there are factions, aren't there? That's what Astaroth said when he gave me my orders. I gather he represents the 'This is a really bad idea' faction."

"And he's got some powerful demons who agree with him. But by no means all. So, there's likely to be, shall we say, something of a fuss once Sargatanas gets back and explains how his mission was terminated, along with Senator Stark."

"How big a fuss are you talking about? Civil war? In Hell?"

"Why not? It happened once before, in –" She pointed up toward the ceiling. "You know."

Peters placed one arm on the back of his chair, and rested his chin on it. "Shit."

"There's no way to know for sure how it's all going to shake out, of course. But it's not an unreasonable scenario, what I just described."

"Astaroth might forget about us?"

"Let's face it, Peters, you and I are pretty small potatoes, in the grand scheme of things. There's no shortage of damned souls in Hell. Or of mid-rank demons, either."

"We'll become small potatoes – once we kill Stark and send Sargatanas back."

"Uh-huh. We wouldn't be ignored indefinitely, I expect. Astaroth – assuming his side wins this civil war that might not ever happen – would get around to us, eventually."

"Define 'eventually.'"

She held up her hands in the universal 'Beats the shit out of me' gesture. "A year. Ten years. A hundred years. Maybe a thousand."

"Get the fuck outta here."

"You, of all people, should know that time has a different meaning in Hell. When you're talking about eternity, what's a thousand years, more or less?"

"Or, your theory could be full of shit, and we might both find ourselves back in Hell within forty-eight hours from now, as they reckon time on this side."

"Entirely possible. Maybe even probable."

"Well, damn."

"My point exactly," Ashley said. She got up, went to the nightstand, and picked up the immense telephone directory that was kept in the bottom. She plopped it into her lap, opened it, and began turning pages quickly.

"What're you looking up?"

She raised her head to look at him, and there was an expression on her face he'd never seen there before. In a human, he might have called it melancholy. "As you said, we don't know what's going to happen to us, a couple of days from now." Then the mischievous grin he was familiar with reappeared. "It's our last night in Washington, and I've decided you deserve the treat I promised you." She went back to turning yellow pages and said, without looking up, "So I'm calling the Elegant Evenings escort service. What's your preference – blonde, brunette, or redhead?"

Chapter 30

THIS TIME STARK'S suite was at the Berkeley Hotel in Richmond. Mary Margaret Doyle came into the living room in a robe, her damp hair wrapped in a towel. Sargatanas sat on the couch, tapping the keys of his laptop and scowling.

"What're you doing?" she asked as she sat down in an armchair and added hastily, "If you don't mind my asking."

"Working on the draft of my new stump speech. Carney gave it to me this afternoon, and, as usual, it's a piece of shit. I don't know why Garrett hired that fool."

"He's supposed to be one of the best."

"Then let us hope that I never have to employ the services of the worst. I wonder what that would entail – first drafts scrawled in crayon on a paper bag?"

"You'll make it better, you always do. Your speeches have been getting favorable news coverage, for both substance and delivery. And it's coming from more than Fox news and the *Wall Street Journal*, this time."

"Yes, I've seen some of it. Several of the media nitwits seem to have noticed that Senator Stark's public speaking began to improve about six months ago."

She smiled at him. "Goodness, whatever could have caused that?"

"Goodness, as you know well, had nothing to do with it. And speaking of nitwits, what about this man Greene? Do you think he has the balls to carry out his latest assignment?"

Mary Margaret Doyle nodded judiciously. "I think so. I've frightened him pretty well. Of course, there are so many factors we can't control – such as whether Greene finds someone suitable and doesn't end up trying to hire a killer who's really an undercover cop. And if he does find an assassin, a real professional, there's the question of whether he'll be able to get the job done."

"You told Greene that there is a time factor."

"I told him to get it done within two weeks. But if it takes a little longer, I suppose we can live with that."

"As long as Leffingwell doesn't."

"Indeed. Even if he were to live, you might well win the nomination, you know. It's your time, now. You're peaking."

"That's true. But the less we leave to chance, the better. There is a great deal riding on this campaign."

"Only everything."

"Once he hires the assassin, Greene's usefulness to us has reached an end. He ceases to be an asset and becomes a liability, given all that he knows."

"I've been thinking about that. We'll have to come up with a suitable way to dispose of him."

"If it should prove feasible, would you like to do it?"

"Well, I hadn't, um –"

"Perhaps you could deal with him as you did that fucking priest. You'd enjoy that, wouldn't you?"

"I really don't know if I –"

"The smell of burned flesh as you run the blowtorch slowly along his body, mingling with the odor of shit and piss as he loses control of his sphincter muscles. The screaming, the begging for mercy, the calls for his mother…"

Her face was beet red. "You're… you're trying to turn me into a monster."

"Not at all, my dear. You were already a monster when we met. I'm simply giving you a chance to exercise your innate monstrosity without restraint – at least, occasionally."

"What do you mean, I was a monster?" she said, with some degree of indignation. "I had never done anything like that before."

"Oh, come, now. You willingly betrayed a man you had served with devotion for… how many years?"

"Eighteen," she said, the indignation fading. "Eighteen years."

"For eighteen years – a long time, as humans view such things. And you delivered him to me like a steer to a slaughterhouse."

"As you said, there are greater things at stake."

"Oh, indeed. The destruction of most of the human race, with you as Queen to rule over the rest with absolute power. Handing over a man you had known, perhaps even loved, for eighteen years seems a small price to pay, don't you think?"

"All right, all right, you win," she said, resting her head against the back of her chair to stare at the ceiling. "I'm a monster."

Several minutes went by. The only sounds in the room were the tapping of keys on Sargatanas's laptop and Mary Margaret Doyle's quiet crying.

Then he said, "I told you to find out where Masterson went while he was on leave."

She cleared her throat a couple of times, then said, in her brisk, businesslike voice, "Yes, I followed your directions and hacked into the major airlines' databases. It seems Agent Masterson flew nonstop to Austin, Texas, returning the next day."

"Is that where his mother lives?"

"I don't know – he's never said, at least where I could hear it. Do you want me to find out?"

Sargatanas thought briefly. "No, let it go. Even if he lied about visiting Mommy, it probably just means he went to Austin to get his rocks off. Unless he did both in the same place, and I understand that kind of behavior is more characteristic of the Southeastern United States than the Southwest."

"That's the stereotype, anyway. Do you know how they define a virgin in Mississippi?"

"I assume this is an attempt at humor. Tell me."

"It's a girl who can run faster than her brothers."

"An attitude of which I approve. But whether Masterson is a motherfucker in the literal sense of the term is of little consequence to us. If he'd made a flight to the Vatican, that might be cause for concern. But I don't see what harm can come to us from his trip to Austin."

"I expect you're right."

"Of course I am. Now get out of here, so I can focus on my speech without being distracted by your stupid crying."

She flinched as if he had slapped her, then got up without a word and walked swiftly toward her bedroom.

"And don't bother to get dressed," Sargatanas said. "I'll be using your body, later."

* * *

THE CROWNE PLAZA bellman, whose name tag said his name was Bruce, let Peters and Ashley into Room 1408 and pulled the baggage cart in behind him. As he unloaded their bags, he carried on a well-practiced monologue about the number of channels available on the room's TV, the hours of the hotel bar, and the number to call if they needed extra towels.

As Bruce picked up the long, steel case and looked for a place to put it, Peters said, "Go easy with that, okay? Bust my guitar, and I'm out of a job."

"I'll be very careful, sir." Bruce finally settled for gently depositing the case on the floor in front of the chest of drawers.

As Peters reached for his wallet to get Bruce's tip, Ashley said, "I need a shower. I hope you've got good water pressure here, Bruce."

"I think you'll find it's nice and strong, ma'am. No guest has ever complained about it, far as I know."

"Great," Ashley said, and pulled her sky-blue knit top over her head and tossed it aside. As usual, she neither wore nor needed a bra. She kicked off her shoes, then reached for the zipper of her gray woolen skirt. The garment fell away, revealing that Ashley wore a red thong underneath. A moment later, it joined the skirt on the carpet. There was nothing coquettish about Ashley's manner. She might have been alone in the room.

Stepping free of the thong, Ashley walked to the bathroom and closed the door without a backward glance. Peters pulled a twenty from his wallet and gave it to Bruce, who was blinking rapidly with the struggle to keep his face impassive.

"Uh, thank you, uh, sir. Hope you and uh, the lady have a real pleasant stay with us." Bruce grabbed the empty baggage cart and got out of there, doubtless in a hurry to tell his co-workers about the visual treat he'd just been given. Peters wondered if they'd believe him.

The door closed behind Bruce, and a moment later, Peters heard the sound of the shower. The bathroom door opened to reveal Ashley, hands on hips, in all her nude glory. "Care to join me?"

"Don't mind if I do," Peters said and started unbuttoning his shirt.

As he approached the shower curtain, Ashley's voice said, "You might want to grab another cake of soap, sweetie. These little things are barely big enough for one person."

Peters unwrapped a bar of soap and joined Ashley. As he tried to get enough water on him to lather up he said, "What was the strip tease about? Were you messing with Bruce, just for fun?"

"What's wrong with fun?" she said, rubbing soap over her breasts. "But I did have an ulterior motive."

"Which was?" Peters washed under his arms.

"Your little story about the guitar wasn't bad, but it called attention to the case, which made it *more* likely he'd remember it, not less, if the FBI should ask him later."

"Hmm. Hadn't thought of that."

"So I, making the immense sacrifice of baring my fair body to a total stranger, have guaranteed that's the only thing he will remember." In a perfect imitation of Bruce's voice, she said, "'Yeah, there was this guy with her, I guess, and they had a bunch of luggage, but dude, you should have seen the ass on that blonde!'"

"That was a good idea. And he's right, too – about your ass, I mean."

"Why thank you, kind sir," she said, and turned to face him. A few moments later he said, "What are you doing?"

She gave the low chuckle that never failed to give him goosebumps. "Assuming that's not a rhetorical question, I'm thanking you for the compliment by helping you wash up. Or would you rather wash this part yourself?"

"Uh, no, you go ahead, you're doing fine."

Later, when they were dried and dressed, Ashley noticed Peters studying the frame of one of the windows.

"Checking for termites?" she said.

"Looking to see if this window will open. It won't, of course, I was just being an optimist. They don't do this in Europe – at least, they didn't used to – but the windows in American hotels don't open. That was true thirty years ago, too. You're supposed to use the air conditioner if you want to cool off."

She thought for a second. "Jumpers."

"You got it. If you're going to practice defenestration, the management would rather you do it someplace else. Even if there aren't liability issues, it would probably upset the other guests to see some guy splattered all over the sidewalk."

"And the hotels' caution makes it hard to shoot somebody from your room, too," Ashley said. "How inconsiderate of them."

She went to the window and tapped the glass with a knuckle. "We could break it."

He shook his head. "Too much noise, plus broken glass on the sidewalk."

"Not if you use the burglar's technique. Get some masking tape –"

"I know what you're talking about. I used it myself a few times, when I was with the Company. Tape the glass thoroughly, then break it and remove the shards by hand."

"Exactly."

"That solves most of the problems, except one. After we're gone, anybody who checks the room will know instantly that this is the one where the shot was fired that killed Stark."

"Hmmm. You're thinking it might interfere with our getaway." A smile warmed the coldly beautiful face. "I love saying things like 'getaway.' Makes me feel like Bonnie Parker – who was a mean, ugly bitch, by the way. Nothing like Fay Dunaway."

"I guess you'd know."

"Indeed I would. Oh, and you're much better looking than Clyde Barrow was, and about three times as smart."

He winked at her as he used one of her favorite words. "Flatterer."

Her smile grew even brighter for a second, then she got serious again. "So, okay, we don't break the window. I trust you have something else in mind."

"After lunch, we'll find a hardware store and get the right size of screwdriver, and maybe a couple of other tools. Once the maid's done cleaning the room tomorrow, well take the window out of its frame – and put it back again, when we're done."

She frowned. "Putting it back's going to take us a while. Once Stark's down, I figured you'd want to waste no time in, as they say, getting out of Dodge."

"Yeah, I've been thinking about that, too. Come on, sit down."

Peters sat on the edge of one of the double beds. Ashley sat cross-legged on the other, opposite him.

"Running is what they'll expect us to do," Peters said.

"With good reason. Killing Stark is going to be like hitting a hornet's nest with a stick. Cops will be swarming everywhere. But you have something different in mind?"

"We stay right here. Act innocent."

"Peters, I haven't been innocent for a span of time longer than you can imagine."

"Don't be so literal-minded. At this distance, there's no way they can trace back the bullet's trajectory. They'll have an idea of the general direction the shot came from, but that's all." He made a head gesture toward the window. "And you may have noticed that there's a hell of a lot of hotels and office buildings in this part of town. The bullet could have come from any of them."

"Still – we'll be questioned."

"Sure – us, and thousands of other people. But my ID's good. It's a product of Hell, Inc. – it ought to be. How about you? Can you create something credible for yourself?"

"Sure," she said, nodding slowly. "That won't be a problem."

"It's gonna be a nightmare for them, trying to get enough cops – federal, state, or local – in here to do the job. Unless we look or act suspicions, I figure we'll spend ten minutes, tops, with some detective who's already thinking ahead to his next interview. But I'll tell you who's gonna get a closer, harder look."

"People on their way out of town right after the shooting, whether they knew about it or not."

"Uh-huh. The cops'll set up roadblocks, and search every car. Be kinda embarrassing to have them find a silenced rifle in our trunk."

"If we stay here, they'll find the gun, too."

"Not if you help, they won't. You can create illusions, right?"

314

"You know I can."

"Can you... I'm not sure how to put this. Can you make it look like there's no rifle here, when there is one?"

"Hmmm." She rested her chin on one hand for a bit, then said, "What you're describing isn't an illusion but just the opposite. Given time to prepare, I could create a variation of the Tarnhelm effect."

"I won't pretend I know what that is."

"It's magic that makes the eye avoid the object you don't want seen. The rifle could be in plain sight, but no one would consciously notice it – which is just as good as not having it there at all."

"You said 'given time.' Is from now to tomorrow afternoon enough?"

"More than enough. It should take me no more than a couple of hours."

"Very nice. I knew there was a reason for having you around. Besides the mind-blowing sex, I mean."

She grinned at him. "Flatterer."

Peters got to his feet. "So, we go get some lunch, then look for a hardware store."

Ashley was putting her shoes on. "Let's eat at a seafood place. I find that I just *adore* shrimp."

LIBBY CHASTAIN WAS alone in the elevator as it took her to the fourteenth floor. After dinner at a nice Italian place down the street, Quincey had offered to spring for the price of one of the hotel's many pay-per-view movies. After scrolling through the selections twice, they had finally agreed on the latest James Bond movie, *Risico*.

They'd each lain on one of the double beds in Quincey's room, the lights out, watching Daniel Craig save the world again, and making occasional sarcastic comments about the movie. Just over two hours later, the elevator deposited Libby at her floor. As she walked to her room, she found herself wondering what would have happened down there if Quincey had invited her to join him on his bed. Would she have agreed, or stayed where she was? And if she'd gone over to lie on the bed next to him, then what?

Libby shook her head, as if to drive stupid thoughts out of it. Sex with Quincey, and the resulting emotional entanglement, would spoil what she'd long regarded as the perfect relationship, plain proof that a man and a woman who liked each other could work closely together without hopping into bed. Getting romantically involved with Quincey was about the worst idea she could have.

Wasn't it?

Libby was about halfway down the corridor that led to her room when she realized what she had been psychically smelling for the last few seconds, while her mind was occupied with goopy thoughts of Quincey Morris.

Black magic.

Libby slowed her pace, a wary expression on her face. The psychic 'smell' was getting stronger as she walked. She reached into her shoulder bag for a strong defensive charm she had in there, just in case.

Is it Stark? Is he staying here – in this hotel, on this floor?

Libby quickly rejected the idea. She knew Stark had Secret Service protection. Surely there would be at least one agent outside his door, perhaps more. Libby could see that she was the only living soul in the hall right now.

316

She focused her concentration, trying to notice changes in the strength of the psychic sensation as she walked. Like a real odor, it became stronger the closer you got to it.

Unconsciously using the words from a childhood game, Libby thought, *Getting warmer, warmer, warmer, warmer still, now colder, colder…*

By the time Libby had reached her room, the sense of black magic was barely perceptible. If it had been this faint the whole way along, she might not even have noticed it at all.

She turned around, and slowly walked back the way she'd come. Gradually the stink of evil grew stronger in her mind. *Warner, warmer, really warm now, colder, colder…*

Libby stopped and went back a couple of steps. Yes, this was it. The emanation of black magic was strongest right outside Room 1408.

Goddess save us, who is in there? WHAT is in there?

Then Libby remembered what Quincey had said about looking into the abyss, and the abyss looking back. She drew in a breath sharply. If she could sense whoever was in 1408, there was a good chance he or she (*or It*) could sense her, as well.

She turned and walked briskly toward the elevator.

INSIDE 1408, MALACHI Peters lay on his back, grunting, as Ashley demonstrated to him the pleasures offered by the Reverse Cowgirl position.

"I'll have better control over my hip movements," she'd said, "and I can put my hands on your knees for balance and leverage, if I need it. Plus, you can grab my ass, if you're so inclined. You'll love it."

"I think I'll be so inclined," Peters had said.

As he lay there, loving it indeed, eyes closed and breath coming in gasps, he suddenly noticed that Ashley had stopped moving. Peters opened his eyes and saw that she was looking toward the door. He could feel the increased tension in her body.

"What?" he said, his voice husky. "Something wrong?"

She stayed that way, like a hunting dog on point, for a second or two more. Then she sighed, faced front, and began moving her hips again.

"It's nothing," she said. "For a second, I thought... It's nothing."

Chapter 31

"IT'S FUCKING BLACK *magic*, Quincey," Libby said, all thoughts of romance driven from her head. "Nothing else smells like that. Nothing."

Morris nodded slowly and scratched his chin. "I agree with you that it can't be Stark, since there's no Secret Service types around up there. I could contact Masterson and ask him, but he'd just be telling us what we already know."

Libby hugged herself, as if from a sudden chill. "Who could it be, then? And what are they doing here?"

"Good questions, both of them. What you sensed – it doesn't mean that they were in there casting spells, does it? Their very presence would announce itself to you, even if they were just watching *Wheel of Fortune*, right?"

"I think so. But based on the strength of the manifestation, this was no dabbler, Quincey. This person, whoever it is, knows the fire."

Morris took a turn around the room, which didn't take him long. "I suppose it's possible this could have something to do with Stark, if our suspicions about him are correct. Or, it could be something innocuous – as innocuous as black magic ever gets, I mean. Even black magicians have jobs, most of them. Evil doesn't pay all that well, so most of them do it as a sideline…"

"Yes, I know that much is true."

"Maybe the guy – or woman – sells industrial casting materials, and he's got appointments with people at three or four of Richmond's biggest factories tomorrow. Then he'll go back home and start sacrificing small animals again. It could be something like that."

"I suppose it could. I hope that's all it is." She hesitated, "Quincey, I don't want you to misinterpret this, but… can I stay here tonight? It's not that I'm afraid, exactly. But if I bed down in my room, knowing what's down the hall from me, I won't sleep a wink, I know it. And I need to be sharp for our little experiment tomorrow."

"Sure, Libby, it's no problem at all. *Mi casa, su casa*, as it were. You've already used the bed near the window. Take that one, if you want."

She gave him an embarrassed smile. "Thank you for humoring me. Now I have to ask you to indulge me a little further."

He looked at her curiously. "Sure, whatever you want."

She held out the card key for her room. "Would you mind going up to my room and bringing down my stuff? I don't want to have to sleep in my clothes, or use your toothbrush."

"I'll be happy to, Libby," he said, taking the little plastic card from her.

"Don't worry about picking and choosing. Just throw it all in the suitcase, and I'll sort it out later."

"Sure, no problem." Morris started toward the door.

"I'd go myself," Libby said, "but I was remembering what you said earlier about the abyss staring back, and all that. If I can sense *them*, it's possible *they* can sense *me*. I've already walked past that door twice tonight, and nothing's happened. But if I do it one more time…"

"'Once is happenstance, twice is coincidence, the third time is enemy action'," Morris said, the way you do when quoting somebody.

"Who said that?" Libby asked.

"A fella named Auric Goldfinger once said it to James Bond."

THE MORNING OF Senator Howard Stark's speech dawned cloudy and cool, but the cloud cover was expected to dissipate by afternoon, allowing the sun to bring temperatures up to around 60 degrees.

The article in the morning's *Richmond Times-Dispatch* said the gates to Kanawha Plaza would open at noon, and the campaign rally would start at 3:00, to include music from the Smoky Mountain Seven, a local country band hired for the occasion, along with an invocation by the minister of the town's biggest Southern Baptist church, a mass reciting of the Pledge of Allegiance by all those present, speeches by a couple of local dignitaries and, just before Stark's appearance, a group singing of the Star Spangled Banner.

Stark was scheduled to speak at 4:00, a fact noted with considerable interest in at least two of the Crowne-Plaza's guest rooms.

"Did you get any sleep at all?" Quincey Morris asked, over the room service breakfast he was sharing with Libby Chastain.

"I managed a few hours," Libby said. "Despite the fact that my roommate snores."

"Sorry about that. Hope it didn't keep you awake."

"No, I found it rather soothing, actually. Kind of like sleeping with a fan on, which I used to do when I was a kid. But I had preparations to make for today."

"I know," Morris said. Several times during the night, he had awakened to find Libby, in the soft light cast from a table lamp with a towel draped over it, sitting or kneeling on the floor. Sometimes, Morris recalled, she was chanting softly. On other occasions, she was drawing elaborate designs on the carpet with different colors of chalk. At least once, she had a candle burning.

"I was worried that the maid would have a fit when she came in and saw what I'd done to the carpet," Libby said, "but I was able to get most of the chalk up with a wet towel. You can barely see my artwork now."

Morris looked, and found that she was right.

"I had more to do than I'd originally planned," Libby said, "given what I found lurking on the fourteenth floor."

"What were you working on?"

"Several different kinds of protection spells, some wardings, and a couple of others which may or may not prove useful. One of the things I did was to enhance my ability to perceive black magic, just in case we can't get too close to Stark. Until the spell wears off, I'll not only smell black magic when it's around – I'll be able to *see* it, in the form of something that will look to me like thin black smoke."

"Sounds appropriate. How long is the spell good for?"

"It'll fade away sometime tonight. Plenty of time for us to assess Stark's nature."

"Paper says the gates open at noon. "I'm not looking forward to standing around for three hours, but if we want to be at the front of the rope line, that's the only way to do it."

"I know. I read the article while you were in the shower. The part that I'm not looking forward to starts at 3:00."

"The rally, with its attendant rhetoric, religion, and rednecks?"

"I don't mind watching preachers lead people in prayer, but it's the smug, self-satisfying way they usually do it that irks me. Also I've never understood where the idea came from that only conservatives are patriotic."

"Well, there's always the music," Morris said with a tiny smile. "The Smoky Mountain Seven. That should be loads of fun."

"Uh-huh. My idea of country music is the Dixie Chicks or Mary-Chapin Carpenter. Wish I'd remembered my iPod – although, come to think of it, I wouldn't bring it over there, even if I had."

"Why not? You could be grooving to the Dixie chicks while everybody else is entranced by the authentic country sounds of the Smoky Mountain Seven, and nobody would know the difference."

"I don't want to compromise my alertness," Libby said. "Not today. I don't know what's likely to happen, but I want to be ready to deal with it, which means I need to be aware of my surroundings at all times."

"You're still worried about the black magician upstairs, or whatever it is."

"Bet your ass I am. That's why I did a Far Vision spell on myself last night, as well."

323

"Far... oh, you mean that thing where –" Morris curled his hands into circles, then put them up to his eyes, like binoculars.

"That's it," Libby said. I figured finding someplace that would carry real field glasses might take us too much time and trouble. The spell will serve quite nicely – for as long as we're likely to need it."

Under the Far Vision spell, Libby could bring her cupped hands to her eyes like Morris had done – only for her the effect would be as if she held a real pair of high-power binoculars, which would adjust to her vision automatically.

"You *have* been busy," Morris said.

Libby shrugged. "Could be it's what you suggested last night – just one of the bad guys on vacation, or traveling for business. But I'm not taking that as a working assumption."

"Probably a good idea. 'You have to plan for the enemy's capabilities, not his intentions.'"

"What's that, another James Bond quote?"

"No, it's from Sun Tzu. *The Art of War*."

"Appropriate choice," Libby said solemnly.

THE KNOCK ON the door of room 1408 came a little after 9:00, followed immediately by a female voice from the hall calling, "Housekeeping!"

"Come on in!" Malachi Peters responded.

There was the buzz of a card key in the lock, and the door opened to reveal a heavyset black woman with short, straight hair, clad in one of the tan outfits the hotel required its maid staff to wear.

"I'm here to clean the room," she announced unnecessarily, "but if y'all want, I can check back later on."

"No, you go ahead," Peters told her, and got up from his chair. "We were just going down to breakfast, anyway." He and Ashley left the woman to her work, squeezing past the immense cart she had parked just outside their room.

Over scrambled eggs in the Pavilion Café, Peters said, "She came to service the room about this time yesterday, so I was hoping today would be a repeat."

Ashley nodded. "Gives us plenty of time to… do what we need to."

"I saw that you stored our guitar case in the closet. After watching you do your stuff last night, I figured we could leave it out anyplace."

Even though both spoke softly, they had agreed that discretion in what they said publicly was probably a good idea.

"Yes and no," Ashley said, slicing into a sausage patty. "Her eye won't perceive it, no matter where it is. But if she trips over it, or whacks it with the vacuum cleaner, that's kind of going to force the issue. No point in making things complicated if we don't have to."

"No, you're right. It's gonna get complicated enough, with… everything else that's on the agenda today."

They had the elevator to themselves for the ride back up to 14. "It just occurred to me," Peters said, "that you don't need to sleep, but you eat. Doesn't seem consistent."

"I don't have to eat, either. But I enjoy food, so why not? 'You only go around once in life, so you gotta grab all the gusto you can.'"

"I remember that. Some old beer commercial, right?"

"Uh-huh. I don't like beer, though. Too bitter."

"Yeah, most American beer tastes like refrigerated piss."

She glanced at him, smiling a little. "And you know what that tastes like? Peters, you have depths I never would have suspected."

He reached over and delivered a brisk slap to her denim-clad ass. "I was just hypothesizing. Bitch."

"Bastard."

"Cunt."

"Cocksucker."

"Termagent."

"Degenerate."

The opening elevator door put an end to their obscene banter.

As they walked to their room, he said. "I'll have to get you to try German beer. I mean the *real* stuff. We may make a convert out of you yet."

"Fine with me. I'll meet you in Stuttgart's best *bierstube*, whatever that happens to be, um, 93 years from today. At 3:00 p.m. local time. How's that?"

"Assuming you, me, and Stuttgart are all still here, you've got yourself a date, lady."

Inside their freshly-cleaned room, Peters went to the window overlooking Kanawha Plaza and pulled the drapes aside. Even without looking through the rifle scope, he could see that work crews were busy on and around the stage that had been erected for the week's political events – and which would be torn down, probably this weekend.

Maybe not, though. Starting later today, it's gonna be a crime scene. The cops may want it left in place a while longer, while they pretend to be doing something useful with it.

He turned around to find Ashley lying naked on one of the beds, looking at him.

"So, what do you think?" she said in what he thought

of as her *Body Heat* voice. "Care to grab a little more gusto before we go to work on that window?"

"You're greedy for your pleasures, lady."

"Maybe because I'm not sure how much time is left," she said seriously. "For either of us."

"Nympho," he said, not without affection.

"Satyr," she replied.

"Slut."

"Pervert."

"Slattern."

"Libertine."

"I have to take a leak."

"Then go take it," she said. "*And hurry*."

THE MAN WHO was known in some circles as The Grocer's Boy believed in the value of research. You could never have too much information about a target.

Most of the problems he was called upon to deal with (that's how he thought of his work – as 'solving problems') could not be addressed by walking up to some guy's table in a restaurant, going *Bang! Bang!* with a .38 and walking out again. If such a simple approach was likely to be successful, a client could find somebody who'd do it for a lot less than the fifty thousand that The Grocer's Boy charged.

In any case, he would never carry out a job in such a reckless fashion. Shooting somebody in a restaurant was full of hazards – witnesses, potential heroes, undercover cops, surveillance cameras – the list was almost endless. The Grocer's Boy enjoyed gangster films, but he thought that most of them represented his profession about as accurately as those old John Wayne movies portrayed the settling of the West.

And so, research. A U.S. Senator spends a lot of time in the public eye – especially if, like Bob Leffingwell, he's running for President. There were hundreds of news items, feature stories, and interviews concerning the man – and most of these were available online. It was a lot to get through, but The Grocer's Boy was a fast reader. He could also multitask – reading, say, a *New Yorker* profile of the Senator while a CNN story about him played on his computer screen.

That was how he came to be reading an article from *The Economist* while half-watching a recording of the Senator being interviewed by Charlie Rose. But he gave his full attention to the computer when he heard Charlie Rose say, "For a man of sixty-four, you seem to be in remarkable shape."

"I work out every day, if I can," the Senator said, "and I watch what I eat, even though it means passing up a lot of the foods I love. As it is, I still get heartburn pretty regularly."

"There are prescription meds that are pretty good for that," Rose said.

"I suppose there are, but my heartburn isn't that serious. I use Gaviscon – I don't know if I can say the brand name on TV –"

"This is cable," Rose said, waving a gracious hand. "Feel free."

"Anyway, I always have a bottle of it handy. Works like a charm."

"You don't like to take prescription drugs, do you?"

"Not if I don't need them, of course not," Leffingwell said. "Most prescriptions are seriously overpriced, even if you have good insurance, like I do."

"Is that why you gave those top executives of Big Pharma such a hard time during the hearings…"

There was more. With Charlie Rose, there was always a *lot* more. But The Grocer's Boy didn't pay attention. He sat back in his desk chair, thinking. Then he logged off, stood, and went to fetch his car keys. He knew there was a big chain drugstore just a few blocks away.

Twenty minutes later, he was back, and in his kitchen. Unlike many other over-the-counter antacids, Gaviscon came in only one size bottle, and there was no generic version available, both of which made life easier – well, easier for The Grocer's Boy. Shorter for Bob Leffingwell, if the plan he was formulating worked out.

Since he'd been told that three drops was the lethal dose, and the little glass bottle Nestor Greene had given him contained much more than that, he had plenty of the deadly liquid to experiment with.

He opened one of the bottles of Gaviscon he'd bought and used the hypodermic needle to let three drops fall into the thick, white liquid. Then he shook it vigorously, as the directions said to do before using, and poured about half the contents into a short, wide glass, the kind some people call an Old Fashioned glass.

He took another bottle of Gaviscon from the drugstore's plastic bag, shook it, and poured the unadulterated liquid into another glass of the same size. He studied the two glasses, and their contents, closely.

Color: identical

Aroma: identical

He knew better than to check them for flavor. Besides, if the poison affected the taste, by the time the Senator realized it, he would have already swallowed the dose and be on his way to cardiac arrest. The Grocer's Boy doubted they would have given him a drug with a strong taste, anyway. It defeated the purpose.

He wanted to see if the passage of time would affect the adulterated liquid. He let everything sit there for twenty-four hours. That should be plenty long enough.

Color: identical

Aroma: identical

He poured the contents of both glasses into the sink, rinsed them, and placed them in the dishwasher. Then he brought two more clean glass of the same type from a cabinet. He wanted to know if sitting in the bottle, away from open air, would affect the liquid in any noticeable way.

He poured the Gaviscon remaining in each bottle into the squat glasses and examined the result.

Color: identical

Aroma: identical

As he washed the results of his second experiment down the drain, The Grocer's boy gave a small nod of satisfaction. He had the means to solve the problem.

What he needed now was access.

Chapter 32

THE SECRET SERVICE agent at the door of Stark's suite, as per standing instructions, used his card key to admit Fernando Garrett into the *sanctum sanctorum*. There was no one in the suite's living room, so Garrett called out, tentatively, "Senator?"

"In here." The familiar voice came from Stark's bedroom, but when Garrett walked in, he still didn't see his boss. More quietly, he repeated, "Senator?"

"I'm in here." This came through the partly-open door of the bathroom. "Something I ate last night seems to have disagreed with me. To answer the question you're about to ask, no, it won't prevent me from giving the speech."

"Glad to hear that, sir," Garret said, "Although I'm sorry to learn that you're not feeling well. Do you want me to send out for some Pepto-Bismol, or something?"

"I have some of that, of which I have consumed the better part of a bottle since last night. I'll be all right. In the meantime, I know time is short. Say whatever you came to tell me – I can hear you just fine."

This was not the first time in his political career that Fernando Garrett had carried on a conversation through the half-open door of a bathroom. Some of his clients had such bad stage fright that they'd tossed their cookies before every major speech or public event – although the idea that Howard Stark would be feeling nervous about something was a notion Garrett found absurd. The man was a rock.

"We've got some new numbers in," Garrett said to the doorway, "and they're very encouraging. You're ahead of Leffingwell in Virginia by three points, and nationally by two – although that second figure is within the margin of error, so it's hard to say for sure."

From inside the bathroom, Stark groaned loudly.

"Senator? It's still pretty good news."

"I know," Stark's disembodied voice said. "That was the diarrhea talking. Go on."

"In the five primaries set for next weekend – Arizona, Massachusetts, Michigan, Ohio, and Rhode Island – You're ahead of Leffingwell in two, less than four points behind him in two more, and your only third place is in Arizona, which is practically Martinez's back yard."

"He's still strong, despite the so-called bimbo eruption?"

"Yes, sir, they like him down there. First Latino to make a serious run at the Presidency, and all that. But the scandal has hurt him some, nationally. The numbers prove that."

"All right, thanks. How long do we have?"

"We need to leave in five minutes, sir, if you want to be behind the podium on time."

"No problem. I'll—uhh!"

"Senator? If you need a little more time, I can probably –"

"No, it's okay, Garrett. I feel better now. I'll wash up and join you in the hall in a couple of minutes."

"Very good, Senator. I'll see you shortly." Garrett turned and went out, and a few seconds later came the sound of the suite's door opening and closing.

Less than a minute later, the suite door opened and closed again as Stark left to give his speech to the assembled throng in Kanawha Plaza, and whatever else awaited him that afternoon.

A little later, Mary Margaret Doyle appeared in the doorway of Stark's bathroom, the knees of her blue business suit dirty and her makeup a ruin. She walked a little unsteadily across the living room and toward her own bathroom, intending to wash her face, repair her makeup, and gargle away half a bottle's worth of Listerine. Then she would try to find a Secret Service agent to drive her to the rally.

LIBBY CHASTAIN LEANED sideways and said in Quincey Morris's ear, "Pity that I was so busy with other things last night that I forget to figure out a spell for sore feet – that, and maybe a potion for an uncomfortably full bladder."

Morris tilted back his hat, which kept sliding down over his eyes. It was a straw boater with images of Stark, the American eagle, and the flag alternating on a banner that circled the crown.

Their strategy of ultra-early arrival at the park had paid off. The two of them stood just behind a length of cord wrapped in red, white, and blue velvet. It was one of a long series of such barriers stretched between portable metal poles that ran the length of the macadam-covered walkway, opposite the cascading fountain that was the Kanawha Plaza Corporation's pride and joy. Uniformed police officers strolled up and down the length of the rope line, to keep over-eager Stark supporters from crossing the insubstantial barrier and posing a security risk. When Stark came by, of course, he would be accompanied by the Secret Service detail.

"Are you going to be okay?" Morris asked.

Libby gave him a tired smile. "Sure, I'm just bitching. A woman's right, you know – I think it's in the manual."

"A Woman's Operating Manual? Now *there's* a book I'd like to read, sometime."

"No chance, buster. It's strictly F.F.E.O."

"Meaning?"

"For Female Eyes Only. Anyway, what's a little discomfort compared to saving the world – or whatever it is we're doing here."

There were vendors everywhere selling Stark campaign memorabilia, and Morris had suggested that he and Libby get some on their way into the plaza. "Protective coloration," he'd called it.

So Morris had his straw hat, and they each wore a button nearly the size of a saucer, featuring a photo of Stark looking resolute, with words around the edges following the button's contours. Above Stark's picture it read, 'Howard – the President we need NOW.' Below the image were the words, 'It's the STARK truth.' Libby also had a smaller button pinned to the light jacket she wore. Its message, superimposed over an image of the flag, was 'Make the STARK choice.'

She saw Morris motioning to a vendor who was making his way slowly through the crowd. He was blocking her view, so Libby couldn't see what the man was selling. She did observe Morris handing over money in return for another button that he pinned to his shirt. Then he turned around so Libby could see it.

The button featured an artist's rendering of a demon – nothing remotely realistic, just the cute, Halloween version in red with a long tail and pitchfork. But the face wasn't a cartoon demon. It was Howard Stark's photo, with red horns added by the artist. The caption along the bottom read 'GIVE 'EM HELL, HOWIE!'

Libby and Morris looked at each other, the button representing a lot of things they couldn't discuss while surrounded by so many people. Morris leaned toward Libby and asked "Bad taste?"

She looked him in the eyes. "I hope not," she said. "I really hope not."

The rally started punctually at 3:00, and it was a little less awful than what Libby had been expecting – but only a little.

The Smoky Mountain Seven (unaccountably consisting of six musicians) were better than the venue would have suggested, the preacher was predictably sanctimonious, the two local politicos surprisingly brief. The recitation of the Pledge of Allegiance was uneventful, 'The Star Spangled Banner' was sung enthusiastically if not well, and then it was time for the great man himself.

Senator Howard Warren Stark, (R-Ohio), looking tan and robust, was escorted to the podium by a man wearing a suit, sunglasses, and an earpiece.

Stark stepped up to the microphone and adjusted it upward for his height. Then, in temporary abandonment of his Yankee origins, he shouted over the applause and cheering, "HEY, RICHMOND! HOW Y'ALL DOIN'?"

The crowd, as they say, went wild.

REMOVING THE SIXTEEN long screws that held the window in its frame was a piece of cake compared to the task of

335

moving the chest of drawers so that it was lined up with the aperture they'd created by taking the glass down.

Peters had been insistent. "Prone position's the most stable, and with sniping, stability is everything."

"But it's going to be a huge pain in the ass getting it over here with so little room for maneuver. And I can't just levitate the fucking thing, you know. Maybe if you'd said something yesterday, I could've tried putting a spell together, but as it is, we're gonna have to do the hard way. It's stupid, Peters."

"No, Ashley, what would be stupid is not doing everything possible to ensure that I make the shot. Firing offhand – standing upright – is the least stable and that makes it the last resort."

"It was good enough for Lee Harvey Oswald."

"Is that right? Oswald really did it, huh? The conspiracy nuts were all wrong."

"I didn't say he managed it all by himself," she said, "and don't change the subject."

"You're the one who changed it." Part of Peters's mind was detached enough to marvel that here he was, arguing with a millennia-old creature from Hell as if he were having a fight with his girlfriend.

"Look, Ashley, I'm not doing this to piss you off. I don't know what distance Oswald fired from, but it can't have been any 500 meters. Firing offhand is the least reliable position. Prone is best, believe me. The whole body supports the weapon. Kneeling and sitting are both more or less in the middle, and the middle isn't good enough, at his range. The sooner we get started, the sooner I can start letting my arms rest from the strain of moving furniture."

"Why can't you use the desk? It's already *near* the fucking window."

"It's too small. Half my body would be hanging over the edge. It's gotta be the chest of drawers."

"Shit!" Ashley spat the word. She'd walked over to the hole in the wall and stared over at Kanawha Plaza, hands on hips. Finally, she'd turned away, and her facial expression was resigned. "All right, let's get it fucking over with."

And so they had, with Ashley cursing the whole way. She was profane in a number of languages, including one that Peters recognized as the tongue spoken by demons.

Even with all the drawers removed, the chest of drawers was extremely difficult to move around. It took forty-five sweaty, profanity-filled minutes, but finally the immense piece of furniture was in position.

"Satisfied?" Ashley asked, giving the clear impression that his answering "No" would be instantly fatal.

"It's perfect, Ashley. Thank you."

She began undressing, which never took her long. "I'm going to take a shower. *Don't* bother to join me."

When the bathroom door closed behind her, Peters shook his head and said, quietly, "Women."

He reminded himself what she really was, and tried to stop thinking of her as a woman, even though she was acting very human at the moment.

He started flexing his arms slowly, to help the muscles relax from the strain of lifting and putting down the chest of drawers, over and over. He'd had enough sense not to remind Ashley that they were going to have to put the beast back in position, once he had killed Stark. He wanted to live long enough to do his job.

Still flexing, Peters walked over to the rectangular hole in the wall where the window had been. None of the nearby buildings came up this high, or taking the window out would have been unacceptably risky. He stared across at Kanawha Plaza, which was already starting to fill up with people. *Five hundred meters. Shit.*

He hadn't checked his watch when Ashley huffed into the bathroom, but it didn't seem to him very long before her voice came through the closed door, over the hiss of the shower.

"Peters?"

"Yes, dear."

"Get your ass in here."

When he was naked and under the water with her, she put her hands on his hips and tilted her head to look up at him. Since she was almost his height, not much of a tilt was necessary. "This body they gave me seems to come with human emotions, too," she said. "Astaroth's idea of a joke, perhaps. How do you humans *stand* it?"

"Guess we just take them for granted."

"Well, I've been acting a little *too* human – possibly to the detriment of our mission. If I were capable of apologizing to a mere human, which I'm not, I'd be doing it now. Okay?"

He grinned at her. "Okay."

She pulled him up against her, her erect nipples tickling his chest. "I want to ask you something, seriously," she said. "Would getting off now make it easier for you to shoot straight later, or more difficult? Say the word, and I'll make myself look like a repulsive old hag who you wouldn't fuck on a dare. I can always change back to my gorgeous, sexy self later. Or do you think it would relax you – coming, I mean?"

"I never had the opportunity to make the choice before," he said. "The CIA didn't send sexy demons along as assistants when I had to use a rifle in the old days."

338

"I might take exception to *assistant*, but go on."

"It'll be at least two hours before I have to pull the trigger." He grinned at her again. "This *coming* you were talking about – it can't hurt, and could maybe help."

"You don't know how glad I am to hear that," she said softly, her face inches from his own. "Maybe emotions aren't such a bad idea, after all."

Chapter 33

AFTER DELIVERING HIS redneck-style greeting, Stark stood there smiling, waiting for the cheering and applause to die down.

Look at them – their pale faces all in a row, like sheep, ready for slaughter.

He held up his hands, asking for quiet. Eventually, the crowd let him have some.

"I can't tell you what a pleasure it is to be here in the Commonwealth of Virginia. I spend so much time in Washington, I almost forgot what *real* people look like!"

More applause, cheering, whistles and rebel yells greeted this, as he knew they would – he had used the line in a hundred different places already, with the same result. In time, relative silence returned.

"And it's real people, people like you and your friends and neighbors, that this campaign is all about."

The cheers and applause were weaker now. The sheep were getting tired. Time to give them something to listen to passively, until he got to the next carefully-scripted applause line.

"Because, you know, it's real people who are suffering, in this great land of ours. People whose jobs have been shipped overseas, or downsized, or just left to wither and die by Wall Street fat cats who just get fatter and fatter, while everyday men and women's lives and bank accounts get leaner and leaner."

The Wall Street fat cats had given millions to Stark's campaign, and would give millions more. They didn't mind being called names out here in Hicksville. They knew what Stark was *really* about – or they thought they did.

"After eight years of socialism at home and cowardice abroad, the choices remaining to us…"

IN ROOM 1408 of the Crowne Plaza, Malachi Peters, facedown atop the chest of drawers, settled the butt of the Remington into the hollow of his shoulder and waited for his heart rate to slow. He was breathing slowly and regularly, and that would soon tamp down the adrenaline rush that occurs in most people when they get ready to kill somebody. There are some who do not experience this excitement. They are called psychopaths.

Peters closed one eye and with the other looked through the scope and its mil dot reticle, which was apparently what everybody was shooting with these days instead of crosshairs. Peters had to admit it was an improvement over what he'd used thirty-some years ago as a CIA assassin. The image he saw through the scope was still in the form of a cross, but now the intersecting lines, instead of being solid, consisted of evenly spaced dots. This allowed for very precise aiming at long distances, and Peters was glad to get it.

He placed the center of the reticle on Stark's head, which appeared so clear to him he might as well be viewing it under a microscope. The chest, not the head, was the sniper's ideal target. It was bigger, didn't move around as much, and a hit anywhere in the chest area was almost guaranteed to get heart, lung, or spine – or some combination thereof.

But diligent research had told him that, these days, more and more politicos wore lightweight body armor out in public. Back in Peters' day, such things were called bulletproof vests. They were big, heavy, and almost impossible to conceal under any clothing tighter than a Hawaiian muumuu. But, as if in compensation for improvements in rifle scopes and ballistics, protective clothing had become lighter, more flexible, and harder to detect.

There was no way to be certain that a chest shot would kill Stark. It would have to be the head.

Now it was time to call on Ashley. His demon companion had proved useful in many ways. She offered fantastic sex, stimulating conversation, encyclopedic knowledge of certain subjects, and a sarcastic wit that kept him on his toes.

And she could do magic.

He had explored Ashley's abilities in several long conversations. No, she could not use magic to simply cause Stark's head to explode. No, she could not make Peters invisible – not to Stark/Sargatanas, anyway, and he was the one who mattered. No, she could not cause objects to appear out of thin air wherever she wished; Peters had been thinking of a hand grenade, pin already pulled, dropped next to Stark's sleeping form late some night.

But Ashley could, within limits, control elements of the weather – like wind.

Wind was the sniper's enemy. At extreme distances, a moderate breeze could blow a bullet as much as ten degrees off course – and that could make all the difference.

The Weather Channel had said the breeze in Richmond (at the last reading, anyway) was 12 miles per hour, with gusts up to 20. There were ways that snipers could overcome wind – that was one of the advantages of the mil dot reticle. You could calculate how the wind would affect your bullet's path, and compensate with the point of aim. But the wind could fuck it all up, if it changed on you. An erratic wind was the factor he'd been most concerned about. The shot was difficult, at best, and at 500-some meters, with the breeze variable, the odds against success would have made a Vegas croupier smile in envy.

But Ashley could, for brief periods, stop the wind. She had prepared magic in advance in order to do just that.

Without moving more than a few jaw muscles, Peters said, "Okay, baby, do it."

Behind him, Ashley began to chant in words that Peters didn't recognize – perhaps one of the more obscure dialects of the demon tongue.

Peters had been concerned about how he would know when the breeze dropped, assuming Ashley was successful. But his first look through the scope had given him what he needed.

Seated on the stage a few feet to Stark's right was a pudgy local politician sporting a comb-over, one of those ridiculous methods by which balding men try to hide their condition and only succeed in calling attention to it. But Peters was glad to see Mr. Comb-Over today. The ebbs and flows of breeze that blew left to right across the stage caused loose strands of the man's hair to rise and fall. Through the scope, Peters could see those dark hairs against the pale scalp clear as crystal, and he watched them now.

Behind him, Ashley chanted for almost a minute – then stopped.

In the scope, the little strands of Mr. Comb-Over's hair moved in the breeze – and then they stopped.

Slowly, Peters shifted the scope's viewpoint a bare inch, from Mr. Comb-Over to Senator Howard Stark, now caught up in the throes of oratory. He centered the reticule on Stark's forehead. With infinite slowness, Peters began to squeeze his hand, applying gradual pressure to the Remington's trigger. That's how you avoid jerking the trigger and throwing your shot off. "You should be increasing tension so gradually that you're surprised when the weapon goes off," Peters's rifle instructor had said at the Farm, all those years ago.

Peters was anticipating his surprise sometime in the next few seconds.

LIBBY CHASTAIN DIDN'T pay any attention to Stark's speech after the first few minutes. It was the usual political bullshit – full of applause lines and empty promises and utterly lacking any serious discussion of the issues. Libby was already in a bad mood from tension and lack of sleep; she didn't need any further aggravation.

She let her gaze wander over the scene in front of her. She couldn't see the crowd, being in the thick of it, so she watched a couple of squirrels chasing each other around the huge fountain, checked out the goods on several young policemen who strolled by, and wondered what on Earth she and Quincey were going to do if it turned out that Senator Stark did, in fact, reek of black magic.

And she made regular checks of a certain window on the fourteenth floor of the Crowne Plaza Hotel, some five hundred yards to her left. If the people standing nearby thought it odd that the woman near the rope line was periodically looking through the circles of her cupped hands as if they were binoculars – and in the direction opposite the speaker's platform, no less – nobody said anything.

Before leaving the hotel, Libby had told Quincey what she wanted to do in order to locate Room 1408 easily from the middle of Kanawha Plaza. In a corner of his suitcase, he had found a roll of black electrical tape, claiming utter ignorance as to when or why he'd put it there. It was exactly what Libby needed.

On her instructions, Quincey had gone up to her room and used the tape to make a big 'X' in the window that faced the Plaza. Since she knew her own room number, it had been easy to spot the 'X,' then count windows from there until she knew which one belonged to 1408. The angle to the hotel from where she stood meant she couldn't see into the suspect room, but at least she knew which hole in the concrete it was – for all the good that might do her.

Libby checked the exterior of Room 1408 from time to time, finding nothing amiss. If asked, she couldn't have said what she was looking *for*, but her witch sense told her something was not right about that room and its occupant, and that was a good enough reason for her to keep an eye on it.

At the moment, Libby was not looking toward the hotel. She'd noticed a bed of tulips that had been planted near the fountain. Too cold for them to bloom in New York, of course, but this was a different climate. Libby was watching the tulips wave back and forth in the breeze when suddenly they *just stopped moving*. She waited for the gentle swaying to resume – and it didn't. Libby hastily wet her index finger and raised it above her head, away from the crowd.

The breeze was gone. Utterly.

Mother Nature is a funny old gal, sometimes. She'll sneak up on you, usually with the wind or rain. You can be walking along, everything's quiet – then all at once you're either being blown off your feet or drenched. Like a well-tuned sports car, Nature has great acceleration.

But, also like a lot of sports cars, she doesn't have very good brakes. Stopping on a dime? Forget it. A breeze will die down, but it takes a little while. The wind doesn't just *stop*.

Except it just did.

Libby curled her hands and brought them up to her eyes at once. She located the fourteenth floor of the Crowne Plaza quickly by coming down from the top. After that, she found, it wasn't necessary to count horizontally. Room 1408 was almost certainly the one from whose window she could see what appeared to her as thin black smoke – the unmistakable sign of black magic in use.

Many people can think fast. Smart people think even faster. And smart witches are fastest of all.

Item: the wind just stopped – dead.

Item: black magic is currently being used in room 1408 of the Crowne Plaza.

Item: the black smoke manifestation wouldn't appear as coming from the window unless the window was open.

Item: windows of modern hotels don't open, to discourage suicides. To get one of those open would require either a strong blow with a heavy object, a small amount of explosives, or a great deal of time and effort.

Item: a candidate for the office of President of the United States is about 500 yards from said building, orating.

Query[1]: why would someone high up in a building go to considerable trouble to acquire an open window and stifle the breeze, while a prominent politician stood out in the open, some 500 yards away?

Query[2]: do the names Kennedy, King, and Wallace have any relevance to the present problem?

Query[3]: what behavioral intervention seems most appropriate?

Conclusion[1]: intended assassination seems the most likely option.

Conclusion[2]: you bet your ass they do.

Conclusion[3]: ohhhhhh, fuck!

This calculation took Libby Chastain slightly less than one second, and it came along with the realization that she had only seconds left, if that.

One of the things Libby had prepared the night before had been an All-Purpose Voice Spell, which would allow her to do a number of interesting vocal tricks, if she had to. Knowing she was going to be in a crowd, outdoors, she'd thought the spell might conceivably come in handy.

It is also worth mentioning that Libby had never made a study of the procedures or jargon of the U.S. Secret Service. However, although she might not admit this to some of her feminist friends, she was a big Clint Eastwood fan. She had seen all of his movies, many more than once. This included the 1993 film *In the Line of Fire*, in which Eastwood had portrayed an aging Secret Service agent. If the movie had been correct, there was one word that would galvanize Secret Service agents like no other.

Libby muttered a few words in Latin under her breath to invoke the spell, then she did three things. She deepened and coarsened her voice so that it sounded like a man's. She projected her voice toward the stage, meaning it would be heard as if she had been speaking from up there. And then, in that male voice, she yelled a single word.

BAT MASTERSON DIDN'T listen to Stark's oratory, either. Even if he had been interested in yet another political speech – which he wasn't – the job dictated that his focus be elsewhere.

Each agent in the detail had his assigned spot. Some were on the ground in front of the stage, others stood at the back of the structure, facing outward, still others were in positions near the speaker's podium. Masterson had positioned himself at the front, about thirty feet to Stark's left. He scanned the crowd restlessly from behind his Oakley sunglasses, looking for flashes of metal, for sudden unexplainable movement, for the one face that was not smiling or intent on the speaker's words.

Then a male voice from close by, one that Masterson didn't recognize, yelled "*Gun!*"

The result was immediate, as each member of the security team began moving, very fast indeed, in a pattern he had practiced many times.

Masterson's pattern took him straight at Stark, like a defensive lineman in football who's just found an open path to the other team's quarterback. He gave no consideration to the effect his tackle would have on Stark's body – as they'd drummed into him at the Secret

348

Service Academy, "Better a couple of cracked ribs than a bullet in the brain."

It took Masterson a long time to reach Stark – at least two, maybe three seconds. He kept his eyes open the whole way, even at the moment of impact, just as he'd been trained to do. One of the last thoughts that Masterson had was to wonder why Stark's left hand, hidden from public view behind the podium, seemed to be making a cryptic sign of some kind in the air, while Stark said several words in a language that Masterson didn't recognize. Then there came the shock of the collision as he hit Stark, followed a bare instant later by an even greater shock, as the .300 magnum rifle bullet penetrated Masterson's rib cage and kept going, all the way through his body to exit on the other side.

Most of the agents, well-trained professionals that they were, got their own bodies between Stark and any potential follow-up shot, then hustled him off the stage, into their nearby car, and away. But Jerry Arkasian, second in command of the detail, had ordered two agents to stay with Masterson.

Like all Secret Service agents, the two who stayed behind were well-trained in emergency medical procedures. But despite their best efforts, Hugh 'Bat' Masterson bled out and died right there, five minutes before the paramedics could reach him.

Chapter 34

THE KILLER SOME people called The Grocer's Boy knew that the best way to catch up with somebody was to get ahead of him. The news sources said that all the Republican candidates were concentrating on Virginia this week. The killer had read a great deal about how these things worked. The night of the primary, each candidate would throw a party for supporters at a hotel. Once the votes had been tallied, the politico would address the faithful – either basking in victory or vowing to do better next week.

The Leffingwell campaign's web site had the Senator's speaking schedule for the week, and all his engagements on Saturday were in Virginia Beach, the state's largest city. That meant he would almost certainly be staying in Virginia Beach Saturday night. Now the question was – where? The campaign website was not quite *that* helpful.

Fortunately, the Devil helps those who help themselves. It seemed that each state had its own Leffingwell campaign headquarters, staffed mostly by volunteers. The Senator's Virginia HQ was in Roanoke.

"Leffingwell for President, may I help you?"

"Yeah, hi. This is Harry Mason at Mason's Fine Wines and Spirits in Virginia Beach. We got a big order for Senator Leffingwell's party Saturday night, but whoever took the information didn't write down what hotel we're delivering to. Can you guys help me out? Like I said, it's a real big order, and we don't want to screw it up."

"Uh, sure, hold on a sec."

There was a soft thud as the phone was put down. The killer got to eavesdrop on the closest volunteer who was making calls encouraging Virginians to vote for Bob Leffingwell, the Man Who Can Make a Difference for America.

A couple of minutes went by before the campaign worker, a guy who sounded like he might be the age of a college student, came back on.

"Hi, sorry to keep you waiting. I had to find somebody who knew where it was."

"No problem at all, man. I appreciate it."

"Looks like you make your delivery to the Hilton."

"Which one?"

"It's the Hilton Virginia Beach Oceanfront, on Atlantic Ave."

"That's great – thanks!"

"Show your gratitude this Saturday – vote for Bob Leffingwell."

"I aim to."

The Hilton Oceanfront's web site said the place had 21 floors, the top three of which were devoted to something called the Empyrean Club, apparently reserved for those with serious money to spend on accommodations. It was a sure bet that Leffingwell would be on one of those three floors come Saturday.

The killer decided he would be there, too. Maybe he and the Senator could be neighbors.

The killer turned off the disposable phone he'd bought that morning and went to look at his fake IDs and credit cards.

"WHAT THE FUCK *happened*, Peters?"

The two of them had put the window back in place and were, not quite frantically, replacing the sixteen screws that had held it in the frame. Peters had possessed the foresight to buy two screwdrivers, so they could work on that task simultaneously, standing back-to-back on the wide window ledge.

"What fucking *happened*," Peters said grimly as he turned the screwdriver, "was that I was putting slow pressure on the trigger, just like you're supposed to. You can't jerk the gun if you don't know exactly when it's gonna fire. I guess I was almost there – another second, and Stark's head would be splattered all over the stage. But the Secret Service guy came out of fucking *nowhere* – I didn't even know he was there, until he was in my sight. I guess I was so startled that my finger moved that last fraction of an inch, and the weapon fired, even though Stark wasn't in the crosshairs anymore. But the Secret Service dude was. And *that*," he said tiredly, "is all she fucking wrote."

"I don't mean *that*," Ashley said. "What the fuck happened on the stage? Why was everybody going crazy, just before you fired? Did one of the Secret Service goons spot you? Give me another screw."

Peters didn't even notice her unintentional *double entendre*. Neither one of them was feeling very sexy at the moment. He passed one of the long screws to Ashley

352

and said, "Uh-uh, no fucking way somebody saw me. The silencer wasn't sticking out the window, you know that. Everything was completely inside the room. And there's no building as high as we are across the way with a line of sight into here. Nobody spotted me, unless the Feds have got fucking pigeons working for them, now."

"*Fuck*," Ashley said.

"My thoughts exactly. Although if you won't hit me for saying it, this particular cloud's got something of a silver lining."

"I could use some good news. Let's hear it."

"We can be pretty sure that Astaroth won't be showing up to take us back to Hell with him in the next five minutes. He wants the job done, that's all he cares about. 'Stark must not take the oath of office.' That's what he told me."

There was a pause, then Ashley said, "As silver linings go, that one's not too bad. Unless, of course, Astaroth gets so disgusted with the way we fucked up, he sends somebody to replace us."

"I don't think so. If he had anybody better than us, he'd have sent them already. We're a good team, Ashley."

"Tell that to the Secret Service guy."

Peters sighed deeply. "Yeah, I know. You done on your side?"

"Just finished. You?"

"Wait one second... okay, that's the last one. I'm done."

"Then let's get down from this fucking windowsill before somebody notices us."

Once they were standing on the floor, Peters said, "I hate to mention this, but the chest of drawers has to go back too."

"Yeah, I know." She blew hair out of her eyes. "Thought I forgot, didn't you? Relax, Peters, I've already had my tantrum on that subject today. And as long as we're talking about silver innings, I've got one for you – and it doesn't even involve sex."

Peters looked across the faux-mahogany furniture at her. "Okay, I'm braced. Lay it on me."

"We're smart enough to learn from our mistakes, right? There was a lot of trial and error involved in bringing this fucking thing over here. But now we know which angles work, and which don't. Getting it back is going to be easier. Not *easy*, but at least eas*ier*."

"Pretty good," Peters said, and took a grip on his end of the chest of drawers. "You're one smart demon."

NOBODY HAD HEARD a shot, but it was immediately clear to most in the crowd that something was very wrong. The controlled chaos on the stage, followed by the candidate's abrupt departure surrounded by guys in suits and sunglasses, was a pretty clear indication.

And if more evidence was needed, there was always the guy in a suit lying on the stage in the center of a rapidly growing pool of blood, while two other guys in suits tried, with controlled desperation, to keep him alive. One was doing rhythmic chest compressions on the downed man, while the other tried to improvise a couple of pressure bandages from folded handkerchiefs. There was a well-equipped First Aid kit in the main Secret Service car, but that had departed with Stark before anyone had thought to say something. It is doubtful that it would have made a difference, anyway.

As soon as he saw what had happened, Quincey Morris said to Libby Chastain, "Come on!" and stepped over the rope line. Everyone else was heading for one of the Plaza's exits, but Morris and Libby fought against the tide and made their slow way to the stage.

Two uniformed Richmond police officers, looking grim, stood at the bottom of the steps leading to the stage. They watched Quincey and Libby approach, and did not seem to like what they beheld.

"Sorry, folks. You can't go up there. It's a crime scene now." This cop was an African-American in his forties whose name tag read 'Monroe.'

"Yeah, you'll have to get your thrills someplace else," the other cop said. He was white and young, and his tag said 'Russell.'

"We're not here for that," Morris said. "The guy who was shot is a friend of mine. We want to see if we can help."

The cops looked at each other, then Monroe said calmly, "Do tell. Well, it's good to have friends." He did not appear impressed.

"His name's Hugh Masterson," Morris said through clenched teeth. "Everybody called him 'Bat,' including him. He was head of Stark's protection detail."

Monroe looked at his partner again. "You catch that Secret Service fella's name?"

"No, but I'm pretty sure I heard one of the other agents call him 'Bat.' I thought at first he was calling him 'Bad', or somethin'. Could be these folks are tellin' the truth. Not that it matters."

Monroe nodded, "Yeah." To Morris and Libby he said, "If that fella up there's your friend, Mr., I'm sorry for your trouble." He turned to Libby for a moment, saying, "You, too, ma'am." Libby nodded her thanks.

"But we got explicit orders," the black cop told Morris. "Unless you or this lady is a doctor, and I don't see either one of you carrying a medical bag, we are not authorized to let you through. Sorry."

Morris looked at Libby. She knew him well enough to understand that he was asking, "Have you got any magic ready that will get us past these guys, and is it worth it to Bat if we do?"

Libby gave her answer to both questions with a slow, sad shake of her head. She did not have any healing magic prepared, and even white magic cannot work miracles. She was fairly certain that Masterson, even if he were still alive, would need a miracle.

Morris nodded glumly. To the two cops he said politely, "All right, officers. Sorry to bother you."

Then he and Libby Chastain turned and walked slowly away. They both knew with sour certainty that they would not be seeing Hugh 'Bat' Masterson again, – not unless they attended his funeral.

To their surprise, the hotel bar wasn't crowded. Most of the spectators at the rally had apparently left for home, there to tell rapt family members and friends about their brief moment of melodrama.

They gave the waitress their drink order, then Morris sat back in his chair. He stayed like that for a while, eyes closed, a finger and thumb pinching the bridge of his nose.

"I'm so sorry, Quincey," Libby said.

"He was a pretty good guy," Morris said, without changing his posture. "I'm gonna miss him."

"Yes, I know, but what I meant was, I'm sorry for the role I played in his death."

Morris dropped his hand from his face. He opened his eyes and leaned forward, staring at Libby. "The part *you* played? Are you *serious*?"

"I'm the one who did the ventriloquist act," she said. "I'm the one who yelled, "Gun!""

"I know that," Morris said. "And it seems like you were right, too."

"Yes, but if I hadn't been so fucking clever…"

The waitress brought Morris's bourbon and water, and Libby's double vodka. They tacitly agreed that a toast wasn't appropriate, so they just picked up their drinks and each took a swallow.

Libby put down her glass and said, "I think I needed that almost as badly as I needed the Ladies Room when we first got here."

"I wasn't exactly sad to see the Men's Room, either," Morris said. "But you were in the process of beating yourself up. If you feel you have to, go on ahead. I'll listen. Not that I agree with you."

"But, if I hadn't used the voice spell –"

"Then Stark would probably be dead, which might or might not be a good thing. We don't know enough to say."

"Oh, that's right, I forgot to –"

"Let me finish, okay? I'm saying something profound here – or at least it sounded that way in my head a minute ago. Libby, I figure two people, and two people alone, are responsible for what happened to Bat. One is the shooter – and I hope to meet *that* sumbitch one day. And the other one is Bat himself. He put himself in the line of fire, just like he was supposed to. He gave his life in the performance of his duty, as they say." Morris stared at the amber liquid in his glass. "There's worse epitaphs a man can have, I guess."

"Amen to that," Libby said. "You know, maybe a toast is in order, after all." She picked up her glass. "To Hugh 'Bat' Masterson, lawman, who died with his boots on, while performing his sworn duty to God and country." She extended her glass toward Morris. He raised his, and the two clinked softly. Then each of them took another drink, in honor of the fallen.

"You said there was something you were going to tell me," Morris said.

"Yes, and it's a doozy, even if I did forget it amidst all the other excitement." She put an arm on the table and leaned toward Morris. "In the second before Bat cannoned into him, I saw Stark make some kind of gesture in the air – with his left hand."

Morris's eyes widened a bit. "Really?"

"Uh-huh, and there's more. Remember how I saw the – *miasma*, for lack of a better word – the miasma of black magic coming out of Room 1408? Well I saw the same thing form above Stark, just before Masterson put him on the floor."

Morris whistled softly. "I won't ask you if you're sure –"

"Pretend that you did. Yes, I'm sure."

"Black magic from the killer *and* his victim? Intended victim, I mean."

"I know. It boggles the mind. Did we wander into the middle of a war between two sorcerers?"

"We don't have enough information to say. But I think I've got an idea about where we might find some."

Libby looked a question at him.

"After we finish our drinks, and maybe have a second round, I suggest we pay us a visit to Room 1408."

Libby frowned at him. "The killer's long gone, Quincey. He'd have to be. Or she."

"Of course. But I'm thinking that he – or she – probably took off in a big hurry. Let's see if anything interesting got left behind."

"Not a bad idea," Libby said. "But if we're going back up there, I think one drink had better be enough – at least for me."

"Yeah, good point," Morris said. He checked his glass and looked to see how much bourbon was left. "I think just one of these will probably do it for me, as well."

THE ELEVATOR BROUGHT them to the 14th floor; after that, they were on their own. As they walked the hall toward Room 1408, Morris said, "Can you get us in there?"

"It should be simple enough," Libby said, "assuming it's the standard hotel lock, and nobody has added any… refinements."

"You're thinking booby traps?"

"Could be. It's one solution to the problem of leaving stuff behind, isn't it? The first person to open the door after our black magician leaves gets blown to bits – and the contents of the room along with him."

"Lot of collateral damage that way."

"Uh-huh. But those Left Hand Path people aren't exactly characterized by their reverence for human life, are they?"

"Guess we'd better be extra careful, then."

"My very thought – Goddess, Quincey!"

"What's wrong?"

"The black magic odor – it's just as strong as it was last night. I would have expected some dissipation by now. This time I can 'see' the stuff, as well, and the hall's full of it. Guess in front of which room it's thickest."

"I only get one guess?"

"You shouldn't need more, cowboy."

They stopped outside 1408, and Libby began sifting through the magical devices in her shoulder bag. While she did, Morris said, "You never know," and knocked firmly on the door. "If a cop answers, we've got the wrong room."

"I'm such a scatterbrain, Officer," Libby said in a sing-song voice. "I'm always getting room numbers confused. I think we want 1208."

"That should take care –" Morris stopped talking, for in that instant the door opened, and he was looking at a tall blonde who was one of the most sexually appealing women he'd ever seen.

The woman looked from Morris to Libby, and back.

"Who the fuck are you?" She sounded more puzzled than aggressive.

"Oh, sorry," Morris said, and stepped back. "We must have the wrong room."

"No, we don't" Libby said tightly. She bent her right wrist oddly, and a wand dropped down the sleeve into her waiting hand. At once it started to glow. "Get back, Quincey – she's Hellspawn!"

Chapter 35

"As soon as I realized I might be in danger," Sargatanas said, "I threw up a quick shield spell I had prepared – although, as it happened, Masterson was my shield. He moves fast for a man his size."

"Were you hurt?" Mary Margaret Doyle asked. "When he threw you down, I mean."

"Some bruises. A rib was cracked, but I had healed it by the time they got me to the hospital. Nothing compared to what would have happened if I had been in the path of that bullet."

"He died, you know. Masterson. I saw it on TV."

Sargatanas shrugged. "He did what he was paid to do. They all know the risks when they agree to do the job." The demon produced a cruel smile. "I wonder if he would have been quick to throw himself into harm's way if he knew who he was really saving, and what it will ultimately mean for his kind."

"If he'd known the truth," she said, "he'd probably have shot you himself."

"Perhaps he and I will have the chance to discuss it in Hell, sometime. But one thing puzzles me."

"The identity of the shooter?"

"That, also, yes. But I was thinking about what happened on that stage. The agents were galvanized into action by someone yelling 'Gun.'"

"I'm not surprised they moved fast," she said. "They probably practice responding to the word, and maybe a few others."

"But none of them will acknowledge being the one who said it. And I didn't recognize the voice – I don't think it *was* one of the Secret Service detail."

"Someone from the crowd?"

He shook his head. "The voice came from the stage, I'm sure of it."

"There were other people on stage, weren't there? Local politicos, and some Bible-thumper to give the invocation? One of them must've done it."

"Then why not *say* so? It would make the man a hero, of a sort. And there's something else that bothers me about all of this."

"What?"

"The police say the weapon was almost certainly a rifle, fired from hundreds of yards away. So what was there for anyone on the stage to see?"

"Well whoever it was almost certainly saved your – Starks's – life. We can be thankful for that."

"Instead of being thankful, you might devote your limited intelligence to determining who wants Stark dead."

She left her chair and went to one of the suite's windows, where she stood in silence looking outside. Finally she said, "The rifle worries me."

"Not as much as it worried *me*, a few hours ago."

"What I meant was, it's outside the pattern. In this country, political assassins mostly use handguns."

"Lee Harvey Oswald, stupid. James Earl Ray. Joseph Paul Franklin."

"I don't recognize that last one."

"The man who shot Larry Flynt. Fortunately, Larry has continued to publish *Hustler* from his wheelchair. Fine magazine."

"You seem to know a lot about these killers."

"Political assassinations are something of a hobby of mine."

"Watching them, you mean?"

"No, causing them. Never mind. My Secret Service protection will be increased, effective immediately. That faggot Arkasian told me so himself, on the way here from the hospital."

"*Who* told you?"

He gave her a look loaded with contempt. "Remind me again why I continue to keep you around."

"Hmmm. Because I'm a good fuck?"

"No you're not. You're just handy. Arkasian was the Number Two man in the Secret Service detail, now temporarily promoted to Number One."

"And he's gay?"

"Of course he is – it's obvious."

"I'll take your word for it. So the Secret Service is adding to your protection. The FBI, I assume, is busy tracking down the killer, who has now lost the advantage of surprise. I don't think we need to worry, overmuch."

"I wonder if you'd feel so blasé if *you* were the one he's after."

* * *

Roland English's Platinum Visa Card had a credit limit of $50,000, almost all of which was available for his use. He also had a Maryland driver's license to prove that the card was his.

Roland English was clearly a man of substance – or he would be, if he really existed. He'd encountered no problem securing a room for two nights in the elite Empyrean Club section at the Hilton Oceanfront in Virginia Beach.

He checked in just after 4:00PM on Friday and was shown to his elegant suite by an aging bellman, whom he tipped generously. The Empyrean Club occupied the Hilton's top three floors – 19, 20, and 21 – and Mr. English was on 19. Noting the absence of large men in suits accessorized by radio earpieces, he concluded that Senator Leffingwell's entourage was on one of the two floors above him. Time enough later to find out which one it was. For now, Mister English had some shopping to do at the nearest Home Depot.

Two hours later, he had purchased everything he needed and had dinner at a small but pleasant restaurant further down Atlantic Avenue. Returning to the Hilton, he left his purchases in the car for the time being and looked for a Men's Room in the hotel lobby. Finding one, he spent a few minutes primping.

Roland English had a full head of carefully styled blond hair. He wore a beautifully tailored tropical suit with an open-collared silk dress shirt underneath. Even though indoors, he still wore the big Wayfarer sunglasses he'd had on in the car. He took off the jacket, hooked the collar with one finger and held it draped over his shoulder. Then he was ready for the trip upstairs.

In the elevator reserved for Empyrean Club guests, he pushed the button for 20, even though that was not his floor. On 20, the elevator door slid open onto a foyer identical to the one on his own floor, and just as deserted. He spent a few minutes walking around, just to be sure, then summoned the elevator again. This time, he pushed 21.

The door opened to reveal two large men in quiet suits who stood facing the elevator from ten feet away, doubtless alerted by the 'ping' of the floor bell. One of the men said, pleasantly enough, "Can I help you, sir?"

Mr. English made a show of looking confused, then checking the cardboard holder for his card key that he'd received when checking in. Without leaving the elevator he said, "Oh, damn, wrong floor. Sorry!" He pressed the button for 19 and smiled sheepishly at the men until the elevator doors took them from his sight.

So Leffingwell and his party were on the top floor. Good to have it confirmed.

Back in his suite, Mr. English went into the well-appointed bathroom and stood over the toilet. He began to tear toilet paper off the roll, seven or eight sheets at a time, and drop it into the toilet bowl. After he had done this eight times, he flushed the toilet. Predictably, the mass of paper bunched together and jammed the outlet pipe.

"Concierge desk, how may I help you?"

"Hi, this is Roland English in 1904."

"Good evening, Mister English. What can I do for you this evening?"

"My toilet bowl seems to be clogged. I can't flush it."

"Sorry to hear that, sir. I'll get a plumber up there right away."

"Great, thank you."

At 9:19 the next morning, a man stepped out of the service elevator onto the 21st floor. He had black hair and a thin mustache, wore the work clothes common to the hotel's maintenance staff, and carried a large tool box. A photo ID card clipped to his collar identified him as Ramon Gutierrez and said his function at the hotel was that of a plumber.

As soon as he left the elevator, Gutierrez was confronted by two large men in suits – one blue, one tan.

"Can I help you?" tan suit said.

"Yeah, hi, how ya doing? You guys are Secret Service, huh?"

"That's right," tan suit said. "How can we help you?"

"Got a work order. He pulled from his shirt pocket a folded sheet and opened it. "Clogged toilet, Mister Laffingwell, Room 21... something. He peered at the paper closely. Looks like 2103."

"Mind if I take a look?" blue suit said.

"Sure – here."

Blue suit examined the work order, then showed it to his partner, who shrugged.

"Okay, Ramon," blue suit said. "You want Room 2106. The man's name is 'Leffingwell,' not 'Laffingwell,' just FYI. One of us will take you down, but first, can you open up your toolbox there for me?"

"Yeah, sure."

As blue suit rummaged through the plumber's tools and supplies in the box, he said, "My partner's just gonna pat you down, okay? Nothing personal, just procedure."

"Whatever," Gutierrez said. "Do what ya gotta do."

The pat-down revealed nothing interesting, nor did the quick search of the tool box.

"Okay Ramon, thanks," tan suit said. "You wanna come with me?"

The agent walked with Gutierrez along the hall and stopped in front of 2106. He knocked on the door, saying, "The Senator and his party left an hour ago, but we're supposed to knock, anyway."

"Just in case, huh?"

"Right – just in case."

When no one inside responded, the agent produced a card key and buzzed the door open. As he and Gutierrez entered the suite, tan suit said, "I guess you know where the bathroom is. I have to remain with you while you're in here. Just procedure. I'll stay out of your way."

"Fine with me, mister."

Gutierrez pushed open the bathroom door, flicked on the light, and knelt in front of the toilet. His body blocking tan suit's view, he muttered, just loud enough to be heard, "Yep, no wonder it's clogged. Somebody took a hell of a big dump this morning."

He removed a plunger from the toolbox and pumped the toilet bowl with it a couple of times. Then he put the plunger down and removed a coiled flexible metal rod, which he slowly unspooled. "Gotta snake it," he said over his shoulder to the agent. "They call these things snakes, ya know, cause they're long and skinny, and kinda bendy. Ain't never heard of nobody getting bit by one, though."

Gutierrez chuckled at his own humor, although the agent did not join in. A moment later he left the bathroom doorway. A few seconds later, Gutierrez could hear a morning news show playing on the TV.

Gutierrez slid the snake into the toilet bowl, and pushed it a foot or so down the drainage pipe. He moved it in and out with one hand. With the other, he popped the lid on large, greasy old can hand-labeled 'Pipe Dope.' Letting go of the snake for a minute, he used both hands and a screwdriver to lever open the can itself. Instead of lubricant, it contained a full but already opened bottle of Gaviscon. After giving the snake another couple of stabs down the pipe, he reached over for the identical bottle of the antacid that he could see on the counter next to a man's shaving kit. Judging the bottle to be about 2/3 full, he quickly unscrewed the cap on the bottle he'd brought with him, and poured some of the thick, white liquid into the toilet bowl. Then he picked a damp towel off the floor and wiped the bottle clean of any oil or fingerprints and placed it on the counter exactly where the other bottle had stood. The original bottle went into the can labeled 'Pipe Dope' which was quickly resealed and replaced in the tool box.

Gutierrez removed the snake and flushed the toilet, sending the tainted Gaviscon down the drain. When the bowl had refilled, he flushed again. He quickly rolled up the snake and replaced it in the toolbox along with the plunger.

Gutierrez got to his feet and went to the bathroom door. "All done," he told tan suit. "Oughta work fine now. I flushed it a couple times, just to make sure."

Fifteen minutes later, Ramon Gutierrez had ceased to exist. In his luxurious suite on the 19th floor, the man who was calling himself Ronald English changed clothes and considered the best way to spend his free day in Virginia Beach. He wondered idly when Senator Robert Leffingwell was going to have his next attack of acid reflux.

THE TWO WOMEN, one blonde, the other brunette, stood tensed, looking at each other like something out of a Spaghetti Western showdown. It's hard to know where that would have led if the tall, muscular man had not come up behind the blonde and gently placed his hands on her shoulders. "Ashley," he said quietly, "easy. Go easy." He looked at Libby, then at Morris. "You folks aren't FBI, are you?"

Morris just shook his head. Libby didn't respond. She was still looking at the blonde the way a mongoose regards a cobra.

"I guess we should talk," the tall man said. "Why don't you both come on in?" He murmured in the blonde's ear, voice barely more than a whisper. "Come on, Ashley. It's cool." He looked at Libby, and what she held in her hand. "Ma'am, if you wouldn't mind putting that away, it would probably lower the tension some."

Libby took her eyes off Ashley for the first time and looked at the man. She appeared to study him for a few seconds before nodding. "All right." With her left hand, she slowly slid the wand back up her sleeve and into whatever sheath had been holding it.

The big man put one arm around the blonde's waist and gently pulled her back into the room with him. Morris followed, with Libby bringing up the rear.

Once they were all through the short hall and in the main part of the room, the man waved his hands toward the beds, one of which was still made. "Why don't we all sit down?"

Libby sat on the side of the unused bed, Morris on its corner. The tall man led the blonde to the room's only armchair, then pulled the desk chair over for himself. "Maybe introductions are in order," he said. "My name's Mal Peters. This lady is Ashley – we won't go into her last name right now, if that's okay."

"I'm Quincey Morris." Figuring that Libby could speak for herself, he turned toward her slightly.

"Hannah Widmark," Libby said, without expression. Morris didn't show any reaction to the lie. In magic, he knew, names were power. He guessed Libby wasn't interested in giving anybody an advantage over her just now.

"Names are nice to know," Morris said. "But right now, a better question than *who* you are is *what* you are. I don't mind going first this time. I guess you could call me an occult investigator, based in Austin, Texas." Looking at Peters closely, he continued, "I'm also a good friend of the man you shot dead this afternoon."

Peters gave a slight nod, but said nothing. When the silence continued, Libby broke it by saying, "I'm a witch of the Right-Hand Path. In theory, that makes me the sworn enemy of those who follow the Left."

"In… theory?" Peters asked.

"I like to keep an open mind – when I can."

"Let's hope this turns out to be one of those times," Peters said. "Our answer to your question is a little more complicated than yours. But you folks being who – and what – you are, maybe you'll understand better than most."

Peters wiped his palms on the thighs of his slacks. "I used to work for the U.S. government, mostly in Europe. No sense trying to glamorize it – I was an assassin. The fact that I did my killing for Uncle Sam was supposed to make it all right. But I guess it didn't – because in 1983 I got myself killed, and for my sins got sent to Hell. I've been there ever since – except last week, I got sprung. There's some weird shit going on over here right now, and they let me out to deal with it."

"Deal with it by killing," Libby said flatly.

"By killing one man. And if you knew who – what – he is, you might want to kill him, too."

370

Peters turned to the blonde. "Tell them whatever you want to, Ashley. I won't presume to speak for you."

Ashley looked at Peters for a moment, then back at Morris and Libby – especially Libby.

"My name isn't really Ashley – any more than this woman's is Hannah. I am one of the Fallen – or, to use a word I heard recently, Hellspawn. Fourth rank, if that matters. I was given flesh and sent here to ensure that Peters is successful in carrying out his mission."

"And the mission is to kill Senator Stark," Morris said. "We know he can use black magic – is he one of the Fallen, too?"

"No, but he's owned and operated by one," Peters said. "About six months ago, he was possessed, against his will, by a big-league demon named Sargatanas."

"That sounds like part of the story," Morris said. "You going to tell us the rest of it?"

"Why should we?" Ashley asked him.

"It'll help L – Hannah and I decide what side we're on. Whether we should maybe work with you – or fight you."

At that last, Ashley gave an unladylike snort, but nobody responded to it. Peters turned to her and said, "I'm gonna tell 'em."

"Of course you are," she said. "Go ahead. I just hope you don't end up regretting it later on."

Peters laid it out for them with admirable succinctness – Sargatanas's terrible purpose, Astaroth's intent in sending them to Earth, the factions in the Netherworld, and the possibility of a civil war there if Peters succeeded – or even if he failed.

When he was done Libby said, "And this demon has been systematically wiping out the competition, using both black magic and old fashioned political dirt."

Peters nodded. "You got it."

"So you say that y'all are determined not to murder innocents" – Morris gave Peters a very direct look, before continuing – "except by accident. But from what you've told us, Stark's an innocent, too. He didn't ask for this, and his real self is still in there, someplace. Even if the demon is in control."

"Since there's more than one *demon* involved in this business," Ashley said, "perhaps you two could start calling him by his name: Sargatanas."

"Sure, not a problem," Morris told her. "We meant no offense."

Ashley raised an eyebrow at him but said nothing more.

"Lets return to my point, Peters," Morris said. "You said you won't deliberately kill innocents, yet Stark sounds like one."

"He's the exception. It's the only way to stop him, to send him back to Hell."

"No, it's not," Libby said.

"What, then – *exorcism*?" Morris thought if there were some kind of prize awarded for contemptuous sarcasm, that Ashley had just clinched it.

"It works," Morris said. "Or at least, it *can*. I've seen it succeed."

Ashley looked at him closely. "And I bet you've seen it fail, too, haven't you?" Ashley shifted her gaze from Morris's face to a point a little lower. "I see you carry Hell's mark on you, Morris. That practically makes us cousins."

"*No, it doesn't.*" Libby's voice wasn't loud, but the force behind it startled Morris a little. He thought Peters might have reacted the same way. Ashley, however, seemed unfazed.

"Exorcism can work, Peters," Morris said. "It can send the d – Sargatanas back to hell, just as well as a bullet in Stark's brain. And that's all your master cares about, right?"

"I suppose so," Peters said slowly. "My orders are that Sargatanas – or Stark, or whoever you want to call him – doesn't take the oath of office. And even if he loses the election, they still want him sent back. The thinking is, if he loses, he'll keep working for the White House. He might make it, eventually."

"We won't countenance murder," Morris said. "But if you're willing to work toward an exorcism, we'll stand with you."

Peters nodded slowly. "And if we're not willing?"

"Then we'll fight you."

Ashley made another one of those snorting sounds. "Doesn't that kind of depend on whether you leave this room alive?"

"No," Libby said, and her voice could have frozen nitrogen. "It depends on whether we leave anything alive behind us when we go."

"Let's everybody just relax," Morris said. "This ain't the OK Corral."

After a few tense seconds, Ashley said, "It didn't happen there, anyway. The Earps and the Clantons fought it out in a vacant lot fifty feet away."

"I'm aware of that, ma'am. I was just taking advantage of a cultural trope."

For the first time since opening the door, Ashley smiled, if briefly. "I think that's the first time I've ever been called *ma'am*."

Libby looked like she had a retort on the tip of her tongue. But if so, she bit it back.

"Okay, so let's see if maybe we can all live with this,"

Peters said, "and I mean that in every sense of the term. Say we agree to cooperate with you toward the goal of an exorcism. But if we can't make that happen – or if it happens, and doesn't succeed – then we kill him. Better one innocent dies than a whole fucking planet full of them."

"'It is fitting that one man should die for the people,'" Ashley said, "'lest the whole nation perish.'"

"That sounds like a quote from someplace," Peters said.

"It is," Morris said. "John 11:50."

"It's more than that," Ashley said.

"What?" Morris asked her.

"It's also a damn good idea."

DELIVERANCE

Chapter 36

"HELLO?"

"Hi, Paul."

"Quincey! How ya doin'?"

"I've been pretty busy, after a brief hiatus."

"That's good – or so I would assume."

"Yeah."

"Hmmm. This is the point in the conversation where you'd normally ask how I am, and since you don't seem to be doing that, I assume it's because you assume the answer might prove awkward for us both. Right?"

"Yeah, something like that."

"Quincey, you're really going to have to start getting over what happened."

"Why's that, Paul? You never will."

"The proper response to that line of bullshit, as any Jesuit will tell you, depends on how you define your terms, my friend."

"If you say so."

"I do, indeed. Now, if by 'get over it' we mean in a physical sense – you're right. I'm going to be blind for life. Unless some eye surgeon comes up with a miracle, like a way to do viable eye transplants. And although I believe in miracles, I'm not really holding out for that particular one."

"Paul, you don't know how sorry –"

"*Stop*! I'm tired of hearing the word 'sorry' from you Quincey. If you say it once more today, I'm hanging up. Understand?"

"Yeah, sure, Paul. I'll try to keep my contrition in check."

"I don't doubt the sincerity of your contrition, Quincey. If this were the Sacrament of Reconciliation, I'd give you absolution. I wish I could do that, anyway."

"Yeah, me, too."

"Of course, if I were a *really* good friend, I'd act seriously nasty toward you, Quincey. I'd pretend to be full of bitterness, and blaming, and self-pity. Then, when you hung up, you'd feel like shit, at one level of your consciousness. But another part of you would be glad to receive some of the punishment it thinks you deserve."

"Very insightful. I guess."

"Freud didn't invent all this stuff, you know. The Church had a handle on it centuries before. There's a reason why Reconciliation used to be called the Sacrament of Penance, you know? I'm sure the Lord was happy to receive all those rosaries and good works we used to assign, but a lot of that had to do with letting the sinner feel some sense of punishment, to partially assuage his guilt."

"Thus, self-flagellation came into practice."

"Exactly. And speaking of self-flagellation, you've been doing some of that anyway, haven't you?"

"Why do you say that?"

"I didn't like the way you said 'hiatus' at the start. You did some self-destructive shit, didn't you? Out of guilt."

"Yeah, I guess I did. I didn't know Sherlock Holmes was a Jesuit."

"One of the Order's better-kept secrets. You haven't done anything really stupid, have you? You calling from jail, or anything like that?"

"No, all my self-destructive shit was done in private. I don't say it was all legal, but nobody saw me do it. Give or take a few whores."

"Whores, plural? You *have* been busy."

"Then Libby came over, and spent a week with me. She helped me get past... some of it."

"Smart lady, that Libby. She's my favorite witch."

"Mine, too. Listen, Paul, there's a reason I called."

"Guilt aside, you mean?"

"Yes, besides that. Thing is, it's happened again, on a much bigger scale, and I need me an exorcist. Paul? Still there?"

"I really don't think I'd be much good to you, Quincey. The ritual's probably available in Braille someplace, but my skills haven't advanced that far, yet. I'm still at the 'See Spot, see Spot run' stage."

"That sounded almost bitter, Paul."

"Did it? Well fuck you, too, asshole."

"Thanks, Paul – I feel less guilty already."

"Sorry, that kind of... got away from me for a minute."

"I appreciate you showing me that you're human, after all. I thought for a while I had St. Francis of Assisi on the phone."

"That pansy? Not hardly."

"Anyway, when I said I need an exorcist, I didn't mean you, Paul. Even *I* don't have that much in the way of stones. But I *do* need an exorcist."

"What's the case like? You said 'on a bigger scale' earlier. What's that mean?"

"It's something big enough that I really don't want to discuss it on the phone, Paul. You never know who's invoking the PATRIOT act to listen in, these days."

"Wow. Must be big, indeed."

"When it's over, I'll come out there and tell you about it personally, okay? Assuming I'm able to."

"What's *that* mean?"

"Assuming I'm not in jail or... otherwise indisposed."

"I'll say it again – wow."

"Thing is, I tried to reach your boss, Father Strubeck, but they tell me he's away indefinitely."

"I'm afraid 'indefinitely' is a shade optimistic. Strubeck's got liver cancer. Terminal. He's moved to a hospice, Quincey."

"Shit, I'm sorry, Paul. He seemed to be a good man."

"He still is. One of the best."

"The lady at the Jesuit Residence says that the guy in charge now is some Father Callahan – but he won't take my calls, or answer my messages."

"Really? That's odd. I don't know Callahan well, but he never struck me as rude. Tell you what, I'll talk to him, find out what's what, and get back to you. Sound good?"

"That's great, Paul. Sooner would be better than later, I'm afraid."

"I call him as soon as we hang up. So, let's hang up now."

"Good idea. You've got my number, right?"

"Sure do. I'll talk to you soon, I hope."

"Okay. Thanks, Paul."

"*Ad majorem Dei gloriam.*"

To THE SURPRISE of Quincey Morris, Hugh 'Bat' Masterson was buried at Arlington National Cemetery, following a funeral service at First Baptist Church in Fairfax, Virginia.

The day was appropriately overcast, but at least it didn't rain. At the conclusion of the ceremony, the carefully folded American flag was presented to Masterson's sister, who, Morris knew, he saw once a year at Christmas. But she was his only living relative, barring some cousins scattered across the country.

The ceremony was attended by a number of clean-shaven, middle-aged men with short haircuts, whom Morris assumed were cops from one or another of the federal agencies. He didn't see any of the FBI people he knew, although he recognized several Secret Service agents from Stark's Richmond rally. Stark himself did not attend, nor did Mary Margaret Doyle. The Senator did, however, send an elaborate arrangement of flowers.

Morris and Libby Chastain were walking slowly toward the parking lot when a male voice behind them said, "Excuse me."

They turned to find one of the Secret Service agents who'd been on the speaker's platform with Stark the day of the shooting. In fact, Morris thought this was the one who organized the other agents' responses after Masterson went down. The man had mahogany-colored hair and very dark eyes. At 5'9" or so, he'd probably just made the Service's minimum height requirement. His thin face was somber.

The man said, "I'm Marty Arkasian. I was second-in-command of the detail the day Bat... died." Saying the last word gave him some trouble. "I was also his very close friend." He put out his hand, and Morris and Libby shook it, in turn.

"I'm Quincey Morris, from Texas. This is Libby Chastain. She lives in New York."

Arkasian looked Libby full in the face for the first time. "You're the witch, right?"

Libby nodded slowly, her face wary. "Yes, that's right."

"I wonder if you folks would care to go someplace and have coffee with me. I'd like to talk with you – and I don't mean sentimental reminiscences about Bat. That would be nice, but we've got more important things to discuss – like the reason Bat went to see you, Mister Morris."

"So you know about that," Morris said. "Obviously."

"I know quite a bit. That's why I think we need to talk."

Arkasian said if they turned left out of the cemetery, they'd find a Dunkin' Donuts down the road about a quarter mile. He suggested that they get their coffee to go, and park behind the restaurant.

"What're you driving?" he asked.

Morris said they had a Black Ford Fusion from Avis.

"Two-door or four-door?"

"Four," Morris said.

"Good. Once we're parked, I'll get in your back seat, and we'll have some conversation. No reason why we need to be seen in public together, beyond this little chat here. Sound okay to you?"

It did.

Twenty minutes later, Arkasian was pulling the Fusion's rear door shut behind him.

"Nice service today, huh?" he said, tearing the little plastic tab away from the lid of his coffee. "Good turnout, too."

"I was a little surprised – pleasantly so – that he was buried in Arlington," Morris said. "I understand that's not easy to get, if you aren't active-duty military."

"You're right. But one of the exceptions is for veterans who've earned one of five decorations, like the Congressional Medal of Honor, Distinguished Service Cross, awards like that. The Silver Star's on that list, and so is the Purple Heart. Bat had one of each."

"I didn't know," Morris said. "He never even told me he'd been in the service."

"Operation Desert Storm, 1990 to '91. Our first little tussle with Saddam Hussein. Bat was doing some kind of Special Ops stuff. He never talked about it very much with me, either."

"Did his sister do all the paperwork to get him in? I didn't think they were close."

"They're not. I did it." Arkasian hesitated. "Bat and I were lovers, Mister Morris. For just over three years. If you've got some kind of problem with that –"

"I don't," Morris said.

"Neither of us does," Libby told him.

"Okay, then. Well, that's why I'm familiar with what Bat knew about the Senator and his pet shark, Mary Margaret Doyle. He also gave me a rundown on the conversation the two of you had last week. And that means I need to ask you something, before we go any further."

"Go ahead."

"I know that the bullet that killed Bat was intended for Stark. The only reason Bat caught it instead was because... because he was so damn good at his job."

382

There was a sob lurking in Arkasian's voice as he finished the sentence.

"Yeah, I think that's a pretty fair assumption," Morris said. "Sad to say."

Arkasian cleared his throat a couple of times. "Okay, then – I don't know if you'd tell me the truth, but I need to ask. Were you or Libby on the other end of the gun that killed Bat?"

Morris saw that Arkasian was watching his eyes intently in the rear-view mirror.

"No, Agent Arkasian, that wasn't either of us. I don't think assassination is a solution that I'd ever arrive at, but in any case I had just started to look into Stark. I wouldn't think of killing somebody over as little information as I had."

"I don't do murder, either," Libby said. "It's against my religion."

After a few seconds, Arkasian nodded. "Okay, thanks. Call me Jerry, by the way."

"Sure," Morris said. "I'm Quincey, she's Libby."

Morris sipped some coffee. "So, what is it you wanted to talk about, exactly?"

"Bat never came right out and said what he thought was going on with Stark. But the evidence he had, mostly from his own observation, all points in one direction. I'm not sure I believe in all this demon stuff. I mean, today's the first I was inside a church since a wedding I went to last Fall. Not really my thing. But I guess I'm more open-minded about it all than I was a few weeks ago. And even more so since... what happened at the rally."

"What do you want from us?" Morris asked.

"I want to know if you've got any more intel than Bat did. I want to know what to believe. Once I've got that straight, I need to figure out what the fuck I'm gonna do about it – pardon my language, Libby."

"We did come across some new information recently," Morris said. "Quite a bit of it, actually."

"I know you said you're developing an open mind, Jerry," Libby said. "But what we're going to tell you is going to push that to the limit. We're going to ask you to believe some things that would be, for most people, simply unbelievable."

Arkasian nodded grimly. "Okay, then. Try me."

Senator Bob Leffingwell was not in a good mood. After all the speech-making he'd done in the past few days, and even with all the money his campaign had poured into this state, the good citizens of Virginia had given him no better than a second-place finish behind Howard Stark.

The ballroom of the Hilton Oceanview was starting to fill up, although Leffingwell wasn't scheduled to address his supporters for another forty-five minutes, when he would do his standard "We almost made it this time, and next time, by God, we will!" speech. As usual, the campaign had paid for a good buffet spread, as well as an open bar, to show appreciation to the many local volunteers.

Leffingwell knew better than to drink in public, but he had been hitting the buffet pretty hard. He tended to eat too much when he was unhappy. Good thing he was blessed with a fast metabolism. Otherwise, given the amount of unhappiness that is often endemic to politics, he'd probably weigh three hundred pounds by now.

"I thought this was going to be an easy first place finish for us," he said to his campaign manager, Simon Charteris. "You said the numbers looked good."

"They did, Senator." From long practice, Charteris stood close to his client and spoke in a voice that was loud enough for Leffingwell to hear without straining, but which would not be fodder for eavesdroppers.

"But our polling was done before somebody took a shot at Stark in Richmond," Charteris said. "My guess is he's getting some sympathy votes out of that – enough to make the difference between first and second, maybe."

Leffingwell shook his head in disbelief. "I know that a lot about politics defies rationality," he said. "But a chain of reasoning goes, 'I wasn't going to vote for Stark, because I don't think he'd be as good a President as Leffingwell. Oh, wait – somebody just tried to kill Stark. Guess that makes him more qualified for the job of President now, and I'll vote for him, instead.' Jeez!"

"Well, I suppose you *could* argue that what happened to Stark adds to his qualifications for the White House, in a way."

"Oh? And what way is that?"

"It's taught him how to duck."

Leffingwell laughed harder than the dumb joke was worth. He and Charteris stood there awhile, discussing plans for the next week's round of campaigning. They were interrupted periodically by half-drunk supporters who came up to shake the candidate's hand.

Then Leffingwell checked his watch and said, "I'm on in fifteen minutes, but my gut is killing me, Simon. Ate too much of the wrong thing again, as usual. I've got to run upstairs and get a hit of Gaviscon before the speech. There's still time."

"Want me to find someone to fetch it for you?" Charteris asked.

"No, I've got to take the dose with a glass of water, and it wouldn't do for these folks to see me taking medicine, even over-the-counter stuff. I'm supposed to be indestructible, remember? I'll see you in a few."

Leffingwell appreciated the work of his Secret Service detail, even before learning that one of their colleagues had apparently saved Howard Stark's life recently. He tried to make it easy for them to do their job. He walked up to one of the agents, who was standing just inside the ballroom door. Frank Turnbull was a broad-shouldered man who looked like he might be of Polynesian descent.

"I've got to go up to my room for a couple of minutes, Frank."

"Yes, sir," the agent said. That meant he would accompany Leffingwell to his room and back.

As they left the noise of the ballroom behind and headed toward the elevators, the agent said, "If you need something from your room sir, I can just radio one of the guys upstairs, have him bring it down for you. Save you a trip."

"Thanks, Frank, but I've got an upset stomach. Too much buffet, I guess. There's medicine in my bathroom that'll fix me up."

As Frank pushed the button to summon the elevator, he said, "You take Gaviscon, don't you sir? I thought I read that someplace."

"Yes, I found that's what works best for me. Why – your stomach acting up too?"

"Not at the moment, sir. But it does sometimes, so I picked up some of these. Sort of on your recommendation."

Frank reached in a pocket and produced a small plastic container that looked like the Gaviscon bottle, but in miniature.

"Gaviscon tablets," Leffingwell said. "Huh. Didn't know they even made these. Do they work?"

"Work pretty well for me, sir. I just chew one, then drink a glass of water."

Leffingwell opened the bottle. "Mind?" he asked Frank.

"No, sir – you go right ahead."

Leffingwell shook on of the white pills into his palm and looked at it. Then the elevator bell pinged, announcing a car's imminent arrival.

"Did you still want to go up, sir?"

"No, Frank, the hell with it. Let's go back in. Maybe you can scare me up a glass of water somewhere?"

"No problem, sir. Happy to do it."

"And Frank? Thanks. You may have just done me a huge favor."

"Glad to be of help, Senator," the Secret Service man said.

Chapter 37

"HELLO, QUINCEY?"

"Yeah, hi, Paul."

"I've got news for you, and I'm afraid it isn't real good."

"Uh-oh. What happened?"

"I made some calls, as I promised. It seems you're poison with the Jesuits right now, my friend."

"You mean, because of what happened to you?"

"Yeah, afraid so. You know that I don't hold you responsible for what happened. We've already had that conversation."

"Yes, and thank you."

"But apparently Strubeck *does* blame you. Before he went into the hospice, he apparently told anybody who'd listen that you'd conned me into performing an exorcism, then failed to exercise prudence during the ritual."

"In other words, I got you into it, then I let go of the girl's arm because I had to scratch my ass, and you lost your sight as a result."

"Yeah, something like that. *You* know that's total bullshit, and *I* know it's total bullshit. But Strubeck's not taking any calls. Apparently the cancer was further advanced than first thought, and he's in kind of bad shape right now."

"Sorry to hear that, even under the circumstances."

"I also wonder how much of this stems from Strubeck's desire, unconscious or not, to free himself from whatever responsibility he may bear in this mess."

"Think that's possible?"

"I do. He doesn't deserve the blame, any more than you do. But good people sometimes feel guilt, even when they don't have to."

"Yeah, I've heard that somewhere. And the Church doesn't exactly discourage it, either. A Rabbi I know once told me, "We may have invented guilt, but it took the Catholics to institutionalize it.""

"Guilty as charged – so to speak. So, anyway, I talked to Callahan, the new Rector. *Nada*. He and Strubeck go way back, and apparently whatever Strubeck said is good enough for him."

"Sweet fucking Jesus. Uh, sorry."

"Don't be. I think the Lord would forgive a little blasphemy, right about now."

"So, Callahan believes a guy who wasn't even there, over the guy who *was* there? The guy who's the injured party?"

"Exactly. I told him what happened, and explained that I went in there with my eyes open, so to speak."

"Please, Paul."

"Sorry. Bad joke. Anyway, Callahan seems to have convinced himself that I'm deluded – as a result of undue loyalty to an old friend, and a psychological need to justify what happened – to myself, if no one else."

"Forgive me for asking this, but can you go over his head?"

"Already tried, but the Father Provincial is apparently buds with Callahan, too. He wouldn't even talk to me. And I got my wrist slapped by the Socius, his Chief of Staff, for attempting to circumvent my Rector, who has apparently been placed in authority over me by the express wish of either the Lord God Almighty or St. Ignatius of Loyola, whoever comes first."

"Sorry you got your butt reamed, Paul."

"Not to worry – my career's not exactly in jeopardy. In my job, it's pretty hard to get fired. Even molesting altar boys doesn't do it, apparently – although it damn well should."

"The stakes are pretty high, Paul. I know I haven't told you why I'm looking for an exorcist, but take my word that if I fail, the consequences are likely to be *real* severe. Maybe if I explained that to your –"

"Forget it, Quincey. Jesuits are human beings, like anybody else, with all the attendant human failings. These guys have their minds made up. They might reconsider, eventually – but it's not gonna happen by tomorrow, or even the day after."

"Well, shit, what am I supposed –"

"What you ought to do is talk to the Dominicans."

"Oh. Them."

"I know you've got an irrational prejudice against those guys, over stuff that happened five hundred years ago, but they're the only game left in town – among religious orders, anyway. Individual parishes sometimes have an exorcist on staff, but unless you know the Bishop…"

"Yeah, I've already been down *that* road."

"Then I guess it's the Dominicans or nothing, my friend."

"Well, shit. The Dominicans it is, then – because *nothing* is just not an option."

NESTOR GREENE HAD spent almost $60 on a bottle of twelve-year-old Scotch, a single malt that its distillers pretentiously labeled 'The McCallan.' As he sat at the desk in his study, the height of the liquid in the bottle already reduced by several inches, he thought, *This stuff is so fucking good, maybe a certain amount of pretension may be excused. Here's to you, Mister McCallan, wherever you are.*

Greene poured more of the amber liquid into his glass with hands that were still steady, but not likely to remain so for much longer. The glass itself was a beautiful piece of Swedish crystal. Nestor Greene liked nice things, and he had always been willing to do what was necessary for him to afford them.

The things he had done for money over the years had never troubled him very much. Until now.

Greene took another sip from his glass, and concluded that Scotch this good almost compensated the world for atrocities like bagpipes, haggis, and The Eurhythmics. *If you could bottle Heaven, this is what it would taste like – just as well, since it may be the only taste of Heaven I ever get.*

Greene was replacing the glass on its coaster when the nearby phone rang. His hand jerked, causing him to spill a few drops of liquid Heaven onto his desk. He reached for a handkerchief with one hand and picked up the phone with the other.

"Hello?"

"You know who this is," said the voice of the ever-cautious Mary Margaret Doyle.

"Why yes, I believe I do."

"Have you carried out your most recent assignment?"

"I have – my part of it, anyway. I found the appropriate... specialist. Came highly recommended. He agreed to take the case. Since I haven't seen anything in the news, I assume he hasn't, um, completed treatment yet."

"He understands the time factor?"

"Yes – I made it very clear to him. As I said, he's supposed to be very reliable. Always delivers the groceries, to mix a metaphor."

"Good. You've done well. There may be other work for you down the road, if you're interested. But for now, I'll send you the balance due, and we can consider our association ended. Look for your payment in a few days."

"Thank you. I think –" Greene realized he was talking to a dead line. He slowly put the phone down, without uttering the obscene imprecations that usually followed any contact he had with Ms. Doyle.

So, another fifty grand was on its way to him, or would be soon. And unlike the money he owed The Grocer's Boy, this tidy little sum would be his, all his.

Nestor Greene took another sip from his glass. Fifty thousand dollars can buy you a lot – maybe even a decent night's sleep. Especially if it is accompanied by about half a bottle of liquid Heaven.

"HE'S BEEN DRINKING," Mary Margaret Doyle said. "I can hear it in the way he pronounces certain combinations of consonants."

"Too far gone to understand what you just told him?" the demon Sargatanas asked her.

"No, he was still coherent. If I'd called a couple of hours from now, that might be a different story."

"Very well. Now we'll make the device that will provide the final solution to our Nestor Greene problem, to borrow a phrase from one of your race's late, lamented statesmen."

On the desk of the hotel suite's living room – this one was in Minneapolis, but seemed identical to all the others – she laid out the various items that Sargatanas had directed her to buy. Fortunately, Mary Margaret Doyle did not receive Secret Service protection when she went out alone, unless she asked for it. She had not wanted witnesses to this little shopping trip.

Her errands had taken her to a hardware store and a laboratory supply house. Her last stop had been an 'alternative' food co-op, there to purchase Belladonna and Mandrake Root – both common ingredients used in black magic. Fortunately, she had not been told to secure Eye of Newt, since she would have had no idea where to begin looking.

"I could create this little device myself," Sargatanas said from over her shoulder, "but I want you able to make it by yourself in the future, so that I won't have to waste my time with such trivial matters."

Mary Margaret Doyle stood bent over the table, wearing only undergarments under the robe she had wrapped around herself. She and Stark were attending a fund-raising event tonight, and she did not wish to wrinkle her outfit before it was time to leave.

"Place some of the magnesium powder on that square of cloth. More. Now cut off a piece of Mandrake Root about the size of your thumb, and place it on top of the powder to that its ends face East - West. Now repeat this invocation after me. I'll write it down for you later…"

Ten minutes later, the device, as diabolical as ancient magic and modern science could devise, was almost ready to be wrapped for mailing. Sargatanas was still standing behind her, where he had been throughout the process, murmuring instructions in her ear.

Now he said, "It's a pity that this is the way we must dispense with Mister Greene, but it's too dangerous to take a more hands-on approach, this time."

"It doesn't matter," she said. "This looks as if it will do the job just fine."

"But it's so *impersonal*," he purred in her ear. "You won't even get to see him burn. Certainly not as enjoyable as the treatment you were able to inflict on the late Father Bowles."

"I'd really rather not –"

"Just imagine poor Mr. Greene, naked and bound tightly to a chair, his eyes wide with terror as he looks at your tools and imagines, quite correctly, what you're going to do to him."

"Since it's not going to happen, there seems no point –"

"You'd have to put a big piece of heavy tape across his mouth, of course, to muffle the screams. Unless you were fortunate enough to find a venue far from people. Then you could leave the gag off, and breathe in the screams like rare perfume. That's what *I'd* prefer."

"Listen, I really wish you –"

"My favorite part of such recreation is the very beginning, oddly enough. After you first draw blood, or apply flame to flesh. Once he's finished squealing – for the time being – and looks at you, with the realization dawning that you are utterly serious in your intentions, that you are about to do unspeakable things to him, and that there is no chance of escape. The despair in their eyes is wonderful to behold. Don't you agree?"

"No, I don't! I'm *not* like you, despite all your efforts to make me that way."

"I thought we already had this discussion, and it ended with you acknowledging your true nature, at last."

"I didn't mean it! I just said that to make you leave me alone!"

"Oh, I was *wrong*, then. My humble apologies for misjudging you. I can see now that you're not the kind of woman who would take pleasure from another's torment."

"Of *course* I wouldn't!"

He stepped back from her. When she turned, he was wearing a smirk that she wished she had the courage to wipe off with a good, hard slap.

"Just keep telling yourself that, Mary Margaret. In time, you may even come to believe it."

He walked toward the door, then stopped and turned back. "Although I really do have my doubts."

To say he ignored the sobs behind him would be inaccurate. In fact, he was smiling as he walked away.

FATHER MARTIN FINLAY was in his faculty office, trying to explain to a graduate student why her proposed thesis debunking the Book of Genesis might not be the surest path to her Masters Degree.

"Two of every species of animal, all living peacefully on the Ark – for *how* long? Give me a break, Father!"

The graduate student, Lucille McBride, was small, bespectacled, and intense-looking. She had taken two theology classes from Finlay already. Privately, he gave her high marks for intelligence and dedication, but somewhat lower ones for common sense.

"There are more than ten million known species and subspecies of animals, Father. It must have been one heck of a big boat, don't you think? Not to mention why all the plants didn't die from being underwater that long."

"Of course, it's absurd – but if you want an argument, you're talking to the wrong guy. If Jerry Falwell were still alive, I'd send you to him, but I'm sure there are any number of fundamentalist preachers willing to fight with you on that subject – but not a humble servant of Holy Mother Church, like *moi*. The Church has never taken the position that the Bible – well, at least the Old Testament – had to be interpreted literally. A lot of it is probably metaphor, in order to give the ancient Hebrews something they could relate to. As long as you grant the essential truth behind it, you don't *have* to believe the literal account. If you write the thesis you've proposed, your committee will just laugh."

The young woman leaned forward in her chair. "But I still think it's important to demonstrate –"

Finlay's phone rang. He said "Excuse me just a second" to Lucille and answered it, intending to find out who it was and offer to return the call later.

But not *this* call.

"This is Father Finlay, can I help you?"

"Father, this is Brother Frank, in Father Voytek's office."

Finlay felt a fist clench in the pit of his stomach, but he tried to keep his voice matter-of-fact. "Hey, Brother Frank. I'm with a student right now, so –"

"Father Voytek would like to see you, Father. Right away, I'm afraid."

"Yes, of course, I'll be there in a few minutes."

He hung up the phone. "Lucille, I hate to do this, but

that was Father Voytek's office. Father 'I'm-in-charge of-this-whole-place-and-don't-you-forget-it' Voytek. Remember him?"

She laughed a little. "Sure, I know who Father Voytek is, although I think your characterization might not be quite fair. He seems like a nice man."

"He *is*, actually – but not to priests who don't respond to his summons. I'm afraid I have to go. Are you free this time Friday?"

She checked her appointment book. "Sure, I can do Friday, if you like."

"Great – just remember: apple, tree, talking snake – maybe not. First parents screwing up big time – beyond doubt."

Lucille stood. "I'll argue it with you Friday, Father." She smiled. "Good luck with the ogre." And was gone.

Finlay walked briskly, wondering if he was being sent for in Father Voytek's capacity as President of the Institute, or as Prior Provincial of the Order. He would know soon.

The fist of dread had not loosened its grip on Finlay's innards. In fact, another big, strong hand seemed to have joined in on the task of constricting his digestive organs. He tried hard not to think of the word *exorcism*.

He opened the heavy door to the outer office, to find Brother Frank looking up expectantly. "Hi, Father – you're to go on in."

"Okay, thanks. What do you think, Brother Frank? Am I in deep shit?"

"Not as far as I know. There's some guy, a layman, who's been in there with him for over two hours. Guess they want you to join the party."

"Let's hope there's cake," Finlay said, and rapped twice on his boss's door.

At "Come in," he pushed the door open to find Voytek and the aforementioned layman – a guy in his forties with slightly graying black hair and a thin, careworn face.

Voytek stood up from behind his desk. "Father Paul Finlay, I'd like you to meet Mr. Quincey Morris."

* * *

Transcript of Oral Message left on the Answering Machine
of Ms. Judith Mary Racine
An Unindicted Co-Conspirator
Case 1443-16
People of the United States
v.
Quincey P. Morris, et al.
Second Circuit Court,
Federal District of Eastern New York
Offered as Evidence Exhibit 1443-16-221
by
Edward T. Richie, Senior Prosecutor
Office of the U.S. Attorney for Eastern New York

Voice on Tape Positively Identified as
Paul Thomas Finlay,
Federal Defendant #1443-16-003

TRANSCRIPT BEGINS

Hey, it's me. I know personal calls are frowned upon at work, so I figured I'd better do this. I wish I could wait to tell you in person, but I've got a plane to catch. I'm not sure when I'll be back – could be as much as a couple of weeks, or even... never mind, it doesn't matter. I wish I could explain to you why I can't say no to this, Judith. The stakes are just too high. I'm sorry for the distress I know this must be causing. Hey – I, like, love you, and stuff, you know? See you as soon as I can. Bye.

TRANSCRIPT ENDS

Chapter 38

THE MAN KNOWN to a few people as The Grocer's Boy had never been very interested in the news. But ever since returning from the job in Virginia, he'd made a point to watch a national news broadcast every day. That wasn't hard to manage, considering the wealth of news available on cable TV, in addition to those four diehard major networks, who were still in there pitching.

He was waiting for the big news story that would surround the death by heart attack of Senator Bob Leffingwell – *so sad, the nation mourns, we'll be back after these messages*. The killer had been home four days now, and no such story had appeared.

Either Leffingwell had been careful about what he ate lately, or the drug wasn't working as advertised. If the poison was at fault, did that mean the stuff was taking longer to work than expected, or that it wasn't going to work at all?

This uncertainty was a new experience for him – but then, he'd never been asked to kill by such indirect means before. His work tended to be pretty straightforward.

The marks were either mobsters or civilians who had pissed off some mobster, usually by not paying money owed or planning to say the wrong thing in court. His means was almost always a firearm – either pistol or rifle, although he used a handgun far more often.

Only twice had he used a knife, and that was because there had been no other choice. In one instance, the mark was never very far away from bodyguards, business associates, or family. Even a silenced pistol shot would probably bring somebody running from the next room, which meant more people to kill, without getting paid a dime for it. In the other blade job, the mark had positively surrounded himself with state-of-the art metal detectors. Fortunately for The Grocer's Boy, neither the mark nor his bodyguards had heard of ceramic knives.

But poison – he'd never used it before, and hoped never to again. There were too many variables outside his control, which led to unpredictable outcomes. Like now.

There was no way he was going to get anywhere near Leffingwell again. After somebody had taken a shot at Stark, one of the other candidates, everybody's Secret Service protection had doubled – he'd heard *that* on the news.

If the mark ultimately survived, it would be either because of bad luck on the killer's part, or extraordinarily good luck on Leffingwell's.

He hated the thought of calling Greene and reporting failure. Apart from personal embarrassment, word might get around. He'd never heard of this Greene before, had no idea how well connected the guy was, or who he might tell that The Grocer's Boy had fucked up – which wasn't even true, dammit.

Maybe the solution to his problems was to kill Greene while he was still waiting for Leffingwell to keel over. The killer would lose his fee, but at least his reputation would remain stellar, and that was worth a lot more than a measly fifty grand in the long run.

He'd give it a couple more days. If Leffingwell was still breathing, then the killer would pay a call on Mr. Greene. After all – in business, a man's reputation is really all he has going for him.

"I WAS HOPING we'd have the nomination locked by now, but I'm afraid this could go all the way to the convention," Fernando Garrett said to Stark, with Mary Margaret Doyle hovering in close attendance. "It's been a see-saw battle since February – you take First and Leffingwell takes Second, then Leffingwell comes in First, and you're right behind him. Neither one of you has been able to pull ahead."

"If we go into the convention more or less tied with Leffingwell, who has the edge?" Stark asked.

Garrett scratched his chin. "Hard to say. It could depend on who makes a deal with Martinez. He's running a distant third, and hasn't got a hope in hell of getting the nomination, but he could end up playing kingmaker."

"Which way is he leaning, do we know?" Mary Margaret Doyle said.

"More to the point," Stark said, "what does he *want*?"

"Regarding the first question, the short answer is 'we don't know.' He hasn't made any public statements indicating whether he favors you or Leffingwell, and if he's made them in private, I haven't heard about it – yet.

I've got some people trying to work back-channel and find out what he's thinking." Garrett sat back in his chair. "As to the second question, that's easy: he wants to be Vice President."

Stark pursed his lips. "If it came to that, we could do worse."

Garrett nodded. "We could for sure do a *lot* worse. The Latino population keeps growing and growing, and so does its political clout. Historically, Latinos have tended to vote heavily Democratic" – Garrett grinned at them – "but maybe that's because nobody ever gave them a good reason to vote Republican. Martinez on the ticket? Yeah, I think that'd be a pretty good reason. It would allow the GOP to take a big bite out of one of the Democrats' core constituencies – and help us shake the image that we're the party of rich white guys."

Mary Margaret Doyle paced the room slowly. "We'd get the conservatives anyway, of course. Even if some of them don't like a Hispanic in the number two spot, what are they going to do? Vote for the Dems? That scenario works only if the other side nominates a conservative for their top spot, and that will likely happen" – she smiled, as if at a private joke – "a week after Hell freezes over."

"About two weeks, I estimate," Garrett said.

"They might just stay home on election day," Stark said, "out of disgust with the idea of this *non-white* person just a heartbeat away from the Presidency."

Garrett shook his head. "Some years, maybe they would. But the Democrats have been in the White House a long time. Lots of conservatives are so hungry to see one of their own guys in power again" – Garrett, who was half Salvadoran, grinned a second time, but now there was a nasty edge to it – "they'll hold their noses and vote for us, even with a *spic* on the ticket."

"It occurs to me," Stark said, "that Leffingwell is going to be having a similar conversation with his own people, if he hasn't already."

"Of course," Garret said. "Those boys can count as well as we can."

"If both camps offer Martinez the VP slot..." Mary Margaret Doyle looked a question at Garrett.

"He'll go with whoever he thinks has the best shot at winning in November," Garrett said. "And right now, a reasonable case can be made for either you, Senator, or for Bob Leffingwell."

Stark nodded slowly. "Well," he said musingly, "maybe Leffingwell will falter before we get to the finish line."

Garrett shook his head dubiously. "I don't know – he'd running pretty strong at the moment."

"Still," Mary Margaret Doyle said, "stranger things have happened."

THE DEMON WHO called herself Ashley flopped down on the bed next to Peters and waited for his breathing to slow until it was something approaching normal.

After a bit, still looking at the ceiling, she asked, "And how did you like *that*?"

Peters raised a hand that was not quite steady. He held it before him, palm down, and waggled it in a *comme ci, comme ca* gesture. "Eh," he said, "not bad."

Without changing position, she knuckle-punched him in the thigh, quite painfully. "I'll give you 'Not bad,' Evespawn," she said with a grin. "That was the best sex of your life – this one or the old one – and you know it."

"It's always the best sex of my life," Peters said. "One of these days, my heart's just going to give out, or you'll give me a stroke."

"They'll find you on the bed, stone cold dead, with the biggest, widest grin any corpse has ever had."

"I'll take my chances," he said. "At least until the job's done – which has taken a quantum jump in difficulty."

The bed they lay on was in a hotel room, and the hotel was in Green Bay, Wisconsin. The 'Stark for President' campaign had rolled through town yesterday, with Stark giving three speeches before moving on to the next primary state.

Peters and Ashley had looked for opportunity, and found it sorely lacking. For Stark's outdoor events, the Secret Service had even placed teams on surrounding rooftops – each team consisting of an agent with field glasses and another agent with a high-powered rifle.

"They didn't have counter-snipers on the roofs in Virginia," she said.

"Because they didn't think anybody was going to be sniping at Stark in Virginia. If Chastain hadn't done her little voice trick with '*Gun!*' this would all be over with by now."

"I think she's kinda cute. Do you think she's cute?"

"You weren't acting like you found her cute the first time," Peters said.

"Obviously, we're separated by denominational differences."

"It looked more like the cats of Kilkenny to me."

"Sorry?"

"The Irish legend about the cats of Kilkenny – they fight wherever and whenever they meet."

"I didn't say I wasn't willing to fight her," Ashley

said. "It may come to that, eventually. But I wouldn't mind fucking her, either."

"Well, you might still get the chance – to do one or the other. Since we can't get to Stark, looks like we'll have to play it her way – hers and Morris's. Which means we better go to that meeting in Newark, day after tomorrow."

"Yes, I suppose you're right," Ashley said, not sounding happy about it.

"Since you've got the magic touch, not only in bed but with the computer, would you be so good as to get us airline reservations?"

"Well, since you asked so nicely..." She got up and walked naked to the desk where they had set up Peters' laptop. She sat down and started pointing and clicking.

"I suppose we'll have to fly into New York, rent wheels, then drive across the river," she said. "Ugh."

Peters was on his way to the shower, but he turned back for a moment. "Come on, baby, we've both been in Hell – I think we can probably handle New Jersey."

Chapter 39

THE SUITE ON the fourth floor of the Best Western in Newark, New Jersey was rented in the name of something called QM Reclamations, Inc., which described itself to the IRS every year as a 'consulting firm.' QM Reclamations could have rented a conference room for the planned meeting (the Best Western offered several), but the CEO and founder of the company decided that such an arrangement might draw undue attention to what was, after all, a very private meeting.

The suite's living room was already furnished with a sofa and two easy chairs, along with a straight-backed chair that went with the room's desk. In addition, the straight-backed desk chairs from each of the suite's two bedrooms had been brought into service. All of this furniture was arranged in a rough oval.

The meeting, which was due to begin at 10:00, actually started at 10:06. No minutes were kept.

Quincey Morris had been sitting in one of the straight chairs. Now he stood and said, "Everybody's here, so we might as well get started. To say 'Thank you all for coming' sounds trite, and doesn't begin to convey the gratitude I feel to each of you for the trouble you went to, as well as the risk you're assuming. But – thanks for coming."

This raised a laugh. A small one.

"Before we go any further," Morris said, "There's something I need to say out loud, even though you're probably well aware of it. Speaking of saying stuff out loud, by the way, I want to assure you that there's no surveillance, electronic or otherwise, directed at this room. It was checked, just an hour ago" – he nodded toward Libby Chastain – "by an expert, and it's now protected by some magic that, I'm told, will make sure whatever we say in here stays private."

Morris paused, as if choosing carefully the next words he was about to say.

"If you stay in this room for the discussion we're about to have, you will almost certainly be engaging in a criminal conspiracy, even if you never do anything about it after you leave. It's also very likely, if we carry out the operation I'm going to propose, that we will be breaking a number of laws, federal and local. We run the very real risk of losing our liberty – even our lives."

He paused to let this sink in. "So if that risk is more than you're willing to take, get out now. I won't insult your intelligence by saying that nobody will think any less of you for leaving. Personally, I'll hate you" – more laughter, a little louder this time – "but it's your life, and your freedom. Nobody should decide to risk them but you. So, anybody feels like walkin', now's the time."

He waited through a slow count to ten in his head. *No point in dragging it out.*

"Okay, then. To save this from looking like a damn encounter group, I'll go around the room and perform the introductions. I've talked with each of you individually about what's okay to say, and what isn't, so nobody should be getting mad about the way you're introduced."

He gestured to his left, toward the woman sitting closest to him on the couch. "This is Libby Chastain. She's a member of the Sisterhood of Wicca, which means she's a white witch. She's also a business associate of mine, and a very good friend.

"Next to her is Eleanor Robb, known as Ellie." He indicated a thin, intense-looking woman in her fifties, with black hair going gray. "She heads the North American circle of the Sisterhood of Wicca. That makes her a white witch, too."

Morris nodded toward one of the chairs. "This gentleman is Special Agent Jerry Arkasian, of the U.S. Secret Service. He's assigned to Senator Howard Stark's security detail. Next to him is Father Martin Finlay, a priest of the Dominican Order – and an exorcist."

Finlay was not dressed in the robes of his order today. Instead, he wore a blue chambray shirt, jeans, and a grim expression.

"Over there," Morris said, "is Mal Peters. He used to kill people for the CIA – until he was himself killed in 1983, whereupon he was consigned to Hell. He has been sent back for an indefinite time, with the job of assassinating Senator Stark."

Peters seemed aware that several people were looking at him with curiosity. He shrugged his big shoulders and nodded a general greeting.

Morris cleared his throat before continuing. "Next to him is a lady who goes by the name of Ashley. She normally resides in Hell, as a demon of the fourth rank. She was temporarily given human form and sent here to work with Mr. Peters on the assassination of Howard Stark."

Ashley gave the room a brittle smile and said, "I'll be pivoting my head around and barfing pea soup later, if anyone's interested." Nobody laughed.

"I don't mean to be difficult," Finlay said, looking at Morris, "but is this young lady's claim to be an incarnated demon supported by anything other than her own word, and maybe that of her companion?"

"I can attest that –" Libby began.

"No, no, the man asks an intelligent question," Ashley said, a tiny smile on her face. "I'll tell you what," she said to Finlay, "I will reveal my true form to you, right here and now. Will you trust the evidence of your own eyes?"

"I would, yes," Finlay said.

"I'm only going to do it for a second," Ashley said. "That's about as much as most humans can stand without suffering permanent mental damage."

She looked around the room. "The rest of you, if you're smart, will look away and spare yourself some bad dreams. But I imagine your own curiosity will get the better of some of you. So be it – don't say you weren't warned."

She looked at Finlay again. "Before we proceed, *Father*, I want to be sure there's no quibbling about it later. Do you have any reason to believe you've been hypnotized?"

Finlay shook his head. "No reason at all."

"Is it possible that someone may have slipped you a dose of some hallucinogenic drug once you got here?"

"Not possible. I haven't consumed anything since arriving."

"So you trust your perceptions, at the present time?"

"Yes. I trust them completely."

"Very well," Ashley said, and then she did it.

410

It is not possible to describe in any human language what an actual demon looks like. The image is, literally, unspeakable – which is another way of saying that it is horrible beyond words.

Several of those present did not look; they knew more or less what they would see, and had no desire to see it again, if they didn't have to.

Quincey Morris, Libby Chastain, Ellie Robb, and Malachi Peters all averted their eyes. Finlay looked, since that was the point of the exercise. Arkasian looked, too, because part of his mind did not believe it was really possible.

One second is not a long time. But there are circumstances in which it can seem a very long period, indeed. Try pressing your fingertip against a hot stove for a full second; when you're done, you'll probably wish you hadn't, but you will have had a good lesson in the flexibility of time.

So Astur Badaktu, once ranked in the fourth choir of rebellious angels so very long ago, and now a denizen of Hades, where the worm dieth not, etc., displayed her real self to these disbelieving humans.

They saw – and believed.

Finlay drew back in his chair as if flinching from a blow. His eyes became huge, his mouth dropped open, and a thin stream of saliva began to run down his chin.

Arkasian, lacking Finlay's years of religious training and devotion, was even less prepared for what he had seen. Unlike Finlay, he did not rear back in his chair. Instead, the Secret Service man sat rock still, as if he had gone catatonic. Then he started to cry.

Libby Chastain got to her feet, and Ellie Robb did the same. "We thought this might occur," she said, "so we have something prepared that should help."

411

Libby went at once to Finlay's chair, while Ellie tended to Arkasian.

Libby squatted next to Finlay, which put her face approximately level with his. She touched the side of his face with her palm and softly said a word that no one else in the room but Ellie Robb would recognize. Keeping her hand in place, she said the word twice more. Then she took from a pocket a small square of cloth, which she unwrapped to reveal a single leaf of clover. She picked it up and reached toward Finlay's still-open mouth. "I'm just going to put this on your tongue," she said. "Leave it there, don't swallow yet." She put the clover leaf in place then lightly touched her fingers to the underside of Finlay's jaw. "Close your mouth, Father."

Ellie Robb was doing more or less the same thing with Arkasian, who now had tears and snot dripping on to his shirt.

Libby rose and went behind Finlay's chair. She gently wrapped her hands around his skull and uttered a sentence in that unrecognizable language. She left her hands there for a few seconds more, then bent and whispered in Finlay's ear, "Now, swallow."

Finlay did as he was told. Then he slowly pulled his head back and took in a deep, deep breath. He let it out, and gazed around the room – without looking at Ashley too closely, perhaps for fear of what he might see again.

Arkasian seemed also to have responded positively to Ellie's spell. He'd found a handkerchief and begun mopping his face. His expression was pensive.

Ellie Robb touched Libby's shoulder and spoke softly to her for a second or two. Then both witches resumed their seats.

Ashley gave an exaggerated shrug. "Don't blame *me*," she said. "I warned them."

"Yes you did, Ashley." There was no anger in Libby's voice or manner. "I think it was important that we had this little... experiment, unpleasant though it was for these poor guys." She glanced toward Ellie, who nodded. "Although several of us here have bits and pieces of information, the definitive proof of Stark's nature comes from you and Mr. Peters," Libby said. "Now there should be no doubt as to your veracity. What you did was necessary, and you softened the blow as much as you could. I thank you for that."

Ashley stared at Libby, and for once there was no instinctive hostility in her face. She looked at Libby for a few seconds, then turned away.

Libby turned to the two men who had just been treated. "Jerry? Father Finlay? You guys okay now?"

Finlay rubbed a hand briskly over his face, as if waking up from a deep sleep. "Much better, thank you Libby. And please, call me Marty, all of you." He looked over at Libby. "You know the theological implications of what I just experienced, not only from Ashley but also from your... spell? Was that what it was?"

Libby nodded. "A minor one, but useful sometimes."

"I'm going to have to think about how that fits into my belief system."

"I don't think my beliefs are incompatible with most of yours, Father," Libby told him. "We'll talk sometime, if you like, once this business is done."

Morris looked at Arkasian, who was still cleaning himself up. "Jerry? You okay, podner? Would you like a glass of water?"

"Water? Yeah, that'd be good." Arkasian's voice sounded phlegmy. "Thanks, Quincey." As Morris stood,

Finlay asked, "Could I have one, too?" and received a nod in return.

"I guess," Arkasian said to nobody in particular, "I'm gonna have to have to start going to church again."

Ashley shook her head in mock disgust. "I was *afraid* that would happen."

Arkasian turned her way curiously, and she smiled at him, then winked. He gave a bellow of laughter that went on awhile and threatened to turn into hysteria. "Jerry!" Libby said sharply.

He stopped, and looked at her.

"It's okay now," she said. "Everything's going to be fine."

Finlay looked across at Ashley. "Frankly, I prefer your present form, which is really quite attractive. If you'd keep that one in place, I'd be grateful."

"I was planning to," she said.

"I'm not sure how I'm supposed to feel about you," Finlay said. "In theory, or maybe theology, you're my bitterest enemy, a representative of something I've been fighting my whole adult life."

"Yeah, I know," she said. "I've been dealing with some stuff like that, myself." She glanced toward Libby. "But we've all got bigger fish to fry right now, don't you think, Marty?"

"Yes, absolutely."

"So why don't you just think of me as a hot chick who comes from a really bad neighborhood, and leave it at that. Okay?"

"I'll do my best."

Morris returned from one of the bathrooms with two water-filled glasses and gave one each to Finlay and Arkasian. Then he resumed his place in the front of the room.

"We know from Ashley and Mr. Peters what some of us had suspected: that Senator Howard Stark is possessed by a demon. As I understand it, this possession took place about eighteen months ago. Mr. Peters, perhaps you and Ashley could fill in some of the details."

"Just call me Mal, okay?" the big man said. "Okay, then. Ashley and I have been told, by those who would know, that it happened last Halloween, in Rhode Island. Some guy named Hassan el-Ghaffar did a summoning. I guess he'd done it successfully before, and Stark was coming down from Boston to watch him do it again. I think he had visions of a battalion of invincible demons wearing the uniform of the U.S. Marines, someday. With Stark getting all the credit, of course."

"But it was a set-up," Ashley said. "Stark had – *has* – this woman who he's depended on for years to run his political career. Mary Margaret Doyle. I don't know how she did it, but she arranged to betray Stark during the summoning, which called up the demon Sargatanas."

"This Doyle woman broke the circle after Sargatanas had been summoned," Peters said. "I guess most of you know what that means – he was freed. But instead of just killing everybody present, he took possession of Stark's body. He and this Doyle chick killed el-Ghaffar, then went off to rule the world, or try to."

"I guess I'm the only one here who isn't part of the club, so to speak," Arkasian said, "so I hope you don't mind some dumb questions. Here's my first one: why would this demon Sargatanas want to possess Stark, as opposed to taking over anybody else?"

"Because Stark was already running for President," Peters said. "With Sargatanas's 'help,' he could succeed. As you can see, he's pretty close already. Maybe you've noticed that funny things have been happening to a lot of the Republican politicos who were competing with Stark for the nomination."

"Okay, here's my next dumb question," Arkasian said. "Why does whoever sent Sargatanas want him to be President? So he can turn America into a bunch of Satan-worshippers?" He looked at Ashley. "No offense."

"I'm not offended, Jerry – in fact, that sounds like a pretty cool idea -- but the stakes are much bigger than that," Ashley said.

She and Peters then explained about the competing factions in Hell – one planning humanity's destruction, another fearful of the consequences if the plot succeeded.

When they had finished, Finlay said, "This is fascinating – or it would be, if the danger it poses wasn't so great. The Church has never really considered the possibility of factions in Hell. I guess we always assumed that it's the evil analog of Heaven – or of what we believe Heaven to be. There'd be one supreme authority, Satan in this case, and everybody else does what they're told."

"Even Heaven has its factions, Marty," Ashley told him. "Well, once, anyway. That's why Hell was created – to exile and punish the losing faction, of which I was one, sad to say."

"I was surprised by that at first, too," Peters said, "but she's right. The relationships among the top demons in Hell is worse than Renaissance Italy during the time of the Borgias. Plots and counterplots, schemes and conspiracies – it never stops."

"Part of it's boredom," Ashley said. "You've got these supremely intelligent creatures without a lot to do. I mean, tormenting damned souls is fun, but it gets old after a few thousand years. And so we've turned on each other. Some of us, anyway."

"You guys need cable TV or something down there," Arkasian said with a shrug. "I'm just sayin'."

"Oh, we have it now," Ashley told him. "But all we get is *The Jerry Springer Show*."

Arkasian looked startled, before he realized she was kidding him.

"Old joke," Peters said. "They do have them in Hell, you know."

"I know, Morris said. "In fact, I've come across that one before, myself."

Ashley looked at him closely. "Yes," she said. "I bet you have."

"Perhaps we could all return to the matter at hand," Libby said. "So, we know that Stark was possessed against his will, that the demon within him is ruthlessly seeking the Presidency, and that if he succeeds he will do his best to destroy the world – and might well manage it. We also know that at least one faction in Hell opposes this plan, which is how Ashley and Mal got here. The important issue, is seems to me, and the reason why we're all here, is what we do about it."

"My instructions were to kill him," Peters said. "I already told you that. Once Stark dies, Sargatanas will be returned to Hell."

"But that way, an innocent man is killed," Ellie said. "I can see how that might not unduly concern the agents of Hell, but it certainly bothers *me*."

"It bothers me and Libby too," Morris said. "That's why we brought in Father – uh, I mean Marty. If he can conduct a successful exorcism, then Sargatanas also goes back to hell, right?"

"Yeah, that's right," Peters said. "They don't care about Stark himself. Astaroth's bunch just wants Sargatanas back home, before he can do something to provoke Armageddon."

"Killing him is still the simplest and best way," Ashley said. "You guys of the white always make things so damn complicated."

"We won't be party to murder, Ashley," Libby said. "That is, unless there is absolutely no alternative. If it came down to the choice between Stark's death, and the destruction of all the world and its people, then, okay. It's justified."

"But even then," Ellie said, "all Libby and I could do is step aside. We cannot use our power for murder, no matter what circumstances seem to justify it."

"But killing Stark isn't the only option," Morris said. "And since, I gather, the increased security around Stark has made assassination virtually impossible, you all need us to help you carry out your mission. Which means you have to do it our way."

"Yeah, yeah, I accept that," Ashley said, sounding weary. "That's why Peters and I showed up. But, boy, I'm never gonna live this down in Hell, even if it succeeds."

"Perhaps," Finlay said, with the tiniest of smiles, "You could tell them that an angel made you do it."

Chapter 40

THE KILLER KNOWN as The Grocer's Boy was not the only one who had been following the news of late, waiting for Bob Leffingwell to keel over. To Nestor Greene, the subject of the man's health, or lack of it, had become a matter of great interest bordering on obsession.

Unlike the professional killer he'd hired, Greene didn't have to change his daily habits in order to keep track of what was going on in the world. He was a news junkie – partly from sheer interest in the great chess game where everybody cheats, and partly out of necessity. After all, he never knew what event in politics or world affairs would provide him with a new client – or a new target.

When Leffingwell was still alive, a week after Greene's meeting with The Grocer's Boy, a knot of tension had formed in his chest, just below the breastbone. With every passing day that found Bob Leffingwell still above ground, the knot seemed to grow a little bigger, a little tighter. Greene had even consulted his physician, to be sure that he wasn't developing some kind of heart problem or esophageal disorder.

Dr. Endicott had performed an EKG right there in his examining room, the results proving normal as could be. He'd even given Greene a piece of the long ribbon of paper that the machine had disgorged, showing the activity of his heart – "in case you ever need to prove that you have one." Dr. Endicott knew something of Greene's work. He was a skilled physician, but in Greene's view, over-fond of his own wit.

Dr. Endicott had also probed Greene thoroughly, both with his fingers and verbally.

Was Greene experiencing undue tension lately?

No, not really.

Was he worried about anything, either in business of his personal life?

No, everything was reasonably copacetic, for an election year. His personal life was confined, as usual, to high-class whores, a fact Greene neglected to mention.

Had Greene been having trouble sleeping?

No – as always, he slept like a rock.

There was barely a word of truth in any of Greene's answers. Even though he knew at some level of his mind that lying to your doctor is extraordinarily stupid, the habit of playing the cards close to his chest was deeply ingrained in him – even when, as now, those cards seemed to be pressing a little too firmly for comfort.

Part of what was wearing on Greene was the uncertainty. He'd always had a low tolerance for ambiguity, and the present situation might well be used to illustrate 'Ambiguity' in some future encyclopedia of politics – or psychology.

Had The Butcher's Boy just changed his mind, figuring he was under no obligation to Greene since he had demanded no money in advance? Had he taken one good, hard look at the security surrounding Leffingwell and decided, "No not for me, too dangerous. There's easier ways of earning fifty grand."

Or had the killer's past caught up with him? You can't kill people, even mobsters, without making some other people mad – maybe that was especially true with mobsters. Could be, somebody who took one of The Grocer's Boy's hits as a personal affront had tracked the guy down and dished out a good, lethal dose of the killer's own medicine. Greene could have seen a news story about the killer's comeuppance and never even known it, since he had no useful name to go with the face he'd seen, and people got themselves murdered all the time.

Or was the heart-attack-in-a-bottle drug that Mary Margaret Doyle had provided for him defective in some way? Greene had no way of knowing where she had obtained it, or under what circumstances, or even what it was. It was not like the ever-efficient Ms. Doyle to fuck up like that, but she was only human. Wasn't she?

Thoughts of Mary Margaret Doyle eventually sent him to the post office. She'd said she was going to pay him another fifty thousand, the implication being that she wasn't going to wait until she'd read Leffingwell's obituary to do so. That was all to the good – if she was willing to pay him for failure, he was happy to accept it.

He wondered if it might be a good idea to go away for a while. Greene's finances had improved significantly of late, thanks to the nasty, well-paying tasks he'd been performing on Ms. Doyle's behalf. Maybe he should take a vacation until the election was over. Then the issues of Leffingwell's death and Stark's candidacy would be moot, one way or the other. She wouldn't take the trouble to exact vengeance by that point. Would she?

Greene had always wanted to visit Brazil. He had a smattering of Portuguese, and he thought he could pick up the rest fairly quickly. Languages had always been easy for Greene, who spoke four. He could work on his grammar while basking on the beach at Rio de Janeiro, enjoying the scenery offered by whatever genius had invented the thong bikini, and sampling the local talent.

At the post office, Greene was gratified to find the smudged, once-white card informing him of a package that was waiting. Even the line to the counter – long and slow-moving, as usual, did not spoil his good mood. It *had* to be from Mary Margaret Doyle. She was his only client these days, and his former associates had never shown any burning desire to keep in touch.

As Greene inched closer to the head of the line, he was using his meager knowledge of Portuguese to piece together in his mind the sentence, "How much for half-and-half?"

BOB LEFFINGWELL WAS feeling good about things. Last weekend's round of six primaries had ended with Leffingwell taking first place in four, leaving Stark to suck hind tit with the other two. Martinez was still a distant third, and his catching up with the front-runners now was not only politically unlikely, but mathematically impossible.

Leffingwell had been thinking that matters had reached the point where he ought to have a quiet conversation with Martinez, or one of his top advisors. It was time for Ramon to face reality and cut the best deal he could before going into the convention. Besides, being the first Latino Vice President, although not quite the social leap forward that Barack Obama's election to the White House had been, was still enough to guarantee you a prominent place in the history books.

The campaign was not on the road today, for once, which meant Leffingwell was able eat all of his lunch in one sitting. But, wouldn't you know it, even a fairly leisurely meal had stimulated the acid reflux that had plagued him during the campaign.

Fortunately, there was a cure – or at least a temporary palliative. He called a five-minute break from the meeting he'd been having with Charteris and a few other top-level people in the living room of yet another hotel suite and made a beeline for his bathroom.

The toilet kit was where he'd left it after shaving this morning, and the bottle of Gaviscon was inside, just as he'd remembered. Leffingwell shook the bottle, like you were supposed to, and drew a glass of cool water from the tap. Thus prepared, he unscrewed the maroon cap from the plastic bottle. The manufacturer said you were supposed to take two tablespoons worth, but Leffingwell never traveled with a spoon or measuring cup. One substantial swallow usually did the trick.

He was bringing the bottle to his lips when one of his aides called from the living room, "Senator! Phone for you! It's O'Brian, from your Senate office. Says it's urgent."

Leffingwell lowered the bottle and shook his head at the reflection in the bathroom mirror. Never a minute's peace. "I'll be right there," he yelled through the slightly open door.

Then he brought the bottle of Gaviscon to his mouth, tilted his head back, and took a big swig.

* * *

THE GROCER'S BOY watched Nestor Greene's Jaguar pull into the post office parking area, and chose a spot for his own car that gave him a clear view of the lot's only entrance/exit. He'd see the Jag when it left.

Taking care of Greene inside his home looked like it would pose some difficulties. Perhaps because of all the enemies he'd made, Greene had spent what looked like a good deal of money making the place safe: floodlights, good locks, and what looked, through binoculars, like a state-of-the-art alarm system.

The Grocer's Boy was a killer, not a burglar. He had acquired a few housebreaking tricks along the way, but he didn't trust his skills sufficiently to test them against Greene's little fortress. Anyway, a fortress only protects you as long as you're inside it.

There were too many people around here to risk popping Greene as he came out with his mail, and the traffic in this part of town moved too slowly for a quick run to the nearest Interstate ramp. He would tail Greene unobtrusively and wait for him to stop in the right sort of place.

Then the killer could put on the big hat and sunglasses he'd brought with him, and get out of the car with the paper bag that contained the silenced pistol. He'd walk up to Greene, take out the gun, and put two bullets into him (one each in head and heart, if possible). Then he would replace the gun in the bag and keep walking to where he'd parked.

If Greene went straight home from here, there was always tomorrow, and the day after. Sooner or later, Nestor Greene would put himself within The Grocer's Boy's delivery area.

It was a good fifteen minutes before Greene appeared again, carrying a small package wrapped in brown paper. The killer watched him return to the Jag and get in, then started his own car, prepared to follow. *Come on, Nestor, take yourself out to dinner. You deserve it. Find a nice, quiet restaurant, maybe on a side street somewhere. Have a good meal in your stomach when you die.*

But Greene didn't start up the Jag immediately. It looked like he was fiddling with something in his lap – probably the package he'd brought out with him. Maybe Mom had sent cookies, and Greene couldn't wait to try one.

Don't eat too many, Nestor. Wouldn't want you to spoil your appetite for dinner.

The explosion when it came wasn't very loud – certainly nothing like your typical car bomb. The Jaguar didn't blow apart. But the inside of the car lit up immediately with the bright glare of something that was burning very fast, and very hot.

The Grocer's Boy watched with professional interest. He could see Greene frantically thrashing around inside the car, and he could hear the screaming from where he sat, even with the windows closed. He was not moved to run over and offer assistance. A couple of local heroes did give it a try, but the intensity of the blaze drove them back. In time, the awful screaming stopped, and the bright fire seemed to be dying down.

He could hear sirens in the distance now. No point in hanging around. He didn't know who hated Nestor Greene enough to burn him alive, and didn't really care. The job was done, even if somebody else did it.

The Grocer's Boy left town with his reputation intact.

Chapter 41

"WE HAVE A lot working against us," Quincey Morris said. "What we're going to do is, in effect, abduct a candidate for the Presidency of the United States, under the noses of what is probably –" he nodded toward Arkasian "– the best security team in the world, get him somewhere secure, and maintain that security long enough for Marty to conduct an exorcism – that takes approximately how long, Marty? I have some experience there, but I'd like to hear your estimate."

"The answer," Father Martin Finlay told the group, "depends on whether you're talking about how long it takes to complete the ritual, or how long to drive out the demon. And the reason those times are different is that it doesn't always work the first time."

"So, you could be at it for a while," Jerry Arkasian said.

"Yes, I could. The process itself, if conducted strictly by the book – the *Ritual of Exorcism*, I'm talking about – without interruption, takes about an hour. Forty-five minutes to an hour."

"Maybe you ought to explain what you mean when you say, 'strictly by the book,'" Morris said.

"The book is the ritual," Finlay said. "But it was never intended to be set in stone. There's room for what, in a less serious matter, I might call improvisation. There are certain prayers that I sometimes use, even though they're not part of the ritual *per se*. I use them because they've been helpful to me in the past. That's all."

"I want to see if I can establish some parameters of what's possible, versus what's likely," Ellie said. "I'm not sure how much help the Sisterhood will be in this endeavor, but we'll do whatever we can. So when I ask about statistics, Father, understand that I mean no disrespect. I'm not treating the sacred ritual like baseball cards. But the numbers may be important."

"Ask what you want, Ellie, and I'll answer what I can. God knows –"

"*Aaaah.*" Ashley had given vent to a short, sharp scream and was now hunched over in her chair, hands clasped tightly over her ears. After a few seconds she straightened up, her face wet with tears. "Well, turnabout is fair play, I guess" she said.

"Ashley, I'm sorry if I –"

"No, it's okay, it's not your fault. I should have realized the obvious – that you can't discuss this subject without using… that name. But it shouldn't surprise you, Marty that hearing it – well you just saw what happens."

Ashley stood up. "I wouldn't ask you to refrain from saying it, Marty. Even if you tried, it would be only minutes before you forgot yourself and said it again. Therefore," she said, heading towards the door," *I* am going for a walk."

Libby was frowning. "Does this mean you're abandoning the… whatever this is… the operation?"

"No, it doesn't, Libby. It just means I'm going for a walk. What we're doing is too important for me to bail out now."

She turned to Peters, "When you want me back, just say, out loud, 'Ashley, please.' I'll be here immediately. Okay?"

"Yeah, sure," Peters said carefully. "I'll do that."

Ashley glanced around the room. "I can't really say that it's been nice meeting all you folks, but I will say it's been interesting. I'll see you in a bit."

Then she was through the door and gone.

"If I had any doubts about what she is," Finlay said, "which I most certainly don't, that would clinch it for me. During exorcism, demons often can't stand to hear the name of God, or that of Our Savior Jesus Christ, or any other holy name."

"Let's get back to it, shall we?" Morris said. "Although Ashley's reaction, and the understandable reaction earlier of you and Jerry here, is giving me the beginnings of an idea. I'll tell you all about it later, if it makes sense."

"You were asking about my experience expressed statistically, Ellie," Finlay said. "This will have to be off-the-cuff, since I've never sat down with a calculator and tried to figure this stuff out."

"I understand," Ellie said. "Now, have you ever succeeded in an exorcism with the first attempt?"

"Yes, I have."

"Can you give us an idea, just approximate, of what percentage of your exorcisms worked the first time?"

Finlay's brow furrowed. "I'd say about a quarter of the time – yeah about twenty-five percent."

"What was the greatest number of times you've had to go through the ritual, in a single case?"

"Successfully, you mean? Hmmm. I'd say it was nine, over several days. Exorcism is exhausting – I don't think there's a priest alive who could do nine back to back without rest. And don't forget, this is a religious ritual – it must be treated with reverence."

"You said 'successfully,' a minute ago," Peters said. "Does that mean sometimes you've failed?"

"Yes, sad to say, it does."

"I don't mean to seem obsessed with this," Ellie said, "but how many times did you not succeed?"

"I can remember four cases where I was unable to bring deliverance to the possessed," Finlay said. "And before you ask, Ellie, I believe that I've performed a total of sixty-four exorcisms, although I could be off by a couple either way."

"So, there's no guarantee," Arkasian said bleakly. "We could risk everything, and it might all be worth diddly-squat."

"Yes, Jerry, I'm afraid so," Finlay said.

"I think I remember an old David Bromberg song," Arkasian said, "that goes, 'A man should never wager more than he can afford to lose.'"

"Good advice," Morris said.

"Yeah," Arkasian said. "Too bad we can't follow it."

AFTER LEFFINGWELL CALLED for a break, the senior campaign staff and their aides were standing around the room in groups of two or three, chatting quietly. The phone rang, and a nearby staff aide named Patrick Connor picked it up. He listened for a moment, said, "Yes sir, I'll get him."

Connor had seen Leffingwell go into the bathroom. The door was partly ajar, so he called out toward the gap, "Senator! Phone for you! It's O'Brian, from your Senate office. He says it's urgent."

He heard Leffingwell's voice say, "I'll be right there." A few seconds later, he heard sounds from the same source that alarmed him – spitting, gagging, choking sounds. He dashed toward the bathroom door and whatever awaited him on the other side.

EVER SINCE HE quit smoking two years ago, Bob Leffingwell had marveled at how sensitive his taste buds had become. That meant that good food tasted better than it used to – and, of course, bad food was worse than before.

Leffingwell knew what the liquid antacid labeled Gaviscon tasted like – it had a slight minty flavor. What he had just poured into his mouth did not taste like mint, or like Gaviscon, or like anything he wanted in there one instant longer.

Without even thinking about it, Leffingwell spit the liquid out violently. Most of it went into the sink, although some hit the mirror, and a little more ended up on the bathroom counter. Leffingwell had never tasted something so vile in his life, and he continued to gag even after his mouth was empty.

One of the aides, Patrick something, burst in, a panicked look on his face. "Sir, are you all right? Senator?"

Leffingwell, incapable of speech for the moment, held out a reassuring hand. He took the glass of water he'd set down nearby and used it to rinse his mouth out, thoroughly. By then Ron Messmer, one of the Secret Service agents, was at the door, shouldering young Patrick aside.

"What's happened, sir? Can you talk?"

Leffingwell could now, even though some of that awful taste remained in his mouth. "I came in here to take some antacid. It's the same brand I always use. Hell, I've used about half this bottle already. But I haven't had any in a couple of weeks, I guess, and the stuff's gone bad – in a *big* way." Leffingwell spat into the sink again. "I didn't think antacid was supposed to do that."

"I've never heard of that either, sir. Is this the bottle?"

"Yeah."

"Mind if I take a look?"

"Go ahead. Keep it, for all I care. I sure don't want any more of that crap."

Messmer held the bottle to his nose and sniffed. Then he got a little of the contents on one finger. He touched the finger to his tongue and immediately made a face.

"*Ugh*! I see what you mean, Senator. Antacid shouldn't taste like this, ever."

"Hell, Tom, *nothing* should taste like that!"

"I agree. Did you swallow any of this stuff, sir? Any at all?"

"No, I'm sure I didn't. As soon as that awful taste hit my tongue, I was spitting it out. None too carefully, as you can see. I made quite a mess."

"I think that may be just as well, sir. That you spit it out, I mean." Agent Messmer capped the bottle. "I'm going to have this sent to the FBI lab for analysis, Senator. You never know."

"You think someone tried to *poison* me?"

"I guess we won't know that until we find out whether it's poison, sir."

* * *

MARY MARGARET DOYLE walked into the living room of yet another hotel suite. I've got good news and bad news," she said.

Sargatanas looked up from the briefing paper he was studying. "Don't play stupid word games with me. If you've got something to say, say it."

"All right. I just saw in the online edition of the *Washington Times* that Nestor Greene, one-time political mercenary and dirty-tricks expert, was killed when a thermite bomb went off in his car, while he was parked outside the post office in Annandale, which is where he lives – *lived*."

"So our little surprise worked. Good. Pity I couldn't have seen his face, in those last few seconds before the pain took him. And what were you characterizing as 'bad news'?"

"Simply the fact that, unlike Greene, Bob Leffingwell is still very much among the living. If he hasn't taken the drug by now, I think the odds are he never will."

Sargatanas put the briefing paper down and sat back in his chair. "Do you think Greene betrayed us – kept the money and never hired anyone to poison Leffingwell?"

"No way of knowing – especially now."

"Did he give you the name of the supposed 'professional' he hired?"

"No – he just said it was someone who was highly recommended."

"Recommended by his grandmother, most likely. Well, this leaves us in an awkward position. Leffingwell's got a few more delegates pledged to him than we do, and the convention is the week after next. That means there will be what your politicians so charmingly call a 'floor fight.' Can we win?"

"Garrett says we can."

"Garrett is paid to be optimistic. Martinez hasn't returned your phone call yet, has he?"

"No, I've heard nothing from him, at either of the numbers I gave his people."

"That spic cocksucker. I bet he's returning Leffingwell's phone calls. If Martinez were to, say, fall off a bridge tomorrow, what happens to his delegates?"

"They'd be free to go wherever they wished. But – you're not thinking of doing something to Martinez, are you?"

"Cold feet, Mary Margaret? It really is a little late for that."

"No, I just meant it would be hard to get to him on such short notice and still preserve our own deniability. Especially now that we don't have Greene as an intermediary."

He looked at her in a way that she had learned to dread. "You're not by any chance questioning my decision to get rid of Greene, are you?"

"No – no, of course not."

"Because if you were, that would be insolent. And what happens to insolent little girls, hmm?"

"T-they are punished. Severely."

He held her in his basilisk gaze a little longer, then said, "Get out of my sight. I have some thinking to so."

She got.

Chapter 42

"I DON'T MEAN to be all gloom and doom," Quincey Morris told those assembled in the suite at the Best Western. "We do have certain things going for us – and they may just be enough to bring us through, successfully and in one piece."

"God willing," Finlay muttered solemnly.

"A consummation devoutly to be wished," Peters said, with a crooked grin.

"Fuckin' A," Libby Chastain added, with a grin of her own.

"Let me run it down for you, and then I'll tell you the idea Libby and I have cooked up to make the most effective use of it."

"We have three essential advantages," Morris said. "I'll start with the smallest and work up to the biggest one. The smallest one is surprise – neither Sargatanas, nor any of the people guarding him, have any idea that we're in the game, or what we're planning to do. And the aggressor always has the advantage."

"It's less of an advantage here than it would be in other situations," Arkasian said. "That's because you're planning to surprise the U.S. Secret Service. I'm not saying that because it's my team, rah-rah. But Secret Service agents are *trained* to react to surprises. Every six weeks, an agent rotates back to the academy for two weeks of testing, weapons requalification, and simulated attacks on a protectee. If you do security work for a long time, and nothing happens, you get soft and slow and complacent. The training is designed to counteract that. In fact, I'm due to rotate through the academy the week of the Republican convention, so I won't even be there when all this goes down." He gave them a sour expression. "Well, at least it gives me an alibi, if I need one."

"Jerry had described for me the intense training the agents receive so they'll react fast in emergencies," Morris said. "That's why I listed surprise on the low end of our advantages. Still, we get to choose when to strike, and how. Even though the agents may well respond very, very quickly, we still get to make the first move. And even Secret Service agents don't train to deal with the kind of stuff they'll be facing in Madison Square Garden this time. And speaking of the Garden, I'll let Jerry discuss our second advantage."

"The next element in our favor is, well, me," Arkasian said. "In other circumstances, I guess you could say that I'd be acting as a mole who is betraying one of our leaders to our nation's enemies. It just so happens that in this case, I know that the country's biggest enemy is the guy who wants to *be* our leader."

"Still, that must be a lot of cognitive dissonance for you to deal with," Finlay said.

"Not as much as you might think, Marty. Okay, so one of the big plusses of having me in this group is that I can tell you with almost 100 per cent certainty how Secret Service agents will react in a given situation. We all get the same training, apart from specialists like snipers. All I have to do is ask myself what *I'd* do, and I can apply it to the other agents as well."

Arkasian stepped over to the nearest wall, where a rolled bundle of poster-size documents was leaning.

"Mal," Morris said, "you wanna help me move this table into the center, please?"

Peters and Morris picked up the low coffee table and brought it into the middle of the oval created by the chairs. Arkasian pulled rubber bands off the bundle and unrolled it onto the table. He and the others found small, heavy objects in the room to place on the corners, to keep the thing from rolling up again.

"It wasn't easy to copy these with nobody else being the wiser," Arkasian said. "I had to do it over several evenings when I could come up with a plausible reason to be alone in the document room. As you folks might imagine, this stuff is classified – just Confidential, though. If it was Top Secret I'd never get near it without two other agents with automatic weapons standing over me every second."

Arkasian pointed to the top document. "This sheet is part of the blueprint for the Garden – it's up-to-date, revised after all the new construction they did there a few years ago. The Garden is so fucking huge, the damn blueprint is spread out over five of these pages. We can come back to those later."

He counted off five sheets, pulled them free from the pile, and put them aside. The next page wasn't a blueprint, but it seemed to be almost as detailed.

"This is the Service's plan for bringing Senator Stark into the garden. It looks like there's going to be a floor fight for delegates this time out, which means each of the three biggies – Stark, Leffingwell, and Martinez – will be addressing the convention at different times. That doesn't usually happen, they tell me. Most years, the primary system determines the nominee months beforehand, and all they do at the convention is listen to speeches, fight over the party platform, and wait to see who the Presidential candidate's running mate is gonna be. But not this year."

Arkasian pointed to the elaborate diagram. "This is the Stark movement plan. There's a different one for each of the three, based on the old military principle that you never follow the same route through enemy country twice. If the Service used the same procedure for each candidate, somebody who observed the first one would automatically know the others. So this is the specific strategy for getting Stark from the Secret Service vehicle – an armored Suburban, like they all are – into the Garden and onto the podium securely, and back out again when he's done orating. Check it out."

He pointed at one edge of the drawing. "Stark will be brought in via the 23rd St. Entrance. From the street door, it is 420 feet to the first side corridor. Turn right, and then it's 190 feet to the elevator."

Arkasian looked up and around at the others. "The public isn't allowed to use the elevators in the Garden, apart from folks in wheelchairs, things like that – and they sure as hell won't be using this one Tuesday night, when Stark is scheduled to speak."

He rested his finger on the spot labeled *Elevator 4 (Stark)*. "The elevator will have agents stationed at the street level entrance where Stark gets on, at the elevator door on Level C where Stark will exit, and there will be armed agents on the elevator itself, before he even gets in it."

The finger moved again. "From the elevator, Stark and his Secret Service escort of twelve agents will turn right, and walk the length of this corridor, which is 628 feet. After that, he goes into a room designated as a holding area, and from there to the podium where he'll speak. I'm glossing over that part, because this corridor is the crucial area." Arkasian looked up at them again, his expression grim. "That's where we're going to hit him."

"And that brings me to our third, and biggest advantage," Morris said. "If we didn't have this one going for us, the other two wouldn't be enough – not nearly enough. But we *do* have it, and it can be expressed in one word: *magic*."

MARY MARGARET DOYLE walked into the suite's living room to find Sargatanas in an apparent good mood, for once. She distrusted this, of course – sometimes he was in a good humor only because he had devised some new sexual degradation to inflict upon her. Many of these had been exciting, at first. But now his torments were just something to be endured.

"There you are," he said. "I want to talk to you about our friend Ramon Martinez."

A jolt of fear made her heart race. He had been obsessing about the Senator from New Mexico for days now. If he had decided to do something drastic about Martinez, it could bring the whole carefully-built structure down around their ears.

"Have you decided on a safe way to... deal with him?"

He gave a bark of laughter. "Deal with him? I'm tempted to send you over there to fuck him. I understand Ramon has a taste for bimbos."

As usual, she ignored the insult. "What do you mean?"

"I heard from the Senator himself, not ten minutes ago. It seems he's been giving thought to his future, has Ramon. And, in return for my pledge to make him my running mate, he's going to throw his support to me in New York."

"Why that's... that's fantastic!"

"This will be during the second ballot, of course. Ramon wants the joy of hearing his name placed in nomination to be President of this Great Land of Ours, which is to be expected."

"Yes, it's common practice – or used to be, back in the days when floor fights were the rule, rather than the exception."

"How well-informed you are. Anyway, during the second ballot, Ramon will release his delegates, with a *strong* recommendation that they cast their votes for the next President of the United States, Howard W. Stark. Little do they know that they'll also be voting for the *last* President of the United States."

"That will put us over the top. Leffingwell won't even be close."

"You know, I think I'm starting to be glad that our little plot to do Leffingwell in didn't succeed. I expect he'll find the taste of defeat to be *far* more bitter than any poison we could have slipped into his iced tea."

"So, I assume that Martinez is no longer 'that spic cocksucker' around here?"

"Don't be stupid. Of *course* he's still a spic cocksucker. But now he's *our* spic cocksucker."

AFTER MORRIS AND Libby had finished explaining the broad outlines of the plan they had conceived, Morris asked, "What do you think?"

After a couple of seconds, Peters said, "I think we better get Ashley back here, since she's got such a big role to play."

"Good idea," Morris said.

"I'll strive to watch my language while the lady is present," Finlay said dryly.

Peters said, conversationally, "Ashley, please."

The words were barely out of his mouth when there was a knock on the suite's door.

"I'll get it," Peters said.

As Ashley entered the room and walked back to her seat, Morris said to her, "We've been plotting – and since you're going to play such a major role, we thought you should be here."

"Fine," she said pleasantly. "I always love a good plot."

After Morris explained what he had in mind for her to do, Ashley clapped her hands together girlishly. "Ooooh, that sounds like fun. I even get to take my clothes off!"

Soon thereafter, they broke for a room service lunch. When the waiter knocked on the door, by prearrangement the others quietly went into one or the other of the bedrooms, and closed the doors. There was no reason why they should all be seen together – even by a room service waiter.

Morris opened the suite's door so that the man could wheel in the big cart with their food. "Just lay it out on the table, if you would," Morris said. "My friends will be back soon."

The waiter complied, then presented Morris with the bill. As he was signing, they could hear from one of the bedrooms a woman's voice yelling, "Yes, yes, right there, right there, yes, oh yesss!" This was followed by some inarticulate grunting sounds. The waiter could not help smiling, but wisely said nothing. Morris added a better-than-average tip and handed the bill back.

"Just call us for pickup when you're done, sir – or wheel the cart into the hall, if you prefer."

As he opened the door to leave, the waiter looked back and said, expressionlessly, "Enjoy your afternoon."

Morris waited a few seconds, then called, "Y'all can come out now!"

From the room where the sex noises had originated came Libby, Peters – and Ashley, who was grinning.

"That's an interesting sense of humor you've got there, Ashley," Morris said.

"What? Me? Oh, you mean those noises?" Ashley tried to look innocent, and failed miserably. "That wasn't *me* – that was Libby."

Morris looked toward Libby, who responded with a shrug and an indulgent smile. "Sorry, Quincey. I just couldn't control myself."

After eating, the group spent another couple of hours finding holes in the plan, and fixing them. They discussed various things that might go wrong, and worked out ways of dealing with them.

Finally, Morris looked around at this, his most motley of crews – the two witches, the demon, the priest, the damned soul and the Secret Service guy – and said, "Anything else you want to say? Anybody?"

Receiving no response apart from a few headshakes, he went on, "Then I guess we might as well call it a day. I'd ask that we meet back here a week from Sunday.

441

Although hotel space in the whole metro area is going to be impossible to find during convention week, a considerable bribe to the hotel manager has got us this suite again for that whole period – which we probably won't need, since it all hits the fan Tuesday night, when Stark comes to the Garden to give his speech. But, you never know."

"One thing," Ashley said. "Maybe this was already discussed during my absence, but why don't we hit Stark at his hotel, before he goes to the Garden? I'm sure Jerry here could find out for us where the guy is staying."

"We did talk about that, actually." Morris said. "Thing is, we'd never get close, not through all the security. And even if we somehow did, there's no way to get out afterwards. At least with the Garden, we know he's coming to us, when and where. We can prepare the ground in advance. And the layout of the place gives us at least a chance of getting clear afterward."

"Okay," Ashley said. "Just a thought."

"We each have our preparations to make in the meantime, and I'd suggest you all make whatever personal arrangements you need to, in case things don't work out for us the way we planned."

"Aw, what's the worst that can happen?" Peters asked with a crooked grin. "We get killed? Hell, I did that once already – it ain't so bad."

Chapter 43

THERE WAS A knock at the door, followed by a male voice saying, "Senator? We'd like to leave in about five minutes, if that's okay."

"Fine, we'll be ready."

Mary Margaret Doyle bustled about the room, but with purpose. "I think I've got everything," she said, "including the final draft of the speech."

"Why bother?" Sargatanas asked. "There are two teleprompters, remember?"

"Yes, and I also remember that in 1994 Bill Clinton was giving his State of the Union address before Congress, and some dolt loaded the prior year's State of the Union into the teleprompter – which Clinton only found out when the thing started rolling."

"Goodness. What did he do?"

"He had the speech he was supposed to be giving memorized, so he pretended to be reading it off the prompter. They got it fixed midway through. Some people said later that it was the best speech he ever gave."

"Indeed? Not bad, for a mere human. I could do the same, of course, if necessary."

"I have no doubt you can," she said. "But a little extra redundancy never hurts."

THE CONVOY OF six black, unmarked Jeep Suburbans made their slow way down Broadway. Stark and Mary Margaret Doyle were in the third one, along with four Secret Service agents, including the driver.

The agent sitting next to Mary Margaret Doyle turned to her and asked, "Ms. Doyle? Everything okay?"

"Yes, fine," she said. "One of these stupid false eyelashes came loose, and it's making my eye tear. I've got it now."

The agent privately wondered why a loose eyelash in one eye would make tears slide down both of her cheeks, but Secret Service agents are trained to discretion.

"Just *look* at all those people," Stark said.

The sidewalks on both sides were jammed the whole way. Some of the pedestrians seemed to be moving, or trying to. But others just stood at the barriers, waving signs and shouting. They had no idea who was in the black SUVs, but it was widely known that those were the Secret Service's vehicle of choice when transporting dignitaries.

"There must be thousands of them," Mary Margaret Doyle said. "What do they *want*?"

"Lots of them are protesting something, ma'am," the agent in the shotgun seat said. "Some are against the war, some are for the war, some of them oppose the federal budget cuts, some favor nuclear energy, some oppose nuclear energy, and some want us to nuke Saudi Arabia. The animal rights people are here, and the anti-timber people, and some anarchists, who are against everything – there's something for everybody."

"But... even if the Senator were already President, he couldn't do anything about some of those things."

"I don't believe they care, ma'am."

The agent turned away from Mary Margaret Doyle and spoke into the radio transmitter on his wrist.

"CX, this is S-3. I have Dragon and Princess about two minutes out." He seemed to listen for a moment, then said "Roger that."

The Secret Service had recently changed the code name designations for Stark and Mary Margaret Doyle. She liked his new one better, but thought that 'Attila' had a certain cachet that 'Princess' just didn't carry.

Soon the little convoy pulled up to the curb outside one of Madison Square Garden's many entrances.

"Please don't exit the vehicle until we give you the 'All Clear,' folks," the agent in front said. Since there was a burley bodyguard sitting next to each door, disobedience was highly unlikely.

The agent spoke into his wrist mike again. "Roger. Disembarking now." He turned to the back seat passengers. "Time to go, folks. Curbside only, please."

Then they were out of the SUV and walking toward the door of the building, agents in front, behind, and on either side of them. In the distance, people yelled and chanted. They entered Madison Square Garden, walked down a hall and turned right, agents standing at all four points of the intersection where they turned.

Then there was an elevator open, agents outside and inside. Into the elevator, a brief descent, the elevator door opening onto a windowless area of hallways and closed doors. "We'll be taking you to the holding area now. You can relax for a while before it's time to go upstairs."

Another long, linoleum-covered hall stretched before them. Two agents walked about fifty feet ahead, four more were directly in front of Stark and Mary Margaret, two each walked on either side, four more were directly behind, and two more lagged further back, looking over their shoulders frequently. Senator Stark and his Chief of Staff were so well protected that nothing could possibly happen to them.

They had covered about half the length of the long hallway when Fright Night began. For real.

SPECIAL AGENT CHARLIE Vincent was working trail on the Stark escort with Pete Brewster next to him. Walking backwards at any speed is clumsy and hard to keep to a straight line; you tend to bump into stuff. So agents in their position walk normally but look over their shoulders a *lot*. Every time it was the same: walk-look-nothing; walk-look-nothing; walk-look-nothing; walk-look-*man with a gun*.

Vincent saw him first, although where the figure had appeared from he couldn't have told you. Vincent yelled "Gun!" as he was supposed to, and very quickly produced his own weapon, the Sig Sauer P229 that most agents use. Brewster's pistol was brought to aim a bare half-second behind his.

What Vincent had seen was a broad shouldered man with black hair and a dark overcoat who was aiming a handgun in their direction. Since a weapon was already in evidence, Vincent and Brewster were authorized by regulations to fire without having to yell "Freeze!" or any such nonsense.

They each fired four times, very fast. Secret Service agents have to re-qualify with a pistol every couple of months, and the standard is high. Every Secret Service agent in the Protective Division is a superb shot. Agents Vincent and Brewster were thus surprised when a man who had surely just been shot at least six times in the chest turned and ran way.

"Body armor," Brewster said.

"Yeah, gotta be," Vincent said, and they took off after the fleeing figure.

The rest of the detail did exactly what they were supposed to upon hearing the dread word "Gun." They moved the protectee (in this case two of them) very fast in the direction opposite danger – here, that meant straight ahead. They were also prepared to deal with danger from the front. Nothing says the bad guys can't work as a team, too. The agents were prepared for any individual brandishing a weapon.

They were not prepared, however, for the naked woman.

They couldn't have said where *she* came from, either. The nearest corner was 200 feet behind her. There were no side doors in this section. But there she was.

She wore noting but black high-heeled shoes, just like porn stars and strippers do. She had no weapon – her hands were empty, and she surely had no place to hide one.

To each of the agents, she was a vision of his personal fantasy – whether movie star, porn star, TV actress, supermodel, Miss February of 2004, or, in one man's case, his sixth-grade teacher, Miss Evans.

She walked toward them, a welcoming smile on that beautiful face that looked so different to each of them. The only two people not affected by her beauty and raw sensuality were Mary Margaret Doyle (who was as heterosexual as a June day is long), and Howard

Stark, who knew something was amiss, but not yet what it was.

When she spoke, her voice was just… wonderful. "Good evening, folks," she said, the smile still in place. "How's everybody doing tonight?"

Discipline, so firmly ingrained in these agents, finally reasserted itself. One man got his Sig Sauer out and pointed at the vision of female perfection. "Freeze! Stand still! Hands on your head!"

She looked at him with raised eyebrows, and stopped. Then she slowly put her hands atop her head, which of course only displayed her perfect breasts more prominently. "You mean like this?" she asked sweetly.

Then, in an instant, the vision of loveliness became a vista of horror beyond description, as the demon known in some circles as Ashley gave these brave agents of the U.S. Secret Service an unfiltered look at her true form.

It only lasted a second; Ashley had agreed, somewhat reluctantly, not to expose these dedicated men to so much of herself that their minds would be destroyed permanently. The effect was essentially what had recently afflicted a priest and Secret Service agent in a New Jersey hotel room. This experience may have been a little worse than theirs, since the agents had no indication that a vision of Hell was on its way.

Three of the men passed out, their brains refusing to accept any more of this horrific sight. Several others fell to the floor and immediately curled into a fetal position. Five of them sank slowly to the floor and sat there sobbing, as if at their only child's funeral.

Mary Margaret Doyle had been looking at Stark when this horror occurred, and was thus largely unaffected. And the demon Sargatanas, once he recognized one of his own kind, let Stark's face twist in anger before growling "*You!*"

Ashley, looking once again like the Playmate of the Year's prettier sister, turned her face to the ceiling and said "*Now*."

Three seconds later, the lights went out. All of them. Every one of the thousands of lights and other electrically-powered devices in Madison Square Garden was extinguished – for seven seconds.

IN A HOTEL suite in Newark, New Jersey – the same suite that the demon Ashley had visited ten days earlier, seven women sat in a circle on the floor of the suite's living room. They had been chanting a series of spells for the last half hour, ready for the psychic signal that their leader, one Eleanor Robb, was waiting for.

When Ellie 'heard' the word 'Now,' she repeated it aloud, and she and the other witches began to focus the magic they had prepared. It was a tough job, taking down the power grid that services Madison Square Garden, even if you're only doing it for seven seconds. But they managed beautifully.

AS SOON AS everything went dark, something happened to one of the walls near where two demons stood and a number of unfortunate human men writhed on the floor in mental and spiritual agony. The painted cinderblock shifted, changed, and became a brown metal door, like so many others to be found on the lower levels of Madison Square Garden.

Magic had not been used to create that door – magic had been employed to *conceal* it.

The door formed quickly, then opened wide. Libby Chastain slipped out, using witch sight to see where she was going. She saw Ashley, and Stark, and a woman in a business suit staring around frantically in the darkness. Ashley, being a full-blown demon and not merely one inhabiting a human body, was stronger than Stark, whom she grabbed and hustled through the newly-appeared door. As she did so, Ashley said to Libby, "This one, too. Yes, we have too!"

Since Libby could see and Mary Margaret Doyle could not, it was not extremely difficult for Libby to drag the woman the short distance through the door.

Ashley slipped back out of the room and slammed the door behind her. The door disappeared and, a moment later, so did Ashley. In two more seconds the power, including juice to the many surveillance cameras, was restored.

MORE SECRET SERVICE agents came running around the corner, slowing when they saw their fallen comrades. Several of the agents knelt next to downed agents, looking for bleeding, or other evidence of wounds – and finding nothing.

One of the agents remained standing and said loudly and firmly into his wrist mike, "I've got men down in Corridor C-9. I say again, we have men down. I'm gonna need ambulances, with stretchers for – let me see – fourteen men. No, Dragon is not among them. Neither is Princess. No, none of the agents are deceased. Their wounds are" – the agent looked about in confusion at the men obviously in pain, and not one drop of blood spilled. Nerve gas? "Their wounds are serious, but undetermined. There is the possibility that some kind of nerve gas or paralyzing agent was used. Now get those ambulances!"

* * *

ELLIE ROBB NODDED with satisfaction. "Nicely done, my Sisters. Thank you. I have another Sister monitoring a police band radio across the river. Once she learns what hospital the Secret Servicemen are being taken to, we can get over there and do our best to sooth the minds of those poor, brave men."

"It's a pity they had to suffer like that," one of the younger Sisters said.

"Yes, it is. And I'm not usually a proponent of situation ethics. But if Stark gets elected President with that demon inside him, those men will ultimately suffer even more, and the rest of the world will doubtless join them."

ROOM C-109 HAD a low ceiling, with a flickering double-tube florescent set in the middle. The walls were painted institutional green over the cinderblock surface; the filthy floor seemed to be patterned gray and white linoleum that was coming up in places. Institutional junk was stacked around the room. One corner held a pile of folded chairs that looked like they belonged at some graduation ceremony. A couple of wooden crates contained what looked like parts for industrial lawn mowers.

In more or less the center of the room sat an elaborate wooden armchair, like something that might be used as a throne in a high school play. A coil of rope lay on the seat.

"Not the most elegant place for an exorcism," Father Martin Finley thought, "but I've seen worse, too – far worse."

Ashley had declined to stay for the exorcism – for obvious reasons. The name of God was likely to be said in this room – many, many times.

Stark drew himself up to his full height. "What is the meaning of this? What is wrong with you people? Who are you? Don't you know *who I am*?"

"Nice try," Quincey Morris said. "But we know exactly who, and what, you are, Sargatanas."

The thing that had once been Howard Stark abandoned the expression of outraged indignation and looked at Morris with narrowed eyes. "You seem to think you know my identity. Who, might I ask, are you?"

"You don't need to know our true names – except for one." Morris gestured toward Finlay, who wore a simple black cassock with a purple cloth stole around his neck. The stole had prayers in Latin imprinted on it, and the image of the cross sewn onto each end.

"Meet Father Finlay. He'll be your exorcist this evening."

Sargatanas looked the priest up and down. "Nice dress," he said. "But I believe most of the cock-sucking faggots in this town usually go for something more elaborate"

"Not very original," Finlay said, "for Hellspawn."

He looked at Morris. "We might as well get started."

Morris looked at Libby, and made a head gesture toward the door. She went over and stood with her back against it. She would monitor the spell that created the illusion of a plain blank wall on the other side, and listen for any activity that might take place in the hallway.

Morris looked to Peters, who had just finished unfolding one of the metal chairs for Mary Margaret Doyle. "Sit down." When she looked at him blankly, he said, "That wasn't a request, lady."

Morris said to Peters, "It's time."

Peters nodded. He pointed a finger at Mary Margaret Doyle and said, "You stay in the fucking chair – no matter what happens. You get out of the chair, and I'll knock you fucking stupid. Understand?"

She nodded, wide-eyed, without speaking.

Peters walked to the large chair and picked up the coiled length of rope.

"We can do this easy," Morris said, "or we can do this hard. The outcome's the same either way – you end up in that chair, tied down securely. Only question is, do you have to get beaten up in the process, or will you just sit down and get it over with?"

"Well, if those are the choices…" Sargatanas seemed to tense his muscles, but before he could do anything with them, Peters punched him in the right kidney from behind. The man screamed in agony, arched his back, and Morris shoved him into the chair.

With a pocketknife, Peters cut lengths of rope from the coil. Some he passed to Morris, who tied Sargatanas from one side of the chair, while Peters did the honors on the other side.

When they were done, the man's arms and legs were tied firmly the chair, and a length of rope passed around his middle secured his trunk in place, as well.

"Pity we didn't buy more rope," Peters said. "I was hoping to have some left to secure the princess over there. Guess I'll just have to keep an eye on her."

Finlay picked up an extra prayer book he'd brought. "Will one of you guys read the responses as we go through this? It's not essential for the ritual, but it does help things go a little faster."

Peters looked at Morris. "Guess it better be you. I'm not sure what my standing is with the Big Guy right now. No point screwing everything up if somebody on that side is still mad at me."

Sargatanas turned his head to study Peters. "So you're not entirely a creature of the white? Maybe you're on the wrong side here, young man."

"Don't bet on it, asshole."

Father Martin Francis Xavier Finley opened his prayer book to the ritual of exorcism, and it began.

Chapter 44

"Look, a U.S. Senator, and maybe the next fucking President of the fucking United States of America *does not just disappear*!"

John Crossman, Special Agent in Charge of the Secret Service detail at the Republican National Convention, was not an excitable man, usually. The Secret Service does not hire hotheads – it values men and women who can keep their cool, even in highly stressful situations.

But this was more stress than Crossman had signed on for.

"You've checked all the cameras, for the last hour." Crossman was talking to Elmer Irvin, whose job was to supervise the technicians who worked the immense security cam system that Madison Square Garden is so proud of.

"Yes, sir, every damn one." Irvin, as a Garden employee, did not work for Crossman, but 'Sir' still seemed like a good idea. The amount of quiet fury that Crossman was exhibiting tended to impress people.

"Then check 'em again."

Irvin grimaced. All of them?"

"Right. Start with corridor C-3 and work outward. Also, look for glitches in the video, any suggestion that a camera's reception might have been interfered with by some kind of electromagnetic pulse, or something, I don't know what the fuck. Just check them!"

Crossman turned his swivel chair away from the perspiring Irvin and took three long, deep breaths. He hoped this would help to bring his blood pressure down into a range that did not threaten imminent cerebral hemorrhage.

"Agent Vincent, Agent Brewser," he called to two men sitting glumly over against one wall. He made a 'come here' gesture.

"Sit," he said. The two agents sat.

"Look," Crossman said, "I want you to work with me here. Nobody is saying you fucked up. Something weird is going on, and I admit we don't have a handle on it yet. But if two experienced agents with spotless records tell me they saw a man with a gun, then I believe they saw *something*."

Crossman sat back in his chair, the springs creaking under his weight. "The guy with the gun – you've independently described his build, what he was wearing. But I don't see anything about his face. What did he *look* like?"

Brewster and Vincent studied their shoes. Without looking up, Vincent said, "He was a man with a gun, sir. That's what we focused on. I guess nothing else mattered to us."

"Did you at least notice his race? People *always* notice that. Was he white, African-American? Asian?"

The two agents just shook their heads.

After a while, Crossman said, "Your shift is over soon, isn't it?"

"Yes, sir. Another hour or so," Brewster said.

"I'd like you to stick around. You're not being punished, understand? But I want you here to answer questions when more come up. And I'm pretty damn sure they will."

"Yes, sir. We'll be here as long as you need us," Vincent told him.

"Dismissed."

"HOLY LORD, ALMIGHTY Father, everlasting God and Father of our Lord Jesus Christ, who once and for all consigned that fallen and apostate tyrant to the flames of hell, who sent your only-begotten Son into the world to crush that roaring lion –"

"Why don't you try praying to Santa Claus? Maybe he'll bring you a dolly!"

"– hasten to our call for help and snatch from ruination and from the clutches of the noonday devil this human being made in your image –"

"That's right, shaman! Shake your rattle over me. Now dance around like a nigger with a bone through his nose!"

"– your image and likeness. Strike terror, Lord, into the beast now laying waste your vineyard..."

"AGENT CROSSMAN SPEAKING."

"Sir, this is Ron Fanyak. I'm at Bellvue with the guys who got... hurt, or whatever they did guarding the Senator."

"Yeah, hiya. Have any of the poor bastards said anything?

"Just fragments. The hospital won't let me in with any of 'em – I have to sneak in when the nurses aren't looking. Then they see me and kick me out again."

"Tell me about these 'fragments.'"

"One of the agents keeps saying something like, 'She was so beautiful, the girl of my dreams...'"

"What the fuck does *that* refer to?"

"Your guess is as good as mine, sir. One of the other guys is saying stuff about the devil. He says he saw the devil, and the devil's a woman."

"Shit. Are these agents being tested for exposure to some kind of gas? Something that would induce hallucinations or psychotic breaks?"

"I asked one of the docs, and he said they're looking into that, but no news so far."

"All right, keep me posted."

"Will do, sir."

Crossman put the phone down and sat there, rubbing his jaw and scowling. Then he raised his head and looked around until he saw the man he wanted, at a computer terminal fifty feet away. "Agent Stevens! Come here a sec!"

When Stevens stood in front of him, Crossman said, "I remember when we started working on the security plan for the convention we had access to the complete set of blueprints for the Garden. What happened to those?"

"No idea sir, but I'm guessing you want me to find out."

"I sure as shit do – and when you find where they are, have 'em brought up here, ASAP. Got it?"

"Yes sir, I'm on it."

"A Lesson from the holy Gospel according to St. Mark.

'At that time Jesus said to His disciples: "Go into the whole world and preach the Gospel to all creation. He

458

that believes and is baptized will be saved; he that does not believe will be condemned. And in the way of proofs of their claims, the following will accompany those who believe: in my name they will drive out demons; they will speak in new tongues –'"

"*I've got a new tongue, too. Wanna see? Know who loves my tongue, Marty? Judith – she just loves the things I do to her pussy when you're away on your little exorcisms. You should hear the way she squeals when I –*"

"STEVENS, LOOK HERE – no, right there. What do you figure that's supposed to be?"

"It's just the architect's rendering of a door, sir."

"A door, just off Corridor C-9."

"Yeah, right."

"You were down there earlier, weren't you?"

"Sure, we all were. So were you."

"Do you *remember* a fucking door in that wall?"

"I CAST YOU out, unclean spirit, along with every Satanic power of the enemy, every specter from hell, and all your fell companions; in the name of our Lord Jesus Christ –"

"Quincey, there're in the hall – a lot of them!" Libby said.

"Can you hold the door?" Morris asked.

It depends on how they attack it – and in how many places. I'll do my best."

"Libby, listen – if they do get through, make yourself invisible, and get out when you can. You've got that spell ready, haven't you?"

'Yes, but I can't just let them –"

"Having us *both* in jail won't help anything. Having you outside just might help. Promise me, Libby!"

"Shit! All right, Quincey. All right. I promise."

Suddenly, in a voice far louder than any it had used before, the demon Sargatanas bellowed, *"We're in here you motherfuckers! We're in here!"*

"Somebody gag him," Finlay said. "Quick – I think I'm close!"

Peters, who had been standing over Mary Margaret Doyle, pulled a bandana handkerchief from his pocket and dashed over to the chair. And that is where he made his mistake.

Sargatanas had been struggling and straining against his bonds, and the chair that secured them, almost from the beginning of the exorcism. The chair was old, the joining not as firm as it could be. Sargatanas had found the left arm of the chair was coming loose. Indeed, it felt like one more good heave would pull the arm completely off.

Sargatanas had been waiting for the best moment to exploit his hidden advantage. Now he found it.

Peters came to stand in front of him, and bent over…

Sargatanas gave a mighty heave with his left arm. The chair arm pulled loose, and its momentum carried it, along with the arm it was tied to, in a vicious arc toward Peters' head.

Peters had no chance to block or duck. The wooden chair arm, with all of the demon's force behind it, took him alongside the head and knocked him sprawling.

Morris started to go to Peters, but Finlay cried out, "No, no – restrain Stark, or he'll get free. I'm nearly there, Quincey! Hold him down!"

Morris stared at Finlay for a long second. Then he

scuttled around behind the chair, grabbed the loose arm with chair fragment still attached, and yanked it back down to Sargatanas's side.

Morris glanced up to see how Finlay was doing – and made inadvertent eye contact with Sargatanas. At once, his burn scar began to hurt, and the pain grew worse with each passing second.

Libby, her back pressed against the ensorcelled wall, was trying to hold it against the impact of sledgehammers from the hall. She saw that was happening. "Quincey! Hang on! Transcend the pain! Let it pass through you!"

Morris' neck felt like a branding iron was pressed against it. He screamed through gritted teeth. Tears of pain rolled down his face. His body began drip sweat.

But he did not loosen his grip.

"Begone, then, in the name of the Father, and of the Son, and of the Holy Spirit. Give place to the Holy Spirit by this sign of the holy cross of our Lord Jesus Christ, who lives and reigns with the Father and the Holy Spirit, God, forever and ever…"

"Come closer, priest! It's not working – come closer!"

Morris felt as if he had been cut in two. Half of him was ready to pass out from the searing pain. The other half gripped the demon's arm with hands that did not weaken, did not tremble, did not move one millimeter.

Dimly, through the haze of agony, Morris could hear brickwork crashing to the floor, the sound of sledgehammers louder, then louder still.

Finlay never stopped, never wavered – until the voice from behind Morris yelled, "Federal officers – get your hands in the air!"

Finlay stepped back at last, reverently put down the prayer book, and raised his hands. Disappointment covered his face like a shroud, Morris finally released his grip and collapsed to the floor. Of Libby Chastain there was no sign.

And the demon Sargatanas laughed in triumph – and laughed, and laughed.

ENOUGH OF THE bricks had been knocked away to allow the Secret Service agents access to the room. They found themselves with one man in a priest's cassock in handcuffs, two other men in civilian clothes unconscious but handcuffed, Senator Howard Stark laughing like a loon but, apparently, unharmed – and the Senator's Chief of Staff, Mary Margaret Doyle, doubled over in a metal folding chair in the corner, weeping uncontrollably.

The agents wasted no time in cutting Stark's bonds. "Senator – are you all right? Have you been injured? Do you need medical care?"

"No, no, I'm not bad at all, considering. I assume you'll be taking these maniacs off to jail."

"Absolutely, sir. We have a long list of charges in mind."

"Excellent. Did you get the woman?

"Ms Doyle? She over there sir."

"No, the other woman – Libby something."

"There was nobody else here when we broke in, sir. We got 'em all."

"I see. Very well. Perhaps I was mistaken."

"Who are these people, anyway? Religious nuts?"

"So it would seem, Special Agent. So it would seem."

Another agent, Stanley Cummings, was helping Mary Margaret Doyle to stand up. She resisted him at first, then suddenly sprang to her feet and began to move very fast, indeed.

Her left hand snaked under Cummings' suit jacket and grabbed the Sig Sauer from his holster. Her other hand, palm flat against his chest, pushed – hard.

Cummings was a big, fit man, but he'd had no reason to expect violence from this obviously harmless woman. He took an involuntary step back, lost his balance, and fell into the pile of metal chairs with a clatter.

Mary Margaret Doyle knew how to shoot – she even had a pistol permit. As a woman living alone in the murder capital of America, she'd thought the gun, and some professional instruction, justified.

Before any of the other agents could react, she had shifted the weapon to her right hand and fired off three rapid shots, two of which found their target – the chest of Senator Howard Stark.

The agents' training took over then, and Mary Margaret Doyle had barely squeezed off her third shot when she was struck by bullets from four separate Secret Service pistols. She fell over backward from the impact of the high-velocity bullets, and lost the gun when her outstretched hand struck the floor.

While one agent not-quite-frantically called for an ambulance, two others used their emergency medical training by applying pressure to Stark's wounds, which were bleeding copiously. A fourth agent, Marvin Brantley, walked cautiously over to where Mary Margaret Doyle lay supine across some metal chairs. Seeing that the weapon she'd used was well out of her reach, he knelt down next to her to assess her wounds prior to employing his own emergency first aid. Then he saw that her lips were moving. He leaned over, put his ear next to her mouth. A few seconds later, as he lifted his head up again, Mary Margaret Doyle's body spasmed twice and then was still for good.

Other agents, now supplemented by Garden employees, began to knock more bricks away, to make room for stretchers. Stan Cummings had regained his feet, and said to Brantley, "Man, I am *never* gonna live this down. "What was she – a fucking psycho? Why the fuck would she *do* that – I thought she worshipped the guy."

Brantley looked down at the still form. "Guess we'll never know."

"Did she say something? I saw you bending over her."

"I'm not sure if I heard it right," Brantley said. "It sounded like, 'Not such a monster, after all.'"

Chapter 45

IN BELLEVUE HOSPITAL'S Intensive Care Ward, Senator Howard Stark lay clinging to life. His doctors listed his condition as 'Critical,' but to each other construed it as 'He could go either way.'

Several miles away, in her condo, Libby Chastain was entertaining a rather unusual visitor.

"I got the idea once I heard that Stark wasn't dead," Libby told her guest. "As you might imagine, getting anywhere near his room in the ICU is going to be difficult, verging on impossible, even for us."

"I bet we could've managed it," Ashley said.

"Fortunately, we don't need to. Absolutely nobody is paying attention to Stark's hotel room. There isn't even a guard on the door. Getting past the lock was child's play, and it took me only a few seconds inside to find what I was looking for."

Libby reached into the black leather bag she usually carried and removed a hairbrush – a man's hairbrush, with plenty of evidence of use still clinging to the bristles.

"This is everything we need," Libby said, "to do a little sympathetic magic."

"Yeah, maybe," Ashley said. "But taking it both ways, that's gonna be trickier than a motherfucker."

"I've always admired your colorful vocabulary," Libby said. "Does that mean you're not willing to try?"

"Fuck no, let's give it a shot. For me it's a win-win. Even if we fuck it up, I still get what I want. You're the one who's taking a risk."

"Yes, but it's one worth taking. So, you brought whatever gear you need for a working?"

"I sure did. Got it right here."

"Do you want to use the coffee table? I'll prepare mine in another room, so we don't distract each other."

"Yeah, here is fine."

"Great." Libby stood up. "Let me just grab some of this hair, and you can have the rest. Give me a shout when you're done, okay?"

"Sure – will do."

As Libby left the room, Ashley pulled some of Howard Stark's hair from the brush, and began to make her voodoo doll.

Less than an hour later, they were ready.

"I feel weird just being here and watching you do this," Libby said. "But since I'm then going to undo it –"

"Or try to."

"Or try to – I guess there's nothing that goes against the ethics of my profession."

"You really care about stuff like that, huh?"

"Yes, Ashley, I really care about stuff like that."

Libby then watched as Ashley proceeded to kill Senator Howard Stark.

She did some incantations in a language Libby didn't recognize, and lit a black candle she'd brought with her. A few more incantations followed.

Then Ashley picked up a long, straight pin, and plunged into the crudely made doll's chest – three times.

In Stark's ICU room at Bellevue, alarms began to go off, warning the nurse's station that something had gone seriously wrong in room 9. Two nurses walked rapidly toward the room, while another picked up a microphone. She thumbed it on and said, calmly, "Code Blue, ICU 9. Code Blue, ICU 9."

Soon Stark was surrounded by doctors and nurses trying to keep him alive. They tried two different injections, chest compression, and, finally, the defibrillator – twice. But the lines on the monitors continued to grow shallower and shallower.

In a condo miles away, a creature known as Ashley leaned over a black candle, and blew it out.

Within two minutes, the lines on all Stark's monitors were as flat as a pool table.

"Damn!" the attending physician, Dr. George LeMay said. He always took the death of a patient as a personal affront. "Well, maybe the autopsy will tell us what happened and we'll learn something out of this. Too bad, though. The guy almost got to be President, I hear. Would someone get me a death certificate, please? I mark time of death as 10:21 a.m."

Ashley removed the pin from her voodoo doll and sat back. "Your turn, Libby. Go for it."

Libby lit a candle of her own – a white one – and began an incantation in ancient Aramaic.

"Doctor – doctor," a nurse said excitedly, "we're getting a pulse. Look!"

"B.P. is starting to rise, doctor," another nurse said. "Respiration increasing, too."

"Get me two units of whole blood, stat!" LeMay said, then more softly, "Senator, this may just be your fucking lucky day."

After ten minutes more, Libby Chastain stopped chanting. Sweat beaded her forehead. On the coffee table, the white candle still burned.

"Think it worked?' Ashley said.

"I'll pull up a 24-hour news site on my computer. If he dies, it'll be big news, and they'll announce it at once. If we don't hear anything – well, no news is good news, as they say. You figure Sargatanas got sent back to hell, once Stark's heart stopped beating?"

"He should have – a demonic spirit can't inhabit a dead body, I know that much. Maybe I'll hear something from my boss, Astaroth – he's the one who sent Peters and me on this little mission impossible."

"Well, we did what we could," Libby said "Hey – how about coffee and some apple crumb cake?"

"Sounds fantastic. Thank you."

Later, as she finished her coffee, Ashley said, "So, you got any ideas on how we're gonna get our guys out of the slammer – short of a jailbreak, I mean. I could probably pull something like that off, but being on the run doesn't sound like a lot of fun for Peters. I bet Quincey wouldn't like it much, either."

"Well, if Stark's alive, I'm hoping he'll take care of that for us, once he's recovered. It'll take a while, which is a pain. But, as you said – a jailbreak isn't really practical."

"Well, thank you for the coffee and cake."

"You're very welcome, Ashley."

"Uh, Libby?"

"What?"

"You like girls, don't you?"

468

Libby looked at her for a moment or two. "Yes, I'm bisexual."

"In that case – wanna fool around?"

Libby repeated the look, for a little longer this time. "Thank you, Ashley. But I think I'm going to say, 'not right now.'"

"Does that mean 'not right now,' or 'never?' It's okay to tell the truth."

"I'm always truthful – it comes with the territory, remember?"

She leaned over and touched her lips, very briefly, to Ashley's.

"It means, 'not right now,'" Libby said.

Epilogue

THE MORNING AFTER his inauguration, President Robert Leffingwell was at his desk early. He was slightly hung over, and had managed about two hours' sleep the night before. Under other circumstances, he might have considered sleeping in, but everybody was going to be watching to see how the new Chief Executive handled his first day, and staying in bed until noon might give the wrong impression.

Leffingwell was normally a man of temperate habits. He'd been a politician for the last thirty-two years, and he took his work of representing the people seriously – not in any goopy *Mr. Smith Goes to Washington* way, but more out of a recognition that he was being paid the people's money to do the people's business, so he'd damn well better give it the importance it deserved – and that was hard to do if the phrase 'party hearty' was anywhere in your vocabulary.

Still, a man only gets inaugurated President (for the first time, anyway) once in his life. When Leffingwell and Sharon had made their entrance at the first of five Presidential balls, and he had heard 'Hail to the Chief' played for the first time in his honor – he thought his heart was going to swell to the point of bursting through his chest, like something in one of those *Alien* movies.

Then, after finally returning to spend their first night – what was left of it – in the White House, Bob and Sharon Leffingwell had torn up the sheets like a couple of teenagers – and who could blame them?

Leffingwell planned to approach the presidency as he had his prior positions in the Senate, the House, and the Florida Governor's office – he would get as much rest as the job allowed, and drink both rarely and in moderation. Still, he offered a quiet prayer that the nation, and the world, would remain relatively peaceful – just for today.

A knock on the office door was followed by the appearance of Jonah Wilde, his Appointments Secretary. "What have I got on my plate this morning, Jonah?" he asked.

"You've got the Secretary of Defense at 9:00, sir, and the Joint Chiefs at 10:30. But right now you've got Senator Stark, who called the transition team weeks ago and asked to be your first appointment on your first day. I thought you wouldn't mind, considering everything he's been through."

"How does he look?"

"Not bad, sir, considering he was at death's door last summer. Hasn't regained all his weight yet, and walks a little slower than he used to – but not bad."

"Bring him in, then."

When Stark came through the door, Leffingwell stood and came out from behind his desk to greet his old political rival – who had ceased utterly to be a rival on the second day of the Republican convention. Stark's Chief of Staff had unaccountably pumped three bullets into him following some kind of bizarre hostage rescue by the Secret Service, before being gunned down, herself.

The details of that uncanny incident were still not all available, but the effect had been to give Leffingwell the nomination in a landslide – nobody wants a candidate who might not even live until election day – and he and Ramon Martinez had won the general election with a comfortable margin of both popular and electoral votes.

"Howard, it's been a long time. How are you doing?"

"Pretty well, Mister President, thank you. Getting around much better lately, although my golf game has suffered something fierce."

Leffingwell laughed at the little joke. Then he said, "Let's sit down over here," and led his visitor to some comfortable chairs arranged near the fireplace. "Would you like some coffee? Tea?"

"No thank you sir. I'd best get to the point, since I know we only have half an hour."

Stark cleared his throat. "I didn't ask for this appointment to offer my congratulations, Mister President, although you have them, and my best wishes, in abundance. Rather, I came to tell you something – and I will admit from the start that it strains belief. I expect before I'm done that you'll be wondering if my injuries haven't unhinged me, in some way – but if you'll hear me out before calling for the orderlies, I'd take it as a courtesy."

"Now you've really got me intrigued, Howard. Please proceed with your… story, or whatever it is."

"There's a lot to tell, but I'll try to be as succinct as possible. Mr. President, I have been on a journey to hell, and it began on Halloween night fifteen months ago."

Twenty-eight minutes later, Stark was saying, "… and it worked. My near-death experience drove Sargatanas out of my body, and, I assume, back to Hell. Among my many regrets is that I never got to tell Mary Margaret how sorry I am about it all, even if she did get me into that mess to begin with."

Leffingwell sat in silence and looked at him.

"If you're thinking about a straitjacket, sir," Stark said with a small smile, "I take a 42 long."

"Howard, I... how can you expect me to give credence to this story? Demonic possession? Witches? Reincarnated assassins? I'm sure you believe that's what happened, but there *must* be some other explanation. There simply *has* to be."

"I figured that would be your reaction, Mr. President – and I don't blame you for a second. In your position, I'd respond in exactly the same way. However, I believe that I can offer proof of my account – or some of it, anyway. Right here, and right now."

"Really? Then, by all means, do so."

"Before I proceed sir, let me tell you that you're in for a shock – no, I wouldn't think of attacking you in any way. I'll stay right here in my chair – but you're about to have trouble believing your eyes."

"For God's sake, Howard, just get on with it, will you?"

"Yes, sir – but I would ask you to refrain from using the Lord's name aloud, in any of its forms, despite what I expect will be a strong impulse to do so."

Leffingwell sighed in a way designed to show that his patience was thinning. "Very well, if you insist. Go on."

"Of course, sir." Stark looked to his left and right. "If you're not really here, ladies, I am going to look like a raving lunatic. But if you *are* here, please make yourselves known."

"Who are you talking – *dear merciful G –*"

"*Sir!*" Stark held an admonitory hand up. "You promised."

Standing on either side of Stark's chair was a woman. One was attractive enough, for a brunette in her thirties. But the other one... was very simply the woman of Bob Leffingwell's dreams.

"Pardon me for the melodrama, Mr. President. But I think you'll agree that nothing else would have been as effective."

Leffingwell looked back and forth between the women – although he gave the blonde the greater share of his attention.

"How – how did you two get *in* here?"

"We walked in behind Senator Stark, Mr. President," the brunette said. "We used magic to make ourselves invisible. Well, I did. Strictly speaking, Ashley here used the Tarnhelm effect, which causes her not to be noticed, even though she's visible."

Leffingwell stared at them, his mouth half open.

With a broad smile that threatened to turn into a smirk, Stark said, "Mr. President, may I present Libby Chastain" – he indicated the brunette – "and a lady who calls herself Ashley."

Libby smiled and said, "I'm quite real, Mr. President. I'd be happy to come over and shake hands – but if you'd rather not, I understand."

Leffingwell got to his feet. "Shake hands – well, yes, of course."

Libby walked over and put her hand out. "A pleasure to meet you, Mr. President, even under some truly odd circumstances."

Her hand felt perfectly normal, the grip firm but not at all uncomfortable.

Then it was the blonde's turn. "Hello, Mr. President. Glad to make your acquaintance – although I am not, in fact, the first of my kind to visit the White House. Not by any means." Her touch was lighter than the other woman's, her voice a caress. Despite having made love with Sharon twice the night before, Leffingwell found himself growing an erection.

The women resumed their positions on either side of Stark's chair. Leffingwell stared at the three of them, then said, "Excuse me for one moment."

He walked to his desk, picked up the telephone, and stared at the plastic buttons for a second before pushing one.

"Jonah? This is highly unusual, and I won't be making a habit of it. But I must direct you to cancel all my appointments this morning. Yes, through lunch. Senator Stark has brought an urgent matter to my attention, and I need to deal with it immediately."

"I know, Jonah. We don't normally do business this way and I likely won't be doing it again. No – everything's fine – I'm under no duress. I didn't say the code word, did I? Don't call in the SWAT team. Thank you, Jonah. See that we're not disturbed, all right?"

Leffingwell replaced the phone in its cradle and looked at the trio again. "Well," he said, briskly, "Let's move these chairs around, so that the four of us can talk. I expect we have a lot to discuss."

"MORRIS – YOUR LAWYER'S here."

Quincey Morris, Prisoner 443429, tossed aside the magazine he'd been reading and stood up. He knew the drill by now.

– *The prisoner will approach the bars, then turn his/ her back, extending his/her arms through the meal slot.*

– *The prisoner will be handcuffed, and will withdraw*

his/her arms from the meal slot when told to do so by a corrections officer.

– The prisoner will turn again and face the bars.

– When the cell door has been opened, the prisoner will step forward into the corridor and allow himself/ herself to be taken into the custody of a corrections officer, which may include a search of the prisoner for weapons or contraband.

– The prisoner will obey all instructions given by the corrections officer while in transit to or from his/her cell.

Morris wondered what Gloomy Gus wanted this time – not that he objected to a little extra time away from his 'house.'

Normally, Morris was allowed out for solitary exercise one hour out of twenty-four. He was permitted two supervised showers per week. He wouldn't have minded more frequent showers, but had no problem at all with being watched by a C.O. while he cleaned up. Morris had nothing against homosexuals, or homosexuality. But if he were going to expand his repertory of experiences, he wanted it to be his idea, not that of some guy named Big Mustapha – and his friends.

Morris' lawyer, Gustav Vollmer, was known among the prisoners as 'Gloomy Gus' because of his perpetually lugubrious expression. It was usually justified by the news he brought to his clients – whether they were serving long sentences or, like Morris, in federal custody awaiting trial.

Morris didn't let himself hope that this visit would be any different. They have a saying behind the walls: 'Hope will kill you quicker than a shank – and hurts twice as much.' It's not hope that does it, of course, but the death of hope – and hope dies a messy death behind the walls every single day.

Morris and the C.O. who grasped him firmly by the arm had almost reached the section where rooms were set aside for lawyer-client meetings. Once inside, the guard would unlock one of Morris's cuffs and reattach it to a stout bracket bolted onto the metal table where he'd sit. This would allow limited freedom of movement – enough for him to hold and sign paperwork, but not enough to strangle his lawyer, were he so inclined.

They reached Interview Room 4, and the C.O. said "Stop." Morris stood still while the guard unlocked the metal door and opened it.

"In." Morris stepped into the room where his lawyer waited – and stopped dead in his tracks, without receiving any instructions to do so. He was staring with amazement at something he'd never seen before, and never, ever expected to see.

Gloomy Gus was smiling.

UK ISBN: 978 1 907519 62 8 • US ISBN: 978 1 907519 63 5 • £7.99/$7.99

Jordan helps kids on the run find their way back home. He's good at that. He should be - he's a runaway himself. Sometimes he helps the kids in other, stranger, ways. He looks like a regular teenager, but he's not. He acts like he's not exactly human, but he is. He treads the line between mundane reality and the world of the supernatural. Ben McCallan's urban fantasy debut takes you on a teffifying journey.

"Black Magic Woman is the best manuscript I've ever been asked to read. Keep an eye on Justin Gustainis. You'll be seeing more of him soon."

Jim Butcher

BLACK MAGIC WOMAN
A MORRIS AND CHASTAIN INVESTIGATION
JUSTIN GUSTAINIS

www.solarisbooks.com ISBN: 978-1-84416-541-4

Supernatural investigator Quincey Morris and his partner, white witch Libby Chastain, are called in to help free a desperate family from a deadly curse that appears to date back to the Salem Witch Trials. To release the family from danger they must find the root of the curse, a black witch with a terrible grudge that holds the family in her power.

SOLARIS DARK FANTASY

UK ISBN: 978 1 907519 95 6 • US ISBN: 978 1 907519 94 9 • £7.99/$7.99

Imagine a place where all your nightmares become real. Think of dark urban streets where crime, debt and violence are not the only things you fear. Picture a housing project that is a gateway to somewhere else, a realm where ghosts and monsters stir hungrily in the shadows. Welcome to the Concrete Grove. It knows where you live...

 WWW.SOLARISBOOKS.COM

Follow us on Twitter! www.twitter.com/solarisbooks